LITTLE MISS LOVESICK

A TRAVERSE CITY IN LOVE CHICK LIT NOVEL

KITTY BUCHOLTZ

Daydreamer
Entertainment

Little Miss Lovesick

Published by Daydreamer Entertainment

Copyright © 2011 by Kathleen Bucholtz

ISBN: 978-1-937719-03-6
ISBN: 978-1-937719-00-5 (ebook)

Library of Congress Control Number: 2012953870

Cover Design: Wordable Design
Illustrations © musillustrations — DepositPhotos.com

Revised edition 2023

DEDICATION

I always said my first book would be for Mrs. Sherry Day, my 6th grade teacher at Kalkaska Elementary School. I can't imagine how I would have gotten here without you. Thank you!

I am so grateful that God gave me so many friends to help and support me along the way! Writer friends in the Tempe Christian Writers Group, my Imaginary Friends, the Reunioners, my Romance Writers of America buddies and my Romance Writers of Australia mates, and all of my other friends who shouted encouragement along the way. A special thank you to Darrin and Stephanie Dennis for helping me edit the final version.

This particular book would never have been written if Lauraine Snelling and Kathleen Wright and Deidre Knight hadn't been laughing so much at the first chapter. Thanks, ladies! You guys make me smile!

And always saving the best for last, thank you, John. You make everything way more awesome!

Little
MISS
Lovesick

Kitty Bucholtz

CHAPTER 1

*W*e were all going to die.

My great escape into the wilderness of Michigan's Upper Peninsula to vanquish Heartbreak from my life was going to end in my early demise. And here I thought it was my broken heart that was killing me.

We'd been driving for over seven hours. The last town snuck past us an hour ago when we'd turned off the paved road. Pavement became gravel, then dirt, then two-tracks. The wooden hand-painted signs with arrows and mileage that marked our way made it feel like we were driving through another world. Like the kids through the wardrobe in the Narnia books. Okay, that part sounded kind of nice, actually.

Dirk would hate it here. No tennis courts in the forest. No skim lattes with soy milk and a sprinkle of cinnamon. And he certainly wouldn't drive his BMW down a two-track through the woods with the top down.

I sighed. This was harder than I thought it'd be, getting Dirk out of my head. If I could exorcise him from my head, I'm sure my heart would heal faster. I was so tired of crying, of whining, of wishing life was different. All I wanted was to settle down with a husband and a house and a dog and 2.4 kids. I knew exactly how I wanted to decorate our home. I'd planned the kinds of parties we would have. We'd be part of the Neighborhood Watch team, and we'd plan block parties for 4th of July. We were going to have the perfect life together.

Then it all ended. Abruptly. Without warning. And I thought I was going to die. But that was four months ago. I had to find a way to get my life back again. Hence the trip into the wilderness.

Then I remembered we were *all* going to die. Who knew there was this much wilderness out there?

"How much gas do we have?" I called from the back of the fifteen-passenger van. I could just see the obituary.

Ten city girls who should have known better died last week when they drove a van through the wilderness without gassing up in the last town.

Yeah, that's the way I can see my life ending right now. Great.

"There's plenty of gas, don't worry," said Patty.

Patty McEntyre had organized this fly-fishing trip — an idea I'd loved before I became convinced of our imminent deaths. Patty had become my Mom-away-from-home since I'd moved to Traverse City two years ago. My mom and I talk, but we don't communicate. Patty's the one I trust to listen and give me good advice. Mom's advice…well, she means well, but she's a big Dirk fan.

See, I met Dirk — Frederick Wayne Schneider III — when we both worked for the same company in Lansing, Michigan, where we're both from. All the girls lusted after him, but I was the lucky one who got to sigh into the mirror and say, "He picked *me*." Naturally, when he moved north to Traverse City, I came with him.

Well, I followed him. Looking back, I see the difference. On the one hand, he didn't want us to move in together to "protect my reputation." On the other hand, he had no compunctions about sleeping with me. Silly me, I thought that if I saved myself for the man I'd marry, he'd actually *marry* me! Instead, after four years of promises, he dumped me. Said he was in love with someone else.

So there I was in Traverse City with a job I loved (turns out I'm a *great* residential realtor), an apartment I'd assumed would be temporary, and a naked ring finger. Completely heartbroken. After four months of tears, I'd decided I needed an escape. Well, Patty suggested it, and my best friend Emily signed us up. A girls-only fishing trip into the wilds of the Upper Peninsula with the Harbor View Nature Club.

Though if we didn't find some kind of civilization soon, I had my doubts that we'd ever be seen or heard from again.

"Only fifteen miles to go," Shelley said from behind the wheel.

"Fifteen miles?" Emily cried. "At five miles an hour, that's three more hours!"

Emily Dodson, my best friend in the whole universe, had been unnaturally excited about this trip. I wanted her to come because she's my best friend and I didn't want to go alone. But I wasn't prepared for her — well, *exuberance*. Emily's a city girl. Well, as city as you can get where we live. She's all about malls and looking great and having beautifully painted nails. She's more *Sex in the City* than *Northern Exposure*. Emily had never even gone hiking with me. In a healthier state of mind, I would've seriously questioned her newfound desire to kill and cook her own dinner.

Patty smiled soothingly at us from the front passenger seat. "She's teasing you. We're almost there. Half an hour at the most."

"That'll make us look even more intelligent in our obituary," I said. "'Ten women died twenty minutes from civilization. It's rumored that they drove in circles saying, 'Just a few more minutes, a few more minutes.'"

Emily grunted. My pseudofascination with how I would die usually amused her. The fact that she wasn't laughing meant she wasn't so sure I was wrong this time.

She waved her cell phone. "It's impossible to die in the wilderness if you're anywhere near civilization in this day and age." She sounded like she was trying to convince herself more than the rest of us.

I looked at her phone and quirked an eyebrow. "Oh yeah? How much longer do you think it'll say, 'Searching for signal'?"

Emily looked at her phone. "Panic" would aptly describe her expression. "Are you sure you know where we are, Patty?"

But twenty-eight minutes later (I looked at my watch so I could gauge time of death), the two-track suddenly opened into a huge yard of sorts, a meadow really. Obviously it was used as a parking lot because there were half a dozen vehicles there.

But wherever tire tracks hadn't crushed them, the lively color of wildflowers sprang from the ground. The pine, birch, and maple trees joined together to form a harmony of forest around us. To the left as we pulled in was a two-story building with a quaint painted sign, "Abundance Creek Lodge and Store," nailed above the door.

Next to the store stood what appeared to be the bunkhouse. Two, no, three little cottages peeked out from the woods on one side of the meadow. The first thing that came to mind when I saw them was *The Three Little Pigs*. It made me smile. So long as the Big Bad Wolf and all of his real life brothers stayed far away. Yikes. I'd forgotten the U.P. (Michigan-speak for the Upper Peninsula) had actual wolves. I tried not to think about it.

Thing is, I expected all of the buildings to be rugged, wooden structures, hardly a step up from tree forts. Wooden they were, but there was a sense of artistry here. Nothing like what I assumed men would build in the wilderness — or even what I figured men would choose if it were this pretty place or a more earthy, flea-infested fishing lodge.

But hey, I'm single, so what I know about men is obviously in question here.

I don't know where I went wrong, sighed Little Miss Lovesick. *I was so close to having it all.*

Ignore her. I'm not Sybil or Eve or anything, but...well, you know those voices in your head? I named them. Not all of them, just the obnoxious ones. I mean, it's nothing weird or anything. Okay, it *is* weird, but it's better than talking out loud, right? Then *everyone* would know. Oh, forget it. *Anyway...*

Shelley parked the van and we all spilled out, groaning and stretching. The feel of real, not-planted-by-human-hands grass under my feet made me take off my sandals. I sighed with pleasure as the long grass enveloped my feet. This trip was a great idea.

"I hope they sell fudge," said Tracey, a marketing consultant I remembered from a previous Nature Club excursion.

"Why?" I asked. "We just drove here from the fudge capital of the world."

She laughed. "But now *we're* the ones on vacation. We can act like Fudgies and the locals can wish we'd spend our money and leave."

It's true. That's what we call tourists in Traverse City — Fudgies. They're always backing up traffic when they try to turn into a fudge shop unexpectedly. Very annoying when you're trying to get somewhere. On the other hand, you have to be grateful for the economic boost. Me especially, since sometimes it's a "Fudgie" buying a vacation home that helps me make rent.

Of course, the fact that you pay rent and not a mortgage is Dirk's fault, said Pride (Sergeant Pride, I call him). *You give the man love, loyalty, sex (!), and what do you get? The old kick in the caboose. Jerk.*

Turns out Mom was right about the milk and the cow, sighed another Voice.

Whatever. I mentally stuck my tongue out at myself. I would be mortified if anyone ever found out about all the voices in my head.

Everyone followed Patty into the store. Everyone but me. I waved Emily off, deciding I needed to breathe in some soothing, wilderness air. The sugar blues that follow a sugar buzz wasn't helping my roller coaster of emotions. I decided to self-medicate. I opened another candy bar and a can of Sprite from our stash.

Starting today, I would force my broken heart to heal if it was the last thing I did. Then maybe I'd lock it away someplace safe.

Don't say that, said Little Miss Lovesick. *Love is the most wonderful thing in the world. You just need to find* true *love.*

True love. That's what I wanted, but if I thought I had it once and I was wrong, how was I ever going to know how to find it for real?

I walked through the grass, trying unsuccessfully not to tread on the flowers. Closing my eyes, I savored the feel of the breeze on my face. Ahh, heaven. Feeling calmer, I folded the empty candy wrapper and stuck it in my pocket. I took a swallow of ice cold Sprite as I climbed the porch steps—

And ran smack into an opening screen door. Which wouldn't have been so bad except the body moving through the door was moving in my direction and crashed into me. Cold Sprite sloshed down my shirt, making me gasp.

"Criminy! Are you all right?" A hand cupped my cheek and moved the screen door away from my face. Cold Sprite dripped all down my front. I took a step backward in an awkward attempt to get away. I felt my balance wobble. The hand firmly gripped my elbow, moving me away from the danger of the stairs.

Sputtering from the pop up my nose and in one eye, I wiped at my eyes and squinted to see what had just happened.

It's The Diet Coke Man, Little Miss Lovesick choked out.

I know I watch too many YouTube videos, but Lovesick may have been right. The Diet Coke Man from the "11:30" commercials was standing right in front of me. A flash of the commercial where the office women ogle the construction worker across the street blew through my brain. Dark hair and piercing eyes, built like a Viking. The way his black T-shirt outlined his muscular form did nothing to remind me that Heartbreak was the reason I had to get away.

Luscious, said Lovesick.

Holy... I tried to squeegee the liquid from my eye. Yeah, he looked equally fabulous with both eyes open. He stared at me in a concerned way that made my stomach flutter. I kind of liked men who looked at a woman this way. Like all you had to do was say the word and they'd fix whatever was broken.

The Diet Coke Man brushed drops of Sprite from my cheek and chin and I immediately sprang back, which only caused him to grasp my elbow tighter as I fell onto a lower step. Theoretically, I liked that kind of man. Realistically, I needed to keep my distance.

"Excuse me!" I found my footing and backed out of reach. He let go when I grabbed the handrail on the stairs.

"Sorry, sorry." He wiped his damp hand on his jeans, and had the grace to look embarrassed. "Are you all right?" He was dangerously appealing standing there trying to help, looking both embarrassed and amused.

I shook my wet right hand, not really wanting to wipe it on my shorts (like a guy), and wiped my face with my left hand. My cold chest caught my gaze and I gasped, pulling the fabric away from my body.

"Fine!" Did I *look* fine? My shirt was white and wet. My bra was black and lacey. I glared at him so he knew I was lying about being fine. He couldn't have noticed my glare, however, because he was staring at—

Look for a ring, Lovesick murmured.

You're not looking for a wedding ring on a stranger who knocked you down and is now ogling your breasts, declared Sergeant Pride.

"Uh, wait right here," said The Diet Coke Man, and he rushed back inside. As he opened the door, my eyes followed his left hand — but *accidentally*. Didn't matter. Couldn't tell. A moment later he was back, ripping a wad of napkins from a plastic package.

I swear, if he started dabbing at my chest with them like Hugh Grant did to Julia Roberts in *Notting Hill*, I'd pour the rest of my pop over his head.

"Here, I'll trade you," he said as he took the can and handed me the napkins.

"Thanks." I tried to blot my shirt without making a peep show out of the black lace. I turned slightly to my right for a bit of privacy. Why did I wear this on a *camping* trip?

I glanced up to see if he was watching. He smiled. My hand paused while blotting my shirt. This man's smile was so — so *gorgeous*. His eyes were an amazing shade of blue. I wanted to offer him the smallest of smiles back. After all, he did look fairly innocent and embarrassed. Instead, I stopped giving him the evil eye. That was as accommodating as I was willing to be.

A Rescuing Hero if I ever saw one, sighed Lovesick.

I tried to think of something to say, something funny to diffuse the tension. Something smart so I wouldn't look like such a dork.

"I, uh…"

"I'm really sorry," he said. He took my damp napkins and handed me back my pop can. With his left hand.

No ring! Lovesick squealed.

"Let me buy you another shirt," he said, nodding at my wet chest. He was trying to pretend he wasn't still staring. Rather gentlemanly for the backwoods.

He was already halfway through the door when I mumbled

something that was supposed to be, "Don't worry about it, I'll get a fresh one from my suitcase," but came out as, "No, I-I..."

A moment later he pressed a blue plaid button-down flannel shirt into my hands. I stared at it trying to remember a time I had ever worn a flannel shirt. Before I could think about it further, he grabbed it, ripped the tag off with his teeth, and handed the shirt back to me.

I blinked at him. He was so not Dirk. I liked that about him.

"Sorry again," he said. "If you'll excuse me, I've got to get a few things done before we get started." He trotted off the porch to a nearby pickup (which he'd left unlocked in a decidedly small town way) and started rummaging around.

Before we what? I stood there staring stupidly after him, a flannel shirt in one hand and a forgotten pop can in the other. A fly buzzed past my nose and I snapped out of my trance.

You could go over and talk to him, suggested Lovesick.

Of all the things I might do on this trip, I was *not* going to flirt with some handsome stranger. No freaking way. My plan was to get over men, not rebound like a basketball.

He wasn't even that handsome. Honestly. His hair was too long, well past his collar. And his hands were too rough, as I remembered from when he wiped the Sprite from my cheek. And...and he smiled too much. Yeah. Seriously annoying.

Before I could think about it much more, I hurried into the store. Girls only. This is a girls-only fishing trip. Say it like a mantra. No boys allowed.

Okay. Deep breath. Close your eyes. Calm. Calm. Girls-only fishing trip. That means nature, which means tranquility, which means peace.

I opened my eyes. The inside of the store was as much a surprise as the outside had been. I expected more of what was in the general store in the last town — tourist trinkets and junk food and fluorescent lighting. The Abundance Creek Store had windows on three sides, letting the sunshine bounce off the polished wood beams in the ceiling and walls, and the well-worn but polished hardwood floor. One full wall held nothing but fishing tackle, most of which I knew was fishing tackle only because this was a fishing lodge.

As I walked around, I noticed fishing poles in a huge wooden barrel, a magazine and book rack, two full aisles of canned and boxed food, even a few kitchen utensils. I walked past a refrigerated unit with a sliding glass top and looked in hoping for a frozen Snickers bar. At first I thought the little tubs might be homemade ice cream or something since they had no labels. Then I saw something move under the plastic lid.

I jumped back, gasping and wrinkling my nose. The sign above the fridge read — Night Crawlers, Fresh Water Shrimp, Black Flies. Ugh! I looked back at the wall of *artificial* lures gratefully. That's where I'd be shopping if necessary.

I smiled as I passed Janice and Shelley, and walked over to the book and magazine rack. There was one copy each of some novels that had been on the *New York Times* bestseller list at some point. Some of the hunting and fishing magazines were special editions. The rest were either May, June, or July issues. I'd hazard a guess that these constituted the entire summer inventory. But still, it was a nice touch. You can never have too much reading material on vacation.

I picked up a copy of *Fisherman's Weekly* and flipped through it.

"If I can help you with anything, let me know."

Startled, I whirled around, bumping my elbow into the person behind me. "Oh, sor—"

I stopped in mid-apology. It was him, The Diet Coke Man. I tried to move away, but my back was against the bookshelf. I felt a little shock, like when you were a kid and put a 9-volt battery on your tongue. It scared me at the same time that it made my heart race.

It's the sugar. I ate enough to throw an entire kindergarten class into a coma. He's not making my heart race; it's the sugar. I slowly turned away and put the magazine down. Don't look at him. Just nod and smile, then pretend he's not there.

A muscular arm reached around me and moved the magazine back to its original spot. I realized I'd put *Fisherman's Weekly* in front of a stack of *Bow & Arrow Hunting* magazines. I felt the heat from his body and got a whiff of his aftershave or deodorant or something. I grabbed one of the books and read the back cover. Safe to be reading. People don't talk to you when you're reading.

His presence sent tickles up my back. Which was stupid. My shirt was still wet and sticky from him spilling pop on me. That was the cause of the ticklish feeling. I couldn't focus on reading the book so I put it back. The arm reached around me again with more magazines, arranging them on the shelf in front of me.

I got the feeling I was invading his precious orderly wilderness. It's wild. That's the point of calling it *wild*erness. What was he doing anyway? He must work here, I guess. But Patty said this place was owned and operated by a friend of hers.

I turned back to him. "Am I in your way?"

Ooo, attitude girlfriend, said a Voice.

Crap, I hadn't meant to sound so rude. But he was unnerving me.

He looked up from straightening candy bars in the snack rack behind us. I watched as a dimple appeared to anchor one corner of his grin. What is it everyone loves about dimples, anyway? They're just big vertical wrinkles.

"No, not at all." He picked up an empty candy box from the floor and broke down the ends, folding it into a neat square.

"Listen, I'm really sorry about spilling your drink." His gaze dropped to my shirt for a second, then popped back up. I folded my arms across my chest and scowled.

His eyes were that shade of bright blue that surely only comes from colored contacts. No one aside from Paul Newman has eyes that blue.

"Do you need any help with the shirt?" He pointed to the one he'd given me earlier, still in my hand.

I knew it! He's some kind of redneck gigolo. "I don't know what you think I came up here for, but it wasn't to be hit on by you. I'm just here to fish, okay?"

I saw his eyebrows raise before I turned on my heel and stalked away. There. That should show *him*. I gave myself a mental high-five.

"I was only going to tell you where the bathroom is," I heard him say.

Little Miss Lovesick sighed. *It's a pretty bad day when you confuse a gentleman with a gigolo.*

CHAPTER 2

*W*hat was wrong with me?

I wandered around the store moping. I just wanted to be my old self again. Have a nice man, a nice house. Heck, even a nice vacation. I didn't need to be ecstatic. Just regular, run-of-the-mill happy. I used to be a very nice person not so long ago. Now even I didn't like my company very much. Not since the night Dirk dumped me.

The most horrible night of my life, said Little Miss Lovesick.

A night I desperately wanted to forget. Even forgetfulness would be happiness for now.

"Syd, isn't this awesome?" Emily gushed as I approached. "They've got everything anyone could need to stay here for *weeks*. There's food, reading material, a phone, *and* we're getting fishing lessons! I am going to *freak out*! Oh, look at this hat! It's like, Indiana Jones Goes Fishing!"

Welcome to Emily-On-Sugar. I smiled as the hat nearly encompassed her whole face. She put it back and walked toward the creepy-crawler cooler.

She took a big breath and closed her eyes, smiling in bliss. "Ah, the smell of earth and fish and worms. Doesn't it smell wonderful? We haven't been here an hour yet and I'm ready to stay for weeks! You brought your camera, right? We *have* to take pictures. Hey, what happened to your shirt?"

I shook my head and smiled. If I could package her exuberance, I could sell it and be rich. Emily didn't have problems; she had dilemmas and challenges. She didn't see half-full or half-empty glasses; she saw a dish cabinet full of possibilities. I sighed and looked down at my damp shirt. I only saw problems. Lately, anyway.

"Someone bumped into me," I said. "Personally, I'd check the expiration date on the food before I decided to stay here for weeks."

Emily rolled her eyes. "It's not meant to completely feed you. It's a *supplement*. That's why we're taking *fishing* lessons. We'll learn to go back to our hunter/gatherer roots. We'll fend for ourselves. It's going to be great!"

She walked along the wall of tackle. I touched a fishing lure that looked like fur. Emily examined some bug-shaped ones. "Besides, think how much money we're saving being away from the malls and the sales flyers."

"What I'm thinking about, Em, is the fact that you spent twice your weekly shopping budget on the new sleeping bag—"

Emily put on her serious face. "Necessary, didn't have one."

"—the new luggage—"

"I couldn't bring my Louis Vuitton bags up here." She looked appalled.

"—the new fishing vest—"

Emily was getting "the look." "Whatever," she said.

"—the new fishing clothes—"

She was trying not to smile now. "*What. Ever.* Whatever. Talk to the hand." She raised her hand and started walking away.

"You've saved a lot of money by getting away from the malls this weekend, Em. I see what you mean."

She turned and gently pretend-slugged me in the shoulder.

As I laughed and began to turn away, she grabbed my shoulders and turned me back to face her.

"Oh. My. Gosh. Do not turn around," she said.

"What?" I tried to turn around, of course, because that's what you do when people say "don't look" — you look.

"I said don't turn around," she said in a whisper and pulled me a little further into the aisle.

Her eyes were fixed like a bird dog's on something behind me. Come to think of it, she really did remind me of a pointer I saw once, completely consumed and unblinking. The dog I remembered was black and Emily's hair is black as night. It made me start to laugh a little.

"Shh," she whispered. "Casually, turn and look but then turn around like you don't see anything."

I tried to casually turn as she instructed. I don't know what I expected — a wild animal or a ghost or something. But all I saw was some of the women from our trip, Sprite Guy, and another tourist fisherman guy. I turned around and shrugged.

"What?" Apparently this was the wrong behavior for our undercover surveillance.

"Shh! Don't act like you're looking."

"But I don't know what I'm looking at."

She groaned. "Oh, now there it is. That is truly *nice*. Okay, over by the fishing poles. Look toward the window. But don't *look*."

I turned slowly in the direction of the big barrel and finally saw what Em was looking at. A *very* fine piece of God's creation was bending over the barrel showing off the back of his Levi's. Nice. Round. And long legs underneath.

I turned back to Emily and grinned.

"See?" She giggled. "Now that is one *fine* sit-down."

"I hate to say it, but I would have to agree with you," I said as I took another peek. Not that I was *looking*-looking, but I was trying to remember that's what girl trips are for, right? To laugh a lot, enjoy the scenery, and go home?

As we both giggled and "enjoyed the scenery," the scenery changed. Up from the bottom of the barrel rose Sprite Guy.

No freaking way. Man, he was everywhere I turned.

Emily giggled again. "Oh, yeah, that's what I'm talking about."

I turned away. "Well, it's *not* what I'm talking about."

"He's cute. But *manly* cute." Emily let the word roll off her tongue in a deep, husky voice, then laughed. "You know who he reminds me of? The Diet Coke Man. Remember, from those commercials. Tall, dark, and handsome? And brawny as — Hey! Syd!"

She finally noticed I had walked away.

She grabbed my arm as she caught up to me. "Seriously, doesn't he remind you of The Diet Coke Man?"

"Yeah, yeah, but he's the Sprite guy." I tried to be sure my tone implied that I had no interest in him whatsoever.

"What? There's no Sprite guy. No, it's Diet Coke that has the commercials with the construction worker and the girls in the office—"

I turned to face her and whispered, "I *know* what you're talking about. What I'm talking about is he's the guy who spilled Sprite on me earlier." I gestured to my shirt. "He's annoying." I didn't mean to, but I glanced his way again. "Sweet, but annoying. This is a girls-only fishing trip and I don't want him to think we would love for him to join us. That's all I'm saying, okay?"

Sweet? Why did I say he was sweet? I picked up a can of peas and pretended to read the label. Hmm, 30% of daily Vitamin C can be found in one serving of peas. Interesting.

In my peripheral vision, I saw Emily look from me to him and back. "Wow. He's sweet, huh?"

Crap! I slammed the can on the shelf. As soon as she said the words, I started mentally shopping for a Sydney-sized muzzle. Emily is quick to play matchmaker, especially since Dirk and I broke up.

Her eyes were alight with mischief. "You actually noticed a man? Did you talk to him? Come on, we'll introduce ourselves."

If I walk backwards, can I have hindsight *before* I get in trouble?

I planted my feet as she started to pull me away. "Emily! I already met him. He may be cute, but he—" I looked around to be sure he wasn't nearby. "He's just trying to pick up women."

"Oh, really?"

You've never experienced "her gaze pinned her to the wall" until you've had Emily stare you down to get information. Escape is impossible.

"Forget him, Em. Girls trip. Who cares? He already used a line on me anyway, but I told him to get lost."

Emily folded her arms and smiled.

Shooty. Hindsight again.

"Now we're getting somewhere. And what, pray tell, was the line?"

In the movies, you can disarm a bomb before it goes off. You just have to choose the red wire or the blue wire.

"It was nothing. Something about helping me change my shirt. It was stupid. Don't worry about it."

Emily peered over her shoulder looking for the man in question. Then she moved closer and grabbed my arm, whispering, "The Diet Coke Man wants to take off your shirt? You should go tell him yes!"

I knew I should've cut the blue wire.

I looked at Emily for an instant, letting my eyes dart over her shoulder to the fine form once again digging something — trash? — from the bottom of that stupid barrel. Emily followed my gaze and let out a low whistle.

Mortified, I darted away. I saw Mikki and Tracey and

another girl named Laura nearby. They followed Em's gaze and giggled.

I peeked out from the end of an aisle, examining a box of Cheerios. The Diet Coke Man stood and walked toward the cash register. He rang up that other fisherman who'd been looking at tackle. He seemed oblivious to the commotion he was causing. Faker. How can he not notice so many women admiring his fabulous form?

His eyes met mine across the room and his smile faded to politeness. Well, great, make me feel bad then. I pretended to study the back of the cereal box. I may be in a cranky mood, but I really don't mean to be cranky *at* people.

I sighed in genuine despair. This vacation was not a good idea.

"Ladies, over here please!" I heard Patty's voice and saw a disconnected arm waving from behind one of the shelves to my far right. She is *so short*. But then look who's talking. I swear people don't take me seriously just because I'm short and I look younger than I am.

Emily came up behind me and whispered, "We should get her one of those fake hands from the Halloween store and put it on a stick for her to wave. Then everyone can see her."

I chuckled as we moved closer to hear. Leave it to Emily to try to make me laugh when I needed it. I leaned against a shelf of various gloves and other outdoor paraphernalia. I always thought the gray gloves with the red stripes on them only looked right on railroad guys. You know, train engineers and stuff.

"Can you all hear me? Quiet down now. We're going to unpack and relax in a few minutes, but first our fishing guide would like to give us the itinerary for the weekend. Matt?"

"Welcome to Abundance Creek, ladies," said a familiar voice. I dropped the ugly green gloves I was playing with and looked up in alarm.

Emily stood on her tiptoes, then grinned back at me and pulled me closer. There he was. The Sprite Guy, who looked amazingly like The Diet Coke Man, was the fishing guide. I closed my eyes and groaned. I can't believe I thought the *fishing guide* was hitting on me!

I thought about everything he'd said to me today. Not once did he say, "Let's play house." Not "I'd like to suck your lips off." Not even "Would you like to have dinner?" Gun-shy. Isn't that what they call women like me?

Hopeless. That's what I call women like me.

He's gorgeous, breathed Little Miss Lovesick.

I ignored her, clueless as to how to argue.

"I'm Matt Engel, and I'll be your fishing guide this weekend. I'll teach you how to fly fish, how to clean your catch, cook it, whatever you want."

Emily leaned over and whispered, "Whatever I want? How about father my children?"

I elbowed her to be quiet. Matt's eyes met mine and I looked away. Picking up a Thermos from the shelf next to me, I unscrewed the top. Nice. I screwed it back on and put it down. Anything to keep from meeting those electric blue eyes.

"Unless you already have dibs on him," Em whispered. "Then we'll have to work something out."

I could feel the blood rising in my cheeks. *"Em!"* I whispered. I knew she was teasing me, but I couldn't keep myself from reacting.

"If you go exploring, please do everyone a favor and let people know where you're going so we know where to send the search party if you don't come back."

Everyone laughed. I bet he was serious, though. It seemed like we drove forever to get here and passed very little on the way. I remembered the wolves and shivered. I'd stay close to the lodge.

"There's plenty of fun and relaxing things to do around Abundance Creek, but if you just want to be left alone—"

He looked straight at me and winked.

"—we're happy to oblige."

He *winked* at me. Why did he do that?

Emily glanced at me and back at Matt. She whispered in a singsong, "Somebody likes you. Somebody likes you."

Little Miss Lovesick grinned inside.

CHAPTER 3

*A*s we moved our belongings from the van to the bunkhouse, I breathed in the pine-scented air. Ahh. I looked around at the buildings snuggled into the woods as if the trees had morphed into a welcoming home for those who needed to leave their troubles behind. No cars, no planes, no noise — just birds and breezes.

Poetically sappy. That's me.

Em and I dropped our stuff into a room, then explored a bit. The front third of the building was a kitchen, the middle third was a dining area, and the last portion was a living room kind of area. A huge stone fireplace served to separate the dining and living rooms. Since it was summer and too warm for an indoor fire, you could look right through the fireplace into the other room. In fact, if you bent down a bit, you could *walk* through it.

On the two long walls of the bunkhouse were eight small rooms, four on each wall, with two sets of bunk beds each. In each corner of the building were bathrooms. Two were clearly marked "Women," and the other two had a large piece of paper taped over the door with "Ladies" written in black magic marker. I bet there were urinals in the "Ladies" rooms.

Only a few trophies decorated the living area. There was a huge fish (don't ask me what kind, but it had teeth), a massive rack of antlers, and a beautiful black bear skin. The décor was understated wilderness: hewn beams and muted colors.

The biggest surprise was the upright piano against one wall. I walked over and played a C chord. It was even in tune. The opening bars of "Piano Man" skittered across my mind, chased quickly away by a desire to preserve my dignity. I wasn't good enough to play in public.

We saw that the other women chose to finish unpacking before relaxing, so Em and I went back to our room to do the same. I was relieved we didn't have to triple up with anyone. I don't mean to sound rude, but I just might have to thumb a ride home if I had to be caged up with someone who snores.

When I leaned over to unzip my suitcase, something hit me in the back of the head. "Hey!" A bag of Reese's Pieces landed on my sleeping bag. I turned to look at Em.

"Ta-daa!" With a triumphant look, she opened a Walmart bag to show me a dozen more Reese's Pieces and a dozen Hershey bars. Our favorites.

"Ah, you know how to make a girl happy," I said and tore open the package, choosing to ignore the Voice that was counting calories. Maybe I'd start my low-sugar diet after the candy ran out. I changed into a dry T-shirt, tossed the flannel shirt on top of my suitcase, and Em and I fell back onto our bunks to eat our candy.

"Seriously, Sydney, our cute fishing guide was definitely hitting on you."

"Which is precisely the reason I don't like him already." Technically, I was lying. He seemed nice enough. But I needed to put a stop to Em's ideas.

"Yeah, right, I forget how that works. Only flirt with guys who ignore you. I always get that one wrong."

I threw an orange peanut butter candy in her direction. "I

didn't come up here to flirt, I came up here to heal. Rebound relationships rarely last because they're rarely healthy. I'll get healthy, *then* start...you know, dating." It felt weird to say it. When I moved to Traverse City, I assumed I'd never have to date again.

"Quoting another Internet guru? I'm telling you, flirting *is* a healthy way to move on. Trust me."

Listen to her, urged Little Miss Lovesick.

I'll admit, it did feel good to have the attention of a seemingly nice and definitely attractive man. And we were only here for the weekend. If Emily was wrong, we'd be safely home again in three days and I'd never see him again.

I sat up on my bunk and stared hard at Em. "You really think it'd be good for me?" Even though she didn't have a boyfriend right now, she always seemed so confident when it came to relationships.

"Healthy and harmless." She crossed a finger over her heart. "I swear."

I ate some more of my candy, pairing up the brown ones with either an orange or a yellow and eating them two at a time. After a minute, I said, "Okay, I guess." I looked up at Em again. "But don't get pushy, okay?"

She grinned. "You're going to feel so much better. Come on, let's go outside."

We wandered out and sat on the porch swing. It was in good shape, but it looked old. I liked that.

"This is the life, huh?" said Emily.

"Mmm," I said as we set the swing in motion.

We both leaned back and closed our eyes. The breeze tickled the leaves and rustled them like quiet wind chimes. I smiled. I just might have to sit here the whole weekend.

Footsteps sounded down the porch. They got closer until they stopped and I heard another chair creak nearby.

"Ah, this is the life, huh, girls?" Patty's voice floated over and we giggled without opening our eyes or changing the rhythm of the rocker.

"I just said those exact same words," murmured Emily.

Creak, swish, creak, swish. The rocker lulled us into a lazy peacefulness. It felt *soo* wonderful. A few minutes later, more footsteps sounded on the grass, getting closer. I opened one eye and saw Matt coming toward us.

Patty waved. "Matt, this is wonderful. You and Ted have outdone yourselves."

"I'm glad you're enjoying it," Matt said as he turned toward us and stopped. "I guess you were right about the swing." He put one foot on the bottom step and leaned against the railing, nodding toward Em and me.

His wavy dark hair was tousled and messy. His eyes and his mouth always seemed to be smiling. I liked people who smiled a lot. Normally, I'm one of them. I thought about Em's suggestion that I do a little flirting. How do you start again? I noticed his biceps and forearms were tanned and covered in muscle. Nice, but I couldn't really say, hi, so how'd you get all those muscles?

He is so sexy, crooned Little Miss Lovesick.

I closed my eyes again. Too relaxed to argue. Especially about that.

Patty laughed. "I didn't unpack quickly enough."

"Did you want to sit here?" I asked. I turned toward Patty, poised to get up.

"I can trade with you if you want," Emily volunteered.

Matt grinned and Patty laughed. "No, no, no. You girls enjoy it. I'm fine for now."

"Patty and my uncle argued all winter about whether he should bring up this swing. He insisted no one would sit on it, but it looks like he was wrong."

"It used to be in my backyard. But we got a new one and I couldn't think of a better place for that one than up here. Worst case, I'd sit in it every time I came up."

"You all know each other then?" Emily finally opened both eyes.

"Oh, where're my manners? Matt this is Sydney Riley and Emily Dodson." The three of us murmured our acknowledgements. "Matt's mother and I were best friends all through school."

"And you still are?" I said.

"Well, she died when Matt was a boy." Patty smiled in a motherly way at Matt and he smiled back. Smiles tinged with a bit of sadness. It made my heart ache a little. Seemed I was sensitive to *anyone* losing someone they loved.

"Are you going to build our little fire?" Patty asked, eyeing the bag in Matt's arms.

"I can't build a little fire. I can only build towering bonfires." Matt's eyes sparkled and Patty laughed. Her eyes widened and she said, "I know!" like there was a story there somewhere.

"What's in the bag?" Emily asked.

"Hot dogs, condiments, s'more fixin's, napkins—" Matt peered inside as he listed the contents.

"S'mores?" Emily interrupted. She stopped rocking and we looked at each other and smiled. "Hey, I know you probably need to get that fire started and, you know, watch it and all. We'll set up the supplies for you, if you like." She elbowed me.

The supplies Emily referred to were, of course, the s'mores makings. If you haven't eaten s'mores on a summer's evening, you haven't lived. A big fluffy marshmallow toasted over an open fire until it was golden brown, then pressed between two graham crackers with a big square of Hershey's chocolate. Yum. So good, you always wanted "some more."

For s'mores, I could pretend to flirt. "We're very good at setting up supplies," I said in a mock serious tone. "We set up supplies all the time, don't we, Em?"

"All the time," she echoed, standing up. "Patty, don't you think he needs help setting up the supplies?"

Patty waved her hand at us and laughed. "I'm sure he'd love your help. You all go start dinner"—she got up from her chair—"and I'll reintroduce my seat to that old rocker."

"Well, if you want to." Matt looked at me like he wondered if I was going to play nice or not. I smiled brightly at him, hoping that was the right amount of flirtatiousness. He smiled and made a manly grunting sound, then led the way to the fire pit.

"Are you ladies enjoying the U.P. so far?" Matt asked as we walked along.

If you're not familiar with Michigan, it's surrounded by the Great Lakes so both land masses are called peninsulas. The Lower Peninsula is where Traverse City is, where I live. The Upper Peninsula is bordered by Canada on the north, and it's mostly just called the U.P.

"Oh, it's wonderful," said Emily. "The flowers and the scenery — and we saw a bear on the way here! Very cool."

Matt smiled at her contagious enthusiasm. (Everyone does.) "What about you?" He turned to look at me. His expression was kind and gentle. For a second, I wanted to put my hand in his and walk for a very long time. Not Little Miss Lovesick. Me. I wondered what Patty had said to him. Why else would he look at me that way?

I mentally shook myself and decided to go the witty route. "Hmm, I've found it to be"—I looked away—"damp and sticky." I looked back to find the tug of a grin beginning around his mouth. I felt a bit of a tug around my mouth, too. I was tired of being mad at people. In fact, the little relaxation I'd gotten on the porch swing had helped a lot. There was no reason not to be friends. Or at least friendly. We'll see about flirtatious later.

"Damp and sticky, huh?"

I noticed below his lovely blue eyes, a day or two of whiskers covered his cheeks. I never had to push Dirk to shave every day because he's the kind of guy who wants to look professional seven days a week. I like kissing a clean-shaven man better than one with whiskers. But there was a certain charm to Matt's unshaven state.

"Any chance of improvement in the forecast?" he asked.

I tried to act like I was thinking. "Mm, I think tonight is expected to be a vast improvement. A fire, food, fun — and s'more food." I couldn't help but laugh a little.

"Definitely, s'more food is in the forecast," Emily chimed in. "Which will likely lead to s'more fun."

Matt laughed. "Okay, point taken. I'll get that fire going."

We'd walked down a wide trail in the woods and into a small clearing. A firepit the size of a small car was in the middle. There were huge logs around it that I assumed were for sitting on because a pile of chopped firewood waited to one side. A couple picnic tables made up the balance of the man-made objects. The simple setting was perfect.

Matt dropped the bag of groceries on the nearest picnic table and walked over to the pile of wood, grabbing some smaller pieces. "Either of you know how to start a fire?"

Emily pulled the hot dog buns out of the top of the bag. She looked at me and grinned as she answered. "Sydney knows how to build a great fire." My eyebrows rose. We had a gas fireplace at my parents' house. You flipped a switch and had a fire. "She used to be a Girl Scout," Em finished.

"No, I, uh, that was a long time ago." I made a *what are you doing?* face at Emily. She nodded her head in Matt's direction. Thankfully he wasn't looking our way. *Stop it!* I mouthed with a glare. Building fires was one of the many things I did *not* learn how to do in Girl Scouts. This smelled like an Emily setup to me.

"Come help me get this thing going and you'll have your s'mores in no time," he said as he arranged the kindling in the bottom of the pit.

This is the point in the movie when the audience yells, "No! Don't do it!" But like all movie heroines, I blindly moved forward, not knowing that this moment just might be the beginning of the end.

I walked over to Matt, feeling a little stupid, and stood there watching him. He took a long-nosed lighter like people use to light their fireplaces and started dry leaves and grass burning under some twigs.

"Hand me some more of that kindling," he said. He pointed behind him to a little pile of sticks. I squatted down and handed them over, and he fed the growing fire.

What is it about a T-shirt and jeans that is such a turn-on? Twice in one day, I was admiring this man's very fine rear end. Women complain about being ogled like a sex object, but we do a pretty good job of doing the same thing to men.

Matt backed up a couple steps as the fire burned higher. I nearly fell over in my haste to get out of his way. The contact I was trying to avoid happened anyway when he reached down and clasped my wrist, pulling me up. "Why don't you move back a step. The fire's going to be hot soon."

Soon? The calluses on his hand tickled the inside of my wrist. I think the fire is too hot already. I was torn between trying a little flirting per Emily's suggestion or backing up and getting away, far away. My not-yet-healed heart made the decision. I pulled back.

"Looks like you've got it going, so...I'll just see if Emily needs any help."

The words were barely out of my mouth before Emily called, "Oh, I've got it under control here. Matt, you need Syd to help you with anything else?"

Matt tossed another couple pieces of wood on the fire and backed up a little more. He looked over his shoulder at me and said, "Wanna help make some hot dog skewers?"

"Sure. What do you want me to do?" I tried to sound cheerful, easy-going, not at all intimidated by his presence or the fact that he was asking me to help with something I was clueless about. Hot dog skewers. How hard can that be? I could keep a comfortable distance between us. It'd be fine.

He pulled a pocketknife from his jeans and took a long, green stick from a pile on the ground. Unfolding the knife, he grabbed the end of the stick and, with a few clean hard swipes, had a perfect skewer for hot dog roasting and marshmallow toasting.

"Okay?" He smiled and handed me the knife and another stick.

I gulped and took the knife very carefully from him. Concentrate on the task at hand. Don't think about his smile. I have a task. I can focus. This is good. I took a swipe at the stick. Not bad. I can do this.

I glanced up as Matt happened to look my way. He smiled. I smiled back. If a butterfly flaps its wings in your stomach, will there be a storm?

I looked back at the stick I held and took another swipe with the knife. Yes, concentration is good. The stick is looking fine. Just have a little knot here. Careful. I'll cut it the other way.

Out of the corner of my eye I saw Matt lean over, grab another log, and toss it onto the fire. The muscles in his arms were amazing.

I pressed too hard with the knife. It hit the knot and went flying along the wood toward my hand. Matt turned to me just as I nearly cut my thumb off.

"Whoa, there!" He jumped toward me and grabbed both of my hands in his, holding the knife hand away and looking closely at the thumb I nearly lost. "You okay?"

He's quite a bit taller than me and he'd bent down to examine my hands for blood and missing digits. His face was very close to mine. I looked for the telltale ring around his irises that would prove he's wearing blue contacts.

"Fine. I'm fine." I felt like I was stuttering. "There was a knot." I held up the stick, but I was still looking in his eyes. No contacts. Real blue eyes. I felt his hands holding mine. *That* was contact. I pulled away. After all, I didn't know this guy. He could be a total lunatic.

He's not a lunatic, he works here, said a Voice.

Remember The Shining, said another.

Patty knows him, so he must be safe.

But I don't feel safe. I feel like I'm being slowly electrocuted. That Voice certainly had the right of it.

Matt let go of my hands and stood to my left, explaining to me how to safely sharpen the end of a stick with a knot in it. But there were too many other Voices and I couldn't concentrate. I pulled the knife down the end of the stick and hit the knot again.

"Hold on, you're going to hurt yourself." Before I knew it, his right arm was around my back and holding my right hand. His left hand covered mine and he moved the knife smoothly over the wood.

I'd always wanted Dirk to teach me something in a romantic gesture like this. Like what you see in the movies. A man's arms around the woman he cares for, showing her how to swing a golf club or swing a tennis racket or...

Or sharpen a hot dog stick. Oh geez, he smells good. I closed my eyes for a moment. Like sunshine and spices and...and fire. Matt shifted his weight. I could feel his entire body behind me. His breath moved my hair, which tickled my ear.

"You see?" he said. He moved the knife again, my hand still held in his.

Should I say no so he'll stay? The Voice in my head seemed logical to me.

I know he was just helping me sharpen a stick without cutting my hand off. I know that. But it *felt* like being held. And I couldn't remember the last time I'd been held. I don't know if I moved closer or he did. But as the knife continued to move up and down the stick, I felt his body wrap around mine. I closed my eyes again, feeling content for the first time in months.

The knife stopped moving. I opened my eyes and turned my head to look at him. A bolt of electricity raced through my body. He must've felt it, too, because he pulled away suddenly with a surprised look in his eyes.

He cleared his throat. "And, uh, that's how you, uh, yeah…"

CHAPTER 4

I'd like to say that the next day, the first day of fishing lessons, I showed no ill effects from playing with fire the night before. But the alarm went off before the sun rose, and Em and I were talking until only a few hours earlier. One particular subject dominated the conversation, a subject that I was about to spend a good part of the day with again.

What I really wanted to do was hide under my pillow and let the world take its course without me. As appealing as that sounded, I didn't want anyone to think I had in any way been affected by — well, by anything or any*one*. Besides, Em was right. I'd spent too much time crying in bed the last few months. Today was the second day of my plan to heal myself if it killed me.

I rolled out of bed, threw on some clothes, splashed cold water on my face — very cold, which woke me up a little — and felt my way in the darkness to the porch. Shelley was dozing leaning against a beam and Patty looked asleep in the rocker. Emily followed me out a minute later, looking a bit more awake. We sat down on the porch steps to wait for Matt.

Em and I both wore new khaki shorts with cargo pockets.

Emily — of course! — insisted on buying them at Dunham's Sports when we bought the sleeping bags. I was trying to decide if I was just tired or if it was too cold for only a T-shirt. Surely it would warm up soon. I checked to see if Em wore a sweatshirt.

"Do you have makeup on?" I asked, thinking I was too tired to see straight.

"No," she said. "Just some mascara and eye shadow."

"Right, just what's absolutely necessary for pre-dawn fly-fishing." I didn't have it in me to put on makeup before dawn on vacation. I could just see myself sticking my eye with a mascara wand.

She leaned her head on my shoulder and said, "Shut up" as she closed her eyes.

I saw movement in the morning shadows and watched Matt materialize. I didn't even realize there was ground fog until he walked through it. With a little imagination, he reminded me of Aragorn in the *Lord of the Rings* movies, coming to save his people. The thought made me smile.

Matt caught me watching him — I was probably the only one with my eyes open so it couldn't have been difficult — and mistakenly thought I was smiling at him. He smiled back. I blurted out "Good morning, Aragorn" in a tired mumble. I have no filter when I'm tired.

He winked at me. "Morning. Ready to go fishing?"

I grunted. "What, we don't look ready to you?"

"I think," he said, sitting on the porch next to me, "that you ladies stayed up past your bedtime last night."

Yeah, stayed up talking about you, Mr. Stud Muffin. I pretended indifference to the nerve endings firing throughout my body. I could feel the heat radiating from him and thought I should probably go get a sweatshirt because it felt really nice.

"You mean, this morning. We stayed up past our bedtime *this morning.*"

"Ouch," he said with a mock pained expression.

Without moving from my shoulder, Emily mumbled, "It had to be done. That's what vacations are for. That's what girlfriends are for."

"Well, in that case, I'm glad I don't have one because I, for one, got a wonderful night's sleep and I'm ready to catch some fish." He nudged my knee with his.

Emily sat up and yawned. Patty and Shelley stretched and ambled down the steps.

"Anyone else coming?" he asked. He started distributing the fishing poles that I hadn't noticed were leaning against the porch railing. He must've brought them down earlier. Wow, talk about an early riser.

"Wait for us, we're coming." Tracey and Janice came through the door, rubbing their eyes and pulling their hair back.

"This morning," Matt began, "we're starting late because I need the light to show you how to tie on the flies. It's pretty overcast right now so it'll be hard to see, but we'll manage. Tomorrow, I'll be down here at five for anyone who wants a good shot at catching some big fish."

"We're going to be here at five sharp," Emily whispered to me amid the groans of the other women.

Like I'm really going to get up at 4:30. On a Sunday morning. So glad this is only a weekend trip. I'm going to have to go back to work to recover.

"The poles I've given you are based on your height, so try to hang on to the same one. At Patty's suggestion, I decided to have you all use artificial lures instead of live bait, so there's no reason not to learn how to tie on your own flies."

Memory of the movement under the plastic lid yesterday whizzed through my mind. Yuck. Why did I come on a fishing trip without even thinking about whether I would enjoy fishing?

To get away from thinking about Dirk.

Oh yeah. Well, speaking of not thinking about him...

"There's a lot of fish in our little stream," Matt continued. "I hope I can help you each catch a few. But trust me, they aren't going to jump up and volunteer to be your dinner."

We all chuckled. An image of a fish that looked like Horshack from *Welcome Back Kotter* popped into my mind. "Oo, oo, oo! Pick me! I want to be your dinner!" I released a tired giggle. Emily looked at me and mouthed "What?" I just shook my head.

"All right. Ready to have some fun?" Matt asked.

"You're excessively chipper this morning," said Shelley with a yawn. "I think everyone else is sleepwalking."

"Well, the fish are awake and they're hungry. Let's go get some breakfast, ladies."

We followed Matt down a path behind the lodge. I tripped twice on the way. (I was tired, and it was dark. I'm not *that* clumsy.) The third time I tripped, I nearly landed on my face. Matt turned around just in time to grab me and set me back on my feet.

"You okay?" He didn't let go of my arm.

"Fine. It's dark." I tried to pull free.

Matt glanced at the women behind him. "No one else seems to be having problems."

Emily piped up from behind me. "That's because we're using Sydney as a guide. We're walking wherever she doesn't."

I started to slide on loose pebbles and grabbed his upper arm with my free hand. I pulled myself close. Oh man, he smelled good.

"What the heck kind of shoes are you wearing?" Exactly how I wanted to start Day Two of my vacation. I ignored him. Besides, they were the most comfortable sandals I owned.

Yeah, but you never thought about smooth leather soles on a slippery gravel trail, did ya?

"Sydney, didn't you bring any sneakers?" Patty asked. "Do you need to borrow some other shoes?"

"I tried to tell you," said Em.

"I'm fine." I turned in her direction. And slid a couple inches on more loose gravel.

"Don't let her fall, Matthew," Patty said in her "mom" voice. "I'll have to talk to Ted about this trail."

As I got my feet under me, I once again tried to pull away. Matt interlaced his fingers through mine.

"Oh, no you don't. Hang on or I'll carry you."

"Yeah, right," I snorted under my breath. I was too tired to be polite, and too nervous I might fall into the river and never be heard from again to risk letting go. Besides, his hand was warm. It was surprisingly chilly out for June. But then, we couldn't have driven much farther north without ending up in Canada.

A short walk brought us to the stream, flashing and gurgling in the early morning light. Along the bank stood silvery birch trees. Soft, green ferns grew thick on the forest floor. The morning calls of robins and chickadees filled the air. I breathed in the smell of earth and water. Mm, thank you, God.

Matt stopped at a wider area of the bank and showed us how to tie on the flies. I can't express how relieved I was to *not* have to use "live bait." Ugh! Then he showed us how to cast.

"What you're going to do is bring the rod back in a back cast, then forward — that's the forward cast — a couple of times until the line is just long enough to toss the fly gently onto the area of the stream you think the fish are at. Watch." Matt demonstrated as we watched carefully. The fly landed with barely a ripple.

I tried not to be impressed. He made it look like he wasn't even trying. I guess that's what you want in a fishing guide, though, someone who knows how to fish. I yawned.

After a couple of demonstrations and a few questions, we spread out along the bank. I tied the lure Matt had given me onto the line and studied it for a moment. "It looks like chicken feathers," I said.

"Mine looks like a dragonfly, only smaller," said Emily, holding it up for my inspection.

As we each practiced our casting, Matt walked up and down the riverbank giving pointers and encouragement. I yawned as I cast the rod back, forward, back, and release. I pulled the string, wire, *line* (whatever, I am *so* tired) back in for another practice cast. Someone please remind me why I'm doing this again. With someone like Emily for a best friend, how were we not at a spa resort right now? Still sleeping.

"Matt, when you're done, I need some help," called Emily.

I watched her for a moment. "I think you're doing great. Better than me."

"Thanks, but I really want to learn how to do this right so I can catch some fish." Emily frowned as she re-cast her line.

Matt went over to help her. Em concentrated on what he was saying, then cast a few more times. Finally, she smiled and nodded. Matt smiled at her, then looked over at me. My stomach took a dive. Must be hunger. Yeah. I need breakfast.

I went back to fishing. Don't look at him. Pull the line in. Back, forward, back — I shivered really hard and broke my very little concentration. I messed up the line, catching it in my hair in the process.

A chuckle near my left ear made me shiver again.

"A bit tangled up, eh," Matt said as he pulled the line from my hair. I'd forgotten to pull it into a baseball cap and my hair was a wavy brown mess. I should've brought my straightener, camping or not.

I tried to joke around. "I shivered and lost my aim. Now I understand why all the stores sell flannel shirts. Even in June."

"Well, you caught us in a warm spell this week." He straightened out my fishing gear and handed it to me.

Then he started unbuttoning his shirt. I shivered again, trying not to watch him and watching anyway out of the corner of my eye. Holy cow, what was he doing? I dug my fingernails into one palm, the hands-full approach to pinching myself. Ow. I was either awake or having a disturbing dream. A wonderfully disturbing dream.

He took his shirt off and put it around my shoulders.

"Hey, what — no, I'll just go back and get a sweatshirt."

He pried my fishing pole out of my hands. It wasn't difficult since I could barely feel them. I just stood there, torn between letting him be the gentleman and insisting on my independence.

"Your hands are freezing," he said quietly. "No wonder you cast into the woods instead of the stream."

Point taken. I'd let him play gentleman for now, but tomorrow I'd remember my hoodie. Matt helped me get my arms into the sleeves as I tried to figure out what drugs I'd taken the day before. I must've been on something to agree to Emily's flirtation plan. It had seemed logical enough when Matt wasn't around. But when he stood so close... How could this be happening? This drop-dead gorgeous hunk in a white T-shirt and jeans was dressing me (okay, unusual in a sexy dream) in his flannel shirt (another point to make one wonder about one's ability to imagine well) while half a dozen women looked on curiously.

Okay, good point. Not sexy exactly, but nice.

Really nice, sighed Little Miss Lovesick.

Matt buttoned his shirt up to the last button, then turned the cuffs back so my hands showed through. I tried to focus on gratitude not attraction, but holy smokes, his hair smelled good. I shivered once more even as I felt ridiculously warmer. I didn't know what to think about his attraction thing. I hadn't spared more than a glance for another man since I met Dirk four years ago.

"You're going to get cold." I eyed him again. Soft white cotton wrapped around his chest. A chest that I could clearly see was amazingly muscular. More than work-out-at-the-gym muscular.

He chuckled softly, moving closer, lighting all my nerves on fire. "I'm an All-American red-blooded boy. I think I can take it."

The last time my stomach felt this way was right before I threw up, the month after Dirk the Jerk dumped me, when I drank too much wine and ate too much Ben & Jerry's ice cream trying to drown my sorrows.

"You okay now? Ready to try again?" He placed my hands correctly on the pole.

No, I am *not* ready to try again. All I wanted in the whole world was to be a wife, eventually a mother, and have a home of my own. One occasionally decorated with unexpected flowers from a doting husband. But I didn't know how to try again. I'd made a serious error in judgment when it came to the character of the man I loved. How could I trust myself not to make the same mistake again? Especially when I didn't know where I went wrong. But being around Matt, oh, I wish I *was* ready to try again.

He leaned closer, adjusting the fishing line. Oh, you smell so good — concentrate, concentrate on the river, casting, don't cast the fishing pole into the water.

I kept my eyes forward and hoped the sudden rush of warmth in my face was not visible in the dim light.

"Remember what to do?" he whispered.

"Why are we whispering?" I whispered back.

"So we don't scare the fish away."

Oh yeah, I vaguely recollected him mentioning that.

I tried again. Now that I was warmer and not shivering, I did a better job. Meaning I landed the fly in the river rather than in my hair. But certainly nowhere near where Matt had landed it.

"Not bad, not bad. Pull it in and try it again," he said.

It was one thing to keep a cool head when Matt was not in sight. It was another thing altogether when he was standing so close I could practically feel the heat from his body.

"It's in the water," I said, pointing (stupidly) in front of me. "It's fine. I don't want to take up everybody else's time."

I glanced upstream but no one seemed to be paying attention. I thought surely everyone would be wondering why Matt was spending so much time with me. Even Emily completely ignored everything around her. Man, that girl is serious about fishing.

"You're not taking up anyone's time. Come on, pull it in." Matt stood there smiling with his arms folded over his chest.

"I got it in the water," I said in mock irritation as I did as he asked.

He responded with mock seriousness, "A very good place to start when trying to catch a fish."

I laughed in spite of myself.

The sun was still hidden behind the tall trees, but it was lighter out and that automatically meant I was waking up. At least mostly.

I yawned.

"Now," Matt said as he stepped behind me and put his right hand over mine on the fishing pole.

I bit the yawn off in surprise and nearly bit my tongue. Why did it seem this man was always putting his arms around me?

"Hold the pole like this." He adjusted my hand a bit. "And the line like this." He let go of my right hand and moved to my other side to put the line in my left hand.

"Go ahead." Matt stood looking at me expectantly, arms crossed over his chest again.

I looked down at my hands and wondered what I'd missed. I turned back to him. He smiled and shook his head a little, his eyes twinkling like the sunlight on the stream.

"Go ahead and cast."

"I'm really not good at—"

Matt cut me off with a wave of his hand. (Or was he swatting at a fly?) "You're fine. You can do it. Go ahead."

I wasn't so sure. My goal in life at this moment was to not look like a complete imbecile. I stood there for a second hoping I wouldn't embarrass myself when I felt his arms wrap around me.

No, I mean really. Not the very discrete and professional thing he was doing a minute ago. I'm talking both arms around me, both hands on mine, the warmth of him behind me, practically cheek to cheek. He moved the pole and the line, explaining everything again as he made my hands go through the movements.

His voice was low and soft near my ear. "Forward, back, and release, letting the line go out...and then you're done."

He moved his hands to my shoulders but didn't move away.

"See? I told you you could do it."

I turned to say thank you (I couldn't think of anything else to say), but as I did I noticed how close his lips were. I mean, it's not that I was looking, exactly. But I'm quite a bit shorter than he is and his lips were right at my eye level.

I risked a quick glance and noticed Emily grin and look away. A movement farther down caught my eye. Patty smiled at us. Great. I can imagine how we looked. Apparently, so could Matt.

He dropped his hands and cleared his throat. "Call me if you need anything." He walked down the bank to help Mikki.

I turned back to the river. Amazingly, the fishing pole was doing its thing without me. There it was in my hands, the fly still floating in the water.

I am *so* not interested in him. I'm just tired, that's all. Maybe if we'd met later when I was looking for a good, healthy relationship. If I even knew what that was.

Mm, something smelled good. I dipped my head closer to the collar of Matt's shirt. Oh my. I closed my eyes for a moment and breathed in — what, soap? Aftershave? Something nice, whatever it was.

This is exactly why your mother told you not to have sex before marriage, the "Mom" voice droned in my brain. *Once you've had it, it's all you think about.*

I turned my face away from Matt's shirt. I am *not* thinking about sex!

I am, said Little Miss Lovesick.

I sighed. It doesn't matter. I've already run the gamut of self-destructive behaviors over the last four months. The last thing I'm going to do — no, not the last thing I'm *going* to do, the one thing I *won't* do — is try to find comfort in some cute guy's bed. Like the wine and the ice cream, it'll likely be something I really regret in the morning.

A booming voice inside yelled, *she* can *be taught!*

CHAPTER 5

*a*s the sun rose above the tree line, I tipped up my face to capture its warmth on my skin. Sighing peacefully, my eyes drifted open. I pulled gently on the line in my hand, trying to interest a fish in my lure — if there were any fish around. My gaze shifted across the water where I noticed a movement. I leaned forward trying to make out the shapes in the shadows of the trees.

A deer! I was almost positive. Yes! There was its white tail as it turned deeper into the forest. Not wanting to lose sight of it — come on, we saw a *bear* on the road on the way here, and now I was yards away from a deer — I took a step forward. In my slippery, smooth-soled sandals. My foot slipped. I spun my arms backward trying to regain my balance. But the grass-covered river bank was wet with dew and I slid right into the river.

Icy water rushed over me. I gasped and choked on water. Gotta get my feet under me. Keep my head above water. Too cold to think.

Something pulled at me. I fought harder to find my footing. My head broke the surface of the water. I coughed and tried to yell. I heard voices yelling back but I couldn't understand them. So cold.

"Let go, I got you," I heard behind me.

The voice came together with the realization that it wasn't some*thing* pulling at me but some*one*. I tried to relax.

And then I was on the bank, holding tight to my rescuer. Shivering and disoriented, I clung to him like a life preserver. Strong arms held me tight.

"You're okay," he said. "I've got you."

Emily and Patty hovered over me, arms and hands and voices wrapping around me as I shook with cold and surprise and embarrassment. The others rushed over and crowded around. As my brain defrosted, I realized everyone was jabbering at me, but my teeth were chattering too hard to respond.

"Is she all right?" Patty asked Matt.

"I think so," he answered. He rubbed his hands briskly up and down my arms. "We just need to get you warmed up," he said to me with a smile.

Keep smiling at me that way and I'll be plenty warm, said You-Know-Who.

I worried about brain damage. Because right now that particular voice made sense.

"Oh my gosh, are you okay?" Emily hugged me tight.

She looked like she might cry. Which would make me cry. Which would be even more embarrassing. Think of something funny to say. Think.

"Can I borrow your shoes?"

Emily pulled back to study my face. She blinked. Then she burst out laughing.

In seconds, everyone was laughing. I could feel the deep sound of Matt's laughter in his chest. For just a moment, all was right in the world. Cold and wet, but right. Which reminded me...

I looked up at Matt, who was still holding me. "I guess the forecast hasn't changed much," I said, trying to keep my teeth from chattering. "Damp and sticky just became cold and wet." Which made him and Em and me laugh even harder.

When Matt felt a huge involuntary shudder shake me, he turned to Patty. "Will you watch things down here? I'll take Sydney up to the lodge and be back as soon as I change into dry clothes."

"I'll come and help Syd," Em immediately volunteered. I smiled gratefully at her.

"Be sure she doesn't fall on that trail," Patty instructed Matt as he stood and pulled me upright. She turned to me. "Take a hot shower before you change clothes. No point in getting sick."

I nodded, clenching my jaw to keep my teeth still. Matt put his arm around me and pulled me close, leading me up the trail to the lodge. The trail wasn't wide enough for three, so Emily followed behind us.

"Matthew, you check in on her later and make sure she's okay," Patty called.

Matt raised one hand in the air, but didn't turn around.

"I'll stay with her," Emily called back.

"I'm so sorry," I said to Matt as he hurried me toward the bunkhouse. I slid and slipped more than ever. He was half carrying me, but I was too cold to care.

"Don't worry about it."

"But it's my fault that—"

"I said don't worry about it." He smiled down at me and brushed river water from my cheek. "These things happen."

I shivered again and tried to smile back.

"I really am fine." I tried to smile reassuringly up at him, my arms crossed tightly in front of my chest to keep from shivering.

His dimple appeared. "That was nothing. I've seen worse."

"At least I didn't get swept away, or attacked by piranhas, or—"

"No obituaries, please!" Emily exclaimed. "That was too close."

Matt laughed and hugged me tighter. "You're funny."

Right about then, my wet leather sandals hit that stupid gravel. I slid backward, but stayed upright since Matt already had me in a death grip.

"Clumsy, but funny."

I gasped. "I'm not clumsy!"

He looked at me and laughed in disbelief. "You're having a pretty difficult time walking and staying on dry ground today." He stopped and made a move to pick me up. "It'll probably be safer if I carry you back up the trail."

I backed out of his arms and pointed my finger at him. "I will drive a stake through your heart if you pick me up. I swear." There was a limit to how many embarrassing things I could survive in one day. And it wasn't even breakfast time yet.

Matt looked at me for a second then glanced back at Em, obviously trying to decide if I was serious. He rolled his eyes and shook his head. "All right, Buffy, but if you fall I'm carrying you."

I couldn't help but grin at the TV reference. He pulled me close to his side and we continued our slip-slide way up the trail.

At the bunkhouse, Matt and Emily helped me up the steps. "Do you need any help?" His hands rubbed my cold arms. Since my teeth were chattering, I gave him a look that said, "As if!"

Emily laughed and rolled her eyes. "Go!"

"Just thought I'd offer," he said. He opened the door. As I brushed past, I heard him chuckle.

Rescuer or rogue? That is the question.

Either one works for me, piped up Lovesick.

An hour later after a deliciously hot shower, I started back to the river, warm and dry in borrowed shoes and my hoodie zipped to my chin. The sun had risen above the tree line while I was inside so I was able to pick my way carefully down the trail. I didn't slip once.

I'd sent Emily back to the fishing lesson after assuring her I planned on staying in the shower for a week. I saw my fishing pole next to her at the river so I headed that way. The fact that Matt was helping her with her casting at that very moment had no bearing on my decision. Pulse, normal. Respiration, normal. Mental state, *crazy!*

Matt turned and looked at my feet, now clad in tennis shoes instead of sandals. "Much better." He winked at me.

He'd changed into khaki cargo shorts and a black T-shirt with *Runs With Scissors* printed on the front. Like his other T-shirts, this one clung to his muscular arms and chest. I told myself I only noticed because he looked so different from Dirk. Dirk was slim and toned, but not muscular. He spent most of his time in a business suit trying to move up the ladder. He didn't have the outdoorsy look Matt had.

Yeah, all I was doing was cataloging the differences. That's it.

I picked up my pole and moved down to a narrower part of the river. A swirling little eddy near the opposite bank looked to be the perfect place to try to sink the fly into. I stayed a good three feet from the edge of the bank, aimed, cast, missed and pulled in the line. Aimed, cast, missed, pulled in the line.

I heard some commotion up the bank, then a happy cry from Emily. She'd caught a fish. Cool!

Matt helped her pull it in. I hate to admit it, but watching it flap around with its buggy eyes and glistening body was not making me want to catch one. I didn't relish the idea of going all girly-girl when Matt came to help me. You know, "Eew! No, I don't want it! You take it!" How embarrassing would *that* be. I'd already met my embarrassment quota for this trip. Maybe I'd just pretend to try to catch fish for the rest of the weekend.

"Hope you're all hungry tonight," Matt said, holding Emily's fish up for everyone to see. "For a bite, anyway."

Oh, I hope it ends up looking like fish in a restaurant. After seeing it alive and jiggly, I didn't think I could sit around a campfire and eat something that still had its head attached.

I grimaced and turned back to my casting. Okay, trying to build a skill. That's it. Not trying to catch a fish. Hey, maybe I should take the lure and hook off the end. Then I *can't* catch any fish. No, then it wouldn't fly over the water right. It needed some weight. Hmm, I thought about it as I pulled in the line again. Well maybe I could—

"Lookin' good there."

I jumped. "Doggon*eit*! Stop sneaking up — are you *trying* to make me fall in?"

"Little jumpy, eh?" Matt smiled and crossed his (muscular) arms over his (muscular) chest. Apparently his usual stance. I needed to stop noticing. The last time I'd seen this many muscles on one man was when Hugh Jackman played Wolverine. Who cared about the storyline when *that* was onscreen the whole time?

Matt's damp hair formed little curls around the sides of his neck. My mother would say he needed a haircut, but I liked it. Pretty adorable, actually.

"At least you're a safe distance from the water here. I don't want to have to dive in after you again."

I looked at him and sniffed, nose in the air. Then I looked away and prepared to cast again. "I was *con*centrating," I said in a mock huffy tone.

I heard him laugh softly, but I didn't look at him. The last thing I wanted to do was look stupid while he was watching me.

I focused and cast the line out. Whew! I made it pretty close to the eddy I'd aimed for. I looked back at him with my eyebrows raised and sniffed again. "See?"

When he laughed, I couldn't help myself. I dropped my act and laughed, too.

But Matt barely glanced at the fly I had cast. I swear he was looking me up and down like, *you* know. I couldn't quite remember what I was going to say. Those eyes were just stunning in their intensity.

Now what was I supposed to do, to say? I panicked as he wandered a step closer. His eyes were mesmerizing.

"Do you wear blue contacts?" I burst out.

Every single voice in my head groaned.

I turned back to the river, making idiot faces at the water as I tried to figure out how to either turn back time or grab the first bus back to Traverse City.

He laughed again. "No, why?"

Now he stood right next to me so I had to stop with the faces.

I shook my head. "Nothing. You just have — I've never seen —" Surely I hit my head in the river and I have brain damage. I'm a freaking idiot.

Just say it. It won't sound stupid if you just say it.

"You're eyes are so beauti- blueti- blue," I stuttered, "I wondered if you wore blue contacts."

I closed my eyes and yanked on my fishing line. That *did* sound stupid.

He moved closer and lowered his voice. "You think my eyes are beautiful?"

"No!" I said quickly. "I said they're beau- *blue*!" Geez, I can't talk.

"You think my eyes are blue?" he said.

"No, I said—" I turned to look at him, completely flustered and saw he was laughing. Laughing right in my face. Close enough to—

I slugged him in the stomach without even thinking. Just left hand, wham! Like he was one of my cousins, always teasing me.

"Ugh!" he grunted, and laughed some more.

I started to do it again, but he grabbed my hand and wouldn't let go. I tried not to laugh as I pulled and twisted my hand.

"You think I have beautiful blue eyes, huh?" He had my left wrist in his right hand, his left arm still casually crossed against his chest, like it didn't take any effort at all to fend me off.

What isn't taking him any effort at all is making my stomach feel like I'm on a roller coaster, sighed Lovesick.

"Say it," he prompted.

"I'm trying to fish here," I said as I stopped struggling and tried to concentrate on the river — with one hand.

"Say it and I'll let you get back to fishing — or whatever it is you're doing while trying not to catch a fish."

"What? I'm trying to catch fish!" I looked at him indignantly and tried to pull away again. What does he know? The big tease.

"You are not. You're pretending to try to catch fish. Emily there is actually trying to catch fish." I looked past him at Emily, but my eyes came back to his.

I didn't want to give away that I'd just turned girly-girl about the slimy beasts. I like being in the middle — not girly-girl, not tomboy, just in the middle. And having the *fishing guide* know that I'd just decided that catching something alive with bulging eyes and a gaping mouth and then killing it and eating it was making me wish there was a grocery store around here — well, that was more than I could take. When I signed up for this trip, I had no idea I wouldn't like the stupid things.

"Fine. Say what?" I asked in exasperation.

He pulled my hand closer and grinned. "Say you think I have beautiful blue eyes."

"You have blue eyes, now let me go." I pulled away and he pulled me back.

"That's not what I said."

"You are a bully," I said trying to inject some backbone into my spineless self. But my insides felt like little firecrackers were going off all over.

"You must like it." His cute little dimples deepened. "Or you'd say it and get your hand back."

I narrowed my eyes and sucked in my breath. "I-do-*not*-like-it-you-have-beautiful-blue-eyes-so-there-let-me-go," I said with the speed of an auctioneer.

He laughed and pressed his lips to my fingertips before letting go of my hand.

"You are so easy," he said. Then at my offended look, hurriedly added, "To *tease*."

I gave him a look out of the corner of my eye meant to say, "It's a good thing you're so cute and funny or I'd bust you one." When he laughed, though, I had no idea if that's what he got from it.

If we were alone, you'd be in so much trouble now, said Lovesick.

I think I'm already in trouble.

CHAPTER 6

*a*fter dinner that night (six big fish — headless — filleted and fried in butter and flour, even *better* than a restaurant), Emily and I settled back against some logs not far from the fire where Matt had cooked our meal.

"So," Emily said, "when you gonna go flirt with him some more?"

Warning! Danger, Will Robinson!

Could I slip away unnoticed and hide from my well-meaning friend? I remembered the bear we'd seen on our way here. Maybe wandering the woods at night would be worse than what I was going through right now, but not by much. The problem wasn't that I didn't want to get to know Matt better. It was that I did. And that scared me.

"I wasn't flirting," I burst out in a stage whisper. "I was fishing."

"There's nothing wrong with it, you know." Emily patted my hand. "It's a normal healthy way to get to know someone, see if there's any chemistry."

"Then you flirt with him."

Em grinned and looked across the firepit to where Matt was

talking with Patty and Janice. "I'm not the one he's flirting back with."

I turned to her in surprise. Matt was flirting with *me*? Well, huh, I guess our playful banter could've been classified as... wow, okay. But I wasn't comfortable with the idea yet, so I said, "I was just fishing."

Emily snorted. "You were not."

"I was too!" Why does everyone keep saying that?

"Oh? How many fish did you catch?" Emily folded her arms and looked at me.

I tried to think up a lie that wouldn't make me laugh. "I caught...one...a great big one...but I had to throw him back... because...it was out of season."

Emily started to giggle. "I don't think you threw him back. You just want me to believe you did."

I turned back toward the fire to try and hide my grin. "No, I did throw him back. I don't much care for fresh fish and I don't need a trophy to take home."

"So don't worry about a trophy. Just enjoy the sport."

I looked at Emily in surprise. "I'm not really the sporting type."

She leaned closer. "It's a vacation. It's not like the fish will follow you home."

I hate to admit it, but Em's arguments weren't easy to dismiss. "I don't know, Em," I said. Though watching Matt, I was sorely tempted to follow her advice. "I'm not sure the cure isn't potentially worse than the disease."

She shook her head adamantly. "No way. No non-psycho is worse than Dirk. And you know someone who knows his family, so he's probably not a psycho. The chances that you'll wind up on the front page are almost nil."

Naive girl found dead this summer in the Michigan wilderness. Known to have bad luck with men, she nonetheless made sport of flirting with the fishing guide. Her last known words were, "He's safe. I know someone who knew his mother."

I could see Em warming to her subject — matchmaking or flirting, I wasn't sure which. I wanted to believe she was right. That flirting could be a safe, fun way to get a little fresh air into my weary soul. But it could also be stupid. After all, I came up here to get away from Heartbreak, not to see if I could go double or nothing.

"Trust me," she said. "When have I led you astray?"

"I don't know," I wavered. "I haven't flirted like that in a really long time. Over four years." The idea was beginning to sound like fun but, when it comes to men, I have a history of making poor decisions. All of which seemed like good ideas at the time.

Em twisted herself to face me and grabbed my hands. "You were doing it today. Just up the amperage. Turn on your charms."

"What do you mean? Kiss him? I can't kiss him. I barely know him!" I could feel panic coursing through my veins. Why do I listen to her?

Emily laughed. "No, you don't kiss him. You — well, I mean, if you want to kiss him, it's dark and there's a fire and moonlight, so it'd be perfect—"

"Em!" I whispered fiercely. I was getting cold feet already. I wasn't sure I could do this with finesse. And without finesse, it would just make me feel worse about myself than I already did.

"Flirting can be the way to recovery. I saw you flirting with him earlier — and enjoying it immensely, I might add." Em elbowed me lightly in the ribs.

I dropped my eyes. I couldn't argue with that. But I didn't mean it to be noticeable. The tiniest of smiles began to creep out. It *was* a lot of fun. And it didn't seem to be hurting anyone. Unless—

"What if he has a girlfriend?" I asked, rearranging myself against the log so we faced each other.

"He doesn't. Remember what he said this morning? He was glad he didn't have a girlfriend to keep him up talking all night? It's just harmless flirting, Syd. It's a fun self-esteem builder, that's all."

I snorted, and cocked my head at her. "And if it backfires, are you going to pick up the pieces?"

"Yes, but it won't." She leaned closer and grinned. "Trust me."

Emily and I had our heads together, whispering and giggling, occasionally sneaking a peek at Matt. A moment later, she tapped her finger on my arm and grinned.

Matt turned toward us and caught us watching him. He looked over his shoulder, then back at us, then over the other shoulder before looking at us again. Of course we laughed. Exactly what he wanted, I could tell. He grinned.

Okay, that was cute.

He excused himself and wandered around the fire to where we sat.

Okay, that was scary.

"Hi," said Emily. I looked at her and giggled softly. In one word she had managed to say, "Hello, tall, dark, and handsome stranger. Come talk to us, your adoring fans."

"Hi there, fisher ladies," he said. He nodded and smiled at Em, then looked at me in my jeans and sweatshirt. He hunkered down beside me. "Warm enough?"

I grinned saucily at him. (Or at least tried. I'm not sure what a "saucy" grin looks like, but it sounds sexy in a cuter way than pure sexy — which isn't me.) "For now," I said.

Oh my gosh, I did it! Even I recognized that as flirting.

"Let me know if you get cold," he said, never taking his eyes off me. "I'll give you the shirt off my back — 'cause I'm that kind of guy." He wiggled his eyebrows at me.

"Very Good Samaritan of you, kind sir. But how many shirts can you give away? Because you've already given me two."

He laughed. It made me feel like maybe I was cute and funny. I remembered his T-shirt from this morning. "So, what does 'Runs With Scissors' mean?"

"It's my Indian name."

I paused for an instant, then laughed. No, *he* was the cute and funny one.

The three of us chatted and laughed and ate s'mores. I could tell that Matt noticed me flirting. And it looked like he was enjoying it. Em was right — I was feeling much better.

After a while, Emily got to her feet. "I think I'm going to hit the hay so I can get up early and catch some fish before we go home tomorrow." She yawned a very ladylike (i.e., fake) yawn. "G'night, you two."

I looked around, suddenly noticing that the three of us were the only ones left around the fire. "Oh! Well—"

"Hey," Em said quickly, "would you mind giving me five minutes of privacy? I need to write a letter."

I looked at her funny. A letter?

"Oh, what am I saying?" She laughed down at Matt and me, still sitting against the log. "It'll take me more than five minutes to write a letter. Would you mind giving me a half hour?"

I chickened out. Couldn't do it. "I promise not to look," I said, getting up and dusting myself off.

Emily didn't give up easily. "I don't want to keep you up with the light on and all."

"Don't worry. I can sleep through anything." A big lie, and she knew it. "Thanks for the s'mores, Matt. See you in the morning."

Before she could say anything more than "good night," I grabbed her hand and hightailed it for the safety of our room.

Fun self-esteem building would have to wait for another day.

THE NEXT MORNING, I SLEPT IN WHILE THE OTHERS TOOK ONE last shot at fresh fish before we left for home. Having reconciled myself to the fact that it's nature I enjoy, not fishing, I sat on the porch swing most of the morning, thinking. I'd wanted an escape from my life so I could figure things out. I got the escape, but still had no idea what to do when I returned home.

I thought about Matt. Did the fact that I was so attracted to him mean my heart was healing? Or did it mean I was a complete basket case, a loser who couldn't go a day without a man in her life? I couldn't figure it out. I'd lost all perspective on my life.

I leaned my head back against the porch swing and rocked. The birds sang choruses all around me. I heard a squirrel chatter. Occasionally the leaves rustled in the breeze. I took a deep breath and let it out.

Maybe now was the time to simply *decide* to feel better. The words of my junior high gym teacher echoed in my head: "Fake it till you make it." Could I do that? Could I hold onto this peace that I felt right now?

Surprised, I opened my eyes and stopped rocking for a moment. Hey, I *did* feel at peace. It's been so long, I didn't even recognize it at first. A lazy grin spread over my face as I closed my eyes and started rocking again.

After a while, I went inside and grabbed a banana and a bag of Reese's Pieces (nutritious, I know) and headed off into the surrounding woods. I wanted to savor the peace and quiet for as long as possible. When we returned to the city tonight, my life would be there waiting for me. Maybe I could come back with a new attitude and that would make the difference.

At least I won't have to wonder about Matt. I have absolutely no interest in trying to see someone who lives so far away. Maybe the flirting this weekend really was a sign that I'm getting over my Heartbreak.

I stuffed my banana peel into the candy bag and put it in my pocket. The trees, the ferns, the birds, the woods — it all calmed me. (I know, calming ferns, weird. But I love ferns. They're like living lace.) I smiled and sighed. It was a fragile peace, but I thought I could hang onto it.

Maybe when I got home I'd keep my eyes open for a guy with some of Matt's characteristics. Funny, good-natured, part Tom Sawyer, part Hugh Jackman. Surely someone like that lives in Traverse City.

Maybe by the time you find him, said a Voice, *you'll be ready to do something about it.*

Yeah, that's a good plan. Take my time. Keep my eyes open. Relax and enjoy the good life I have. Then when I meet someone, I won't have any baggage to deal with.

I made my way back to the lodge, arriving as the others were packing up their fishing gear. Matt stood by the porch, collecting the fishing poles. He smiled as I approached. Yeah, I'd like to meet a man with such a kind smile.

"Have a nice morning?"

I closed my eyes dreamily. "Wonderful," I said. "I sat on the swing, then explored the woods. Eavesdropped on about a hundred conversations between the birds."

He chuckled. "I'm glad you enjoyed yourself."

"I just wish I could stay longer and wander around some more."

"I wish you could, too." His smile warmed. He stopped working on the fishing poles and leaned forward. "You know, I—"

Before Matt could finish, Mikki brought him her pole and regaled me with stories of "the ones that got away." As much as I was thrilled no one caught anything this morning — I hated to think about being in an enclosed space with several dead bodies for seven hours — I wanted to know what Matt was going to say. But he'd gone to put the fishing tackle away.

When everyone was packed up, we hauled our stuff to the van. Patty loaded everything in, often interrupted by Ted or Matt who had a better idea on how to make it all fit. The three of them were funny together, arguing and muttering like people who've known and loved each other for a long time. Half way through, it became obvious they were putting on a show for our amusement.

The men hugged and kissed Patty goodbye, and shook hands with the other women. Ted's handshake and smile conveyed a warmth I'd sensed in Matt. It must be a family trait. I added that to my mental list of what to look for in a man.

Don't make that list too long, grumbled Sergeant Pride.

Gotta start somewhere, right?

When Matt shook my hand, I got that 9-volt-battery-on-your-tongue feeling again. That was definitely going on the list.

"I'm glad you enjoyed Abundance Creek," he said. His dimple appeared as his smile widened. "Of course, you quite literally experienced the creek." He squeezed my hand.

I laughed. "Thanks for saving me."

He still had my hand in his, which was doing funny things to my insides. Heck, I was never going to see him again; I'd let him hold my hand as long as he wanted. His hands were rough and calloused, and his thumb traced little circles on my skin. When I got home, I was going to have to have tests done for nerve damage. 'Cause every nerve ending in my arm was firing.

Can we take him home with us, asked Lovesick with a sigh.

I tried to think of something to say before I embarrassed myself. After all, there were ten other people standing around talking. Someone was going to notice Matt and I staring at each other wordlessly.

"Thanks for the lessons," I said.

"If you wanted," Matt paused, cleared his throat, continued, "we could exchange phone numbers."

A thousand Voices created a cacophony of sound in my head, much like the sound of rushing wind. The sound people say they hear just before they pass out.

Logic prevailed — as it does so infrequently in my life, pretty much only when I'm working. "That sounds great. If you ever want to buy a house," I dug through my purse looking for my cards, "give me a call." I found a card and handed it over.

I couldn't read his expression. "Right. Exactly," he said as he squeezed my hand one last time and released it. He pulled a card out of his wallet and gave it to me. I was too nervous to do anything but shove it in my purse and smile.

As he walked away, I wished I knew what he was thinking. Emily sidled up next to me and whispered, "Oh. My. Gosh."

"Shh!" I whispered. She giggled as we got in the van.

I tried to resist, but as we pulled away, I looked out the window. Matt and Ted stood watching us. Matt raised his hand and smiled. At me. I couldn't help it. I grinned like the Cheshire cat and waved back.

"So, did you give Matt your phone number?" Patty turned in the front passenger seat to smile broadly at me.

I kept my tone light. "We exchanged business cards, but I came up here to learn to fish and I did. Now it's back to the real world."

Patty gave me a funny look. "I thought you two were getting along pretty well. Don't you want to see him again?"

I laughed and shook my head. No need for matchmaking. I'd started a list of qualities I wanted to find in Mr. Right. Heartbreak had its moment. Now it was time for me to move on. When I got home, well, maybe I'd look around a little.

CHAPTER 7

When Monday dawned, I was ready to go again. I came to work early, determined to catch up on anything on my desk by noon. My Starbucks iced mocha with whipped cream (yes, sugar *and* caffeine) rested on a sandstone coaster as I booted up my computer and looked over my mail.

Carmen, the office manager, stopped by with my phone messages when she came in. "Okay, girl, tell me everything." She leaned against my desk and sipped her coffee.

"Well, let's see. I saw a bear, fell in the river, and found out I don't like to fish." I laughed at Carmen's expression. Obviously not what she was expecting.

"Sounds terrible!"

I leaned back in my chair and sipped my coffee. "Actually, it was nice." I licked whipped cream off the lid. "Unbelievably beautiful up there. Wish I could've stayed longer and done some hiking." I thought about Matt. Definitely wish I could've stayed longer.

Do not *mention him to anyone*, said Pride.

"Emily kicked butt in the fish-catching department, though. Caught three, better than anyone else."

"Good for her. Tell her I said 'nice going.'"

"I will." I sat up and set my drink back on the coaster.

Carmen started to return to her desk, then paused. "Any chance you met any fascinating men up there?"

Play it cool. I smiled and said, "Just the fishing guide and lodge owner." Completely not a lie.

Carmen pointed her finger at me. "It's time, girl. There's plenty of good men out there. If you don't know how to meet them, I'll introduce you. Pretty Boy is gone, and I say good riddance."

I grinned. It's good to be loved. "Thanks, Carmen."

She harrumphed and went back to her desk. I shook my head and went back to work.

Over the next couple of hours, people trickled in and out of the office, some stopping to ask about my fishing weekend. I repeated what I'd said to Carmen and got the same reactions. It was fun to be the center of attention for a few minutes.

"Hey, Sydney, how was your weekend?" Trent pulled up a chair and sat down.

I finished typing and turned away from my computer. "It was nice." On the corner of my desk sat a bud vase with two fresh roses. I shook my head as I picked up the vase. "You've got to stop doing this."

Trent had a habit of doing nice things for me sometimes like bringing me roses from the rosebush in front of his apartment complex. It was sweet. I always told him he should get a girlfriend and give the roses to her. He'd always laugh and say all the good ones were taken. Such a sweetie.

Trent laughed when I stuck my nose in the flowers. "I will when you stop enjoying them. Come on, tell me about the fishing trip."

I grinned. "I saw a bear, fell in the river, and found out I don't like to fish."

"Well," Trent raised his eyebrows, "you don't believe in boring vacations, do you?"

I laughed. "I certainly didn't plan it that way."

"Speaking of vacations, what're you doing over Fourth of July weekend? Going home?"

Something in Trent's tone made me look up. Was he...? Oh. Oh dear. I had a feeling he was about to ask me out. Before he did, *if* he did, how should I reply? I know I said I was ready, but...am I? I did a quick comparison against the list I'd made in my head yesterday. Trent was kind, rather funny, good-natured. Not bad, I guess.

Yeah, piped up Little Miss Lovesick, *but not like with Matt where you watch him and accidentally brush up against him and have dinner by firelight and—*

Enough! Matt's too far away to date. Trent is here.

But do I want to date him?

"My parents are going to Disney World, if you can believe it," I told him. "Emily's work is having a picnic on the beach before the fireworks, so we're going to hang out there all day. Swim, eat, get a tan. What're you doing?" I tried for a nonchalant tone. I didn't want it to sound like I wanted him to invite me anywhere, but I didn't want to sound like I hoped he wouldn't, either.

"Some friends are going sailing, then we'll watch the fireworks from the bay. Probably spend most of the time on the boat." His eyes met mine and darted away. He fiddled with the vase I'd put down on my desk.

"Sounds fun." Man, this flirting thing was so much easier this weekend.

"Let me know if you'd like to go out sometime — on the boat, I mean." Trent got up to leave. "Remember, you owe me dinner."

"What?" I snorted and wrinkled up my face. Humorous faces definitely lighten the mood.

"Last week you gave me a rain check."

"No, I gave you a rain check for lunch."

"Fine, what's your schedule? I have to show a house today at 12:30." Trent waited expectantly. Did I walk right into that or what?

"I'll check." I didn't make any move to open my calendar on my laptop.

Trent cocked his head. "Tomorrow or Thursday?"

I chuckled. "I'll check my calendar, I said."

"Fine, Thursday then. Around one. The office may close up early and we could have the rest of the afternoon for a long lunch." He smiled like he'd just checked my king.

I needed to learn to play a better game of chess. "If I'm free." I shook my head at him. "Which I won't be if you don't let me get back to work. Go!"

He grinned and left. What was I going to do with him?

He likes you, said a Voice. *You kind of like him. Maybe he's The One.*

I still like the other one, said Lovesick.

The phone rang and saved me from having to think about it. It was the newlyweds. It's possible I might have to kill myself if they don't find a house soon. They kiss in every room. They stare at each other with googly eyes every moment they're together. Once, I took her out alone and the only thing she talked about was him. They were so sweet, they were giving me cavities.

Only because you desperately wish that was your life, said a Voice.

Today they'd called to discuss the pros and cons of buying a "fixer-upper." I gave them my opinion and they were off the phone in a flash to "conference." That's what they always said when they wanted to discuss something and get back to me. "We have to conference. We'll call you back." Don't they know "conference" is a noun, not a verb?

The fact that you could be a happy newlywed right now if things had turned out differently is making you cranky, said Little Miss Lovesick.

No, the issue, said Sergeant Pride, *is that Dirk's a jerk and that's why you aren't a happy newlywed right now.*

That's enough. Remember, I've decided to feel better now. Focus. I choose to be happy. I choose to feel peaceful. I choose to stop thinking about Dirk.

Another Voice whispered a word I try not to use, though it *was* an apt description of my ex.

The phone rang again. Thank you, God! I need a distraction from all this noise in my head.

"By the Bay Properties, Syd Riley speaking."

"Darlin' Sydney! How are you, sweetheart? It's GT!" I put my hand over the mouthpiece and groaned. I hit my forehead on the desk twice. It didn't help.

"Are you there, darlin'? This is Gerald Turkelbain. You remember me, don't you? You helped me buy my cottage last winter."

Oh, I remembered him all right. Remembered every touchy-feely, Southern charming detail about him. He'd gotten a reputation for being a difficult-to-please client (in three months, he'd gone through seven realtors in four agencies without buying anything), and I had the reputation of being able to work with anyone. Of course, I ended up with a massive commission check when I found him a house. But I swore to myself and to Perry that I would never, *ever* work with the man again.

"Good morning, Mr. Turkelbain." I tried to smile as I said it.

"Oh, come on now, darlin'. It's GT between friends. Listen, I'm looking to buy another house, one for Merci's mama, and I was hoping I could sweet-talk you into helping me out. You're about the nicest realtor I've worked with. What do you say?"

I ran one hand through my hair. I didn't want to say yes. He was a pain in the patootie. But I wasn't really the kind of person to say no. Which is why I was often banging my head against hard surfaces.

"Uh, let me check my calendar. Did you have anything specific in mind?" I brought up the calendar on my laptop. Not even a dental appointment. Darn!

"I sure did! I figured you come pick me up at the cottage — I'll show you around and let you see the renovations — then we'll have lunch at the Boathouse." GT loved the best in everything, especially the best food. The Boathouse was arguably the nicest restaurant in town.

I closed my eyes, pinching the bridge of my nose. "I meant, did you have a specific kind of property in mind?"

"Now, that's what we're going to discuss over lunch, darlin'. Merci's mama is *ver*-ry par*ti*cular. I love her, but I'd rather get her her own cottage than have her here with me and Merci. Lawd!" GT made a noise in the back of his throat that sounded like he was having an attack.

"Well, we could discuss it now, on the phone. Then I can get started that much sooner." I hoped my voice conveyed polite enthusiasm, not a deep-seated desire to spend as little time in his company as possible. Apparently, it conveyed both.

"Aw, Sydney, honey. Ain't you something? You're safe from me." He laughed again. "I'm a reformed man! Didn't I tell you I got married? Mercedes Tobias. Well, Mercedes Turkelbain now. But I just call her Merci. Oh-h, *Mer*-ci!"

"You're married?" I inhaled a deep breath of relief. Well, that changed things. I hoped. "Congratulations, GT. You sound very happy." I hoped I didn't sound too relieved. "I'm not available during lunch today, but tomorrow looks open."

"I've got another lunch tomorrow. Hang on now." I heard papers rustling, then GT talking to someone else. "Oh, here's the contractor now. Can't keep him waiting. He's making my dreams come true with these renovations. I'll call you back and we'll schedule a time ASAP. Maybe a dinner meeting would work better for me. All right now, darlin'." And he hung up.

I opened my mouth to agree, but dial tone was all that remained.

CHAPTER 8

*T*he next couple days consisted of catching up on work from the weekend and getting ready for another three-day weekend. (Boy, I really know how to schedule my vacations, huh?) Emily and I didn't have time to see each other because she was doing the same thing, but we always had time to talk on the phone.

"Just say no, Syd," she said when I called her Tuesday night. "It's that simple. I remember how stressed out you were when you worked for him last winter. You don't need that."

"I know, but I made almost $30,000 on that sale." I ate chocolate chips out of a bag while we talked. "And he's married now."

"Then have him meet you at the office. Or make sure his wife will be home. The money's not worth the stress if it turns out he's not so reformed."

That particular period of my life was not what I wanted to think about. Bad enough that my boyfriend was completely unsupportive of my problems with a touchy-feely client. But Dirk got all bent out of shape about my insistence that all the money go into our House Fund. Said it was the man's job to provide for a house. Said I should buy something pretty for myself. Suggested a flat-screen TV for watching movies together. Hmm, in retrospect, maybe the TV thing was a warning sign in our relationship.

In the end, he convinced me it would be better to buy my Kia Sportage with cash and not have to worry about the $400 a month payments since real estate is such a feast or famine kind of business. Now I had no house (which I probably would have by now if I still had that money) and no man providing one.

But you do *have an opportunity to replenish the House Fund*, said a Voice.

Price tag, sanity, said Sarcasm.

I decided to think about it until GT called back, and make a decision then. Or maybe after we had our first meeting.

Thursday, Trent reminded me about lunch while we were standing in the kitchenette. Before he knew it, two more co-workers had invited themselves along. Trent did not seem one bit happy, but he was too polite to say anything. Me, I was afraid to say anything for fear the others would think Trent and I had a thing going. So the four of us went to lunch and, honestly, had a pretty good time.

Back at the office, though, Trent followed me to my desk. "So, have any plans for dinner tonight?"

Boy, you give an inch...

I laughed nicely. "I'm still full from lunch." I sorted through my messages.

"Going to lunch with the whole office wasn't what I had in mind when I asked you earlier."

I started to interrupt, but he held up his hand and kept going.

"Just in case I'm not being clear, would you like to have dinner with me, just the two of us, tonight?"

I stared at him for a moment. Sweet Trent had a backbone, a trait I admired in a man.

"I can't tonight," I said in a tone that conveyed my willingness to consider a different date. That was as helpful as I could be right now. Getting back into the dating scene, knowing what to say and when, was harder than I remembered.

Trent's expression softened a little and he moved a step closer. "How about after the weekend, say Tuesday?"

I smiled a little and turned back to my paperwork. I was afraid I might be blushing, which was too ridiculous. "I don't have anything Tuesday night." I looked back at him.

"Right after work, beat the Happy Hour crowds?"

"Sounds good. Where do you want to go?" My chest tightened. I was really going out on a date. Oh geez, I didn't know if I could do this.

"We'll figure it out then. Someplace fun, I promise." He smiled and walked away, looking inordinately pleased with himself, I might add.

As for me, I was having an attack of serious nerves. Time to finish things up and start the long weekend.

Emily met me at my apartment just before lunch Friday. Our plan included nothing more than ordering a Crusted Creations pizza to go and then lying out in the sun all day at Clinch Park beach. Ahh...bliss. I told her about lunch with Trent and next week's dinner.

"Way to go! See? I told you flirting is a self-esteem builder. Now you're out there again. Good for you!" Emily gave me a big hug, which almost made me cry. I mean, you know your friends love you, but sometimes you really *know* they love you and it kind of takes your breath away for a moment.

I laughed a little to keep from crying as I hugged her back. "You're such a good friend, Emily."

We lathered on the sunscreen and talked while we sunbathed. It was perfect 4th of July weekend weather — hot enough to want to be in the water, but not a scorcher. Brilliant blue sky, a couple of pretty white clouds drifting along, and the smell of dozens of barbeques. The beach was ridiculously crowded because of the holiday. But we were in the portion that had been roped off for Em's company picnic. No kids to kick sand on us. Yee-ha. So it was startling to be lying there, eyes closed, and hear a voice so close.

"Hey, Emily. Not doing any fishing today?"

I looked over as Emily literally jumped into a sitting position. "Geoffrey!"

"I didn't mean to startle you." He laughed, a deep, rich sound. Nice. I didn't know who this guy was, but he was pretty easy on the eyes. Thick wavy blonde hair, brown eyes, a face that looked like it smiled a lot. Very nice.

"You didn't," Emily said breathlessly. "I mean, you did, but that's okay. What're you doing here?" This man had Emily's undivided attention. I couldn't remember the last time I'd seen her so flustered. So *breathless*. Interesting. I continued watching the conversation, not even trying to pretend I wasn't riveted.

"Same thing you're doing here, I'd guess. Is there room at the inn?"

I looked around at the rather large roped off area we were in. But neither Em nor Geoffrey the Mystery Man even glanced at the open sand. I considered pinching myself to be sure I hadn't fallen asleep and dreamed us into a soap opera.

"Sure, of course." Emily glanced at me quickly, eyes wide. I sat up and tried to figure out what to say or do to help.

Before either of us could move, Geoffrey had unrolled his beach towel right next to Emily. He put his cooler and beach bag at the top of the towel, then stood and stripped off his shirt and shorts. Emily and I gaped.

He was breath-taking with his hard muscles flexing under perfectly tanned skin. "Adonis" came to mind. And not because I was reading a romance novel. He was simply that gorgeous.

As he sat down, he looked at Emily and his smile faltered. "Is something wrong?"

"No, nothing, no. It's just — I've never seen you without—"

Emily! I wanted to scream at her, don't say it!

"—without a tie."

Whew! Good save.

His smile returned as he looked her over. "Yeah, I've never seen you without—" He gestured at her navy blue bikini and straw hat. "You know."

"Yeah."

I giggled. I couldn't help it. I couldn't see Emily's face, but I could hear the big, fat smile in her voice.

They both looked over at me like they'd forgotten I was there. Which I also found vastly amusing.

"Oh! Geoffrey, this is my best friend, Sydney. I've told you about her." Emily gestured toward me while talking to him, then turned to me. "Syd, this is Geoffrey. From work." Her eyes pleaded with me not to ask questions. Yet.

"Sydney, I've heard so much about you. It's great to meet you." He leaned over Emily to shake my hand. I saw her bite her lip as she stared at his face, inches from hers.

Who was this man who could turn poised Emily inside out? And why hadn't I heard of him? "It's great to meet you, too," I said.

Moving back to his own towel, he saw Emily watching him. His smile became a great big grin. She grinned back and started to turn red. I couldn't believe it. Emily blushing!

An hour went by before Em and I could get two minutes alone to talk. By then, more of her co-workers had arrived and Geoffrey was engaged in conversation with two of them. She and I walked down to the water's edge and put our feet in to cool off.

"Emily!" I squeaked. "What's with Mr. Hunk-a-licious?"

She giggled like a schoolgirl. "Isn't he di-*vine*?" she whispered.

"Come on, give me the thirty-second version before he

follows you over here." I glanced over to make sure he was still out of earshot.

She looked, too, and smiled like she was a fairy tale princess seeing Prince Charming for the first time. "We work together, but he's all-business, all the time. I couldn't figure out how to talk to him about anything else. Then one day he started talking about this fishing trip he went on and how much he adores fishing."

I put the pieces together in my head. "So you decided to learn to fish."

She giggled again. (It was so weird. Em does *not* giggle.) "Yeah. Then on Tuesday, I told him I'd just got back from a fly-fishing trip in the U.P. We had lunch together the last couple of days and talked about fishing and...stuff." She looked over at him again. "Now he doesn't seem to have any problem talking to me."

"He definitely likes you," I told her emphatically.

Her head zipped around and she looked me in the eyes, her face a cloud of doubt. "Do you think so?"

I laughed. "Emily, look at him. He's looked over here twice already. He put his towel next to yours the moment he got here. He came early probably to see if you were here. And he smiles at you every time you look at him. He's smitten."

She sighed. "Oh, my. Me, too."

The rest of the afternoon and evening passed with a mix of laughter, food, and shoptalk, capped off with an amazing display of fireworks over West Bay. Geoffrey (not Geoff, Emily made a point of telling me) kindly included me in the conversation when the three of us were together, and Emily introduced me to a bunch of her other friends and co-workers. During the fireworks, though, I eased myself away a bit in case the lovebirds wanted to take advantage of the romantic moment in the dark.

It was nice not to be the needy one for a change. Nice to be the person who tries to do kind things for her friends. It was one of those days when I genuinely liked myself. And there hadn't been a lot of those in the last six months or so.

Em and I spent most of the rest of the weekend together, shopping, swimming, sunbathing, and of course, talking about Geoffrey. Now that the secret was out, Emily couldn't shut up about him. Which amused me to no end.

We were going to have lunch after church, but she called me about twenty minutes before we were supposed to meet.

"I'm *so* sorry. Please don't be mad, but I'll do anything for you if you wouldn't mind canceling our lunch."

Since I was in the car, driving to meet her, my first thought was, you've got to be kidding me. But then I realized.

"He called, didn't he?"

"He did! About a minute ago! Oh, Syd, you don't mind, do you?"

I chuckled. She sounded desperate and happy. "Of course not. But if he starts coming between us, I'm going to have to take action," I teased.

"You're the best! I owe you! Wish me luck!" And she was gone.

Now, what to do about lunch? For about ten seconds, I thought about calling Trent. I mean, we're friends. We just had lunch. We're having dinner next week. What's the big deal?

I put my phone away. The big deal was that this "maybe I'll start dating again" idea was going way faster than I was ready for.

CHAPTER 9

*T*uesday morning, GT called to schedule a meeting to discuss buying a "cottage" for his mother-in-law.

He chuckled. "Darlin', you don't know how bad I hafta find one. Quick! Or she may move in with me and my bride. That would certainly cramp my romantic style."

I laughed a tad uncomfortably. Oh dear. Do we know each other well enough for this conversation? But...this is what I do. I smiled into the phone. "I completely understand. We'll make it a priority."

Hey! yelled a Voice in my head. *What happened to "I'll think about it" or "No"?*

House Fund, think House Fund.

Nah, House Fund or not, I loved my job and I wanted to see if I could help GT find what he was looking for. My parents and Dirk had always pushed me to get into higher end real estate, or move to commercial properties. They wanted me to have a reputation as a go-getter, a successful business woman — and no doubt they thought making a ton of money was the only real proof of success. But I was more interested in finding people houses that could become homes. Didn't matter to me if it was a little fixer-upper first home or a multi-million dollar summer home. It was the "home" part that made me happy.

My parents, God bless them, were very interested in appearances, and that's probably why they liked Dirk so much. We lived in a really nice house with lots of antiques and fancy furnishings. The dining room was covered in plush white carpet, so we only used it when we had guests — special guests. It sat empty about 360 days out of the year. That was how I grew up — don't touch, don't go in there, don't walk there, don't, don't, don't. I was determined to push people to make their houses into homes, to relax and be happy.

GT finally found a place that made him happy last time I worked with him. It was a challenge to see if I could do it again.

"Now that's what I like to hear," he said when I agreed to work with him. "I'll fax over my specifications today and you'll pick me up tomorrow at my cottage. Meet me there at 2:00 and we'll get to work."

I raised my eyebrows. My style is more along of the lines of *asking* people if they're available rather than ordering them around. But...deep breath...just chill...I gave him the agency fax number. Checking my calendar belatedly, I was relieved to find it clear in the afternoon. GT's take-charge attitude had thrown me. I was used to being the one in charge. My usual clientele tended to have no idea where to begin in a house hunt.

Remember, he was like this before, a Voice reminded me. *And he just kept getting worse.*

Well, now I know what to expect, so I can make it work this time. I'll find him a house without losing my mind. I will.

When Carmen handed me the fax from GT, well...oh my...

I finished scanning it and carefully read it again. Did a house like this even exist? No wonder he was willing to pay me a bonus to find it. I thought about calling GT back and telling him this was impossible. But no, I wouldn't quit that easily. I'd tell him in person tomorrow.

It's best to meet clients where they're comfortable. You find out what they really want, not just what they say they want. (Trust me, there's a big difference.) I'd find out what he wants, get it for him, move on to the next client. Okay, no worries.

I hit the spacebar on my keyboard to shut off the screensaver and clicked on my MLS online. (The Multiple Listing Service is a realtor's primary tool of the trade.) I read, scanned, printed, and searched for the next three hours. I called over to That'sa Pizza for lunch and ate it at my desk in the nearly empty office. One way or another, I was going to begin our meeting on the right foot — with a folder full of possibilities.

The day went by quickly, as busy days do. I must've gotten two dozen phone calls. Trent called around three-thirty to remind me of our dinner plans that night. I was surprised to find myself eager to get going.

Workplace romance is working for Emily, mused Little Miss Lovesick. *Maybe it can work for us.*

She didn't sound convinced. Neither was I. But I was still looking forward to dinner.

As it turns out, I had good reason. He didn't hang on my every word, but Trent was attentive. He was charming as he argued with me occasionally. He was sweet and funny. More relaxed and confident than I'd seen him before.

And completely spark-free, complained Little Miss Lovesick.

Yeah, well, it's only one dinner. Give it time.

The sparks started way *before dinner with* Matt, she pointed out.

It was a bad idea to use that man to create your list, mumbled Sergeant Pride.

I was getting a little defensive with myself. It's a good list. And Trent's scoring high.

"So..." Trent said. He smiled at me and I smiled back. "Think you can handle dessert? They have the best Italian ice cream you've ever had."

I looked at my to-go bag next to me. Half of my lasagna cooled inside. I looked back at Trent — who had no to-go bag. "Do you have a hollow leg?"

He laughed. "You have to admit, the food is good."

"It's great, but I really don't think I can eat any more."

Trent waved the waitress over even as I spoke. "We'll have one dish of the Italian ice cream to share, please."

"You do have a hollow leg."

Trent shrugged. But the last laugh was on me. He was right. The ice cream was so good, I ate *at least* half of it.

By the time he dropped me off at my car back at the office, we'd been talking and eating and laughing for four hours. I don't know why I kept feeling so surprised to be having a good time.

Probably because of You-Know-Who, said a Voice.

I'd been reading the Harry Potter books again and it made me laugh to think of Dirk and the evil Voldemort in the same category.

"What's so funny?" asked Trent as I searched my purse for my keys.

I looked up. No mentioning past boyfriends. Completely taboo. "I can't believe I'm playing the part of the stereotypical woman who can't find her keys," I said, rolling my eyes.

"Sure they're not in your pocket?"

I patted the front of the Capri pants I had on. Sure enough. I pulled them out and jingled them in front of Trent's face. He took them and unlocked my door.

"Women," he sighed.

"Gimme my keys, please." I held out my hand and he dropped them in.

"I'm glad you came tonight," he said, standing next to my open door.

"Me, too." I smiled, then looked down at my keys. I wasn't sure what to do or say. Again.

When I looked up, he was smiling at me. No stomach flips, but still nice. I could do worse. In fact, I had.

I don't think you're supposed to have to try this hard to like someone, said Lovesick.

It's not hard to like Trent. He's very likable. I like him.

It's not the same, she sighed.

"So…" he said.

"So…"

"Big day tomorrow?"

"Kind of, yeah." Was I supposed to just stand there and wait for him to leave, or could I get in my car? Was he going to kiss me? I wasn't sure I wanted him to, but I didn't want him to think I didn't want to kiss him. That seemed rather…rude.

"Guess I should let you go then." He stepped back so I could get in.

I turned on the engine and rolled down the window before I closed the door. He leaned against the doorframe and watched me buckle my seat belt. "Thanks again, Trent. I had a great time." Once again, surprised that I meant it.

"Me, too. Thanks for coming." He remembered something and looked past me.

"Got your leftovers? Yeah, you do." The bag sat on the passenger seat next to my purse. "I guess I'll be seeing that again tomorrow."

I stuck out my tongue at him and slapped his arm. He laughed and jumped back.

"What? There's nothing wrong with that. My mom is the queen of leftovers."

"Yeah, that's what every woman wants, to be compared to someone's mother." I rolled my eyes.

He laughed. "See you tomorrow. Drive safely."

I pulled out and waved as I drove away. My plan to choose to feel better seemed to be working. It wasn't all fireworks and chocolates, but it was nice. I really couldn't complain.

Then I will, said Lovesick.

I DROVE STRAIGHT TO GT'S FROM HOME WEDNESDAY MORNING. I was used to GT canceling and rescheduling, so I half-expected my cell phone to ring telling me to turn around and go home. I probably wouldn't have turned around though.

The sun sparkled over West Bay as I drove up Peninsula Drive. The water reflected the brilliant blue of the sky. The grass and trees shone in a dozen shades of green. This was one of the prettiest drives in town. If I didn't have to work, I'd keep going until I reached the lighthouse at the end of the peninsula, maybe take off my shoes and walk along the beach up there.

Maybe another day. I could see where I was headed from a half mile away. The right side of the winding lakeshore road was lined with pickup trucks. Pulling into the driveway, I maneuvered around a backhoe and parked under a tree. Looked like more than a simple renovation to me, but then GT had a fondness for doing things in a big way.

I took the folder of listings from the seat beside me and climbed out. I didn't bother rolling up the windows — which after two years in Traverse City, still amazed me. In Lansing, I wouldn't have even gone to the ATM without rolling up every window and locking all the doors. But I liked this small town feel.

I picked my way carefully around to the back. (The front door was covered with a plastic drop cloth.) I wore my favorite sandals with a stylish cotton blouse over Capri pants. Professional, yet comfortable. The sandals, along with the rocks and debris in the driveway, reminded me of sliding down that gravel trail in Abundance Creek. Better be careful. No one to catch me here if I fell.

I found another door, obviously the one being used by the construction workers. A large piece of dirty carpet lay haphazardly in front. GT had told me to knock and walk in since it might be noisy. I knocked and heard a "come in" that I guessed was directed at me. I walked in and shut the door behind me, having to move the chunk of carpet a bit with my foot to get the door closed all the way.

I had entered the kitchen, also being remodeled. A man at the counter studied some papers, making notes. From the look of him — T-shirt and jeans, hardhat, scribbling away on what may have been floor plans — I guessed he was the foreman, maybe even the contractor. He probably knew where GT was.

"Hi, do you happen to know..." I didn't finish my sentence, but my mouth was still open. Wide open.

The foreman's head shot up in surprise as soon as I began to speak. He didn't say anything. He just stared.

It was Matt. Right there in front of me. Not in a fishing lodge. Not hours and hours away. Not in a dream. (Ignore that. No comment.)

Right there in GT's kitchen. With a hardhat on.

"Sydney!" He took a step toward me. "What — what are you doing here?" He looked shocked and maybe a little pleased to see me. Not unlike what I was feeling at the moment.

"What are *you* doing here?" I looked again at his hardhat and the floor plans. "You're a fishing guide," I reminded him. Like he had forgotten.

He smiled that really cute smile I remembered from the very first day, the one with the dimple in his left cheek.

"Yeah, sometimes. I'm a general contractor the rest of the time." He took another step closer and looked at me like I was water in the desert. It felt like that to me, anyway.

"But why are you here?" Not that it mattered. He was *here*. Who cared why?

Matt skimmed my appearance and something in his expression lit up. What was he thinking?

Hopefully the same thing I'm thinking, exclaimed Little Miss Lovesick.

"I'm just doing him a favor."

I walked farther into the kitchen and stopped a foot or two away. Geez, he was more handsome than I remembered. Not just his looks, his whole — *self*. "Who?"

Matt's smile widened. He could tell the effect he was having on me. "GT. I've worked with him before on commercial projects. He asked me to help out when the other guy he hired had a family emergency."

"Oh."

Dang, but he looked fine. This shirt seemed even tighter on him than the ones he'd worn up north. Of course, it was hotter now and he didn't have a flannel shirt on. His biceps were... more...*appealing* than I remembered. And his smile...*my* water in the desert.

"So, how've you been?" He moved closer, his hand reaching out to touch mine, then pulling back.

His touch made me shiver. I couldn't stop staring at him, at those incredible blue eyes staring back at *me*. I reached out my hand. Our fingers touched, intertwining a little, pulling away and coming together again.

I've died and gone to heaven, breathed Little Miss Lovesick.

"Well, I—"

The door opened behind me. I jumped away from Matt like a junior high kid caught behind the bleachers. Matt moved back to his papers. I looked over my shoulder to see who had come in.

GT, looking spiffy (and expensive) in a short-sleeve silk shirt, lightweight slacks (that also appeared to be made of silk), and leather shoes (probably Italian, it's GT, after all), filled the room. Of medium height, he had the protruding stomach so many older men get, but he was solid. Still, it wasn't his size, but his presence. GT moved like the world revolved around him.

"Well now, Syd Riley. How are you, darlin'?" GT stuck out his hand and grasped mine with both hands. He held it rather than shook it. Southern charm, I guess. I pulled my hand back on the pretense of adjusting my purse strap on my shoulder.

We exchanged pleasantries while I pretended Matt was not in the room. But my mind was spinning. Why was he here in Traverse City? Where did he live? I found it difficult to concentrate on my client while thinking about the gorgeous man behind me. My imagination ran wild picturing him working, arms bulging, shirt on the ground...

I swallowed hard. I shouldn't have watched that Diet Coke commercial on YouTube again when I got home from the trip.

I tried to focus on GT. He pointed around the kitchen and through the window, his lips moving and sound coming out. No idea what he said, though.

"I see you met my contractor here." GT motioned for Matt to join us near the window. He clapped his meaty hand on Matt's shoulder with a grip that probably would've brought me to my knees. "Matt Engel, builder of dreams, meet Syd Riley, dream weaver."

Matt and I chuckled politely at GT's descriptions and quickly shook hands as if we were just meeting. His hand was hard and rough and strong. Mine was shaking.

"Syd here," GT continued, "can see the potential in anything. I didn't want this house at first, didn't want any of the houses she showed me."

Boy, I remembered *that*.

"But she has a way of seeing beyond what's in front of you. She can give you the *vision* of what could be." GT patted my shoulder.

"Matt, now, he's a man who takes the vision and builds it. Some of this is your idea, Syd. Look around. He's an artist!"

Matt looked down at his feet, then nodded at GT. He looked at me out of the corner of his eye. I was grinning like a wild woman, I'm sure. His dimple appeared as he kept eye contact.

"You two should work together. You'd make a great team," GT said, thumping Matt on the back. Then he winked at me and turned back to Matt. "Best be careful, though. She's spoken for."

Mayday! Mayday! All the Voices in my head were screaming — or fainting.

Matt's eyes narrowed. My words stumbled over each other. "Oh — no, GT, that's — we, uh—" My eyes dropped to my wringing hands. This was embarrassing beyond imagining.

GT looked at me in surprise. "You're not married? What happened?"

Pull yourself together, woman, yelled Sergeant Pride. *Repeat after me, things didn't work out.*

I took a deep breath and tried to relax my hands. "Things didn't work out." I avoided Matt's gaze and tried to show a composed, professional demeanor to GT. "It happens."

Now, hightail it outta there!

"So, shall we look over the listings I brought?" I tried to smile brightly.

"Well, that's just a crying shame!" GT sputtered. "What a fool to let you get away." He turned back to Matt. "You're not seeing anyone, are you?"

CHAPTER 10

I sat on my balcony Saturday morning, feet up on the railing, chair tipped back the way teachers always yelled at you for in school. A tall glass of orange juice rested on the table. Next to it lay my cell phone. And Matt's business card. A card that plainly showed a Traverse City area code...had I ever looked.

I stared into the woods that extended behind the back of my apartment building, looking for answers. A pair of chickadees called to each other up in the leaves. I wanted to call Matt, but I didn't know what to say.

He had my number and hadn't called, so maybe he wasn't interested. I remembered how we'd looked at each other earlier at GT's. He couldn't have shown his disinterest any more plainly.

I thought about calling Emily, but she and Geoffrey went out on a real live date last night, and since I didn't know what time she got in, I hesitated to call and wake her up. While I tried to decide, the phone rang. I looked at the number but didn't recognize it. The last thing I wanted to do was talk to clients right now.

By the third ring, I sighed heavily and answered. I love my job, I love my job, I love…

"By the Bay Properties, this is Sydney," I said with as much enthusiasm as I could muster. I toyed with the edge of the business card waiting for the other person to speak.

"Hi, uh… This is Matt."

My feet came off the railing so fast I lost my balance and nearly tipped the chair over. The table wobbled precariously. I made a grab for the juice. The phone book landed with a thump on the floor.

"Hello?"

"Uh, hi, sorry, I dropped something."

"Sydney?"

"Yeah. Hi." Crap! I had no idea what to say. My heart started such a drumbeat in my ears, I couldn't hear myself think.

"How's it going?"

"Uh, it's good, it's good. How's it going with you?" Man, I am a freaking idiot. I think I heard him laugh. Was it a good laugh or a bad laugh?

"I'm good." He paused. I scrambled to think of something to say but he beat me to it. "So, what're you doing?"

Easy enough question. Safe.

"Sitting on my balcony with my orange juice." Okay, that was true. Not very witty. But tone of voice was good. I was smiling while I was speaking, so that's good. Adds a friendly tone.

"Haven't, uh, had breakfast yet?"

He's nervous! exclaimed Lovesick. *Listen to him!*

"Not yet, I'm waiting for Wolfgang Puck to start a delivery service. Great omelettes."

"Really? Huh." He chuckled.

Good, Syd, good. Make him laugh. Men like women who make them laugh.

"Well, maybe you'd settle for The Omelette Shoppe. They make a pretty mean omelette."

Pause. What's the right answer? What exactly is the question? Noncommittal is the best bet when you don't know what the heck is going on. He didn't exactly ask me out.

Who cares? cried Lovesick. *Just say yes!*

"I've never eaten there. Is it good?"

"Wanna find out?" He paused again. I blinked. Was he asking me out? He was totally asking me out! "How about I meet you there in half an hour? My treat?"

I realized my mouth was hanging open when I almost swallowed a mosquito.

"Uh, sure, yes. Which one?"

Matt suggested the downtown location on Cass Street as I looked over what I'd put on this morning. It's not a date. It's a let's-get-together-and-catch-up.

It's not a date. Emily and I treat each other all the time.

It's morning. Breakfast. Not a date.

"I'll see you in half an hour," he said and just like that he was off the phone.

Holy smokes, I was going on a date with Matt!

I ran and brushed my teeth. It's ridiculous to brush your teeth right before you eat, I know. Crest and orange juice, yuck! Equally ridiculous, however, was the idea of going on a date *without* brushing my teeth.

I grabbed my purse and headed for the door. I was practically humming. I couldn't remember the last time I'd hummed. I giggled. I knew I was nuts, but I didn't care. Thank you, God! Thank you, thank you, thank you!

My tires squealed as I backed out of my parking space. I took a deep breath as I put the SUV in drive. Calm down. You don't want to get in an accident on the way. It's Saturday, after all, and every idiot with a car is on the road.

Whew. Okay. Better.

I opened my cell phone, dialed one, and got Em's voice mail.

"Em, call me the *minute* you get this message. I mean it. You're never going to believe this! Bye!"

I thought I was going to throw up by the time I pulled into a downtown parking lot. I took a deep breath, then another, trying to calm my nerves.

Don't check your hair or anything, warned a Voice. *He might see you from the restaurant and think you're vain. Or worse, overeager.*

Good point. I hope I look okay.

It doesn't matter. It's not really a date; it's just breakfast.

That's right, it's just breakfast.

Breakfast on a Saturday, *which is like a date because he could be out with anyone right now and he chose me.*

Okay, everyone quiet! I can't breathe.

When I got inside the restaurant, Matt wasn't there yet. I gave the waitress my name, then saw Matt jogging up the sidewalk.

He's jogging, Lovesick squeaked. *That must mean he really wants to see me!*

Or it could be starting to sprinkle, said another Voice.

Yeah, it is so not raining, she purred.

"Hey, sorry I'm late," he said when he walked in. He wore a rugby shirt, shorts, and Tevas. It was a new look on him. I liked it. There was a rugged manliness barely covered by a civilized veneer.

"No problem, I just got here," I said, trying not to smile too broadly.

"Good to see you." Matt leaned in and kissed me on the cheek.

He kissed me! shrieked Lovesick. *At the* beginning *of the date!*

"You're looking great today," he said as his eyes gave me the once-over.

I looked down. White tank top with a blue button down tied at the waist and sleeves rolled up, khaki shorts at mid-thigh, sandals.

"You do the thing—" Matt pointed near my belly button. "With the knot — and the open…" His finger was sort of wiggling around. He reminded me of Joey on *Friends*. "You know. It's nice."

I moved my hand self-consciously over my stomach. Yup, skin showing. I tried not to tug my shirt down, but left my hand covering the open skin. Elle McPherson I was not. I really should work out more if I'm going to be comfortable with the ogling.

I love the ogling! (Oh, you'll never guess who said *that*.)

He winked at me.

My stomach did another flip. How was I going to keep breakfast down with him around? I grinned like an idiot and tried not to look at him.

"Your table is right this way."

I almost tripped the waitress in my hurry to follow her. I let out a breath through pursed lips and tried to act natural. Difficult when I knew he was two steps behind me.

The waitress stopped at a booth and laid down the menus. I slid in one side, half-hoping Matt would slide in right beside me. He thanked the waitress who must've said something waitress-y but I didn't catch it.

"Hungry?" He smiled at me, then looked over the menu.

"You have no idea," I murmured as I opened mine.

He chuckled.

Oh crappy, did I say that out loud? Recover, recover!

"I usually eat earlier than this." I moved the tall menu high enough to hide for a moment. Oh geez, I've got to gain some control.

"See anything you like?"

"Nope!" Can't see you. Won't flirt with you.

He laughed again. The sound made my senses whirl.

I lowered my menu. "I'm not on vacation anymore. No more

flirting." I tried to look like I meant it. Couldn't hold eye contact. Returned to the menu.

I could feel his stare and looked back at him.

"I'm a big boy. I don't think you can tell me what to do."

"Oh really?" Stomach flips! Change the subject, quick!

"So tell me, what brings you to Traverse City, Mr. Fishing Guide?" Okay, getting to the heart of my curiosity was one way to change the subject.

"Dr. Willard. He delivered me thirty-two years ago."

"Uh, okay." I chuckled in complete confusion. "I thought you lived in Abundance Creek."

Matt folded his menu and laid it beside the water glass a bus boy had brought. "That's my uncle's place. I was just helping out while GT was in Greece."

"Ah." I wasn't following.

"GT likes to change things, but he's a bit, uh, controlling. So he doesn't like the changes to take place when he can't be there." Matt shrugged. "It amounted to a ten-day paid vacation for me and my crew."

"Interesting." Generous. Quirky, but generous.

I turned another page in the menu. Too many choices. A dozen kinds of omelettes. Eggs and meat. Eggs with biscuits, on croissants, in burritos. Where did it say just "eggs" with nothing else? I couldn't focus.

"So, you're from here. And you knew I was from here. When we were both up there." It's not that I was mad, but if I'd known, I *definitely* wouldn't have flirted with him. Way too risky.

I looked up to find his eyes measuring me. "Yup." That's it. No explanation. Interesting.

I could do that, measure him with a look. I kept looking. The first one to break eye contact loses, right?

Even if I lose, I win, sighed Lovesick.

"Are you ready to order?" Saved by the waitress.

Matt ordered one of those huge meals that I frankly can't

believe one person can consume alone. I asked if I could have two scrambled eggs with cheese, even though I couldn't find it on the menu. No toast. No bacon. Just eggs.

Matt looked at me like I was crazy. "I take you to the best breakfast place in town and you want plain eggs you could have at home?"

I didn't know what to say. "I asked for cheese." Brilliant. Bravo.

He narrowed his eyes. "Are you one of those girls who pretends not to eat in front of people?"

I leaned closer and lowered my voice. "Do you remember how many s'mores I ate on vacation?"

He grinned and leaned closer, lowering his voice. "I can't count that high."

I playfully smacked his knuckles with my knife.

"Fine, I'll have the quiche, please," I said to the waitress. She took our order and left. "But don't complain when we can't eat all of this food you're buying."

"You think I can't eat mine and yours, too? I'd protect my plate if I were you."

That's when I decided to just relax and enjoy breakfast. No big deal. We lived in the same town. Yes, we flirted shamelessly for an entire weekend, but that was ages ago. (Okay, two weeks in real time, but it seemed like longer.) We were both adults. We could have a mature relationship working in proximity to each other.

So I decided not to flirt with him. Not vacation flirting anyway. Not the all-out-because-I'm-leaving-tomorrow kind of flirting. Not that I didn't want to appear cute and funny. I laughed when he was funny and argued when he was wrong. Very normal. Very non-flirting.

Very intoxicating.

By the end of our meal, I was about as relaxed as I could get under the circumstances. I'd eaten, laughed, (been ogled, let's not forget that), and basically had a great morning.

As I raised my coffee to finish the last swallow, I happened to look out the window. A tall-ish guy with sandy brown hair and a tennis build was walking past.

No way.

He walked with the grace that comes from working out at the gym for two hours a day, four times a week, and playing tennis and racquetball besides.

His clothes were the "look at me" kind that make you look in the beginning and make you sick at the end.

No freaking way!

A moment later, a red Beamer pulled onto the street.

My hand started shaking. The coffee cup clattered against my plate as I tried to set it down without dropping it.

"Guy in the white sun suit?"

"Tennis whites," I corrected automatically. Dirk liked to call the white shirts and shorts "tennis whites." My voice came out in an unnatural monotone. Like it was dead. The way I suddenly felt inside. Again.

"I thought I saw him looking."

I was taking deep breaths of air. Deep calming breaths. *So* not calm.

"I have to go to the ladies room," I whispered and tried to get out of the booth. I tripped and Matt grabbed my elbow to steady me.

"Syd—"

"I'll be right back."

I won't throw up. I won't throw up. I'm okay.

I kept repeating it and breathing deeply. Or trying anyway. I felt like I couldn't catch a breath. Okay, seriously, what does it matter? He dumps me. I don't see him for five months. Then he catches me on a date.

It's not a date!

It *is* a date and I'm glad he saw me. Laughing! And having a good time. A *great* time!

Breathe.

You're fine.

I stood in a bathroom stall, leaning against the wall, grateful no one else was around. I didn't realize how badly shaken I was until I felt a few drops fall from my chin onto my collarbone. I wiped my face. I wasn't crying. It was shock. After a few minutes, I felt calmer.

I left the stall and splashed water on my face. Definitely calmer. I patted my eyes and removed the makeup smudges with a paper towel. See? Doing fine. I let out a big breath. This is a good thing.

I took one more cleansing breath, blew it out pursed lips, and went back to the table. I'm fine. I'll nod and smile and laugh it off. Perfectly fine.

"That him?" Matt asked.

I nodded, meeting his eyes for a microsecond. I smiled briefly and picked up my coffee cup, then set it down again. I might be feeling better, but I'd lost any appetite.

"I could take him," Matt said matter-of-factly.

I burst out laughing. He grinned, and then really, I felt *much* better.

CHAPTER 11

"So then what happened?" Emily waited breathlessly on the other end of the phone that night.

"Matt asked if I wanted to go for a walk. So we drove down to Lighthouse Park and—"

"Separately or together?"

I giggled. "Together. In his truck. And we walked around on the beach for a while in front of the lighthouse." I fingered a pretty shell Matt had picked from the sand for me.

Emily sighed. "How romantic."

I laughed. "It was eleven o'clock in the morning and there were dozens of people down there. But yeah, it was…nice. Wonderful." I dropped from a sitting position on my couch and fell onto my back. I stared at the ceiling and thought about walking hand-in-hand on the beach with a handsome, funny man I couldn't stop thinking about.

"I'm so happy for you, Syd. Really. I told you life would get better."

"Speaking of which, tell me about last night. How'd it go?"

Now it was Emily's turn to go all breathless and dreamy.

"Oh, he's *so* sweet and charming and gallant and handsome and — I think I'm going to die of happiness."

Her melodrama made me laugh. I'd never seen her like this. "So how many children are you going to have?" I teased.

"Two," she replied with a sigh.

"Emily!" Boy, she'd been hit hard. We giggled some more.

Monday, I'll stop thinking about him so much. Monday, I'll start acting like an adult, a professional. Monday, it's back to work, and that means friendly but no flirting.

I hope Monday never comes, whispered Lovesick.

But tomorrow did come. And it brought with it the spawn of Hades.

"HE'S BACK."

"I beg your pardon?" I looked up to find Carmen from the front desk hovering.

"He's back. Dirk's here."

For crying out loud. I looked at her like she was out of her mind, which I sincerely hoped she was. "Dirk Schneider? My..."

It's because he saw me Saturday with Matt. He's decided he hasn't ruined my life enough yet.

Carmen looked at me with a mixture of pity and apprehension. "What do you want me to do?"

"Well, it's not like I forgot to give him back his key," I muttered. Several really bad words went through my head. It was so tempting to ask Carmen to do my dirty work for me.

So tempting.

I thought of Matt's "I could take him." Well, okay, I could take him, too.

I got up and walked to the front. I started going for the "regal" look, nose in the air, too busy to be bothered with him, then decided "professional" was more the thing. I wouldn't be upset in any way. No room for him to push my emotional buttons.

"Hello, Dirk," I said. Cool, professional, unruffled. "How can I help you?" See? I'm good at this.

"Sydney." Dirk turned from a painting on the wall — Gorman, I think. He walked over to within a foot of me. I wanted to back away, reclaim my personal space, but I held my ground. I didn't want to, but I did.

You go, girl, said Sergeant Pride. *Show him your backbone.*

Dirk took a deep breath, like he was preparing himself. "I wanted to tell you I'm sorry and that we should get back together."

Holy crap...

Danger! Danger, Will Robinson!

Never give in, never surrender.

The voices in my head were an overwhelming sea of noise. I thought I might faint for a moment.

"What do you think?" Dirk stood there in his pale green golf shirt and unwrinkled khakis, hands in his pockets, head to one side, looking at me with a tiny half smile on his face.

It was his classic "aren't-I-cute-so-do-whatever-I-ask" Dirk look. He had it perfected. And apparently it worked on more women than just me.

Thankfully, I've come to hate that look.

"Please leave."

Wow, impressive. So cool. So brief.

"Come on, Sydney." He notched up the smile a few watts. I never noticed before that perfect teeth are really not that attractive. They look fake. Huh. Interesting.

I raised my eyebrows at him and looked toward the door.

"I'll pick you up after work and we'll have dinner and talk. How about six?"

"How about I call the police?" Ooh, nice one. Normally, I would've thought of that ten minutes later.

Unfortunately, Dirk wasn't easily put off. I knew that, which is why the complete silence from him since Valentine's Day had been so hard. I didn't expect him to vanish. But I didn't like the new reappearing trick either.

"Okay, I'll call you and we can pencil each other in for lunch."

"Carmen, do you know the non-emergency number for the police?"

"I'll look it right up," she said. I heard her tapping her keyboard.

"It's great seeing you again, Syd." Dirk took a step back. "I'll call you."

He turned toward Carmen and gave her the full effect of his charm. "Nice seeing you again, Carmen." He waved and was out the front door a moment later. Carmen glared at his back.

I watched the BMW pull away, trying to figure out how I felt. Well, triumphant, for one thing. At least I should feel triumphant. We'd just ousted the little snake with no blood, no tears, and no police.

I took a deep breath and smiled at Carmen. "Well, there we go."

I turned around and nearly ran into Perry, my boss. My fairly large boss. My boss with a thundercloud over his head. Bye-bye, triumph. I guess Dirk was more scared of Perry than of me or the police. Well, hey, it's nice to have friends looking out for you.

I waited for Perry to say something. He knew all about my problems with Dirk. More than a boss should, but Perry and his wife had become friends over the last couple years. I'm pretty sure it was the "friend" part, not the "boss" part, that was reacting. A muscle twitched in his jaw. No wonder Dirk was scared. Perry squeezed my shoulder and walked back to his office. I'd never seen him so angry. Yikes.

Carmen practically tip-toed over and handed me a sticky note. "You might need this later," she said quietly.

On it was the number for the police.

I sighed. I don't watch soap operas. How in the heck was I supposed to live in one?

THAT AFTERNOON, WHILE I WAS OUT LOOKING AT A PROPERTY, I called Emily. She would never believe what was happening. When it went to voice mail, I left her a message to call me back immediately.

I couldn't believe the mess I was in. What was I supposed to do? Certainly not call the police. I could just see them arriving at my apartment with the crew from *COPS* in tow. "Domestic dispute" would be superimposed on the bottom of the screen. Dirk would see the camera and smile, give his business card to the police officers and apologize for the inconvenience.

I, on the other hand, would have just woken up, with pillow hair, no makeup, and no shower.

"We're suggesting she see a therapist," the cop would say into the camera. "No one can figure out why she wouldn't want to be with a guy as great as Dirk here." Wide view of the cop slapping Dirk on the back while Dirk waved at the camera. The cameraman would get a close-up of his business card for the audience.

No, I can't call the police. Which means I can only bluff about it so many times. Which means I need a new plan.

"My new plan," I said aloud as I turned into the driveway of a nice little single-level home on 9th Street, "is to sell this house today."

I got out of my car and looked around for Todd and Rosie Slocum. I recognized their Chevy Malibu next to the curb. They were around my age, late twenties, married almost two years and about to have their first child. They needed a first house to go with it. Preferably before the baby came.

Motivated buyers. You can't ask for more than that.

I walked to the back yard. Not there. I knew they weren't inside because I had the key. Huh.

Maybe they'd walked around the block. I'd told them to check out the neighborhood if they arrived before I did.

I looked over my notes. This was a great starter home. Three bedrooms, two baths, sunny kitchen, large backyard, two-car garage. And the price was right.

I heard laughter and looked up. Todd and Rosie were walking up the street, hand in hand. Rosie's other hand was on her stomach. Her quite large stomach. Yeah, they needed to make a decision.

I unlocked the door and, after we exchanged pleasantries, I ushered them in. We entered a tile foyer separated from the living room by a half-wall. A roomy closet opened behind the front door. A fireplace was in the front corner of the living room next to a huge picture window.

I could love this house.

Don't think about it. You don't have enough money yet.

Soon. And you'll find a house even better than this one.

We walked through the living room, across thick Berber carpet, and into the kitchen, tiled like the foyer. There was a large space to the left to put a dining table. An antique dish cabinet would look perfect in the corner, I told them. A sliding glass door opened onto a patio and a lush green backyard.

A wide counter separated the dining room and kitchen. The tiled counter was U-shaped — plenty of room for cooking and baking. Lots of counter space meant there were lots of cabinets above and below.

Back through the dining room, a short hall opened into the rest of the rooms. A large "mud room" opened on the right with space for a washer and dryer and another door to the back patio. Two small bedrooms on the left, separated by a bathroom. Then the master bed and bath in the back corner. For a small house, it was spacious.

"Well, it's everything you said it would be," said Todd. "What do you think, honey?"

Rosie was looking at the master bath, then out the bedroom window into the back yard. "I like it…" She paused.

Ah, doubt. I knew how to handle this.

"It's a big decision, buying your first home," I said. "The second time you go through it you know better what to expect."

Rosie rubbed her stomach and smiled at me. "That's what they say." We laughed.

I'm not a hard-sell, but I really thought this house was perfect for them. And I'm pretty darn good at my job, if I do say so myself.

"Here's what you need to ask yourself. What do you want your home to say about you?" I started back toward the kitchen/dining area with Todd and Rosie trailing behind.

"Do you want it to say, 'Hi friends! *Mi casa es su casa.* There's food in the fridge.'"

They grinned. I changed the inflection of my voice. "Or 'Welcome, beautiful people, to my beautiful home.'" I sniffed. "'Notice my lovely antiques. For heaven's sake, don't sit down on the Queen Anne settee. It's 18th century, you know.'"

Todd and Rosie laughed at my impression.

"That's not us," Todd said.

"What do you think this house says?" Rosie asked.

And there it was. Where the right house sells itself.

"This house definitely says, come in and make yourself at home." I waved my arm around the kitchen and the back yard. "It says, this is a safe refuge from work and worldly cares. Bring your kids over. They can play with ours in the backyard while we drink iced tea and play cards together. This is the kind of home where you can hear the echoes of 'Merry Christmas' and 'Happy Birthday' long after the day is over."

I took a deep breath. Don't cry. You can't buy this house, but you do have to sell it so you can buy one someday. And if you're really lucky, maybe you won't have to live in it alone.

I looked at my clients. They both had a dreamy look in their eyes, and now Todd's hand cradled his unborn child, too.

"Since this particular home"—always use *home*, not *house*—"is not in need of any major repairs, you can think about what you'd like to change when you feel like it. No pressure."

I opened the sliding glass door and stepped onto the patio. "Depending on your personal tastes, you could put in a larger window here," I pointed to a kitchen window, "with a ledge. If you planned to do a lot of outdoor entertaining, it would be much more convenient."

I walked toward the master bedroom and pointed. "This wall could come out and you could put in French doors. If you saw Junior racing to climb that tree, you wouldn't have to run through the house to get outside."

They looked at the three trees in the backyard and nodded. It would be easy to see how a rambunctious child would need to be watched.

"For your adult entertainment," I grinned and winked, "you could put a hot tub right here. From bedroom to hot tub and back with no neighbors the wiser." I indicated the rooftops on all sides of the fenced back yard. "Since all the houses here are single-story, you'd have all the privacy you'd want."

Todd grinned and kissed Rosie. He whispered something and she giggled.

That was a very good sign. "Why don't I wait out in the front yard? You two wander around and see what you think. Take as much time as you like."

"Thanks," Todd said before turning back to his glowing, pregnant wife.

I walked back through the house to the front porch. I'm not that interested in babies, but I think that could change with the right man. The Slocum's lives seemed perfect. Love, house, baby.

I sat down on the front steps and sighed. It was all Dirk's fault. Four years I wasted on him. All the while thinking I was only moments away from that wonderful time that precedes happily ever after — engagement. Then to be dumped over the lobster bisque on Valentine's Day. Humiliating.

Todd and Rosie came out to the front porch, beaming. I have no doubt they were practicing their kissing technique in one of the rooms.

"We'd like to make an offer," Todd announced.

"Great, let's do it."

It wouldn't do to sound too grateful.

By the time I finished the Slocum's paperwork, it was time to go home. I stopped at Meijer's for a few groceries and rented a movie at Redbox. A chick flick, of course.

I called Em's cell phone while I was driving. No answer. Voice mail again.

"Emily," I half-whined, half-laughed into the phone. "There's something wrong with your cell phone. It keeps going to voice mail. Call me if you get this message. Bye!"

As I pulled into my apartment complex, I looked around for a red BMW. All clear.

I hurried up the stairs to my second-story apartment and locked the door behind me. Whew. Safe. Even if he came over later, I simply wouldn't open my door.

Now, what to have for dinner as I watch my movie? It was one with Kate Hudson that I hadn't seen yet. I love Kate Hudson. I want to be Kate Hudson. Well, maybe just have her life. Okay, what I want is the life of one of her characters.

Maybe Andie in *How to Lose a Guy in 10 Days*. She's sweet and pretty and loyal and intelligent and street smart and...

I sighed. I can't imagine myself being nearly as cool as Andie.

I put my Godiva chocolate raspberry truffle ice cream in the freezer and pulled out a Healthy Choice frozen dinner. Don't laugh. The calories saved in the diet food mean a few more spoonfuls of ice cream.

I picked up my home phone while the microwave hummed and called Em's home number.

Voice mail. Darn it!

"Em, you've got to call me as soon as you get this message. It's 911. I swear. I'll tell you one tiny bit if it will make you call me back sooner. Two words. Dirk Schneider. Call me!"

Stupid voice mail. Why doesn't she have an answering machine? I know, they're so twentieth century. But you can screen calls. Even with Caller ID, if the number doesn't show up, you still don't know who it is. Em's folks live out of state and their number shows up as "unknown" or something. Trust me, an answering machine is much better.

Halfway through the movie, my cell phone rang. Em's name appeared on the display.

I hit Stop on the DVD player and Talk on the phone. "Where have you been?!"

"Out. What's going on with Dirk?"

I leaned my head back on the couch and laughed. No humor involved. "Emily! I can't tell if my life is getting really great, or worse by the second."

"Tell me, tell me!"

I sighed. "The Jerk came to my office today."

"Noo!" Emily breathed.

"You're never going to believe this. He actually said he was sorry and he wants to get back together."

"Screw that! No, Sydney! You are not getting back together with that sleazeball."

"You don't have to convince me!" I punched one of the pillows on the couch.

"So what'd you do?"

"I told him to leave or I'd call the police."

"And?"

"He left."

"Just like that?" Emily sounded skeptical.

"Well, after he left I turned around and saw Perry standing behind me. He looked like he was going to throw Dirk out the door. Or *through* the door."

"Yeah! Go Perry! So now what?"

"I have no idea." I frowned and cuddled down into the couch cushions. "Emily, today's the fourteenth. Do you think he did that on purpose?"

She was quiet for a minute, considering. "Honestly, Syd, I doubt he knows what he's put you through. I'm sure he's clueless. He's a horrible person, but a clueless one."

I felt tears pushing to escape. Deep breath. "He said he'd meet me after work today to talk about it. But, *thankfully*, I got out of there before he came back. If he came back."

"Think he'll come over?"

"Probably. I checked the parking lot for his car when I pulled in, then locked the door behind me. If he knocks, I just won't answer."

We both knew this was *not* a long-term solution.

We hung up and I un-muted the TV. Matthew Broderick was singing in a remake of *The Music Man*.

"Yes, we've got trouble! Right here in River City!"

I hit Play on the DVD remote.

Boy, I sure hope not.

CHAPTER 12

*T*uesday dawned gray and damp. It had rained overnight and it looked like it would again.

Gee, weather that matched my mood. That's...great. I hadn't slept well, what with the great dreams of kissing Matt that turned into nightmares of being forced to marry Dirk.

In a fit of moodiness, I pulled on my gray knit slacks and a gray v-neck knit shirt. I found my old tennis shoes in the back of the closet, definitely more gray than white. I looked at myself in the mirror and smiled in spite of myself. I looked like a black and white photo. One where they color in only one thing, in this case my hair.

I grabbed a Balance bar from the kitchen and, at the last moment, an individual size chocolate milk instead of a bottle of juice. Breakfast I could eat in the car.

"Well, lookey here, Matt," GT said as I walked in his kitchen door. "It's a beautiful little rain cloud come down from the sky."

Oka-ay. Sweet in a weird kind of way.

I smiled at them both and wished them a good morning.

"I'll be right with ya, darlin'. Just give me one more minute." GT looked back at the papers in his hand.

"Morning," Matt said with a smile, then went back to his work. More papers and blueprints it looked like.

Fine. Work was work. Great. Terrific. We don't know each other. Fine.

GT finished reading and left the room with a "Be right back."

Two seconds later, I heard "Psst!" behind me. I turned to see Matt looking apprehensively at the doorway to the living room. I watched with curiosity. What was he doing?

"Hey," he whispered. "Do you have dinner plans?" He was looking at me now, but I wasn't so sure he was talking to me. I looked around the kitchen.

"Who are you talking to?" I asked.

He screwed up his face into a look I think I was to interpret as "Quiet down, you fool!"

I whispered, "What are you doing?" I couldn't help it. I laughed.

Okay, now that was definitely a look of exasperation. I tried not to laugh, but I couldn't help it, so I just put my hand over my mouth.

"What?" I whispered.

"I like to keep my business life and personal life separate, that's all. And GT's been grilling me about you."

"Oh." I paused. "Am I part of your business life or your personal life?"

He blew out his breath in a way that sounded like "Stupid idea." Then he whispered, "Forget it," and went back to his paperwork.

I took a step closer, still whispering. "Well, how am I supposed to know? We're both standing in this kitchen on business you know."

He looked up impatiently. "Did we talk about business on Saturday? Over breakfast? A decidedly personal event?"

I could match *that* tone. "No, but you didn't ask me about

dinner *then*. You asked me *now*. And in my line of work, dinner is part of business."

He sighed, then glanced toward the doorway when he heard footsteps. "We'll finish this later."

GT came into the kitchen. "Ready?"

Not really. But I wasn't going to embarrass Matt — or myself — by trying to continue our conversation. I wasn't sure what Matt was trying to ask, and I had absolutely no idea why he was so grumpy about it. Professional smile in place, I said "Sure" and led the way to my car. I didn't give Matt a backward glance.

As I drove, GT told me more about the renovations, his new wife, and what he needed for his mother-in-law.

"It's very generous of you," I said, pulling up next to a house he might like a few miles down Peninsula Drive from his "cottage."

He patted my knee and chuckled. "It's not generosity. Time is money. The closer Yolanda is, the less time I have to spend driving to find my wife." He stared out the window at the house, but made no move to get out of the car. "I like to have Merci with me, but she likes to be with her mother when I'm working."

I motioned to the single-story ranch house. "What do you think?"

"Let's see the next one." He kept looking for a moment as we drove away, checking out the side yard, and what could be seen of the back yard.

It was a nice house, but I remembered GT had a habit of not even walking inside if he didn't like the outside. The praise he'd given me about being a visionary was well earned. Without that particular skill, I'm sure he'd never have bought a house from me.

He pointed to another place as we passed, one without a "For Sale" sign. His other hand rested on my shoulder. "That's more along the lines of what I'm looking for."

I nodded. "All right, well, the next one might not work for you. It sits fairly close to the street."

What wasn't working for *me* was his hand on my shoulder right now. And on my knee earlier. Why, oh why, did I put up with this?

Chill, he doesn't mean anything, said a Voice.

We barely pulled to the curb in front of the next property before GT urged me to drive on. But at the third house, we actually got out and looked around. GT put his hand under my elbow and guided me around a soggy spot in the yard. He held on until we were on the sidewalk — and still showed no signs of letting go. So I pointed out the lovely front door — stretching my arm all the way out and forcing him to let his hand fall.

Boy, it would be a long summer if he kept this up.

Since the house was empty, we peered in several of the windows. GT shrugged. I took that as a good sign, all things considered. Don't get me wrong, it's *way* better to have a client who knows what he wants and can't find it, than one who looks at everything and can't decide. And GT seemed to be quite certain about his needs.

Since he had a lunch meeting at his home office, we drove past one more house and headed back. Not a bad first effort, all things considered.

"Let's try this again in a few days," he said. "I'll talk to Yolanda about some of your suggestions and get back to you."

"Great. Meanwhile, I'll keep looking." You bet I'd keep looking. Property on Old Mission Peninsula is rarely under the quarter mil mark. The words "commission" and "House Fund" flashed in neon in my mind's eye.

I pulled into the driveway and drove all the way up to the back door. "You've got my numbers. Call if you need anything."

GT took my hand and held it again, rather than shook it. "You hang in there, darlin'. You'll find the right one. That last one must be no good to leave you like that. Your time is comin'. Mark my words."

At first, I thought he was talking about the house hunt. Mortified, I realized this man was talking about my *love* life. Will this humiliation have no end?

As GT walked to the back door, I couldn't help myself — I looked around for Matt. He sure was in a snit this morning. But I'd like to clear the air. I saw him talking with another guy in a hard hat. They both pointed at the papers in Matt's hand.

Should I do anything? Walk up to him and try to talk? I could go ask him for his business card. For referrals. Yeah, that's a good one. I could actually pull that one off.

As I sat there trying to decide, Matt looked up and saw me. I stared back, unsure now. When I was about to smile, he turned back to his papers as if I wasn't even there.

Fine! I put the car into reverse and backed down the driveway and onto the road. I was proud of myself. I didn't kick up any mud or squeal my tires or anything.

I GROWLED IN FRUSTRATION. THIS WAS ALL DIRK'S FAULT. I WAS never unsure of myself or other people until Dirk. The Jerk!

I pulled into the McDonald's drive-thru on my way back to the office. A chicken sandwich and French fries would go a long way toward cheering me up today. Parking in the office lot, I heard thunder and grabbed my stuff as quickly as I could. As I opened the car door, I felt the first drops of rain. I sprinted.

Apparently rain, like bears, will only chase you if you run. By the time I got to the front door, I was drenched. When was the last time the sky opened up like that? Michigan rain usually starts out gently, gives you a head start. Trying to get in quickly, my wet hand slipped on the door and I almost dropped my jacket. Hastily, I fumbled to catch it and knocked my wet McDonald's bag against the closing door. The soggy paper gave way and my lunch fell.

Into a puddle. Outside the door. Almost. The chicken sandwich kind of wedged the door open. I looked at my saved jacket, which wasn't in a mud puddle, then back at my lunch — which was.

I closed my eyes tightly. Inside my head I yelled a swear word. I was at the office. A place of business. Where you have to act like a professional. Where all the yelling had to stay bottled up.

"Oh no." I heard Carmen approach. "Let me help you." She took the items still precariously balanced in my arms and put them on a chair. I set the rest of it down, then opened the door to clean up my mess. Carmen brought some napkins — undoubtedly from *her* lunch, fresh, dry, and already eaten — and I finished picking the last of the fries out of the water.

I threw it all in the trash by Carmen's desk, then grimaced at my spectacularly wet self. A ridiculous thought came to my mind.

"Hey, got a scale? We can find out how much I weigh soaking wet."

Carmen burst out laughing and I let myself chuckle a little. Well, it made me feel better for a minute anyway. Still hungry, but better.

I took my things back to my desk and sat there trying to keep my wet hair from dripping onto my laptop keyboard or the papers on my desk.

"Hey, I've got a turkey sub. Wanna share?" Trent stood in front of my desk, Subway bag in hand. A plastic, waterproof bag, by the way.

"Thanks, I'm fine."

"My eyes are bigger than my stomach. Got a foot-long, but I

won't be able to eat it all." He looked down at his stomach and chuckled. "Well, I *can* eat it all, but I shouldn't."

I looked at him warily. "You see that?"

He was trying not to laugh. "I don't think you meant it to be a spectator sport, but...I was only a few steps ahead of you... Yeah, I saw it."

He was grinning now. It was a cute grin. And he was being so nice...what could it hurt?

"You're only gonna get hungrier."

"Well, if it'll help you keep your boyish figure," I said with a smile.

He cocked his head over to his desk and I joined him. We talked while we ate, making each other laugh or grimace with our shop talk tales of crazy clients. Very relaxing after my crazy morning.

When we were almost done, a delivery person came in asking for me. She gave me a vase of tulips and irises and a wrapped box. A gold-wrapped box. Godiva chocolate. I know because Godiva chocolate is my all-time favorite and, well, I hate to admit it, but I buy rather a lot of it.

I looked at Trent. He shrugged. "Beats me." I opened the card. *All her favorites for my favorite girl, Love, Dirk.*

I sighed dramatically. "Why me?" I pretend cried.

"What's wrong?" I handed Trent the card. "Ah," he said as he read it. He put it on the desk and patted my back.

I folded one arm on his desk and beat my head on it. How could one woman have so many man problems? It's against all odds.

Maybe you should go buy a lottery ticket, suggested a Voice.

Don't! You'll get struck by lightning, warned Another.

I rubbed my finger on some of the flower petals. So soft. It's not their fault they were paid for by Dirk. I sniffed them. Hothouse flowers never seem to have much scent, but they're still beautiful.

I picked up the box of chocolates. What purpose would it serve to throw them in the trash if Dirk wasn't here to see it?

He'll know you ate them, and that'll be his victory.

He won't know. How could he know if I ate them or not?

'Cause he knows you, said a Voice.

Why would you throw expensive chocolates in the trash? You aren't going to throw the flowers away, are you? Enjoy them and let the money flow from Dirk's wallet. You didn't ask for them.

Finally, I looked at Trent with narrowed eyes. I opened the box and took out a truffle. Taking a deliberate bite, I closed my eyes in pleasure. "Mmm."

I passed the box. "You provided lunch. I'm providing dessert." I'd share the expensive chocolate with *another man.* So there. "Come on, have some."

Trent laughed nervously. He watched me but didn't take any. Which only fueled my anger and resentment.

"I know what I'll do," I said. "When he calls, I'll thank him politely and tell him you and I enjoyed the chocolate immensely."

Trent gave me a pitying look. I know he pitied me. 'Cause I'm pitiful.

"Come on, Trent. This is the best chocolate on the planet." I pushed the box at him. "And neither of us had to pay for it. Have some." I took another. Ate it in one bite.

"Are you okay?" Trent laid his hand on my shoulder. The gentle touch was my undoing.

"Do I look okay?" I glared at him. Then I felt guilty and dropped my eyes. Then I felt angry that Dirk was making me feel guilty about something and he wasn't even here. I put my hand over my eyes and breathed deeply.

Trent put his arm around me and pulled me closer. Oh my gosh. That felt good. I leaned into him and soaked up his strength. Of course, his shirt soaked up a lot of the water from my shirt and hair.

"Everything's going to be okay. You'll see." He stroked my back.

After a moment, I pulled away. I didn't know how to say thanks without getting even more embarrassed. "Have you ever had Godiva chocolates?" I asked quietly.

He leaned his elbows on his desk and looked into the box. "Don't think so."

"Well, you don't want to miss out. They're amazing." I met his eyes for a microsecond, smiled and looked back at the truffles.

I pointed out the ones that I thought were the best. Trent magnanimously insisted that he save them for me. We ate four or five each, Trent finding ways to make me laugh and cheer me up. Then it was time to get back to work.

"By the way," I paused on the way to my desk, "I like your roses better."

Trent smiled.

I took Dirk's flowers and the half-empty gold box to my desk. As beautiful as the flowers were, they were making me nauseous. I had a thought. I walked up to the front desk.

"So, who are the flowers from?" Carmen grinned the way all women do when someone gets flowers at the office.

I gave her a wry smile. Hers faded. "Oh, honey, I'm sorry."

I shrugged a little and tried to smile a bit. "It's okay. I have an idea, though. I don't want to throw them away because they're gorgeous, but I don't really want them at my desk."

I gestured at her desk, very neat and organized — and devoid of sparkle. "I thought we could decorate the office with them. It'd be nice for clients to see fresh flowers when they walk in, right?"

Carmen smiled like a co-conspirator. "Perfect." She moved her inbox and we arranged the flowers on the corner of her desk. Beautiful.

"Oh, and here." I held out the chocolates. "Help yourself." I handed her the open box.

"Ooo, thank you," she said as she took a couple. She caught my eye. "Don't let him get you down." She motioned to the flowers and candy. "See? This is you in control. You're not his puppet. You're making your own decisions. Don't let him bother you."

My smile was the first real one since the delivery. "You're such a good friend, Carmen." She got up from her desk and gave me a big hug.

"I know." We both laughed. I urged her to take one of my favorite truffles, then went back to my desk.

I sat down, staring at my wet belongings. I opened the Godiva box and ate a raspberry truffle. Even better than the ice cream.

I called Emily and got her voice mail on the first ring. Phone must be off. Or broken. Or lost. She's been hard to reach lately. Maybe her battery's dying. I ate another chocolate. I really should get some work done.

Carmen brought me a fax from GT. It was a revised list of things the new house needed to have. It was longer and more complicated than the last list. Everything is a need, everything is a priority. There is no wish list, just a list of demands.

I crumpled it up and threw it in the trash. I couldn't deal with demanding men today.

I ate another truffle.

You're going to make yourself sick, said the Mom voice.

The air conditioning was making me shiver in my damp clothes. I looked outside at the pouring rain. I couldn't get much wetter. And at home I could change into something warm and dry.

I sat and thought for another minute. Should I feel guilty about leaving work so early? Another look outside and I knew no one would call to look at a house today. I gathered my things together and headed for the door.

I waved at Trent. "Going home to get dry." He smiled and waved. "Thanks again for lunch."

"Any time," he said.

I got almost to the front door and stopped. I turned back, muttering under my breath, and grabbed GT's fax out of the waste can.

Maybe I *should* buy a lottery ticket on the way home. If I win, I'm moving to a deserted island away from everyone. And buying Emily a new phone.

CHAPTER 13

*a*t home, I opened my windows just a crack so the smell of the rain could come in but not the rain itself. I'd had enough things ruined lately, thank you very much.

I changed into dry clothes (and felt better immediately) and put the Godiva box in a kitchen cupboard (out of sight, out of mind). It occurred to me that Dirk might stop by the office to check out his flowers. Good thing I came home.

I connected my laptop to the Internet and got back to work. The afternoon passed quickly between paperwork, phone calls and emails. My stomach growled and I looked at my watch. Nearly six. Wow. I love it when time flies like that.

I wandered over to the refrigerator and checked out the contents. Forgot I made egg salad. I pulled out the bowl and grabbed a fork.

As I was taking a bite, my cell phone rang. Swallowing quickly, I picked it up.

"By the Bay Properties, this is Sydney."

"Hi. I'm looking to buy a house, preferably one with a full dinner prepared and hot on the table. Say, in the next hour."

I smiled. "We can all dream, can't we? Is this Matt?"

"Hey, Syd, how's it going?

"Fine, now." Oh gosh, that sounds like I was waiting for his call. "I mean, the first half of the day was filled with disaster after disaster—"

Which, by the way, you were a part of, grumbled Sergeant Pride.

"—but I'm home with dry clothes on so..." Geez, could I sound more stupid? I closed my eyes and covered my face with my free hand.

"I was wondering...are you busy tonight?" He didn't sound like the confident, knows-where-he-belongs-in-the-world guy from the fishing trip. Which — ironically — gave me more confidence.

I thought of this morning's "business or pleasure" conversation. It had been kind of funny to me, which apparently aggravated him. Which I suppose was the reason he ignored me in GT's driveway. Which pretty much ticked me off.

"You didn't seem like you wanted to be seen with me this morning," I said, swirling patterns around the egg salad with my fork.

He cleared his throat. "Yeah, well...like I said, I don't like to mix my business and personal life. GT can be...I like my privacy."

I thought about GT's intrusion into *my* personal life earlier. "I understand."

"So...have you had dinner?"

I laughed and glanced down at my artwork. "I was standing at the counter eating egg salad out of a bowl when you called."

Matt chuckled. "Sounds delicious. Can you drag yourself away?"

He was too funny to stay mad at. I wanted to say yes to dinner, but how was I going to feel later when he again acted like he barely knew me? "I'd like to, but…" My feelings had been trampled on too much lately for me to walk willingly into a risky situation.

"You can choose the restaurant," he urged.

I wasn't trying to make him beg. "Can I tell you why I'm not sure it's a good idea?" My stomach rolled. I wasn't used to being so honest.

"How about you give me your address and we'll talk about it over dinner. Can I pick you up around seven?"

Pick me up? Holy cow! Like a *date* date. A real date. I looked around my little apartment. Well, there's no time to get ready for a date and clean the place up, too. I just won't let him in.

"Seven sounds great." Oh geez, I sound breathless, breathe girlfriend, it's-cool-it's-no-big-deal.

The calming pep talk at the speed of an auctioneer did *not* help me relax.

I'm going on a date with Matt! A real date where he picks me up and everything! Lovesick practically swooned.

Don't do it, warned Fear. *You're setting yourself up for a fall.*

I ignored the warning, gave Matt my address, and hung up. I stood there for a second then threw my arms up in the air and whooped!

I hurried to put away the egg salad, shut down my computer — oh, leave the papers, I'm not letting him in anyway — and ran to my room. If I hurried, there was time for a shower and fixing my hair.

I looked in the mirror as I shed my clothes. Oh yeah, the hair was just a big mess of brown frizz springing everywhere. Out of the shower, I rubbed some no-frizz, leave-in conditioner into my wet hair, dried it, and worked on taming it with my straightener.

I opened my closet to see what was available. Huh. I looked over at the dirty clothes hamper. Brimming over. Okay, so the good stuff was gone.

I whisked through all the hangers. Nope, nope, absolutely not, huh-uh, nope. Hmm, I came to the black lace top Emily gave me for Christmas last year. Lined in front, and short enough that an inch or so of stomach showed.

I don't know, too sexy? I remembered how Matt looked at my skin showing Saturday at breakfast.

Do it! Wear it! urged Little Miss Lovesick.

I pulled it out of the closet. What else? Oh, I've got that cute black skirt I bought a couple months ago when Em thought shopping would cheer me up. That would look great with this.

I got dressed and looked in the mirror. Hmm. I looked like a girl who wants to impress a guy on a date. I looked good, but... I pulled off the skirt and grabbed a pair of newer, nice-looking jeans from the closet.

Back to the mirror. Yeah, nice. Casual, but obvious that I dressed with care. Jeans on a date on a summer evening? Sheesh. And I had freshly shaven legs so...

Do it! yelled a couple different Voices.

I put the skirt back on.

Time. I looked at my alarm clock. 6:45.

I ran to the bathroom and grabbed some eye shadow and mascara. I brushed my teeth and put on some lip-gloss. (Again with the teeth brushing before eating.)

Time. 6:53.

Oh, I know! I grabbed a black Scrunchi and pulled my hair back into a cute little ponytail. It would do. One last look and I went to grab some black sandals.

I heard a knock, grabbed my purse, and looked through the peephole. Matt. I took a deep breath, turned off the lights, and opened the door.

The crisp, cool scent of the recent rain washed over me. As did the light scent of men's cologne. Matt looked great in jeans and a dark blue golf shirt, hair still wet from his shower.

"Hi there," I said cheerfully as I stepped out and closed the door. I locked it, then turned to face him. He looked me over in the fading light.

"You look…great."

I grinned up at him. "Thanks!" Feeling frisky, I gave him that same once-over look he'd given me. "You look…blue."

It loosened him up. He grinned and took my hand, pulling me close as we walked down the stairs. "I hope you're hungry."

"I'm starving. Drive fast."

"Did you decide where you want to go?"

"Are you sure you're letting me choose?"

Matt glanced at me warily as he opened the passenger door of his black Dodge Ram pickup. The inside was significantly cleaner than I expected from a construction worker. I wondered if he'd cleaned it before he came over. "Yeah," he said in response to my question. But it came out more like "Ye-ah?" I smiled mischievously just to make him worry.

Twenty minutes later we walked into a tiny little Asian restaurant off the beaten path. Nonetheless, it was full of customers.

"I can't believe you've never had Mongolian barbeque. It rocks!" I showed him how to choose one of the frozen meats and press it down into the bowl. Then add noodles and sprouts and pineapple and tofu and — I can't even remember what all we stuffed into our bowls.

We handed them over to the cook. Matt watched him as he spread out the food over the round grill, keeping each bowlful separate for each customer, turning the food with wooden sticks. Then the mess was scraped onto a plate and handed over.

"You're gonna love this," I told him. We slipped back to our little table for two.

After the first bite, Matt smiled. "This is good stuff."

We ate. And talked. A lot. About hiking and fishing and water sports and movies and everything that came to mind.

"Maybe you'd like to go out on my boat with me sometime," Matt asked, taking another bite of food.

"You have a boat?" I speared a piece of pineapple and ate it. My stomach felt stretched already and I was only halfway done.

He shrugged. "It's not that big. Twenty-foot motor boat. I tool around the bay in it, go out to Lake Michigan, tow it to the smaller lakes around here to go fishing."

"Sounds great. I'd love to." Funny how much easier it was to say yes to Matt than to accept a similar invitation from Trent.

He grinned at me with a devilish look in his eye. "I promise I won't make you fish," he said, "if you promise to wear a life jacket in case you fall in."

I slapped at his hand. Quick as a rattlesnake, he grabbed my offending hand and didn't let go. I felt breathless laughter escaping. I loved the way Matt was looking at me, like I was fun and cute and maybe even interesting. Without breaking eye contact, he kissed my fingers.

Little Miss Lovesick sighed.

I'm sure I was all googly-eyed, but I didn't care. This guy was fabulous.

Still holding my hand, he said, "You finished?"

My food was only half-eaten, but I was full. "Yeah. I'll eat the rest tomorrow."

Matt gestured to the waitress to bring a to-go box. "All right. You chose dinner, so I get to choose dessert."

He took my hand as we walked back to his truck. I don't know what it is about holding hands, but...I love it.

Matt drove (both hands on the wheel now) downtown and parked across the street from the beach. Even after eight on a damp Tuesday night, there were dozens of people milling around. The shops stayed open late in the summer because of the tourists. That made it fun for the locals, too.

We walked a couple blocks and stopped in front of a dark storefront.

"Noo!" Matt put his free hand on his hip. "How can they be closed?"

I looked in the darkened window of Kilwin's, one of Traverse City's famous fudge shops. At this one, they rolled out the fudge in the front window. Definitely brought people in. In fact, I'd seen people stand on the sidewalk watching even if they weren't buying. A bigger crowd meant the confectioners were pulling taffy inside. Pretty cool.

Matt pulled me closer and wrapped his arms around me. "Huh? How?" He put his chin on my head and sighed.

Okay, *seriously* loving *this*. I don't care how goofy it sounds, it's the little gestures that please me most.

"Um, they turn off the lights and lock the door?"

Matt leaned down and nipped my neck. It tickled and I shrieked.

"Be good, smarty-pants, or I won't bring you back. Trust me, this is the best chocolate shop in town."

He let me go, but took my hand again. He looked up and down the street, then decided to go back the way we came. We walked and talked and looked in the store windows. As we approached a shop that sold Moomers ice cream, Matt asked, "Like ice cream?"

"You have no idea!" I went crazy and ordered a scoop of cherry praline pecan and a scoop of chocolate raspberry cabernet. Matt got the chocolate orange and the mocha almond fudge. We laughed as we fed each other a bite of our desserts.

"Well, lookey here! If it ain't my contractor and my realtor, out for a stroll together."

Matt and I looked up to see GT and a beautiful blond woman walking toward us.

Matt's laughing grin morphed into a professional smile. He dropped my hand and stepped away from me. His tension washed over to me, and I pasted a professional smile on my face as well.

"Honey, you know Matt," GT said to the blonde. "And this here's Sydney Riley, the lovely lady who's finding your mama a summer cottage. Sydney, this beautiful young thing is my wife, Mercedes."

Matt and I both shook Mercedes' hand as she giggled and said, "How do you do?"

How do you do? My grandmother was the only person I knew who said "how do you do." Huh. Maybe it was another Southern thing. Though I wondered sometimes if GT really was from the South or if he used the charm to manipulate people.

"What are you doing out with this alley cat, darlin?" GT asked me.

I laughed nervously and tried not to look at Matt. Alley cat? Southern charm or not, the only images that came to mind were derogatory. Did GT know something I didn't, or did he think that was funny?

"Oh, we're just...out having dinner." I glanced at Matt.

"So, are you up for the rest of the summer, Mercedes?" Matt asked.

"Oh, you silly!" She giggled again. "I can't live in the house if you're still working on it." She laughed and batted at Matt's arm with one hand. The other one was clinging to GT's arm.

My gosh. It was Marilyn Monroe. Mercedes could've been Norma Jean's sister.

"Merci and I are staying at Chateau Chantal for a couple weeks. We've missed each other, haven't we darlin?" GT gazed into Mercedes face with — love?

GT tore his gaze away and turned back to us. "We just went and enjoyed us a good movie. Now we're on our way back to the hotel to have some fine wine and chocolate. My little gal here loves wine and chocolate."

"Oh, GT," she gushed. "Now I'll have to spend all day at the gym tomorrow because of you." She fluttered her eyelashes at him. Mercedes had "come hither" down pat.

Oh, stop! I had an instant picture of them together, alone. Eew. I like the idea of people being married "happily ever after" and "till death do us part," but I don't like mental images of people I know having sex. Yuck!

"Well, we better let you go then," Matt said. He reached for Mercedes' hand. "Nice seeing you again Mercedes. I'll see you tomorrow GT."

Matt was obviously in a hurry to get away. GT was not.

"Now, hold on a minute. I just had me a fine idea." GT's face lit up. It was the kind of look that inspired cartoonists to put light bulbs over people's heads when they had a thought.

"Merci and I have no one to dine with tomorrow. Two is fun, but three is only business and that bores my little chick. The four of us will have dinner tomorrow night. Someplace nice. My treat."

I didn't know what to say. It didn't sound like a request, but an edict. So I did what I'd been doing during the entire conversation. Nothing.

Matt did what he'd been doing the whole conversation — he immediately tried to get out of it.

"That's very generous of you, GT, but I don't know when—"

GT waved his hand. "Generous nothing. It's all about entertaining my wife. Nothing is too good for her. Is it Muffin?" GT smiled at her and she clung closer to him and giggled again.

I felt something hit my elbow. I glanced at Matt. He didn't look at me, but I knew it was him.

"GT, really, that's very sweet," I tried again. "But I don't have my calendar with me. I really need to check it before I—"

"I'll call and make the reservation for seven. Whatever is on your schedule, I'm sure you're free after seven. Everyone has to eat." GT chuckled. Then he pumped Matt's hand. "Now you show this little lady a good time tonight. I want her in a good mood so she can find me another house."

I held out my hand to shake, but GT brought it to his lips. "Sugar, you keep this one." His eyes darted to Matt and back. "He's hard-working, dependable, always does what he says he will." He let go of my hand. "Now you two have a nice night. We'll see you tomorrow."

CHAPTER 14

*M*att and I stood on the sidewalk trying to recover. I risked a glance at him. Oh yeah, he looked irate. I wasn't sure exactly why, but I wanted to lighten the mood.

"I'm not sure, but I think he just gave you a reference." I laughed a little.

Matt didn't.

Okay, my funny bone's not working so well tonight. What to do?

I ate my ice cream and meandered down the street. Maybe Matt just needed some breathing room. I turned to look at him. Still fuming, he shoveled ice cream into his mouth. He caught my gaze. Thunderclouds. Yikes.

Why is he so mad? Is it such a horrible thing to be seen with me?

This is exactly why you should've said no tonight, said a Voice. *You don't need this right now.*

Matt ate his ice cream like his throat was on fire. I thought he might choke he ate so fast. I turned back to mine and ate quietly. Surely he'd get over whatever it was soon.

You should've brought your own car, said a Voice.

I looked at him again. He'd finished his ice cream. If only he would relax and smile. Without thinking I stuck my tongue out at him. Then I grinned. Nothing.

I moved to look in another shop window. Great, this store sold knives and swords.

I looked at Matt. "This is your kind of store, buddy. Look — all kinds of ways to skin him."

He stepped closer to me, looked in the window, and humphed.

"Of course, if looks could kill, *I'd* be dead." No response. I put my hand over his eyes. "We'll have to get you one of those visors like Cyclops has."

Another grunt. But with a tiny bit of almost-smile.

"Seriously, I'm beginning to be afraid for my life. I don't want to even *think* about driving with you right now." Teasing tone, real worry. "Can you handle walking a bit more?"

"Fine." Well, at least he spoke.

I decided the best course of action was to give him time to cool off. We walked without speaking, pausing occasionally to look inside a window. At the end of the shopping area, he took my hand and pulled me to a stop.

"Hey."

He turned me to face him. His lips were so close, but I refused to look at them. This wasn't really a kissing moment.

"Thanks," he said.

I shrugged and smiled. "What're friends for?"

He looked away, then back at me. "I'm sorry. It's not you."

I didn't know what to say. It was the perfect time to ask the obvious question — "Then what the heck is it?" — but I'd never been the confrontational type.

He smiled a little. "Maybe we should get back. I've got to be at work early."

I tried not to look disappointed. I knew in construction,

particularly in snow country, the hours were dawn to dusk. He'd probably be pounding nails while I was still curled up in bed.

"Sure." Sure? What a stupid response. It all but shouts disappointment.

Matt kissed the back of my hand and let it go. I figured he didn't want GT to see us holding hands again.

Whatever.

We didn't, of course, see GT or anyone else we knew on the way back to the truck. The drive home was not silent exactly, but uh, *muted* might be the right word. He could have been my brother the way he treated me. You know, nothing wrong, perfectly nice, but completely uninterested in, say, whether he could see my abs under my shirt.

We pulled into the parking lot at my apartment complex.

"Thanks for dinner, Matt." I didn't want to say too much. I was definitely getting the vibe that he didn't want to be seen with the same woman too often. I should count myself lucky that we went out twice in a week. It likely wasn't ever going to happen again.

Well, except for tomorrow night. And any fool could see how much he was looking forward to that.

He pulled into a space and turned off the engine as I opened my door. I looked at him in surprise.

"It's late. I'll walk you to your door."

"It's okay. It's a safe neighborhood." I was trying to let him get back home and nurse his attitude somewhere else.

He ignored me and followed me up the stairs.

As I paused on the landing, fumbling for my keys in the light there, I heard a horrible sound. Dirk's voice.

"Hey, Sydney."

I froze.

This couldn't be happening. I looked toward the bottom of the stairs. There he stood.

"I thought I'd stop by and say hi. You haven't returned my calls. I got worried about you." His eyes shifted to stare at Matt.

I narrowed my eyes, frowning. "What are you doing here? How long have you been waiting for me?"

"Not long. We were going to get some dinner remember?"

I glanced at Matt. He stared down Dirk, expression cold and hard. What was he thinking? He didn't know me well enough to know that I didn't play one guy against another.

Crap. Nothing I could do about it now.

I sighed. "Dirk, go home. Go home and stop sending me flowers and chocolate and stop calling me and don't come over anymore, okay?"

Suddenly, I was just exhausted.

If there is any chance that ESP really works, please let Matt know that I just want him to act like we're together for two more minutes.

I dug the keys out of my purse, but dropped them because my hand was shaking. Before I could move, Matt picked them up and took my hand, walking me up the last few steps.

He started to try a key, and I whispered, "The green one." He opened the door and ushered me in. I didn't look, but I could feel the testosterone-based staring match for a few seconds. Matt came in and shut and locked the door.

"Thank you," I breathed.

"You're welcome."

"I'm sorry. I don't know what he's doing here."

That's *a bit of a fib, now isn't it,* said a Voice. *You've been expecting the son of a—*

I don't want to think about it.

"So this is your place, huh?" Matt looked around from his position by the door. "No roommates?"

I looked at the disarray and belatedly remembered that I hadn't cleaned up earlier because I wasn't going to let him in. File folders and papers covered the dining room table. Mail and magazines made a pile on one living room chair; clean, unfolded laundry filled another.

He must think I'm a complete slob. Of course, that's why he's asking if I have roommates, someone to blame the mess on before he makes his judgment.

"Ah, no. I'm sorry about the mess. I was working today and—"

"Don't worry about it. I was just wondering if you'll be safe. That's all."

"Oh." Well, isn't *that* sweet? "That's...kind of you."

He stared at me.

I bet you a hundred bucks he never asks you out again, said a Voice.

He was waiting for an answer. "Oh, right, yes, I'm safe. Dirk isn't any trouble. He just never does what I want." Like stay when I want him and leave when I don't. "Thanks for coming in. I appreciate it." I noticed he still had my keys in his hand. I took them and hung them on the little "KEYS" hook by the door.

Matt chuckled. When I looked at him, a bit of the fun, not-angry Matt was re-surfacing.

"What?"

"It just seems — out of place."

I looked at the cheesy plastic word K-E-Y-S with hooks under each letter. "Well...if I don't put my keys in the same place every day, I lose them. This isn't — I'm not keeping this forever. I just haven't found the right piece yet. I'm looking for a shallow, brass wall sconce. It'd be perfect as a key holder. But I want an old one, something antique looking. Not a new one."

Matt's brow furrowed as he considered it. "Yeah, that could be good."

I stood there looking at him nervously. "Well, thanks again for dinner."

Should I invite him to sit? He said he had to get up early

for work. Or he might think I want him to stay only to make Dirk mad. Or he might think — no, he wouldn't think I might be willing to — no way. He hadn't even kissed me on the lips yet.

I fidgeted.

Apparently my discomfort came through. "You want me to go?"

"No!" Oh boy, too quickly and too vehemently. Compensate. Compensate! "I mean, I understand you need your sleep."

What are you saying? screamed a Voice.

"Not here!" I could *hear* the blood rushing to my face. It roared like a flash flood. "I mean, you said you had to go home earlier."

Matt smiled, his dimple showing. "So you want me to stay and—"

I slapped at his shoulder. "No! You know that's not what I mean." So embarrassed. I walked toward the kitchen, calling over my shoulder, "You want a drink, you big oaf?"

He followed me. "What've you got?"

Opening the fridge, I tried not to think of what it might look like to someone else. Everything I bought was pre-cooked, pre-packaged, pre-made. My mother would die. My dad would love it. He and I didn't like to waste time cooking. We liked to eat and run.

"Juice, chocolate milk, lemonade…water." I could feel him right behind me, looking over my shoulder. I was afraid to move because I didn't know what I'd do if he didn't move out of the way. My heart was beating in my ears.

He's just a guy! It's no big deal! yelled one of the Voices.

"Come on, you're letting out the air. Whaddaya want?" I made my voice pretend-snappy. Play-mad. It worked. He laughed.

But he still didn't move.

Well, yes he did. He put his hand next to mine on the

refrigerator door, our skin touching. A little shiver ran up my arm, but it was from the cold air. Really.

"What, no beer? No tequila? Not even any wine?" he teased.

"Here's some whine — *choose something*," I said in my very best whiney voice.

He laughed and reached his other arm around me to take a bottle of chocolate milk out. For a moment, he about had me in a full body hug.

Then he backed away. In relief, I started to close the door, then remembered I hadn't picked a drink myself. I plucked a bottle of lemonade off a shelf and let the door close.

I twisted the cap off and turned to throw it in the garbage. Matt leaned against the counter, looking like the cat *just before* he ate the canary. I stuck my tongue out.

"My, my, you are just full of invitations tonight."

"Stop teasing me!" I pretend whined again and stomped into the living room.

This was *way* worse than the flirting we did up north. *Way* more fun, too. And *way* more scary.

I turned on a lamp near the couch, stacked a few magazines on the coffee table to clear some space, and sat down. Matt followed me and sat a decent distance away.

Shoot, complained Lovesick.

"So." For the life of me, I couldn't think of a single thing to say.

"No, I don't, do you?" Matt asked when the pause lasted too long.

"No," I giggled. "I don't sew either." Another pause. He was just sitting there looking at me. "Come on, help me out here!"

"You're nervous," he said like it'd just occurred to him. "Why?"

"Well, duh," I replied sarcastically. "I haven't had a man — lover, friend, or foe — in my home in months."

I took a big swallow of the lemonade. "I can't remember how

it works." The truth of that, and the strange thought that Matt would understand, made me laugh nervously even as I said it.

"I don't know either," he said, shaking his head. He leaned back on the couch, glanced at me, smiled, and looked away. Then looked and smiled some more.

From outside, we heard the squeal of tires and a racing motor. A pause as the car came to the end of the driveway, then more squeals as it pulled onto the street.

"Well, I guess Dick's gone." Matt saluted me with his chocolate milk and took a swallow.

I didn't know if he said "Dick" on purpose, but I didn't correct him. I hid my grin behind my juice bottle.

Matt looked around the apartment, leaning forward with his elbows on his knees. He must've stayed just to make sure I was okay. That was nice of him.

"So, I guess you have to leave now?" I couldn't hide the disappointment from my voice so I counteracted it with a smile. I thought about adding a yawn to show that I understood it was late, but I don't know how to make a fake one look real.

Matt shifted his position. "I haven't finished my chocolate milk. You don't want me to drink and drive, do you?"

I chuckled and shook my head, studying my juice bottle. I had no idea what to make of him. Fun, angry, quiet, fun. I may not be ready for this roller coaster ride. But it'd be a fun one if I were.

He leaned back on the couch again. I drank some more lemonade. He swung his knee to hit mine and I looked at him. His face was significantly closer. The little bugger. I thought he was fidgeting because he wanted to leave. He was just moving closer to me on the couch!

"What are you doing?" I asked.

"What? I'm sitting here drinking my chocolate milk." Again with the innocent Tom Sawyer look.

I raised my eyebrows at him.

"And trying to get closer to the pretty girl I'm with?"

"Yeah, yeah, I bet you say that to all the girls." I sat up with my elbows on my knees and gulped my lemonade. He was too close for me to think straight. Very bad. Because I needed to think about how to tell him this wasn't going to work. I thought I was ready, but...

He imitated my position. Getting closer.

"You're right. All one of you." He winked at me.

I raised my eyebrows again. "You haven't gone out to dinner with any other pretty girls?" I teased. "No breakfast dates? Lunch appointments?"

"Yes, but that's not dating. That's eating."

"Riighht." I looked at him for a moment, trying to figure him out. "Like what we're doing," I said slowly. "We're eating."

I told you this was too good to be true, murmured a Voice.

Matt's cheeks and forehead turned a dull red. Well, *that's* a good sign.

He turned his chocolate milk around in his hands. "Listen, I don't play games. I'm not good at them and they annoy the heck out of me. If I run into someone I know and we eat together, that's one thing. But dating is when I consciously call a girl up and invite her out. A lot."

I was quiet for a second, trying to decide if I was going to speak my mind. Four years of being with Dirk had taught me that choosing your battles is often the better part of wisdom.

I decided to speak. "Listen, I've enjoyed...*eating* with you. You've called me twice and I've said yes twice, so I suppose that's a sign I could be interested in 'dating' you." I used my fingers to make air quotes. "But sometimes when we're together and someone you know is around, you get embarrassed and act like you barely know me."

"I told you, it's not you. What more do you want me to say?"

We locked eyes for a moment. He was clueless. Completely

freaking clueless. I huffed air through my nose and shook my head.

"Nothing. I'm not trying to get you to say anything. But here's the thing. I've already been hurt more than I thought I could take. I can't get attached to someone who doesn't want to be seen with me. My heart just can't take it."

Matt appeared to think about what I said. Then he downed the rest of his chocolate milk. He carefully set the bottle on the coffee table.

I looked away, eyes closed, shaking my head almost imperceptibly at my own gullibility. I'm the stupidest person I know.

He picked up my hand and kissed the back of it. "I finished my chocolate milk, so I better go."

I met his gaze for a second. "Sure." I walked him to the door.

"Lock the door after I leave," he instructed in a big-brother voice.

Oh gosh, what a good idea. Too bad I didn't leave the door to my heart locked. How could I accuse Matt of breaking and entering when it was my fault for letting him in?

CHAPTER 15

I don't know what it is about GT. I wish I had his way
with convincing people. I'd be rich! (And he *was* rich,
so there you go.)

Apparently, neither Matt nor I came up with good enough
reasons why we couldn't go to dinner the next night because
there we both were in Trattoria Stella at Grand Traverse
Commons. But...we're professionals. Business dinners are a
part of life. So really, we were doing exactly what we should be
doing. That was my view, anyway.

Matt, however, looked like "polite" was as far as he was
willing to go. He interacted with everyone, listened, asked
questions. It's not like he was sulking about being there. But in
the time I'd gotten to know him, I could feel that he wasn't fully
engaged.

Or maybe this is just his business persona, said a Voice.

I liked his fishing guide persona better, said Lovesick.

In any case, GT was a surprisingly gracious host. He and
Mercedes chose a restaurant so far beyond my means it
would've been embarrassing, except that I'd learned to act like I

belonged at any meeting, wherever the setting. But GT didn't act like we were someplace special. He didn't make mention of how wonderful the food was, or urge us to order whatever we liked. He simply engaged us all in entertaining conversation. The meal seemed to be a magnificent bonus, as far as he was concerned.

While we waited for the appetizers, we chatted about business, real estate, architecture, vacationing. Matt never gave up much information about himself. Personal information, that is. I learned that he'd never been to Hawaii, but would like to go. He'd worked with GT on commercial projects in the past, and this was his first renovation. He knew a lot about architecture, construction, and real estate. (Like that was a big surprise.) But the only personal details I knew about Matt were the ones I'd learned on the fishing trip. Why did he open up then when we were just flirting, but not now that we were sort of seeing each other?

In comparison, the rest of dinner conversation was filled with the hundred or so references to how much GT and Mercedes adored each other. I (skeptically) imagined she loved his money and he loved her looks. But as the night wore on, I began to think they really might love each other in that "happily ever after" kind of way I used to dream of.

Just before the entrée was served (this was one of those three-hour-dinner type of restaurants), I excused myself to go to the bathroom. Mercedes immediately excused herself, too. I sighed inwardly, smiling outwardly. I didn't know her well enough for the chatty girl-talk that group bathroom trips inspired. And this polite distance from Matt was taking its toll on me. (Though I told myself it had just been a long day.)

Mercedes played with her hair in the ladies room. While I dried my hands, I watched her in the mirror out of the corner of my eye. Her hair was perfect. Mine was so — unruly. I tried to add a little elegance with a curling iron tonight, but the loose curls weren't quite hanging right. Dirk always liked me to wear it back or up. Maybe I should've done that.

Mercedes sighed and looked at me in the mirror. "I would kill for your hair."

A bubble of laughter worked its way out. "Why? Yours is perfect."

She fluffed it some more, played with a few loose strands, then looked at mine. "Yours is so curly. I always wanted curly hair. I got a perm once, but it was awful."

"I used a curling iron tonight, actually," I said. "And I think your hair's beautiful."

She pulled her lipstick out of her purse. "GT likes it this way. I don't mind."

"With that pseudo-Southern charm thing, you wouldn't know if he didn't." My eyes jerked up to meet her surprised ones. Crap. That sounded so insulting. "I meant, maybe he's just being nice and he'd be happy however you do your hair."

Boy, I hoped she didn't take that wrong. Or repeat it to GT.

Mercedes smiled a small smile that said she knew what I was thinking and she wasn't offended. She looked back in the mirror and blotted her lips. "The pseudo-Southern charm thing catches more flies than honey." She looked at me again and smiled. "So does the pseudo-ditzy blonde bit. That doesn't make it dishonest."

In that moment, I realized Mercedes was much smarter than she let on. She might truly love GT and not just his money.

Mercedes giggled in the mirror. "Isn't it great to be treated so well by our men?" The ditzy blonde was back.

"Oh, Matt's not my — we aren't — we just met."

Mercedes laughed. "Sugar, I could see the way you two were looking at each other last night. Yeah, you broke apart like teenagers caught in the act when you saw us. But remember—" She turned to face me. "We saw you first."

I wish I could control when I blush. It would certainly help in the lying department. "No, we both happen to have GT as a client, and yesterday was a long day so we had dinner. No big deal." I smiled politely.

"No big deal, huh? That's what every woman says when she's trying not to lose her heart. Denial doesn't help, you know."

I didn't know what to say so I laughed. "Mercedes, just because you're happily married doesn't mean—"

She took my arm as we walked out of the ladies room. "Come with me." We stopped when our table came into view. "Look at him there."

About three seconds went by before Matt looked our way. "See? He's trying to pretend not to notice you, but he notices everything about you. If he was so engrossed in shoptalk, he wouldn't even see us sit down, let alone be watching for us. GT was the same way. Trust me."

Mercedes was just like GT. She could talk you into a place where you didn't know what to say.

She giggled in my ear. "Watch. He won't be able to keep himself from smiling at you."

"No, he hasn't smiled at me all evening," I said without thinking. Mercedes gave my hand a squeeze.

Right on cue, Matt looked our way again. As he caught me watching him, a slow smile appeared. I couldn't help myself. Mercedes had gotten me all crazy. I smiled back.

Mercedes giggled again and pulled me forward, back to the table. It was like a signal had been given. And I mean that in all seriousness. She didn't whisper to GT or anything, but from the moment she and I sat down, the evening became very personal.

They wove dozens of innocuous questions into the conversation. Did we like that movie? Had we read this book? Had we been to that concert? I tried to be candid, but cautious. I felt like we were being interviewed by a matchmaking service. I couldn't tell if Matt suspected anything. But I had the odd feeling of wanting to protect him, so I tried to keep the conversation relatively superficial.

I didn't know whether to be amused, annoyed, or encouraged that someone thought Matt and I belonged together. No, not encouraged. In my current state of mental health, I was not ready to be pushed into another relationship.

Not yet. But maybe with time I'd relax and see what happened.

I tried to glance casually at Matt during the meal to gauge his reactions. His professional demeanor was amazing. I didn't see him blush or stumble or anything.

I wonder if he's a good kisser...

Startled by that wayward thought, I choked on a scallop. I reached for my water while GT patted my back.

"You all right?" Matt asked.

I couldn't look at him. I nodded and swallowed some more water. "Went down the wrong way."

It's not like he hasn't kissed you, idiot, said a Voice. *And now is not the time to think about it.*

Not the time to think about the fact that he's never kissed you on the lips, you mean? said Lovesick. *Kissed your cheek once, your hand several times, but never really* kissed *you? That's what it's not the time to think about?*

See, that proves it. That proves he's not interested in you the way you're interested in him. It's the best thing in the world that you've decided not to pursue this anymore.

The Voices in my head were making me dizzy. Too many opinions and maybes with no conclusive evidence in any direction.

I took a mental deep breath and told myself it was perfect. I wasn't ready for another relationship, and Matt had made it perfectly clear last night that he wasn't looking for one either. He was making it rather clear tonight, too. So no more thinking about kissing.

I remembered what Mercedes had said about Matt watching me all evening. She and GT may be enjoying their matchmaking game, but she was just wrong. That's all.

Dinner ended around ten and we all walked out to the parking lot. GT gave his slip to the valet and we stood and talked for another minute. Thanking GT for his hospitality, Matt and I waved as they drove away.

"That was relatively painless, wasn't it?" I asked.

He grunted. "It could have been worse, I guess."

Protecting his privacy or not, this guy had a bug up his butt and I wasn't interested in taking it out. "Well, good night." I started toward my car.

I heard him take a breath like he was going to say something, then nothing. Then, "Good night." I didn't turn around to acknowledge it.

I walked to a far corner of the parking lot, the only place I could find a space when I pulled in. By the time I unlocked the door and got in, I felt fifty years older. Heartbreak with a capital "H" had been traumatic. But even with a little "h" it was exhausting.

You're just tired. Get some sleep and everything will be better tomorrow.

Remember, said another Voice, *you chose to be happy, grateful, at peace. Keep it up, girlfriend. Count your many blessings.*

I put on my seatbelt and started the car. That is I *tried* to start the car. Several times. Nothing but a click. I let my forehead fall to the steering wheel. Just my luck.

My eyes swelled with tears. This time I didn't do any deep breathing exercises to keep them from falling. No positive thinking was going to undo the last few horrible days. Maybe if I let myself cry for a minute, all the pain would seep out and I could start over. I let the tears fall. I pretended they were all the negative feelings and hard times and pushed them out of my head. Then there would be room for happiness and peace again.

It didn't take long before the crying stopped. I did feel a modicum of relief.

I jumped when I heard a knock on my window.

I glanced over. Matt.

I tried to hide the evidence of my tears and hit the button to roll down the window. Quickly realizing the futility with *electric windows*, I opened the door.

"You okay?" He sounded worried.

I turned away toward the dark passenger seat and wiped my face as unobtrusively as I could. "Yeah, just uh…" I gestured at the steering wheel.

"Dead battery?" Matt asked.

"Yeah." I sighed. "I'll call triple A."

"Come on, I'll take you home." Matt reached inside the car and took my hand.

I pulled it away. "It's okay. The auto club will take care of it."

"Come on," Matt urged. "It's late. You can come back for it in the morning."

It was tempting. To have just one opportunity to walk away from my trouble. You never get to do that in real life. It would be a pain in the butt to get back here tomorrow and still have to go through calling AAA and waiting in the car. But tonight, I could walk away.

Tonight there's potential for more trouble if you go home with him, said a Voice.

Matt reached in and took my hand firmly in his, his face close to my ear. "When was the last time you let yourself be rescued?"

My eyes watered again even as I tried to smile a little. Don't cry. Make a joke. "I seem to remember a river being involved."

As Matt's truck pulled into a parking space near my apartment, I wondered briefly if Dirk would be skulking in the shadows again. I really, truly, honestly couldn't deal with that tonight.

Matt turned off the engine. "I'll pick you up at 7:30 and take you back to your car. If you call triple A before you leave, you might only have to wait a few minutes."

"Thanks, but you don't have to do that. I'll be fine."

"No, I'm the one who told you to leave it. It's not that far out of the way." Matt looked around the parking lot as we walked up my stairs. Neither one of us mentioned why.

I pulled out my keys and unlocked the door. "Thank you for driving me home." My eyes met his and dropped away. "I'll call a cab tomorrow to go get my car. Thank you anyway."

Matt watched me without saying anything. I opened the door and turned on the living room light. I didn't want to close the door in his face. But if he didn't say "Good night," I'd be forced to.

"Good night," I said and started to close the door.

Before I realized he'd moved, he stepped across the threshold, cupped my face in his rough hands, and pressed his lips to mine. He was soft and warm and hard all at once. I inhaled sharply in surprise. Then, without thinking, I leaned into the kiss. All the frustration I'd felt the last few days poured out in a burst of passion. I tasted my tears on his lips and hoped he wouldn't notice.

My hands moved to his waist. The shirt he wore was so soft. One of his hands brushed tears from my cheek, then tangled in my hair as he pulled me closer. I let my arms wrap around his back. Soft shirt and hard muscle and warm kisses, all making me crazy with sensation.

Matt backed off the kiss.

In embarrassment, I rested my forehead on his shirt. I sniffled and tried to pretend our first kiss had not been marred by tears. Matt's arms wrapped tightly around me, one hand stroking my hair. I felt safe and protected for the first time in a really long time. I squeezed my eyes tightly shut. Now would *not* be the time for a good cry.

I cried anyway.

I felt him kick the door closed and lean against it. He held me close and stroked my head and back while all the stress of the last week rushed out. In a few moments, I felt drained but better. *Embarrassed*, but better.

"I'm sorry about last night," he said, his cheek on my hair and his voice soft near my ear. "And tonight. And the times I've ignored you."

I didn't know what to say. I didn't know what was coming, either. He must've felt my tension because he started rubbing my back again.

"I've worked for GT for a long time," he said. "He's a good guy, but he gets too involved in other people's personal lives. He doesn't understand boundaries."

I humphed. Boy, did I know that.

"I was..." Matt paused, either trying to find the words or trying to decide if he should speak them. "...involved with a woman a few years ago. I thought it might become, you know, permanent."

Wow, this guy couldn't even *say* the word marriage. Did I know how to pick 'em or what?

"We were working things out in our own way, but GT got it in his head that we needed help. Instead of patching things up, we ended up not speaking to each other." He sighed. "Have you ever met someone and right away you just clicked?"

I smiled into his shirt.

Oh, have *we*, exclaimed Lovesick.

"But you weren't prepared and you acted stupid and then you had to figure out how to fix it?" He pulled away a little and tipped up my chin, looking into my watery eyes.

"That's what happened with her?" I asked.

He smiled and shook his head. "Tell me what to do to fix it."

I stared up into those beautiful blue eyes and felt safer than I had in years. Getting a glimpse of Matt's heart, I felt the raw wounds of my own heart begin to heal.

CHAPTER 16

*T*he next week flew by. Matt and I were both "summer-busy." In Northern Michigan, particularly in our fields, the lion's share of the work has to be done during the non-snowing months. Which forced our relationship to a snail's pace. But we made important progress on "fixing" it.

When I came over to show GT some houses Friday morning, Matt smiled and talked to me for a moment like we were old friends. I didn't embarrass him by acting like anything more than a fellow professional. He didn't embarrass me by pretending I didn't exist. Then we went back to work. Easy. Simple.

In a better mood, I didn't take offense to GT's touchy-feely nature as I walked him through a house. (Of course, I was so relieved we'd found one he actually wanted to *see*, nothing could've bothered me.)

Emily and I got in a couple quick conversations on the phone, enough to catch up on each other's blossoming love lives. She about swooned when I told her how Matt asked "what to do to fix it." We giggled and sighed. She said Geoffrey had nervously asked her if she wanted to go fishing next weekend.

She was afraid she'd make a fool of herself, but she was excited. I assured her she'd be great.

I was doing paperwork in my office one afternoon the following week when my cell phone rang. Absently, I picked it up and hit Talk as I continued typing on the computer.

"This is Sydney."

"Hi, Sydney."

My hands stopped on the keyboard. My stomach tightened.

"What do you want?" I tried to take a deep breath and relax. I'd thought I was getting over him until he showed up again. Life was *not* showing me its best side lately.

"I want to see you again."

"No." I resumed typing.

"Too busy with your new boyfriend?"

Breathe. Don't let him get to you. "Dirk, you're the one who ended our relationship."

"I know. I made a mistake. That's what I want to talk to you about."

"No." I backspaced a typo and tried again.

"Did you like the flowers? And the chocolates?"

I'd gotten a fresh vase of flowers and another box of chocolates on Monday. "Please don't send any more."

"I bet you didn't throw them away."

"I'm hanging up now."

He laughed. "I didn't think so. They're sitting on your desk, aren't they?"

"No. They're not." It was true. The newest ones were sitting on Carmen's desk. Last week's flowers still looked nice, so they decorated the conference table. I shared the truffles with everyone who came by. That was going over *great* with new clients.

"Listen, I understand that you might be seeing someone just to get back at me, or because you're lonely or bored—"

I clenched my teeth and hung up.

The phone rang again. I let it go to voice mail.

I went back to work, finishing the paperwork at a slow burn. I was *so angry*. I knew I had to let it go, but boy! I wanted to punch something.

Done with the office work, I went out to look at some properties. I had three other ready-to-buy clients besides GT, and I was hustling. Driving made me feel better. The tourists were annoying and the traffic was always clogged and slow in the summer, but I love driving, especially since I bought the Sportage. I'd never had a new car *or* an SUV. Awesome.

I pulled through a drive-thru for lunch and drove up the East Bay side of Old Mission Peninsula. The weather was perfect today, breezy and blue and eighty degrees.

I sighed with pleasure. This is better.

My mind wandered. What was I going to do about Dirk? Maybe if I heard him out, he'd leave me alone. It was something to consider. But it was *not* true that I was lonely or bored and that was why I was seeing Matt.

We'd had lunch on Sunday and — of all things — made a trip to Home Depot. We both needed to go and so — we went. Matt dropped me back at my car, we unloaded my things from his truck, talked for about twenty minutes, then decided to get ice cream. It was nearly five o'clock by the time we were back at my car again.

We talked for another couple of minutes, then Matt kissed me goodbye. It was a very nice kiss, too, considering we were out in public. Warm and sweet and — well, leaving me wanting more. But it was nice.

I turned down a side road looking for a house that might interest an older couple I was helping. I sighed in frustration. I couldn't find it. I turned around and tried again.

GT had faxed me another list that morning of things he wanted for his mother-in-law. I tried to point out that some of them were contradictory like "low maintenance" and "pool and spa." But he told me when I called that he didn't have time. He had to fix a problem with a company in New York. And he left.

Okay. Fine. We'll discuss it when he gets back. Meanwhile, I'll continue to look for houses that have *most* of the qualities he wants.

Darn it! I pulled the car over and took out the listing. It read "1764 E. Plough Road." There's 1748 and 1770. And nary a house in between. What in the world?

A mailbox on the side of the road caught my eye. Painted neatly on the box was "1748 W. Plough Road."

"Oh, for crying out loud." I turned around again. This was *West* Plough Road. I had to go farther to get to *East* Plough Road.

Pebbles flew as I hit the gas. Everything in my life was further away than I wanted it to be. I figured I'd be married by now. I thought I'd own my own home by now. Nothing was turning out the way I expected.

By the end of the day, all I wanted to do was go home and take a long bath, maybe read a book. Maybe a really good romance novel where the girl ends up with the perfect man for her. Maybe a crime novel where the detective has to figure out if the girl really did murder her ex.

That evening, I was running the water in the tub, reading the backs of two novels, trying to decide which one to start, when I heard someone knocking. I opened the door and there was Dirk. Note to self: *look through the freaking peephole next time!*

I sighed in exasperation. Nice and long and loud so he'd get the point.

"Ten minutes," he said. "You can time me."

If it would get rid of him, I'd give him ten minutes. Good thing I bought a six-pack of Mike's Hard Lemonade on the way home. The kiddie stuff wasn't going to cut it tonight.

I opened the door further to let him in and took off my watch. I looked at it, then back at Dirk. "Go."

We stood in the living room facing each other. He took a deep breath.

"Sydney, I meant it when I said I'd made a mistake. Lisa was — we weren't suited. We're not together—"

"So you're coming back because you don't have anyone else? Flattering, Dirk."

"That's not how it is. I love you. I'm just a typical idiot guy who doesn't know how to — I don't know. Have a relationship."

"Pardon me, but I would think that four years together would rather disprove that theory."

"I know, I know." Dirk rubbed the back of his neck and looked at his shoes. "But that's exactly what I mean! Why was I feeling like we were a mistake? Am I afraid to get married? Am I too old to enjoy sex with—"

The shocked look on my face must've stopped him. What? Sex with me? Sex with multiple partners? Sex with one person forever?

"What I mean is I miss you. Not, I miss someone. I miss *you*. And I want to show you that you are the most important person in my life."

I frowned at him. "Did you get fired?"

"No, I didn't get fired." He sounded angry. Obviously his work was as important to him as ever. Insulting that was worse than insulting his mother.

"Do you have cancer? Do you have six months to live?"

"No!" Now he was mad. Good.

"Then what made you suddenly change your mind after *months* of silence? You never even called me to see how I was doing. That really doesn't sound like someone who's been pining away for his lost love."

Oh crap, I forgot about the bathtub.

"Sydney, part of loving someone is forgiving them their faults and weaknesses."

I held up my hand and marched toward the bathroom. "Shut up!"

"Syd—"

"Just hang on! And don't follow me!"

I turned off the water and stomped back out. I hoped the downstairs neighbors weren't home.

"Go on." I said between clenched teeth, glancing at my watch.

"I was just saying that that's what love is about. Marriage is forever. Are you saying if you got mad at me when we were married you would've just walked out? That's it? No forgiveness?"

"If I walked out? If *I* walked out? *You* walked out! You told me you were in love with another woman and that you were so sorry but you had to follow your heart! Do you remember any of this? Does it ring a bell?"

I felt like throwing something, and I would've if we were at his place. But I wasn't about to break my own stuff.

"You're right. I'm wrong. That's what I've been trying to say. I've been trying to say it with words, but you won't talk to me. I've used the time-honored tradition of apology — flowers and chocolate, but I—"

"And I told you to keep your flowers and chocolate! You're wasting your money."

I looked at my watch. "You have two minutes. Anything else?"

"Just one thing." Dirk stepped closer and I forced myself not to retreat. "I love you. If you felt nothing, you wouldn't be so angry. I want you to stop seeing that other guy and let me show you how much I care."

I opened the door. "Let me show you how much I care."

Dirk started through the door but paused on the doorstep. "I mean it. I'm going to prove to you that I love you."

"Goodbye, Dirk." I closed the door with enough force that he had to move or get hurt. I turned the lock as loudly as I could. Maybe the symbolism wouldn't be lost on him.

I marched into the kitchen, grabbed two bottles of Mike's and headed for the bathroom, picking up my two abandoned books on the way. I paused, tossed the romance novel onto the couch, and continued toward my bath with the crime novel.

I hoped it was bloody and awful.

As I eased into the hot water and closed my eyes, I thought about how long it had taken Dirk to even discuss what had happened.

I sighed. And waited. Nothing.

I looked over at the Mike's and grabbed a cold bottle. It was a shock to my bath-heated hand. I took a couple swallows and rested the bottle and my arm on the side of the tub, so I could hang onto it with two fingers.

I just sat there staring at the bathtub wall. Waiting for the tears that always came.

"Huh," I said aloud. "Two beers, but no tears. I'm making progress."

CHAPTER 17

Since GT was out of town for a week, I didn't "run into" Matt at his house. I had no reason to go over, but don't think I didn't try to come up with one. I hadn't seen him or talked to him (Matt, not GT) since Sunday, practically a week ago.

I wanted to call him because I felt cranky from Dirk's visit the night before. But I couldn't screw up enough courage to do it. With Emily out of town for the weekend, I couldn't think of anything to do except work. Sounded...fun.

However, I reminded myself as I sat at my desk Friday, I do have to work *now*. I called the mortgage office to check on the closing paperwork for the Slocums. I wanted to help them get moved in before the baby was born. It looked like we would close next week.

The older couple hadn't liked any of the houses I'd shown them — especially the one on East Plough Road. I was hoping something would hit the market before fall. There's a lot of action in late summer as moving families try to get settled before school starts.

Perry made the rounds, asking everyone for a progress

report. He was a great guy and I loved working for him, but I got nervous every time he did that. I'd never gotten over that whole fear of the principal thing from grade school.

"How's everything going, Syd?" Perry stopped at my desk.

"Great. Should close with the Slocum's next week. The Rasmussen's haven't seen anything they like yet. GT is out of town. The O'Brien's are having a financing problem." I waited for him to move on.

He nodded. "Let me know if Turkelbain takes up too much of your time and doesn't look like he's buying. He's got a reputation for that and we don't have time to waste around here."

"Okay." I waited for him to move on.

"I see we're still getting flower deliveries." He cocked his head toward the front desk.

This was so embarrassing. "Yeah, sorry, I'm trying to get him to stop but he won't listen."

Perry waved his hand as if at a gnat (which is what Dirk was). "Don't worry about it." He chuckled. "If he wants to decorate my office with fresh flowers, I don't care. But are *you* all right?"

One of the many things I liked about Perry was that he genuinely liked all of his employees. Birthdays and Christmas were wonderful, and if you got married or had a baby, you always got an amazingly lovely gift, something that shouted "from the heart."

I smiled. "I'll be okay. Gram always said, 'This too shall pass.'"

Perry laughed. "A wise woman." He moved on. I breathed a sigh of relief.

After lunch, my cell phone rang. Matt's number flashed. My heart skipped and I grinned like a wild woman.

"This is Sydney." I didn't want him to know I knew it was him.

"Hey, Syd, it's Matt." My stomach did a little dance at the sound of his voice.

"Hi, how's it going?" I bent my head and kept my voice low in an attempt at a private conversation. The joys of working in a fish bowl office.

"Better since it stopped raining. Hey, are you doing anything Saturday?"

"I have an Open House from one to four. But I'm free after that."

I couldn't wipe the smile off my face for anything. Not even at gunpoint.

"Well, I was thinking, I haven't had a chance to use my grill all summer. You said you like steak, so I thought we could have a little barbeque. What d'ya think?"

"Sounds great." Oh my gosh! He's inviting me over to his house! A first!

"I hope you don't think this sounds weird, but I won't have time to shop before then, so I was thinking I'd pick you up, we'll go to the store, then over to my place. I'll drive you home after dinner."

"Sounds great," I said, trying to inject just the right amount of enthusiasm into my voice. Then I closed my eyes and raised my free arm in the air like a football hero, mouthing yyeesssss!

"Great, I'll pick you up at your place Saturday at five."

"I'll be there."

We hung up and I pounded my hands on my desk. Then I leaned my forehead on my arm and just grinned. That way no one could see me.

"I take it that was Lover Boy," said Trent as he walked past my desk to the kitchenette.

"No-oo," I said, trying to hide my grin. "There is no Lover Boy."

"Sure, sure," he said as he disappeared through a doorway.

I grinned again.

When Saturday dawned clear and bright, all I could do was lie in my bed and say, thank you, thank you, thank you, God. No rain cancellation on the barbeque!

The Open House went very well, no doubt in part due to the weather. By the time I was back home, I had high hopes of selling the house in the next few weeks. Maybe sooner.

I'd barely changed into shorts when I heard a knock on the door. I opened it with a Scrunchi in my mouth and a sunny, "Hi Matt, come on in."

I finished putting my hair up, found a comfortable pair of sandals, and grabbed my purse.

"Oh, wait! Let me find a sweatshirt in case it cools down."

"You don't think I can keep you warm?" Matt asked with a wicked grin. At least, I interpreted it as a wicked grin.

"Are you offering?" I asked coyly.

He pulled my hand toward him until we collided. Then he kissed me breathless. "Let's go," he whispered.

Little Miss Lovesick fainted.

We pulled into the grocery store parking lot talking about what we each thought made a barbeque perfect.

"How can you have a barbeque without potato salad?" Matt asked, taking my hand when we got out of his truck.

"But not store-bought potato salad. That's all I'm saying. It has too much mayonnaise in it."

"I thought you were a city girl. What do you know about food that's not store bought?"

I looked at him in mock exasperation. "Even city girls know how to cook."

FREE PUPPYS *Nice Peeple Only Please*

Matt and I read the hand-lettered sign as we approached the store entrance. Three tow-headed children stood by a box, alternately reaching inside and calling out to shoppers.

"'Nice people only' — that's cute," I said.

"Hey mister, do you need a dog? If you're nice, we could give you a really nice puppy." The oldest child, maybe eight years old, called out to Matt in his childish, singsong voice, eyes wide and hopeful.

Matt smiled at the kids and looked into the box. "What kind of puppies are they?"

"Uh, just regular puppies." The boy looked back at his mother sitting on a folding chair, smiling indulgently at her progeny.

"The mother is a mongrel of unknown heritage, and we guess the father is, too," she said. "But the vet says they're healthy, and they're a friendly lot."

I already had my hand inside the box. Before I knew it, I was on my knees with a puppy in my arms. Matt reached over to pet it. The pup was velvety soft, with black, white and sable fur.

"Are you a good dad?" asked the youngest.

Matt looked at the child in surprise. She was a cute little thing, probably four or five, very serious though, and waiting for a response. I smothered my laughter in the puppy's fur.

"They need a good fam'ly," she explained.

"Do you have kids? They love kids," the middle boy volunteered enthusiastically. "Especially kids my age."

Matt smiled. "No, I don't have any kids." He leaned down and scratched one of the puppies in the box. Wet noses crowded against his hand as the pups fought for his attention. I put back the one I had and picked up another one.

A particularly enthusiastic puppy climbed over her siblings to rest her front feet on the back of Matt's hand. She looked up at him with her liquid brown eyes, whining excitedly in her high puppy voice. Her tail wagged so hard her whole body shook. Within seconds, she tumbled over backward. Matt and I laughed as she twisted herself upright and climbed back up on his hand. With his other hand, he scooped her up against his chest and stood.

"You sure are a friendly one, aren't you?" he said as he

scratched her head. The puppy responded by licking his cheek. As Matt turned his head, the dog kept licking whatever skin she could reach. Soon both of Matt's cheeks, his chin and his neck were covered in puppy kisses.

Oh, look at him, sighed Lovesick.

Don't lose your head, warned another Voice. *Puppies and kids may bring out some of his cuteness, but that doesn't mean he's The One.*

"All right, all right, you little germ-carrier. That's enough," he said as he laughed and pulled the pup away from his face.

"She's nice, huh?" The older boy spoke as the others looked on hopefully. "She's housebroken, too. And she's smart. Everybody needs a smart dog."

I looked at the kids' mother. "Looks like you've got yourself a good salesman."

She laughed. "They've already given three away, and the day's not over."

Matt looked at the young salesman. "How do you know she's smart?"

"If she wasn't smart, she'd be dumb, and she's no dummy!" The boy thought for a moment. "Her mom can do lots of tricks."

"Yeah? You think she'll be as smart as her mom?"

"Oh, yeah." The boy nodded his head vigorously. "I'm almost as smart as my dad and I'm only seven. He tells me that all the time." The boy frowned in consternation. "But I don't know who the daddy dog is, so I guess I don't know for sure she'll be smart."

Matt tried to suppress his mirth. He caught my eye and winked. I smiled and put back the puppy I had. I stood up and stroked Matt's puppy's ears. If only they stayed this cute and soft forever.

Matt held the pup in front of his face. She craned her neck to try to lick his nose. I laughed. I desperately wanted one, but I'd settle for visitation rights if Matt took one home. Between the puppies and the kids, he looked thoroughly wrapped around someone's finger.

I'd love to have him wrapped around my finger, purred Lovesick.

Don't let him catch you looking at him like that. He'll likely turn tail and run, warned another Voice.

"She looks pretty smart," he said to the boy. "I guess I'll have to take your word for it. You think I should take her home and give it a shot?"

The kids looked at him with a mixture of excitement and wariness. The younger boy spoke up. "We don't got no returns, mister. You gotta be sure."

Matt laughed out loud. I turned away when I laughed so I wouldn't hurt the kids' feelings. I elbowed Matt in the ribs, and he tried to control his expression into one more befitting the children's serious purpose.

"You're right. This is a long-term commitment. Let me think. I've got money to buy her food. I live on a farm with a house and a big yard. I've got plenty of time to play with her. Yeah, I think we'd be good for each other." Matt looked from the boy to me. "What do you think?"

You aren't *falling for him,* said a Voice. *It's the puppy. That's all.*

He's got my dream life in the palm of his hand, said Another.

And the power to crush it, warned the first Voice.

"You live on a farm? With cows?" the little girl asked. Matt turned to her and I closed my eyes against wanting him.

"A cow might step on her. Maybe you shouldn't take her." The oldest boy reached for the puppy.

"No, there aren't any cows. I call it a farm, but I don't have any animals. It's just a lot of fields and woods." Matt thought that was a pretty clear answer, but the kids no longer looked convinced he was worthy.

"I promise, she'll be safe there." Matt waited for the trio to give him their unanimous blessing.

How did they manage to let go of three puppies already?

The boy spoke to me for the first time. "No dogs on the bed. That's the rule. So you gotta get her a doggie pillow. And she needs to be petted every day, and brushed and washed. But you can't yell at her too much 'cause it'll hurt her feelings."

I opened my mouth to say he'd gotten the situation wrong, but how to explain? I looked at their mother. "We're not — we don't—" She waved my explanations away with a smile.

I looked at Matt, afraid of what to say or how to react. But he didn't appear to mind that the kids included me in their "Care and Handling" lecture.

The oldest looked back at his siblings and put his hand over his heart. They followed suit, and the three turned to Matt and me.

"Put your hand on your heart," said the little girl.

Matt smiled, moved the puppy into his left hand and covered his heart with his right. The puppy immediately began licking the back of his right hand.

"You, too," the middle boy insisted, looking at me. I glanced apprehensively at Matt.

"You heard him," he said. I relaxed and smiled back.

"I promise to be really nice to this puppy, and make it happy forever and ever, amen." The kids spoke in unison.

Matt bit his lip for a moment to choke back his laughter. I pressed my lips together to keep it in. Then, as solemnly as we could, we repeated the oath.

"Yay!" The kids jumped up and down and ran to their mother. "That's four, Mom! Only three left! See, we told you we could do it!"

Matt laughed and looked down at his new roommate. "We better leave before they con me into taking one of your brothers."

CHAPTER 18

*O*ur shopping expedition changed course a bit after that. I stayed in the truck with the puppy while Matt ran in for the necessary groceries. There was a PetCo nearby ("Where the Pets Go" — sorry, TV addiction, getting counseling), so we drove there next. Matt bought *so much stuff* for that dog.

"You don't have to buy everything today, you know," I teased when he picked up an adult-size collar as well as a puppy collar. He stuck his tongue out at me and put the larger one back.

The drive to his place was fun, but a tad dangerous. We were so busy watching and playing with the puppy, we nearly rear-ended someone. I was crazy curious to see where Matt lived and what it looked like. The description he gave the kids could mean anything. Some of the countryside right outside of town was gorgeous and expensive. Some areas were little more than personal junkyards. Heck, maybe he didn't even live that close.

Out on M-72, the main road heading east out of Traverse City, we passed one of the fancy golf resorts. I knew from work that a competing nearby resort planned on adding another nine holes next summer. The price of land out here was skyrocketing.

Matt turned onto a country road near Williamsburg. A few minutes later, he pulled into a tree-lined gravel driveway. A two-story, white farmhouse with a wrap-around porch sat in a clearing in front of me. A medium-size barn sat back a little farther, at the end of the driveway.

Matt parked the truck in front of the barn. "Well, here we are." He glanced at me, then looked out over his backyard. "What do you think?"

Think? I was too stunned to think. "Wow," I said. "This is yours?" Stupid question. Comes with the "too-stunned-to-think" territory.

The corner of Matt's mouth quirked up. He looked proud and...content. "Yup," he said.

"Wow." I desperately wanted to ask *how,* but I didn't want to showcase my bad manners. Either he was independently wealthy, or he didn't want to be. If this was family property, I can assure you Matt has been hounded by developers to sell it. And if he personally just went out and bought it... No, it must be his family home.

Matt opened the door and grabbed the groceries from behind his seat. "You comin'?"

I clipped the leash on the puppy's collar in case she got away from me and got out. We walked through his backyard and onto an obviously new extended deck. It basically gave the house a huge back porch in addition to the front porch. I saw Matt's new built-in grill.

"I put the grill where I could use it as close to year-round as possible." Under the porch roof and close to the back door. "Unless there's a blizzard, I think I'll be able to get to it."

He unlocked the back door and motioned for me to precede him. "Just because we live in snow country is no reason not to grill."

"Ever heard of George Foreman?" I teased as I entered the kitchen.

"Got one of those, too. Meat is my specialty." He set the groceries on the counter and went back to the truck for the dog's belongings. I turned in a slow circle, absently petting the pup while I stared.

The huge country kitchen had been renovated in the last few years. A large, wheeled butcher-block table dominated the center. Modern appliances and countertops highlighted the spaciousness of the room. A room that was probably four times the size of the kitchen in my apartment.

Welcome to Envy, population one.

Matt entered with the dog bed and several bags. "What do you think?" he asked.

Will you marry me? That's what I was thinking. Probably not an appropriate response under the circumstances, however.

"It's nice," I said. "Very nice."

He nodded. "It works." He found a place for the bag of dog food in the walk-in pantry, and put the food and water bowls on the floor. He hung the leash on a hook near the door, then looked down at the puppy in my arms.

"Welcome home, missy." He took her from me and ruffled her ears.

She gave a yelp.

"Did you say she's a girl?"

"I did, but—" Matt held her up and looked. "Yup, she's a girl. I didn't exactly check before. She just seemed like a girl."

"What do you mean, she seemed like a girl?" said I, eyes narrowing in mock defensiveness.

"Well, she was all over me the minute she saw me. She's barely stopped kissing me since I picked her up. And I have a feeling she won't be sleeping in her own bed tonight."

"Oh! You are such a schmuck!" I gasped and slugged him. He jumped away from me as we both laughed.

"Come on, dog, you're supposed to protect your master!"

Matt yelped as I got him in the stomach. The puppy yipped excitedly in his arms.

Matt made a grab for me, and I lost my balance. To keep me from falling on my butt, he pulled me toward him with his one free hand, and I landed right in his arms.

Laughing, I tried to get free. Matt's laughter echoed right behind my left ear, his breath warm against my cheek. I liked the sound and closed my eyes for just a second, enjoying the closeness of another human being. His cheek brushed against mine, scratchy with a day's worth of whiskers.

I twisted to see Matt's face.

Big mistake.

An inch from mine, I felt his breath warm against my cheek and mouth. His eyes were a beautiful darker blue in the low light, laugh lines spreading out like ripples on the water. His skin was brown from the sun, and smelled of sunshine and water — and puppy. I smiled at the thought.

Big mistake number two.

Matt's laughter died into — something I couldn't quite define. He stared at my face, my eyes, my lips. My insides went all warm and fluttery. Yikes. My breath came in shallow gasps as I stared back. Our lips were so close they were almost touching. I could feel the heat from his forehead so close to mine. I would barely have to move at all and skin would be touching skin.

His arm tightened around my waist. The intimate moment was suddenly peppered with memories of Dirk. Memories of being loved and then betrayed. How could I know that it wouldn't happen again? I scrambled to get out of Matt's arms. Our eyes never lost contact, but I was sure mine must be conveying my sudden wariness. It terrified me how much I wanted what Matt had to offer — but wasn't offering.

I leaned toward the puppy and scratched the wriggling mass. "My goodness! You have such puppy breath."

I looked back at Matt. He was still looking at me. He smiled a little and his dimple showed. I smiled just a little back. He studied me for a moment, then sighed and handed me the dog.

I let out my breath. I hadn't realized I'd been holding it. That must be why I was feeling a little light-headed.

Matt started unloading the groceries. "If you're too much of a city girl to cook, you might at least help me pick out a name."

Retreat. Whew.

"Do you have any ideas?" I asked, sitting down at the wooden kitchen table.

"I was thinking maybe Rover," he said, as he washed his hands and began preparing the meat.

"Rover? What kind of name is that for a girl?"

Matt laughed at my appalled expression. "She's a dog, not a girl. She doesn't care what her name is."

"Then how about Juliet? Hey, Juliet. Do you like that name? Huh?" The puppy wagged her tail and leaped up to lick my chin. "See? She loves it!"

"Hey, Rover! Come here, Rover!" Matt clapped his hands and the puppy tumbled over my legs and ran across the kitchen to him. "Aha! She loves 'Rover.'"

I rolled my eyes and groaned. "She just came because you clapped your hands." I pulled her away from trying to climb up Matt's jeans. "That doesn't mean she thinks Rover is a good name."

"Exactly." Matt tilted his head at me, one eyebrow raised. He went to get something from the fridge.

"Wha-at?" I put on my best innocent face, then ruined it by laughing. I sat back down at the table.

"What about Boots?" I suggested, fingering one velvety soft sable paw.

"Mm, nah. Maybe Blackie?" Matt looked questioningly over his shoulder.

"Neither one of those is original enough." I puckered my brow as I thought. "How about Clementine?"

"Clementine?" Matt said with a frown. "I think maybe I should name her myself, come to think of it." Matt widened his eyes and nodded at the puppy, tapping his head as if I were a little off balance. I laughed.

"All right, smart alec, so what are you going to name her?"

"Hey, these things take time. Don't rush me. I don't want to end up with a common name like Sydney." Matt ducked as I threw a nearby towel at him.

"You name your dog after me and I will never speak to you again!" I pointed my finger at his nose and tried to look angry. Of course, I didn't come close.

Matt put his hand over his heart and looked at the dog, currently chewing on my hair. "Sorry, pup. I had a beautiful name for you, but it would've displeased the lady. I hope you can live with Rover, buddy."

I rolled my eyes. "Like Sydney and Rover were the only choices."

"They're the only *good* choices." Matt winked at me.

My stomach did a double back flip. It must be hormones. That's it. It's PMS. That's why I want to jump his bones. That's why I want to spend the rest of my life right here in this moment.

Matt marinated the meat, then we put away the rest of Rover's belongings. I couldn't believe he'd named her that, but maybe he was teasing. Like he said, she didn't seem to mind.

He gave me an impromptu tour as we moved around. What used to be his mother's sitting room (she really did bring guests there and use it in that old-fashioned way) had become a library. I sat down in one of the comfy chairs and told him I was never going to leave.

"Okay," he said, "but you'll miss the rest of the tour."

I sighed loudly and followed him. The living room was a man's dream world. Boze speakers were mounted in the corners. A wide flatscreen TV hung on one wall. Stereo equipment, CD racks and DVD cabinets were positioned against the other walls. Every available seat faced the TV.

I glanced at the nearly empty bowl of stale popcorn on the coffee table. "Fall asleep watching TV last night?"

Matt cleared his throat and grabbed the bowl. "Uh, yeah, sorry about that."

I chuckled. "Don't worry about it. I'm teasing you."

We had to return the popcorn to the kitchen because Rover was trying to eat it. Then Matt showed me the rest of the house.

"I remodeled the master bed and bath the way I wanted it," he said, dropping one of the two dog pillows next to his bed.

I liked the room. It had kind of a mission-style look to it. The dark wood shone in contrast to the light colors of the curtains and bedspread.

"I haven't decided what to do with the other three rooms." He opened and closed doors as we walked. "Well, one will be a guest room. No hurry there since I never have any guests. Uncle Ted sleeps in my old room."

Matt opened that door. A loud, unladylike laugh burst out of me. Wallpaper with trains of every description covered three walls. The outer wall with the window was painted a faded blue. A blue comforter covered a twin bed. Shelves held a variety of model planes and cars.

"It's so cute! It reminds me of my brother's room. When he was five."

Matt pushed me out the door and closed it. "I told you I haven't gotten around to it yet. Whenever I've had time, Uncle Ted is here and he doesn't want me messing with it."

I grinned up at him. "I said it was cute. I just never thought of you as a little boy before. That's all."

Matt looped his arm around my neck in a gentle headlock and dragged me that way to the last room. He opened the door, said "See?" and closed it again. All I saw was a glimpse of pale yellow walls and some furniture. I started laughing. He put down the puppy and started tickling me.

"You think that's funny? Huh? I'll show you funny." I screeched and jumped around, trying to be careful of the animal underfoot.

In a moment, Matt had his arms wrapped around me from behind. My arms pinned to my sides, I laughed and tried to catch my breath. Matt's head was next to mine. He turned it slightly toward me.

"Your hair smells great." His voice was quieter.

It made me stop laughing.

Don't tense up. Don't pull away.

Tingles ran up and down my spine.

Then he started laughing, his forehead leaning against my temple, his arms loosening. "I'm sorry. I just heard my mother's voice in my head. 'No girls upstairs.' I don't think I can kiss you up here. The downside to living in my parents' house."

I chuckled and turned in his arms, wrapping mine around his waist. Feeling safer made me a little bolder. Looking in his eyes, I tried to think of something to say.

"If you don't mind hearing my professional opinion, you've done an excellent job with the remodeling." For a second I wondered if that was a stupid thing to say. Then he smiled and rested his forehead against mine.

"Thanks."

Rover yipped and whined from the floor.

We laughed and Matt picked her up. He took my hand and started down the stairs. "Hungry?"

Within an hour, dinner was ready and Rover was tied to the porch. (Unhappily, I might add.) A roaring bonfire lit up the night in a fire pit between the house and the barn. A short table, the perfect height for eating on the ground, held our food.

Matt brought over two cans of pop and nodded at the space next to me. "May I?"

I smiled at him, somersaults in my stomach. "Please."

We leaned against a log. It reminded me of the night by the fire in Abundance Creek.

"I'm getting a little chilly. Mind if I sit closer and share body heat?"

Oh my gosh. He was *so* cute. As if he needed to ask. "You could always get closer to the fire."

He looked at the big log against our backs. "Nah, too much trouble to move the furniture."

I giggled. "You could put some more wood on the fire."

He sighed. "Can't. I almost caught the barn on fire once." He moved around a little, presumably making himself more comfortable, but noticeably inching closer to me.

"What? How?"

"The fire pit was much closer to the barn then. Patty and her husband Duke were over and—" he shrugged. "I was trying to impress all the grown-ups. My mother swore she'd never let me build another fire again, but Uncle Ted calmed her down. He and I moved the fire pit, tested how many logs brought the fire to what height and—" He grinned at me. "Uncle Ted made the Six Log Rule." He nodded back toward the house. "Two Log Rule for inside."

I burst out laughing. "That explains Patty's teasing up north."

He nodded. "So now, if I get too cold, my only recourse is to get closer to you."

"Ah, I see." I paused for effect. "You know what they say, hope deferred makes the heart sick."

He laughed at me in surprise. "Oh, so I won't get any help from you should I begin to freeze to death? I'll keep that in mind the next time I think about giving you *my* warm shirt."

We ate our dinner — the best steaks *ever* — and laughed and talked. When we were done with the meal, Matt brought Rover over — which made her *much* happier. Soon it was dark enough to see almost every star in the northern hemisphere. We pointed out the constellations we knew and argued about the ones we couldn't remember.

Matt took Rover back to the porch, put her on the dog bed, and picked up a grocery sack. At my questioning look, he pulled out a bag of marshmallows.

"Got room for s'mores?" he asked with a teasing smile.

"Duh!" I said, laughing.

We toasted marshmallows and ate s'mores and talked until it really did become chilly. Matt brought me one of his flannel shirts from the kitchen. "If I put another log on," he said, "we'll be here all night. If I let the fire die out, we'll both be cold."

My chest tightened. I didn't know what to say. My eyes dropped to his mouth — whoops! They dropped to his chin. "Huh," I said.

"If you ask me," he said in a conversational tone, "We have about"—he looked at his wrist, which I noticed didn't have a watch on it—"twenty-six minutes before we have to decide to go inside or call it a night."

I laughed.

Matt leaned to pick up a stick he'd been poking the fire with. He prodded the logs apart so they fell with a whoosh of sparks and the flames dropped lower.

"What is it about fires and firelight that people like so much?" I wondered aloud.

"They're warm," said Matt.

I swatted him. "I *mean*," I said, "even in Arizona and California and New Mexico people have fireplaces. I heard one couple joke that in Arizona they turned on the air conditioning on winter nights when they wanted to cuddle so they could sit comfortably in front of the fire."

"Well, that's the reason." Matt poked the embers again and put down the stick.

"What's the reason?" I pulled my knees up and wrapped my arms around my legs.

"People want to cuddle. It's natural." He looked at me and smiled.

I smiled back and looked away. I shivered a bit. This man was making my nerves crazy. I stared at the fire.

"Cold yet?"

I shook my head. "I'm fine."

"Bummer," he said softly. He poked at the fire some more. "Would it make a difference if I said I was getting cold?"

I smiled a little and shivered again.

"Want me to build the fire back up?"

"No, I know you have to—" I looked at the fire, really looked at it. What was leaping flames two minutes ago was now a pile of embers. I whipped my head around. Sure enough, he was trying not to laugh.

"You did that on purpose!" I smacked him in the chest and he started laughing. "You're trying to make me cold so I'll — so I'll —" I was laughing now but still couldn't finish the sentence.

"Let me keep you warm," he finished for me.

Geez, he's got a beautiful smile. And beautiful eyes.

"Cheater."

"Hey, I told you I had to put out the fire, and you stayed anyway, didn't you?"

I ignored him.

"Didn't you?"

I stuck my tongue out at him and he laughed.

"So unless you want to go home, we can sit here and enjoy some quiet conversation until the fire's out. And hey, if cuddling is involved, it's only because you put the thought in our heads."

I stared at him with my mouth hanging open. "I put the thought — I did not!"

"You were talking about all the people who cuddle in front of the fire. I hadn't really thought about it until then, but now—" He poked the fire again with his stick.

"You were like, what, a prosecuting attorney in another life?"

He laughed. "I'll take that as a compliment."

I sighed and narrowed my eyes at him. "No funny stuff, understand? Just for warmth, that's all."

"I promise not to touch you anywhere I haven't touched you before."

I was starting to settle against the log next to him when he said that. But when I sat up a little to give him my version of Emily's "look" it only gave him an opportunity to put his arm around me, which he did. He pulled me snug against his chest.

"Ahh!" he said with mock seriousness. He gave a little shiver. "Much better! I was beginning to think I was going to get frostbite."

I chuckled. "You were not." But I could feel the difference already. Two warm bodies on a relatively cool night was really quite pleasant. When was the last time I'd done this?

CHAPTER 19

I could feel myself getting tense again. Did I want to go home? Did I want to stay? When we were up north, Emily and I hadn't discussed what was on the acceptable flirting list. I'd warned her that I couldn't remember. Being with one person for so long…well, you act differently.

Matt loosened his hold on me and took one of my hands, massaging my palm. That both helped me to relax and made me wonder just what he wanted. Truly, I think I've seen too many movies and too much news. In all the flirting and cuddling that goes on in the world, it can't turn out badly *that* often.

After a moment, Matt said, "What are you thinking about? Suddenly you're quiet as a mouse."

"I watch too many movies," I said in my usual blurting-out style.

He chuckled. "Oh, really?"

I decided I didn't care if I was good at flirting. I was just going to be myself. If he didn't like it, then I'd get to sleep sooner.

"You know, in the movies when two strangers cuddle in the dark, either a psychotic killer comes up behind them, or the guy *is* a psychotic killer, or he's a brute and takes advantage of her or—"

Matt started laughing. "What kinds of movies do you watch?"

"You know, all of them."

"In horror movies, yeah."

"Yeah, horror movies and action movies and—"

"No, in action movies the good guy always saves the girl from the bad guy."

"Well…" I had to think for a moment.

Matt dropped my right hand and picked up my left, massaging it in a way that made me want to shut up and enjoy it.

"I'm right," he said.

"No, I just have to think for a minute. I can't think when you're doing that."

He laughed low by my ear and kept massaging my hand. "I think," he said quietly, "that if you're going to think about movies while we're sitting here, you should think of the one where the girl gets away from the bad guy, goes on a fishing trip and meets a good guy who just wants to make her feel better for a little while."

I couldn't think of a single thing to say to that.

"After all," he continued as he let go of my left hand, "he's seen her cry and he's seen her laugh. Given the choice, he'd rather see her laugh again."

You're being so nice that it makes me want to cry. I tried to casually move my hand up to my eyes, as if rubbing smoke from them.

He pulled me closer.

"Ah, now the pressure is on," he said, "to make her laugh. Hmm…"

He banged his head gently on mine.

"My mind's a blank. It's like hitting a brick wall."

"Hey!" I chuckled and pulled away. "That's not funny."

He pulled me back into his arms. "I'm trying to think of something funny. Just give me a moment." He put his head next to mine again, then put his nose in my hair and breathed in. I remembered what he said upstairs. I closed my eyes and sighed.

"Hey," Matt said. He breathed in my hair some more, then made sniffing noises. "Do you smell a skunk? We have a problem with—"

I laughed and yelled and tried to pull away, but he wrapped me up tight against him and kept sniffing my hair.

"—skunks during the summer. Actually, all kinds of critters. Skunks and—"

I wiggled away, giggling. (Now *this* is fun, I was thinking.)

"—raccoons and porcupines—"

A moment later, I was in the air and then on his lap, still laughing because he was so funny. I wouldn't have stayed there except he was still making me laugh. And making me feel safe.

"—and the occasional pretty girl." He put on a pirate's leer and changed his voice. "Aye, matey, I like the pretty girls best. Harder to catch"—he put his forehead against mine—"but easier on the nose." He rubbed his nose against mine as we both laughed.

Took about a second and a half for both of us to notice how close our lips were. I saw him take a deep breath (I held mine), move a tiny bit closer (I didn't move at all), then it was the Fourth of July all over again!

After a couple of (*fabulous*) moments, he pulled away.

"The question always comes down to," his pirate voice went deeper, sexier, "do we sail away with 'em or—" he opened his legs and I fell between them to the ground, "drop 'em overboard?"

I let out a surprised gasp when I hit the hard ground.

He laughed and pulled me close to his chest again. He had

one arm wrapped around my shoulders and the other around my waist. Very snug. Very nice.

"You're crazy." I grinned against his chest. I snuggled a bit closer.

"You got a problem with that?" He tried for a thick Brooklyn accent, but it was terrible and I told him so.

"Fine," he said. "If you're going to make fun of the way I talk, I won't talk anymore."

And he didn't. He pulled my head under his chin. One hand ran up and down my arm. Sighing, he pulled me closer.

I breathed deeply against his chest and smelled smoke and woods and whatever else made up the scent of him. And I decided that perhaps I would just stay there forever.

How many times are you going to say that? asked a Voice.

Until wishing makes it so, sighed Lovesick.

He ran his fingers through my hair. He put his nose against the top of my head, breathed in the smell of my hair (which probably smelled like wood smoke), then cuddled me back under his chin.

Quietly, he said, "We've only got about twenty minutes left. Then you're going to have to let me go."

I giggled. "First of all, it's been way more than six minutes. Second of all, you're the one holding me."

He moved his arm from around my shoulders as he looked pointedly at his waist. "Uh, excuse me!"

I giggled again. One arm was tucked between us, but my other arm was wrapped around his waist.

He growled in my ear and put his arm around me again. "Trying to blame all this on me, are ya?"

"Yup," I said into his shirt. I giggled as he tightened his grip. He kept tightening it until I finally yelped, "Okay, uncle, you win, I lose, let go!"

He raised his head and laughed like an evil cartoon character. "Ha, ha, haa!"

I laughed again. I snuggled into his arms and closed my eyes. So wonderful…

It seemed like forever may have passed when I felt myself being moved and heard a groan. I couldn't think of where I was except that I was being moved away from the warmth.

I moaned in protest and tried to move back to where I was. I heard a chuckle and someone kissed me on the forehead. Then kissed me again. I sighed.

Then I was moved again. Where was I? Rubbing my eyes, I looked around. Still sitting on the ground in front of Matt, but the fire was completely out. A light from the kitchen cast a dim glow onto the deck. The rest of the yard was covered in moonlight.

Matt rubbed his seat and tried to flex his legs. "My rear end fell asleep," he said with a quiet laugh.

I smiled sleepily at him. "What time is it?"

"I don't know." He grinned at me. "But I'm sure it's been more than a half hour."

I grinned back as best I could. I was beginning to shiver, and I realized my butt had no feeling in it either.

Matt hoisted himself onto the log we'd been leaning against and tried to rub feeling back into his limbs. I started to stand and nearly fell. We both started laughing, then tried to be quieter when we heard it echo across the clearing.

I made it to my feet, then started the "Oh, oh, oh!" dance as the pins and needles raced up and down my legs. Matt laughed and grabbed my hand, pulling me over to him. He rubbed my legs as I hopped from one foot to the other. Soon the circulation was working again and I moved away.

"Hey, I'm cold, get back over here," he said as he pulled me back.

He wrapped his arms around my waist and put his head on my chest. I hugged him and giggled. He snuggled deeper and mumbled, "Back to sleep."

From where he was sitting and based on my height standing next to him, well, his head was snuggled in the *middle* of my shirt.

"Uh, excuse me," I laughed. He snuggled more, moving his head back and forth, left to right.

"Hey, mister, I think we've crossed the line between flirting and being fresh." I tried to back up but he had me tight.

"Hmm? What's that? I can't hear you."

I was still trying to keep my laughter soft enough so it couldn't be heard by whatever neighbors he might have. "Come on, Matt. We have to go to bed."

At that he looked up. "Woo-hoo! I found me a girl and she's *easy*." He sounded like Jim Carrey and I laughed again.

"In your dreams!" I pulled away and tugged on his arms to get him up.

"Again with the bedroom references." He grinned lecherously at me. "I *like* you."

He rose and swung me up into his arms.

"Hey!" I said, startled.

"Mm, this is familiar. Oh yeah, we just slept together like this."

I giggled and tried to move my head away from his. We were inches apart, sleepy enough to forget about good manners, and well, I wanted to kiss him, so I figured it would be a good thing if I didn't.

He could see it in my face. I saw his eyes drop to my lips. I made a point not to move them, not to lick them, not to do anything at all enticing. I opened my mouth to tell him to put me down.

His mouth covered mine in the sweetest way. I moved my hand to his cheek. One kiss melted into another. My hand slid into his hair. So soft. Soft, wet kisses. I tried to move closer. I felt Matt lower my feet to the ground and pull me against him. I wrapped both arms around his neck.

His mouth moved down my neck. I shivered. I pressed closer and kissed his neck. He smelled amazing. It made me want more. I turned my head so he kissed me on the lips again. My stomach had that same sweet/sick feeling that it has when a roller coaster drops down fast.

"We should decide if you're staying or going," Matt whispered.

"Uh-huh," I whispered between kisses.

I felt myself walking backward as we kissed. Matt's hands were running up and down my back, my sides. They moved almost to my breasts and back down again. It tickled like crazy, even though he hadn't touched them. I pressed closer.

The deck railing hit my back. We stopped moving backward. Matt kissed my cheeks, then my ear. His whisper tickled and I dug my fingers into his back. He whispered again, but not as close to my ear.

"Am I driving you home now or later?"

"Mm-hmm," I said. Sort of said.

He pulled back more. I leaned into him. He put his hands on my shoulders to keep me from moving closer. "Come on, Syd, decide."

Barely a moment passed as I tried to clear the fog in my brain, then he kissed me again, hotter than before. His lips and tongue were hard and demanding. I poured myself into him with renewed passion.

Just do it, urged one of the Voices in my head. *You'll feel so much better.*

I knew that was true. I felt light-headed already and we hadn't even done anything to be embarrassed about yet.

I thought about giving in. But I heard my mother's voice and my pastor's voice and all their reasons why I shouldn't.

Why should they ever know? said one of my Voices. *It'll be worth it to feel better, to feel loved.*

I leaned forward and kissed Matt again. So hot and sweet.

I thought of Dirk. He'd made *way* more promises than Matt. And look where that ended up.

Isn't better to be loved for a little while than not at all?

I felt Matt's skin under his shirt. I didn't remember pulling it out of his waistband. He felt hot and—

Stop!

I pulled away so fast, I hit my head on the deck railing. Ow!

I opened my eyes and my mouth in shock at the pain. My hand met Matt's hand at the back of my head.

"Are you okay?" His voice held a mixture of surprise, empathy and laughter.

"I think that might have been God's way of knocking some sense into me," I said a little breathlessly. My ears were ringing. Definitely not thinking about sex at this moment.

Matt laughed, which made me chuckle. Which made me wince.

He took one long deep breath and blew it out. Stepping away from the porch railing, he took my hand, guiding me over to the kitchen door. "You sit here for a minute. I'm going to get two ice cold Cokes and my car keys."

I sat down and put my hand on the back of my head. I thought I heard him mutter, "And a cold shower to go."

CHAPTER 20

*S*unday, I got to church early because I could barely stay asleep. Life just seemed too fine to stay in bed. I sang loudly with the praise band, said a hundred thank you's in my head when we prayed, and complimented Pastor Mark on the sermon. Afterward, I stayed and chatted with my friends for nearly an hour.

By then, we were starving, so we decided to have lunch together. I hadn't gone to lunch with them in *forever*. We went to Paesano's, the best pizza place on this side of town. They have the most amazing Chicago-style pizza — outside of Chicago, of course.

I carpooled with Rhonda, Carlo, and Dave. It was immediately obvious that Rhonda and Carlo had been getting to know each other better while I wasn't noticing. They shared the front seat and acted, you know, like an item.

If you haven't experienced it for yourself, let me tell you, a large church's 20s and 30s singles group can be one step away from a meat market. Just like in a bar, everyone is trying to meet someone, either to hang out or to permanently end bachelorhood. It's a regular Marriage Mart.

I tapped Dave on the arm and gestured to the two in front, arguing about the best route to the restaurant.

"Are they—?" I whispered and raised my eyebrows.

"Over a month, now," he whispered back. "We're taking bets on how long until the 'I dos' take place."

I giggled.

Rhonda turned around to look at us. "All right, you two. Hand check."

Dave immediately pretended to put his hands over my breasts. I laughed and pushed him away.

"Are we there yet?" I whined loudly at Carlo.

"I have to go to the bathroom," Dave whined.

"He's on my side of the seat."

"She's kissing me."

I inhaled in surprise and nearly choked. Everyone laughed while Dave thumped my back.

After a loud lunch with more laughter than I'd had in months, we returned each other to our cars. What a really fabulous day.

Rhonda gave me a hug. "It's good to see you again. You look great!"

"Don't be a stranger!" Carlo waved and smiled. Then they were off.

"It's good to see you smiling again," Dave said. "I've been praying for you."

"You have?" My throat tightened. That touched me like little else could.

"We all have. We've been worried about you."

I gave him a big hug. "Thank you."

We said goodbye and walked to our cars. Thank you, God. I am *so* lucky. You love me. They love me.

Who knows who else might come to love you, suggested Lovesick.

I tried not to think about *that*.

That afternoon, I took a book out to the patio and dozed in the dappled light. So relaxing. I hadn't felt so good in forever. Except for bits of branches that kept falling from the trees, it was immensely peaceful.

Ow, that felt like a pebble, not a leaf or a branch. I swiped at my leg with my eyes still closed.

Another pebble hit me, then another. I sat up, staring into the tree. A squirrel must be having a party up there.

I heard a sound as another pebble hit my ankle. I looked down. Matt grinned up at me. He dropped his stash of pebbles on the ground and dusted his hands off.

"What are you doing down there?"

"I knocked but you didn't answer. I saw your car so…"

"So you went trespassing," I teased.

"You got it. Wanna lock me up?" He held out his wrists to me.

I grinned and shook my head in warning. I could just imagine what that would lead to. And by the look on his face, so could he.

"Get around to the front, you bad boy," I said with mock severity.

He bowed and grinned and ambled off to the front of the building.

On my way to unlock the door, I tried not to go crazy. Matt had come to visit! Uninvited. When we'd just seen each other the night before.

This was *awesome*!

Okay. Calm down. Deep breath. It might not even mean that much to him. Probably not as much as it means to you.

I opened the door. Matt swooped in and kissed me, swinging me around and shutting the door by leaning our bodies against it. Still kissing me. Running his hands all over me.

Still kissing me.

Yeah, right. This doesn't mean anything to him? How could it *not* mean anything?

Just when I thought I was going to pass out, he pulled back and said, "Hi." No, not "Hi," but "Hhiii" with all that his deep male voice could do with two letters.

I just grinned. I couldn't even say hi back.

He leaned in and kissed me some more. Man, he was *very* good at this. He put one hand behind my head to pull me closer — and hit the bump. I winced as he pulled away in surprise.

"Hey, are you okay? Let me see that." Matt tried to look at the back of my head. I moved away from his hand.

"I'm fine, don't touch it."

"There's a big knot on the back of your head. Let me see it."

I grabbed his hands and tried to keep them away. "I *know* there's a big knot. That's why I don't want you to touch it!" I half-laughed.

"Hold still, for crying out loud." He forcibly turned my head and examined the damage, prodding some more and making me grimace.

"Ow! Stop!" He let go and I stepped away, frowning at him. "Like *you'd* know anything." I covered the back of my now-throbbing head with my hand.

Matt raised his eyebrows and cocked his head at me. It was a look I was coming to know as his "you don't know it, but I'm right" look. "Between working at a wilderness camp most of my life and working construction, I've seen things that would make you faint. I do know a little about first aid."

He pointed to my head. "And you should put some ice on that."

I made a face at him. "Yeah, *now* I should 'cause you made it hurt again."

He turned toward the kitchen. "Whiner. Hope you never decide to head-butt anyone."

"Whatever." I followed him.

He pointed toward the living room. "Go sit down."

"I don't need—"

"Sit!" He turned me around and slapped my butt.

It made me laugh so I went. He brought me a soft ice pack from the freezer. Ah, that did feel a little better.

"I still say it was fine before you poked it," I told him.

Ignoring me, he sat close and held his hand over the ice pack.

"Ow!"

"You have to put the ice *on* it, not just dab at it." He shook his head at me again. "Trust me, you'll thank me tomorrow."

I grunted. "Doubt it," I muttered under my breath. He turned his "I'm right" look on me again so I changed the subject. "So what're you doing here?" I said in my pretend-grumpy voice. "And where's the puppy?"

"She's at home. I *was* going to see if you wanted to get some dinner, but now I think we should stay in."

I rolled my eyes. "Yes, right, because the invalid shouldn't exert herself. I made it twenty-eight years without you, mister. I think I can manage."

"I don't know." He shook his head. "It seems like I've bailed you out a lot in the last month. The river, your vehicle, now your head. You obviously need someone to look out for you."

"And you're volunteering for the job?" I asked skeptically.

He grinned. "Depends. What are the benefits?"

I laughed and stuck my tongue out.

"Really?"

I hit him in the chest with the back of my hand. He laughed and kissed my forehead.

"So what do you want to do?"

"I don't know." I shrugged. "I was relaxing on the deck before you came over and made my head hurt."

"You were sleeping."

"I was *relaxing* with my eyes closed. Besides, who can sleep when you're being pelted with rocks?"

He picked up my free hand and twined his fingers through mine. "Stay up too late last night?"

I glanced at him out of the corner of my eye. "Something like that."

"Couldn't sleep?"

"Maybe." I put the ice pack on top of a magazine. He was so quiet. I knew he was staring at me, waiting for me to look at him. I finally gave in.

His dimple dented his cheek. "Me neither. Wanna take a nap together?"

"Yes," I said emphatically. "Which is precisely the reason we shouldn't." The cold pack had helped keep my wits about me. "You," I teased, "are a very dangerous man."

"I thought women like dangerous men." He wiggled his eyebrows and pulled me closer.

"Listen," I kept my voice teasing, "it was all I could do to keep from ripping your clothes off last night. So—"

"I like where this is going," he interrupted.

"Matt!" I laughed. "I'm not having sex with you!"

He swung his arm and snapped his fingers. "Aw, rats!"

I giggled. "Seriously, I told myself I wasn't going to have sex until I got married. Then I did with the guy who was *going* to marry me — at that point, I thought it was just a matter of timing — but then he didn't marry me. So...now I guess I really am going to wait."

He didn't say anything. Which made me nervous. Had I been too serious? Was the timing wrong? Did he fall asleep?

"So we're going to have to think of more things to do with our clothes on." I ended with a little laugh.

I didn't want to look at him.

"You want something to drink?" He got up off the couch and headed for the kitchen without waiting for an answer.

I sighed and let my head fall back against the cushion. Ow. Why are guys so hard to talk to?

"Matt?"

"Lemonade or Snapple?" he called.

"Snapple, please."

I heard the refrigerator door slam shut. Matt walked in with two Snapples and an attitude.

"Just for the record," he said, slamming a bottle on the coffee table in front of me and twisting the top from the other, "we've barely even gotten to first base yet. There's an awful lot of ground to cover — *fun* ground — before we need to have a discussion about sex. And I think you're seriously ahead of yourself to be talking about marriage! We've known each other for what? A month?"

He gulped down a third of his juice.

I glared at him. "Well, excuse me for wanting to give you a heads up about my boundaries. Men always say women act like a tease, act like they want to have sex and say no at the last moment. Here I was trying to be nice and not let it get that—"

"Tell me, have I asked you to have sex with me? Huh?" The way he was waving his juice bottle, I was going to have a mess to clean up later. "Have I been less than a gentleman around you? Tell me!"

Kind of last night, yeah! said one of the Voices.

"I'm just saying I'm not the kind of girl to sleep around."

"I never said you were!"

I huffed and grabbed the ice pack off the table. I stomped into the kitchen to put it in the freezer. Stupid, idiotic, why I bother—

"Put that back on your head!" He followed me into the kitchen.

"I don't feel like it!" I slammed the freezer door. I faced him, hands on my hips. Glaring, waiting.

He glared back. Then he shook his head. "I gotta go." He marched to the door, muttering under his breath.

"What'd you say?" What was he saying? Whatever it was, I wanted to know!

"Nothing!" He turned at the door. "I'd kiss you goodbye, but I wouldn't want you to take it wrong."

My mouth opened to say something — *anything* — but he was gone.

"I'll see ya," he muttered as the door slammed shut behind him.

I was so angry, the smoke from my ears could've set off the fire alarm. I paced into the living room. Back into the kitchen. I heard his truck pull out. No squealing tires like Dirk, but driving faster than one should in a parking lot. Idiot.

I grabbed my cell phone and punched "1", pacing while I waited.

"Hey you, guess what? I caught two fish today." Emily sounded like her usual cheerful self. Out with a man who was happy to have her around.

"Great!" I stomped onto the deck and threw myself into my chair.

"Oohhh, what happened?"

I shook my head. "He's an idiot. That's what happened."

I heard Emily murmur, "Do you mind? It's kind of an emergency," in the background. "Okay, tell me everything."

"He just ran out of here in a fit because I said I wouldn't have sex with him! He's such a jerk!"

"Who? Matt?"

"Yes, *Matt*! I was trying to be nice and he got mad because he thinks I don't think he's a gentleman which I *do* or I wouldn't be going out with him though I probably won't be *now* which is just fine since he's afraid to be seen with me anyway!" I stopped to take a breath.

"Wow," Emily said slowly. "How did all this come up? Start at the beginning."

I got up and paced my porch while I told her about the last twenty-four hours. The puppy, dinner, falling asleep, kissing, hitting my head — and today, which started out great and ended up in a crash and burn.

"Huh," Emily said. I knew that tone.

"What?" My guard went up.

"Did you want to vent, or did you want my opinion?"

I *knew* I knew that tone. I thought for a moment. I probably shouldn't ask, but… "Tell me."

She took a deep breath. "Well, in my opinion, most people get mad without warning when they get too close to a truth they don't want to face."

I knew I wasn't going to like this. Wait, she must mean Matt. Okay, that's fine then.

"So what truth do you think Matt doesn't want to face?" I thought I heard her laugh, but there was a lot of background noise so maybe not.

"Maybe he *does* want to have sex with you, but he doesn't want to admit it because he doesn't want a relationship. Or maybe your talk of marriage scared him and he thinks that's what you're fishing for. Or maybe he's just a nice guy who thought you were moving too fast."

I grunted. "Yeah, right." Was there such a thing? "He seemed to be moving fast enough last night."

He did say you were only on first base, said a Voice. *Maybe it was only in your imagination that you already saw the entire play.*

I dropped down in my chair again. Don't want to listen to that Voice.

"What about you?" Emily asked.

"What about me?" Defensive. Don't want to listen to Emily's voice either if she's going to say something I don't want to hear.

"Is there anything you're afraid to admit?"

"Matt's the one with the problem, not me." I kicked little pebbles off my deck with my toe. Matt's pebbles.

I did hear her chuckle that time. "Oh, well, in *that* case. So you don't want to have sex with him?"

Desperately. "No! I just said that!"

"Okay."

"Okay what? What am I supposed to do?"

She sighed into the phone. "Well, it looks like your choices are a) have sex and see if that fixes the problem or makes it worse — not the best plan if you ask me, b) break up and see if you both feel better, or c) cool down and apologize and see what happens. Personally, I think you two are good together." She chuckled. "Obviously, you've got chemistry."

"Thanks, Em," I growled. I picked up a pebble and threw it as hard as I could at a tree. A couple birds flew out of the branches. A squirrel skittered away.

"Hey, anytime," she said, all cheerful. "I'll call you later and see what you decided."

I closed my phone. "Blah, blah, blah," I said. I liked it better when she just listened instead of helped.

CHAPTER 21

*W*hen I walked into GT's kitchen a few days later, my prayers were answered. Matt stood at the counter. Surrounded by papers and on the phone, he looked busier than ever. I wondered if I should wait to apologize. (I'd decided Em's Plan C seemed like a good first choice.) As I paused, thinking about it, he hung up.

"GT's in his office," he said without looking up.

"Thanks," I said, moving a couple steps closer. "Um, I wanted to apologize about...the other day." I waited for him to look up.

He dialed another number on his phone.

"I'm sorry we...I didn't mean to—"

"Listen, I've got a major problem here, okay?" He looked at me for the first time. "Can we talk about this later? Ed, Matt here. Yeah, he wants to change it."

Well, *that* was a dismissal if I've ever seen one. I took a deep breath, trying to remain calm. Okay, I'll take care of business first, see if Matt has a moment later.

I walked down the hall and around the corner. GT's office door was open but he wasn't in there. A moment later, I heard him come barreling around the corner, talking to someone.

Nope, cell phone. I jumped out of his way as he rushed into his office with a "'Scuse me, darlin'" in the middle of a sentence.

He flipped through some papers on his desk, found what he was looking for, and sat down. I tried to stay inconspicuous near the door. We had an appointment so I knew I wasn't interrupting. If Matt weren't in the middle of something, too, I'd go hang out with him for a few minutes. (*So* not an option today.)

A minute later, I heard GT say, "Can you hang on? Just a moment." He looked up and caught my eye. "I'm sorry, darlin', but I've gotta take this. Can we reschedule?"

"Of course, GT. Give me a call." I smiled my professional smile. Great, one of the houses I wanted to show him would probably be sold before we could make it over there. I waved and left him to his phone call.

When I left, Matt was nowhere to be seen. Yet another thing that had to be put off till later. Big sigh. I drove back to the office to re-plan my day. Perry walked by my desk on his way to get coffee.

"What are you doing inside on such a beautiful day? Can't find anyone to show a house to?"

I pulled my laptop out of my briefcase and plugged it in. "GT had to reschedule."

Perry shook his head. "I don't know about that guy. He might be dead weight." He had a smile in his voice — he always did — but this was the second time he'd mentioned his concern.

I sighed. "He's eager to buy, he just hasn't found it yet."

Perry handed me a fax. I looked at it. Another impossible list from GT. I *really* wanted to crumple it up, but not in front of my boss.

"If he keeps this up, he never will." Perry watched me unload my briefcase. "You have a battery in that thing?" He pointed to my computer with his empty mug.

"Yeah," I said, pausing to look up at him.

"Take it down to the beach. You need some fresh air."

I looked at all the files on my desk. So much to do.

"Nothing that can't wait a couple hours," he said, reading my mind. "Why live in the palm of God's hand if we don't take the time to enjoy it? Grab a smoothie. Breathe in the scent of dead fish. It's good for the digestion."

Surprised laughter floated up. Perry had a knack for knowing how to show his concern without making you cry. Which I might've done if he'd continued acting so nice for another thirty seconds.

As I stood there undecided, he pushed one of my buttons. "Besides, I need someone to drive past the Lockwood estate and give me an update on the landscaping. I don't have time."

"Oh, well, I can do that for you." Call me a brown-noser, but I enjoy helping Perry out. He's so good to his employees, as a boss and as a person, it just makes you *want* to work hard.

He knows you, said a Voice. *He knew you wouldn't go unless he gave you some pretend work. I bet he could find out what he needs to know with a phone call.*

Whatever.

As I repacked my stuff, I wondered if Perry knew driving relaxed me. Round trip to the Lockwood place would be a minimum of two hours.

He said he didn't have time, said another Voice. *That's why he asked.*

Yeah, that's true. I'd become a basket case after Dirk broke up with me, and I didn't want my boss or co-workers to ever see that side of me again. Hide stress at all costs. That's my new motto.

I called Em from the road. "Hey, in a minute, look out one of the windows and wave." I had to drive past her office on my way to the Lockwood's. (No, I didn't go to the beach. I wanted to, but if I relaxed, I'd mope about Matt. Better to keep working and not think.)

"Here, I'm waving on the inside."

Definitely tense. Poor thing. "Bad day?"

"You could say that."

"Well, I've got a cure. Wanna have margaritas Thursday?"

"You have a closing? That's great."

Not very enthusiastic. Must be a really bad day. "My treat."

"I don't know if I can make it."

"Oh, no, you've got to, Em," I teasingly whined. "We've haven't missed Closing Margaritas in a year! It's like my lucky socks."

"If I can I will, but it looks like we'll be working late all week."

"How about we go whenever you get off work? If you have to work late, we'll have dinner, too."

"Listen, Syd, the world doesn't revolve around you, okay? I can't be at your beck and call whenever you need something. I've got my own problems."

I opened my mouth and blinked in shock. The car in front of me slowed down abruptly and I hit my brakes, checking my mirrors to be sure the guy behind me braked, too.

"I better get off the phone before I rear-end someone," I said quietly. "Call me later if you want to talk about — whatever."

"I don't want to talk about it, but thanks."

Ouch. I've never known Em to be so short with me.

"Emily, are you okay?"

I heard her sigh.

"Are you mad at me?" I tried to think of what I might've done or not done recently that I should apologize for. Had I been treating our friendship like the world revolved around me?

"Syd! I just said it's not about you, all right?"

"Okay, okay. I'm sorry. I'll talk to you later."

"Bye." She hung up.

I let out my breath in a huff. Fine. Hang up on me. I tossed the phone onto the passenger seat. My day was becoming an endless chain of one lousy argument after another.

By Thursday, I was thoroughly stressed out and trying not to show it. The Slocum's closing was scheduled for two. I needed to order flowers and buy a teddy bear for the new baby. (I learned from Perry that gifts from the realtor are unexpected and so doubly appreciated. Happy clients make good word-of-mouth advertising.) Plus I had paperwork to prepare for another closing next Friday.

The good thing about Heartbreak is that you can become a workaholic and kick your career into high gear. If I'm going to be alone for the rest of my life, I might as well be successful. Not that I think of myself as Heartbroken any longer. I'm over him. Dirk, I mean. And since Matt's not talking to me, I don't care about him either. I'm just sayin'.

I called the florist, then grabbed my purse. It would take me nearly an hour — an hour I didn't have — to drive to the store where I wanted to buy the bear. I knew I should've done it last night, but I was exhausted then.

"Going to lunch?" Trent called from his desk. He got up and walked over. "Wanna get some Chinese?"

"No, I don't have time." I rummaged through my purse, then my briefcase, looking for my keys.

"Anything I can help with?"

"No, I've got to run out near the mall to buy a closing gift for a two o'clock." I found the keys. "Lunch is going to have to wait until dinner today."

I stuffed my computer into my briefcase along with the file I'd have to work on tonight at home. I looked at my watch. Crap.

"Maybe tomorrow then."

"Geez, Trent! Just back off, okay?"

I looked up to see him raise his hands in the air and retreat to his desk. Great. No time to apologize now.

I hurried to the front door, let loose really bad swear words in my head, and ran back to my desk. The file for *today's* closing was still on my chair. So I wouldn't forget it. I grabbed it and ran for my car.

I bought the softest bear ever made and made it to the mortgage office before the Slocum's got there. The flowers had arrived minutes before me. Pink and blue carnations stuck in a lush potted plant. The carnations would die in a couple days, but the plant could last forever. A good omen for their new life.

When I heard Todd's voice in the lobby, I went to greet them. They both looked beyond excited. And Rosie looked like she was ready to burst in other ways, too. It's hard to believe babies are so small when they actually get here.

"We did it, honey," Rosie said when they finished signing everything. "You were right about that stupid plan." She laughed.

Todd kissed her soundly and turned to me. "I told her, the way to get what you want is to develop a strategy. You know, 'plan the work and work the plan.'" He looked back at his wife. "And now we've got everything we ever wanted."

I couldn't stop thinking about what he said as I drove home. Yes, home, not out for margaritas. Emily really had cancelled on me. I still could hardly believe it. Anyway, I wondered if I needed a plan. Get my life together somehow. But where to start?

I actually thought I was doing okay with the plan I made on the fishing trip to force myself to get over Dirk and start feeling better. Life had gotten a lot better...and then it got worse again. Todd and Rosie talked about a written plan, step by step. Maybe writing things down would make a difference.

At home, I changed into a T-shirt and shorts and sat on my couch, hugging a pillow and staring into space. What did I want — *really* want — and how would I get it? I snorted. If I didn't figure out the answer to the first part, I'd *never* figure out the answer to the second part.

A knock on my door startled me from my musings. I opened it to find — wait for it — Dirk. You guessed it. (What's with my inability to use the peephole?)

Too tired and depressed to even get upset, I just stood there, waiting for him to speak. He put his foot on the doorsill so I couldn't close the door in his face. Smart move. In another mood, I would've been irritated or amused. Today, nothing.

"I thought of a way to prove to you that I love you," he said quickly, without even a hello.

I waited.

"I want to hire you to buy a house. But you can pick it! See? It'll be a house for *us*, something you've always wanted." He paused. "Well, what do you think?"

I sighed. Six months ago he would've been completely correct — it *would* prove to me that he loved me. But six months ago, I didn't doubt that he did. Today was another story.

I started to tell him to go home, but what came out instead — tears, lots and lots of them. What happened to my plan to feel better, *to stop crying?* Embarrassed, I tried to pretend nothing unusual was happening. I tried to say "go home." Just two words. That's all I needed.

Four years of memories overwhelmed me. Good memories. I could smell Dirk's clean, manly scent. I could feel his strong, hard body. I remembered falling asleep with him spooned up against me. I remembered arguing about what movie to see and watching two.

Then I remembered *her*. I'd never met her, never even suspected, but I remembered the night I learned about her. I tried to compose myself. That's when I realized Dirk was rocking me in his arms. I struggled to get away.

"Get out," I whispered.

"Sydney..."

"Please. Just go."

If I'd still loved him, I wouldn't have been able to bear the hurt look on his face. But I didn't care anymore. The not caring didn't even bother me.

Maybe it *was* time for a new plan.

CHAPTER 22

I yanked some paper from my printer and found a pen. Throwing it down, I picked up a black Sharpie instead. I needed to make a statement. Scrubbing my face against the shoulder of my shirt, I ignored the black streak of mascara left behind and sat down at the dining room table. In big, block letters across the top, I wrote:

THE PLAN — STEP 1 —

Okay, what to do first? I sniffled. Staring at the paper, I tried to concentrate. Sniffling again, I got up and found a box of Puffs. I blew my nose and wiped my eyes. Picking up the Sharpie, I decided to just write everything down in no particular order.

Next to "Step 1" I wrote, "Tell Dirk no more flowers and chocolate, and stop coming over uninvited."

I paused, then crossed out the word "uninvited." Yeah, that's good. Speaking of which — I got up again and grabbed the latest box of truffles from the kitchen counter. I popped one in my mouth and put the box on the table beside me.

Don't think, said a Voice, *just enjoy.*

Step 2 — Tell Emily that if she's mad at me, she should tell me, and if she's found other friends to hang out with, she should tell me.

I re-read it. A little childish. Well, I'll say it in a way that doesn't make it sound "all about me" as she put it.

Step 3 — Tell GT I can't help him find a house if he gives me conflicting/opposite needs.

The hard part was going to be explaining that to him in a way he understood. So far, no luck. A thought occurred to me. I wrote in parentheses, "Go look at the house he keeps mentioning and study it."

The house he pointed out that first trip — the one that wasn't for sale — seemed to have caught his attention in a way nothing else had. Maybe I could figure out what he liked so much about it and find something similar.

Oh! I added to step three, "Tell GT to keep his hands to himself." It's not like he's trying to be fresh, but geez. He needs to understand boundaries.

Let's see. What else. I tapped the marker against my chin. Oh!

Quickly I wrote, "Step 4 — Tell Perry to let me know if he wants me to drop a client, otherwise I'm doing the best I can."

Lately, it felt like I wasn't living up to anyone's expectations. Least of all, mine.

Step 5 — Tell Trent...

What? Tell him what? That we might be the right match at the wrong time? That he deserves more — or in my case *less* — than he can get from me? He's so sweet and kind and really rather good-looking and...

I sighed. My life is a disaster. Trent deserves less drama. I crossed out the first two words and wrote, "Figure out what to do about Trent."

I thought about Matt. He seemed *so mad* when he left last Sunday. And he didn't act any better when I saw him yesterday. All I did was tell him I'm not the kind of girl to sleep around.

Okay, *maybe* that sounds like I think he thinks I am. But I tried to apologize and he blew me off!

I sighed, tapping the pen furiously against the table. No matter how I looked at it, it still came down to me apologizing. Not for what I said, but for fighting about it. I could've been far more calm and rational. Just not when he's nearby.

That's it! I'll apologize on the phone or with an email or something. When he's close, all I can think about is kissing his lips off. (Or, in yesterday's case, kicking his butt.) If he's not actually in front of me, I could think better.

Step 6 — Tell Matt I'm sorry about the misunderstanding, and that I'm not going to have sex with *anyone.*

I hope that *doesn't stay true forever,* said Lovesick.

I wondered if he would accept my apology or just refuse to see me anymore. I started getting mad again and wrote one more line. "If that's a problem, too bad."

There. I felt better. I might not actually say it, but then, hey, maybe I should.

Let's see. What else? I tapped my pen on my lips. (Yeah, I'm a pen tapper when I'm agitated.) That covers just about everyone in my life. At least everyone I've been having any, let's say, *issues* with.

Seems like there should be more to planning your life than just resolving personal conflicts. I wondered what Todd and Rosie had written in their plan. Couldn't just call them up and ask. I'd sound stupid.

But you could call Matt, said a Voice. *Get the apology over with and see what happens.*

Not yet, warned Another. *You need to think this through first.*

I'm tired of fighting with him, sighed Little Miss Lovesick. *I want him back.*

I picked up my cell phone and dialed Matt's number.

Don't do it! screamed Sergeant Pride. *Hang up!*

"Hello?"

"Hi Matt." I cleared my throat. "It's Sydney."

"Hi."

Brr, is it cold in here? "Listen, I've been thinking about... about our conversation Sunday and I just wanted to let you know that I'm sorry about the misunderstanding."

Silence.

"The fact is, I'm not planning on having sex with *anybody.* That's all I was trying to say."

"All right."

All right? What does "all right" mean?

I looked at my notes.

"And, uh..."

Say it! said a Voice.

No, I can't. He'll take it wrong.

Just say it!

Don't do it!

"And I just — what I'm saying is, if you have a problem with that..."

Is he trying to torture me by not speaking? A nice person would've broken in by now, said they understood, wouldn't have made me finish.

So say it already!

"Well, it's just too bad."

I winced. There had to be another way to say that.

Too late now, said a Voice.

Had my cell phone died? I pulled it away from my ear long enough to see that it was still on.

"Matt?"

"Anything else?" Ouch. Scary monotone voice. I don't think he's taking this well.

"Uh, no, that's — I just wanted to apologize for the misunderstanding. That's it."

"Okay. Thanks for calling."

"Uh, okay."

The phone went dead. I had a funny feeling I wouldn't be seeing him any more.

"Fine!" I said out loud to no one. "Who needs him anyway?"

I got up and paced my apartment. This sucked! I picked up two truffles from the table as I paced that direction. I ate one whole as I walked down to my bedroom. Biting into the second one, I paced back to the living room. I tossed my cell phone on the couch and stood there chewing, staring sightlessly out the window. Finishing the second truffle, I fell back onto the couch. Put my feet up on my coffee table. Leaned my head back and closed my eyes.

Now what?

I did what came naturally. I picked up the phone again and hit "1." Emily picked up on the second ring.

"Hey, what's up?" She sounded like she was in the middle of a funny conversation. Her voice sounded like she was laughing.

"Hey, I decided to go with Option C, as you suggested. I just called Matt and apologized. But I don't think we'll be seeing each other anymore."

"Oh, Syd, that's too bad. Listen, I hate to cut this short, but I've got to call you back later, okay?"

Cry or get mad? Cry or get mad? I was really sick of both.

I looked at The Plan. She was on the list. Maybe this was the time.

"Listen, Emily, I don't know what's up, if you've got stuff going on that's private or what." As long as we'd been friends, we'd never had any secrets from each other, but I guess it could happen.

She laughed quietly and whispered something to someone, then came back on the phone to interrupt me. "Nothing's going on. Come on. If it were, I'd tell you eventually anyway. Lighten up."

Something was definitely going on.

"Well, if you're mad at me or found some new friends to

hang out with or something, just let me know and I'll stop calling you, okay?"

"Syd, stop. That's ridiculous. I've gotta get off the phone, but I'll talk to you later, okay?"

"Whatever."

The phone clicked.

Cry or get mad? That was so stupid. I *am* childish. What is wrong with me? I swear I haven't been this awful my whole life. Have I? No, I distinctly remember being a mature, well-adjusted human being not that long ago.

I lay down on the couch and hugged a pillow. I wasn't sure if The Plan was going to work. The fact that I knew Emily was right, that I *was* being ridiculous, didn't help. I felt absolutely miserable. Still. I thought working The Plan was supposed to make things better.

I sat up and stared at the dining room table. I got up, grabbed the marker and put a big, black check mark next to Step Two and Step Six.

Six. Sex. Well, that's unfortunate. I should've made Matt Step Five. Now every time I look at the list—

You know what? No. Sex is Matt's problem, not mine. Not that I wouldn't like to have some, too. But a person's got to get their priorities straight. And right now, I want lasting love more than I want love for the moment.

I sat tapping the marker against the paper.

Maybe love for the moment would be better than no love at all, though.

Hang tough! yelled Sergeant Pride. *You can do this!*

"I can do this," I muttered aloud.

Grabbing the box of truffles, I went back and flopped on the couch. I hit the remote for the TV, opened the box, and began to trough-feed. If I was going to finish what I started, I'd need my strength.

CHAPTER 23

"*O*kay, I'd like to see the houses in this order — the Maple Lane house, the Walnut Street house, and the Baker Street house."

I pulled out of GT's driveway and onto the main road. No sign of Matt when I came in today. Fine by me. Hadn't seen or heard from him all weekend. And a peaceful weekend it was.

Liar, whispered Lovesick.

"Why don't we see the Baker Street house first?" I suggested, trying to ignore that particular Voice. "It's closest. Otherwise, we'll be driving around in circles."

GT patted my knee. "That's no problem. This order works fine for me."

Now's the time, urged a Voice.

"GT, I think we need to establish some boundaries. I'm sure you don't mean anything by it, especially after meeting your wife, but I'd be more comfortable without—" Should I just come out with it, or beat around the bush? "You know, you patting my knee, kissing my hand, that sort of thing."

I glanced over at GT who was looking at the printouts of the listings.

"Aren't there two houses on Baker Street you were going to show me?"

I closed my eyes briefly, praying for the willpower to *not* drive him into the bay. No, then I'd lose my cool little Sportage. That would be a bummer. I *love* this car.

"Did you hear what I said?"

GT absently patted my shoulder. "You're tense. That always happens when you have a lover's spat. Don't worry, it'll all work out."

"What?!" I'm pretty sure at that volume and pitch, it's considered screaming.

He smiled with his pseudo-Southern charm. "Oh, Matt didn't say anything. A gentleman wouldn't, you know. But I could tell as soon as I saw you, both of you."

He rubbed his hand up and down my arm in a way that I might interpret as comforting — *if he were my father!*

We were just coming up to a turnoff with a picnic area. I pulled in without slowing down. Gravel went flying and GT looked alarmed for the first time ever.

I stopped the car and put it in park. Turning to face him, I ground out my words through clenched teeth, afraid I would be more — direct? honest? — than I should be with a client.

"GT, I'm sorry. It's my fault for not mentioning this sooner, but your constant touching makes me uncomfortable. It's unprofessional and I need you to stop it if we're going to continue to work together."

"Well, if it bothers you to be touched, I'll try to—"

As if somehow *I* was the one with the problem. My left hand gripped the steering wheel with white knuckles. "No, not try. It needs to stop. In a lot of companies, this would be a big problem."

I was not going to say the words "sexual harassment" because I truly believed he wasn't trying to harass me. "But it's *not* a problem. It's a matter of respecting my personal boundaries. That's all I'm asking."

"All right then, darlin'. If it's that important to you."

His face hardened and his eyes lost their sparkle. He looked a little more Detroit Tough Guy now and a little less Southern Gentleman. Still, it was now or never.

"The other thing is, we need to sit down together and decide what it is you need versus what you want in a house—"

"I've told you everything I need." Detroit Tough Guy tone. Definitely.

"And I've told you that what you've listed is impossible. You can't have a low-maintenance house with a one-acre lot covered in grass and shade trees, with a fountain in the front and a pool and spa in the back. All of those items require quite a bit of maintenance. That's just one of the things I've been trying to discuss with you over the last few weeks."

"I would think with the commission and bonus I'm paying you, Miss Riley, that you'd be doing everything in your power to find me what I want."

I threw my hands up in the air. "I only get paid, Mr. Turkelbain, if you *actually buy a house.* I have other clients who also count on me to help them buy or sell their homes. My boss is breathing down my neck because you ask for a huge amount of my time, but you don't act interested in anything I show you. I'm trying to help you, but I need your cooperation."

"So you want to quit? Leave me in the lurch? That happened three times before I hired you!" GT shook his head, his hands gesturing in front of him, agitated. "I am having the hardest time—"

"Nooo." I took a deep breath. "GT, I'm not quitting. But we need to reorganize how we're handling this."

It was like a light bulb went on in his head. "Reorganization? Of course, *kaizen!* I implemented the 7-S framework with my New

York company and it's had amazing results! I think the Gestalt theory will work best in this case. Have you considered using the Balanced Scorecard approach to your business? I think you'd be—"

I had absolutely no clue what he was talking about. It was still English but...did he even hear what I said? When he was done spouting nonsense (at least it was nonsense to me), GT apologized and suggested I decide the route today since I knew the area best. Then he wanted to go back to his office and make a list of what conflicted with what on his other lists. We'd do better to work one day a week, he said, so he'd be focused on house-hunting when we were together. He promised to set aside Monday mornings if that would work for me.

I nodded and stuttered, "Th-that sounds fine." I don't know what I said to turn things around but, for the first time, The Plan seemed to be working!

I returned to my office in much better spirits. GT hadn't liked any of today's houses, but we both felt we'd made progress. Some of the buoyancy left my step, however, when I approached my desk. There sat another bouquet of flowers and another box of heaven — I mean, chocolates. I sighed and pulled my list out of my briefcase. Yesterday I crossed off Step Six, Matt, and Step Two, Emily. I took a pen and drew a line through Step Three, GT.

I looked at Step One, Dirk, then back at the flowers on my desk. This bouquet had a few roses, a couple irises, and some others I wasn't sure about. Very colorful. Fragrant. Beautiful.

I opened the Godiva box. Truffles again. I'm sure I'd get sick of them eventually, but not yet. Thinking about this morning's clothing change (stupid cotton, always shrinking), I wondered if Godiva, not Dirk, was my number one problem. I sucked in my stomach.

Be a Nike and Just Do It, said a Voice.

I inhaled the scent of the world's most delicious chocolate

and picked up the phone. Dialing Dirk's home number was easy
— I knew he wouldn't be there. His voice mail picked up.

"Hey! Dirk here! You know I'd love to talk to you, but I am
unavailable at the moment. Leave your vitals after the beep and
I'll get back to you just as soon as I can. *Ciao!*"

I rolled my eyes. What an idiot. Mr. Don Juan-a-be. I heard
the beep and said, "Dirk, this is Sydney. Listen, there's a new
plan. You may not have noticed, but I am *not* interested in
getting back together with you. *So*, no more flowers, no more
chocolate—"

I can't believe you just said that, said a Voice.

"—no more coming over to my office or my apartment.
Nothing. Just erase me from your memory banks, okay?
Thanks. Bye."

Hmm, a little harsh, maybe, but necessary.

I leaned back in my chair and smiled. I am woman; hear me
roar.

I picked up my pen and crossed Step One off The Plan. This
was *such* a good idea.

CHAPTER 24

*T*his was *such* a bad idea. I got all excited about working The Plan — things seemed to be going smoothly with GT and Dirk earlier this week — that I didn't even consider that any part of it might not work.

"By the Bay Properties, this is Sydney." God bless the person who invented hands-free earpieces, or I'd have such a crick in my neck.

"Hey By the Bay Properties, whatcha doin'?" It was Emily.

I stopped working. What a surprise. We hadn't connected since the call where I implemented The Plan, Step Two. "Hey! You just caught me. I was walking out the door."

"I only have a minute. I just wanted to say hi and see how things are going."

Things are great. And awful. Does she really want to know or is this a guilt call? Why do I even think that? This is Emily. *Emily.*

You wonder because you know something is wrong, said a Voice.

"Things are great. I have another closing this week. That means margaritas after. You game?" This was the big test. Was she going to back out on me again?

"What day?" Her voice sounded worried.

"Friday." One word, major attitude.

Pause. "Uhh, Friday's not going to work. How about Thursday? It'll be a pre-closing celebration." Her voice sounded hopeful, but there was no way I was letting her off that easily.

"Pre-closing celebrations are only good for jinxing the actual closing." I knew I sounded grumpy but I didn't care. Emily knows these things are never really a done deal until the check is in the bank.

"Well, I can't, Syd. I'm sorry, but—"

"Don't worry about it. Listen, I gotta go."

"Hey, come on, I can't get together Friday night but let's have lunch this week. Okay?"

I stared hard at the phone. "How about now? I could be there about one."

"Today? Well, how about tomorrow or—"

"Forget it. Call me when you have time." I started to hang up. Today I chose anger over tears.

"Sydney, wait! Don't be mad." Imploring voice. Almost worked on me.

"I'm not mad. Just"—confused—"busy. I'll talk to you later." She said goodbye (reluctantly, I was happy to note) and hung up.

Good. I hope she feels guilty. I sure don't.

Liar, whispered a Voice.

Today might be a get mad *and* cry day. What was I doing wrong? Why wasn't this working? I thought about my stupid cell phone bill. When I got home last night, it was waiting for me. No problem. Except that my mobile-to-mobile usage was only *783 minutes!* That means Em's talking to me *half* the amount of time she used to. That is definitely a problem.

I need to add a Step 7 to The Plan — *feel better!* Why was everything upsetting me so much?

Because it doesn't seem like anyone cares—

Shut up! yelled another Voice. *That's not true.*

But it feels true.

As I sat there trying to breathe and think and not cry, the phone rang again. I gave two seconds' serious consideration to flushing it down the toilet, then I answered.

"Sydney! Hello, sweetie. It's Patty. How are you?" Voted World's Most Cheerful Person by, well, *me*.

"Hey, Patty. I'm fine. How are you?" I tried to sound half as cheerful.

"What's wrong?"

Apparently, I'm no good at half-cheerful. I should've gone for the full thing. I sighed into the phone.

"A little of everything. Fighting with Emily and Matt and clients and…just one of those days." Belatedly, I wondered if Matt had already given her his version of events.

"You and Matt are fighting?" Definitely surprised. And interested. "I'm sorry, I shouldn't pry."

I'm so contrary. If she'd tried to get me to talk, I would've clammed up. But since she was being so respectful of my privacy, I had the sudden urge to tell her everything.

"No, it's okay. Maybe you're the exact right person to talk to since you know him."

My frustration must've been audible because she laughed. "I was calling to see if you wanted to go hiking with the group Sunday afternoon. But how about the two of us take a little walk Saturday morning?"

Translating Patty's use of the words "a little walk," I knew it'd still be a hike, but at a slow enough pace to talk. Relief rushed through me. I hoped she could tell me what to do.

She chuckled. "We'll see," she said. She told me to meet her at the Old Cannery Trailhead at seven o'clock. Then we hung up.

The rest of the day went better. I bought a lovely blown glass vase for my client who was closing on Friday. While I was out, I checked my phone messages and found that someone had put in an offer on one of my listings. Yes!

I called the client, Mr. Dahl, and gave him the offering price over the phone. He said he and his wife would get back to me by tomorrow, but he sounded happy. Cool.

The next few days were crazy busy. By Friday I was juggling phone calls for the closing that afternoon, as well as calls from the Dahl's and the realtor whose client wanted to buy the Dahl's house. (Isn't that funny? I'm selling a Dahl house. Ha ha!)

I was never so glad to see five-thirty arrive and happy homeowners depart. I was *exhausted*. But hey, I'd sold another house. Margarita time!

And no one to share it with.

I tried to forget Emily and whatever was going on with her. I thought about calling Don and Bridgette, but they have a toddler and probably wouldn't want to go out. Maybe Kerri? No, I talk a lot, but she talks *a lot*. More of a running monologue. Can't take that tonight.

Since I wasn't in a hurry, I drove back to my office to drop off the closing paperwork. In fact, I decided when I walked in that I was leaving everything. Taking the weekend off. 'Cause I deserved it. Yeah.

I walked through the deserted office to my desk and pulled the files out of my bag. I've got this great briefcase/bag that I bought at Wilson's a couple years ago. It's natural-colored leather, soft as butter — I know it's cliché, but it's *so* soft — with these great inside pockets that keep me organized. The strap is padded so well I can carry it around practically forever and it doesn't hurt my shoulder. Anyway, I was unloading my stuff when—

"Hey, Syd."

I jumped in the air and dropped a folder. "Holy crap!" The folder and its contents went skittering across my desk and spilled onto the floor.

Trent tried to hide his chuckle. "I'm sorry, I didn't mean to scare you." He came over and picked it all up. "Are you okay?"

I closed my eyes and took a breath. "For crying out loud, Trent, you scared the crap out of me!" I looked at him, kindly trying not to laugh, and smacked him on the shoulder. That made us both laugh. Great stress reliever, laughter.

Trent set the folder on my desk and leaned against a filing cabinet. "Hey, aren't you supposed to be in Margaritaville?"

Back to the stress again. "Yeah, yeah. Emily's 'busy' tonight." I did the air quotes with my fingers.

"So?"

I looked at him and frowned. "I'm not such a lush that I'm going to go out drinking by myself."

"Right. As if Emily is your only friend." Trent crossed his arms and looked at me with a somewhat cross expression. "So you're going to go home and drink by yourself."

Bingo!

"Yeah, right," was all I said. I straightened the mess I'd made on my desk and got ready to leave.

"Come on, you've gone out for margaritas every time you close since you've been working here."

"Before that," I said without thinking. He was making me feel worse. Obviously, he didn't know about last week's missed celebration.

Trent pushed himself away from the filing cabinet, took my arm, and steered me toward his desk.

"What?"

"Hang on," he said as he turned off his computer and grabbed his briefcase.

"Oh, Trent, no, don't worry about it. I'm just going to go home." I started to back away from his desk. This was sweet, but unnecessary. And it only made me more upset that Emily was ditching me.

"Nope, come on," he looked at his watch. "There's only an hour left." He took my arm, presumably so I couldn't get away. Or maybe because he wanted to take my arm.

Huh. I looked at him as we walked. He caught my gaze and laughed.

"What?"

He let go of me to open the door. "What?" He looked pretty happy. I wondered if this was a bad idea.

How could this be bad, asked Lovesick. *A cute guy whose company we already enjoy is going to save the evening!*

Enough with the "saving" already! I'm not a damsel in distress.

"Nothing," I said as he locked the office door.

"Two cars or one?"

Warning! "I'll take my own car, thank you." I needed to be sure he didn't get the wrong idea. I wasn't in a good enough mood for a date.

Oh, for Pete's sake, exclaimed a Voice. *Don't get so full of yourself. He's just a co-worker cheering up a co-worker.*

Go home while you still can, warned another Voice.

"Actually, Trent, I'm just going to go home. It's been a long—"

"Actually, no, you're not," he said, looking me in the eye. "Margaritas for you are like lucky socks for a baseball player. If you break the cycle..."

That's what I tried to tell Emily!

"We'll have one margarita to celebrate," he said, "then go our separate ways. If we worked at some corporate job downtown, we'd be doing this every Friday night."

I guess he could see me caving because he said, "If you don't follow me there, I'll come find you."

"Okay, okay. I'll meet you there." I laughed in that "I give in" kind of way and walked to my car.

CHAPTER 25

rent was waiting for me by the door at La Señorita on Garfield. Walking in, we passed the restaurant on our right and entered the cantina on our left. Not a seat to be found — duh! it's Friday — so we ordered our margaritas from the bartender. Trent went over to the buffet and brought back a basket of chips and some green chili picante sauce, making a standing-room space for us at a corner of the bar.

He held up his glass to mine. "Here's to another's happiness. May our clients make us enough money to buy our own homes!"

I laughed. "Cheers!" We dinged our glassed together and drank. It never occurred to me that other realtors felt the same way. I usually thought of Perry — homeowner. Carmen — homeowner. Me — renter. I never thought of Trent one way or the other.

Maybe you should, suggested Lovesick.

Trent ate some chips and motioned for me to dig in. "I figure I have to sell about twelve more properties before I have a big enough down payment to have a manageable monthly payment. How about you?"

"Eight. I thought I was the only one who counted that way." I took another drink. Friday night, margaritas, a free weekend ahead. I was finally beginning to relax.

"I count everything. Twelve properties till I buy a house. A little over a year from now at my current sales rate. So I've got a year to find the right girl and court her and propose to her, and then I'll give her a house for a wedding present." Trent popped some more chips into his mouth. The salsa dripped onto his finger and he wiped it off with a napkin.

"Court her? You're going to *court* a girl?" I laughed. "Don't you date like everyone else?" I dipped a chip into the green sauce and ate. So hot. I loved it.

Trent shrugged and took another drink. Liquid courage to say what's really on his mind? Yeah, I know that one. "I'm looking for a wife, not a one-night stand. Been there, done that, bought the T-shirt." He drank some more. "I want kids. Nice girls want a house and a steady income. I want a nice girl. Besides, I'm under the impression romance is high on the priority list for women. Am I wrong?"

I quickly shook my head. "No, no. You're right. I just...I never thought that you...I just never thought about it."

Trent looked at me and didn't say anything. You can always tell when someone wants to say something, then decides it's the wrong thing or the wrong time. I couldn't help myself. Curiosity killed the cat.

"What?"

He shook his head and took another drink. At this rate, we'd be ordering refills soon. I didn't think he'd tell me what he was thinking. Then he spoke. The bar was so loud, though, I couldn't quite understand him.

"Ice swirls?"

"Nice! Nice girls." He leaned over and spoke close to my ear. "I said I think it's a crime that nice girls are all too often with the wrong men."

"You mean, not with you?" I teased.

He tried to put salsa on my nose. I laughed and leaned out of the way.

"You know what I mean." He didn't look at me.

Yeah, I know what you mean, said a Voice.

I took a long drink myself. I was going to have to sit here for a while if I continued to drink this fast. But it drowned my musings. Musings about whether *I'd* ever be the nice girl who found a nice man.

"So where is Emily tonight?" Trent practically shouted over the din. (Why do we call it atmosphere in a bar and love it, then get mad if our neighbors have their radio on too loud? Weird.)

"Busy." I stuffed chips into my mouth. I didn't know where Emily was. If I were honest, I'd admit that I was hurt and jealous of whatever had taken her away from me. Was it Geoffrey? How could it be? She'd introduced us, so now he wasn't a secret anymore. Whatever was going on, she wasn't telling me a thing.

But enough with the morose ramblings. I'd sold a house, for crying out loud! I was *happy*!

"On a date?"

I stopped with a chip almost to my mouth. If she were on a date, she'd *tell* me. Right? I wouldn't be mad at her for being on a date, for heaven's sake. Picante sauce dripped onto the bar. I put the chip in my mouth.

"She didn't say." No, but now I remembered the giggling and the whispering. Telling signs, if ever there were any, that there was a man nearby, right? She didn't have a new best friend. She had a *boyfriend*. That would be awesome, if it were true.

Pictures flashed through my mind of Emily and Geoffrey acting silly over each other at the 4th of July picnic. Then my mind conjured up images of Matt and me kissing and giggling by the fire a couple weeks ago. I suppressed the wave of loneliness that threatened. Emily must be out with Geoffrey. But why wouldn't she tell me?

Trent and I sat munching for a few moments without talking. He watched the TV over my head. I glanced up but it was ESPN. Don't care.

Don't care about much right this minute, whispered a Voice.

I am *happy*. I sold a *house*. I have more *money* in my House Fund.

Trent said something but I couldn't hear him. I leaned closer. "Sorry?"

"I asked if you were still seeing that guy."

"Oh. Uh, not really. I don't think so." Could I sound more stupid? It's a yes or no question.

And do you know if the answer is yes or no? asked a Voice.

Whatever. Doesn't matter. Think of something funny to say.

"Have you found that girl you're going to court and buy a house for?" I asked with a smile. Teasing. That's what you did when you were out with friends, when you were drinking and having fun. You teased.

I drank some more margarita, making my way along the salty edge. I liked to have some of the salt with every sip. Yum.

Trent took a drink, too, but it looked like he was covering up a blush. Could it be?

I hit my knee against his. "Awww, come on, tell me."

He sort of smiled but didn't look at me. "I don't know yet."

"Yeah, that means you met a girl and you like her. Have you asked her out?"

"Sort of."

"Come on, Trent, you've got a timetable to keep to here. Tick, tock."

"My timetable is a year from now." Trent excused himself to refill the chips and salsa bowls.

I noticed two chairs emptying a couple seats down. I grabbed our drinks and took possession of the space. When Trent came back, I jumped right into teasing him as if he were a girlfriend. "Spill it, dude. I want to know."

"Dude?" Trent raised his eyebrows at me.

I kneed his knee again. "Come on. If you want to go out on Friday with friends from work, you have to be ready for the alcohol-induced inspection."

"I can't do it on one drink."

"So order another one."

"I don't like to drink alone." He eyeballed me in a challenging manner.

I laughed and waved my arm at the crowded room. "You're *so* not alone."

Trent smiled and said, "Nope. If you want the scoop, we stay for another drink and we get some food."

"I don't have anywhere to go." And I'm trying not to think about it.

"Great, what do you want? My treat."

"Well, in that case, the seafood nachos. Have you had them? They're fabulous."

Trent ordered two more margaritas and a large seafood nachos.

"Wait!" I put my hand on his arm and waved my other hand at the almost-retreating bartender. "Get the small. The large is so big we'll be here all night."

Trent waved the bartender away. "I'm hungry."

I laughed. "All right, but don't say I didn't warn you." I drank a few more swallows of my drink to make way for the new one and moved closer so I could hear the whole story. "So, tell me everything."

We were sitting elbow to elbow now, along the bar. Easier to talk this way than at a table where you're far enough away from each other that you have to yell.

This is fun, said a Voice.

And he's cute, said Little Miss Lovesick.

I told someone to smack Lovesick and waited for Trent's story.

He was playing with a chip, drawing in the picante sauce. He looked at me out of the corner of his eye with a little smile. "There isn't much to tell."

"Ah, you like her, I can tell," I said in that singsong voice you tease your friends with. "Come on, where'd you meet her?"

I finished the rest of my margarita and waited for the next one. Maybe I was a little light-headed, but I felt good. Happy.

He shrugged. "I've seen her around."

"And?"

"And...I think she's sexy and nice and sweet. And she's one of those girls I told you about who goes out with the wrong guys."

"Is she seeing anyone now?"

He shrugged again. "I don't know. I think so, but I'm not sure."

I leaned my chin on my hand, thinking. "Well, it's bad form to try to break in. I mean, some people do it, but I think it's bad form. On the other hand, if you're waiting around and she doesn't know you like her and she's not dating anyone, you could seriously lose out."

Our new drinks appeared and we both sipped and thought.

"Does she know that you like her?" I asked.

Another shrug. Apparently a means of communication. Slightly tipsy, I got silly. I leaned against him and shrugged a couple times. "What does this mean? She knows? She doesn't know? You need a massage?"

He laughed. "It means I don't know. I don't know if she knows. I think she does. Maybe." He shrugged again and laughed.

The biggest plate of steaming seafood nachos landed with a thud in front of us. "There must be three pounds of food on that plate," I said with some trepidation. I made a funny face that was meant to look like I was scared.

He hefted the plate. "More like five. Wanna race?"

I held up my hand in protest. "No way. Let's just say you win and be done with it."

We dug in. Delicious!

"So, you need a plan to let her know you like her. And to find out if she's dating anyone. Where have you seen her? You could kind of bump into her again."

Trent's mouth was full of food.

"How about the beach? You go out with your friends on their sailboat a lot. Do you see her at the beach?" I took a none-too-dainty bite with a scallop and lots of cheese.

Trent nodded and swallowed. "She looks hot in a bikini." Again, he didn't look at me and his face was getting red. It was so cute. He really liked this girl.

I giggled and said, "You probably better not tell her that until she knows you like her for herself first." I took a drink. "On the other hand, she might like that you noticed her. In which case, you should definitely let her know she looks good."

"So how do I know — say it or not say it?" Trent put a shrimp on a cheese covered tortilla chip and held it up to my mouth.

I ate it and thought while I chewed. "Well, uh—" I swallowed "—when in doubt, be a gentleman. But cute and funny and charming. But not too much."

Trent shook his head and fed me another chip. "This is why men don't understand women. Everything is walking a line, never sure what to do or say." He ate a huge chipful of seafood.

I grinned. "Yeah, well, it's the same with men. You guys give out advice like 'stand up for yourself' and then get mad when it comes back on you. You answer surveys that say you like it when women make the first move, then when one does, you say she's forward — or worse! It's a no-win situation." I pulled some melted cheese off the plate and ate it.

"That's for sure." Trent had seafood sauce on his chin so I handed him a napkin.

"I probably shouldn't be giving you advice anyway," I said.

"Why's that?"

I cocked my head and looked at him like he was an idiot.

He laughed. "Yeah, you're right. Your love life is messed up."

I socked him in the shoulder. He twisted away and laughed.

"It's one thing for *me* to say it." Then I laughed. This bantering thing was fun.

We sat around for another hour or so, talking and eating. When the nachos were gone and we both felt comfortable driving, Trent paid the bill — very chivalrous — and we headed out.

The next few moments were almost surreal. As it happened, I thought, *this only happens in movies.* We walked past a table of men laughing and watching ESPN and I happened to look toward them. One man was not laughing, not watching TV, but watching me.

Matt.

I paused by the table. I felt my mouth open, but no words came out. It was like I had tunnel vision for a moment. All I could see was him, looking at me, angry and cold. I think I said hi but I'm not sure.

One by one, I sensed the other men at the table turn to look at me, too. Dirk's hand was under my elbow, tugging lightly, pulling me away from Matt. I wanted to push it away. Then I blinked. I looked over at *Trent* and back at Matt. *Crap.*

I tried to smile politely. "See ya."

Then I moved my feet, one in front of the other and out the door, Trent still steadying me with his hand. We walked to my car and I dug my keys out of my pocket. Trent took them and unlocked the door, opening it for me. Such a gentleman.

"Sorry," I said, smiling sheepishly up at him.

"Was that him?"

I looked down at my shoes. "Yeah." I didn't know what to say.

"If you don't mind my saying so, it didn't look like the two of you were happy to see each other."

I looked away and shook my head, then shrugged. I half laughed. "I guess. I tried to...I just wanted him to...I don't know." I tried to laugh again.

Trent took a deep breath. "You want to see a movie tomorrow? Maybe grab a bite afterward?"

I looked up at Trent and cocked my head to one side, studying him. "Why can't I just fall for you, huh? Have a comfortable, happy life with no drama, no fireworks, no tears. Sweet, cute guy who only wants to make me happy. I should apply to be a candidate on the Who Will Be the New Mrs. Oswald show."

It was the alcohol that made me say it. And it must've been the alcohol that made Trent kiss me. Not a peck on the cheek either. But a full contact, lips on lips, hands in my hair, Ross and Rachel kind of kiss. It was the TV reference that made me realize I wasn't moved to tears. No sparks, indeed.

Trent broke the kiss first. He looked at me, chuckled humorlessly and shook his head, his hands sliding down my cheeks and falling to his sides. "My point was to show you that we could have fireworks." He took one of my hands. "I guess it's not the sort of thing you can force."

I sighed. "I'm sorry, Trent."

I really was. What was wrong with me? I went out with him tonight because I wanted to like him more. He had all the qualities I was looking for. But that didn't seem to be enough.

He squeezed my hand and let go. "Don't be. I've had it in my head for months that you could... I *do* want sparks and the occasional drama with the woman I love. But I'm afraid," he chuckled self-consciously and looked away, "I didn't feel any either."

I gazed at him for a moment, wondering if we should try again, try harder. We were perfect for each other in so many ways. But maybe we both deserved more than mutual desperation.

Impulsively, I leaned over and hugged him. He returned it with affection. Yes, this felt much better. I wondered if he'd be upset if I said the words so many men dread hearing.

"You think we could be friends?"

He kissed my hair and pulled away. "I'd like that."

I studied his face. Didn't look like he was lying. It's possible, just maybe, one thing in my life went right today.

Trent handed me my keys. "Be careful."

The way he looked at me, then over his shoulder toward the restaurant door, I'm sure there was a double entendre there.

"Thanks, Trent. For the lucky socks."

"Glad to be of service, ma'am," he said with a little bow. I laughed.

"I'll see you Monday," I said. "Drive safe." He smiled and waved as I pulled away.

Trent had definitely salvaged what had looked to be a pitiful, lonely night for me. But seeing Matt, well, it looked like the night would still have a pitiful and lonely end.

CHAPTER 26

I didn't sleep well that night, dreaming of Matt. And Trent. And the good parts of the evening as well as the bad. For the most part, it was one long nightmare. Even though I was awake (sort of) by five, I barely got myself out of bed in time to meet Patty at seven. She looked me over, gave me a hug, and said, "Let's walk while we talk."

I hadn't decided how much I wanted her to know, but by the time I finished venting, she knew everything. At the very least, I felt *so* relieved to get it all out. Maybe now I could make some sense of it.

"I swear I didn't know he was in the bar last night. I would've gone over and talked to him. By the time I *did* see him, he looked seriously ticked off." I gestured with my walking stick. "*He* should've come over and said hi to *me* then!"

Patty chuckled. "Men don't always see things the way we do."

"Well, that's stupid," I grumbled. "I can understand him being mad if he saw the next part, but I'm sure he didn't."

Patty looked curious. "Why? What was the next part?"

"Uh, Trent kinda kissed me. It's embarrassing now, in the light of day." I refused to look up to see Patty's reaction. "But he was talking about wanting a wife and liking a girl and I didn't get that he meant me. Then I said I should apply to be his wife even though there are no sparks, and then he kissed me to prove there could be, only there wasn't. Then we went home. Just friends."

I grimaced as Patty laughed. "It's not that funny, Patty."

"I beg to differ." She laughed some more and put her arm around my shoulder, giving me a quick hug and letting go.

"Well, *anyway*, I was hoping you could tell me what to do." I waited for her words of wisdom to pour forth like a geyser, or at least a spring, but we walked in silence.

I looked over at her. "This would be the part where you share your life's wisdom," I whispered.

At least I made her laugh.

We reached a part of the trail where a deep, green valley stretched off to one side. A couple of well-placed boulders provided seating of sorts. We sat and opened our water bottles.

"What do you want me to tell you?"

I looked at her like it was obvious. "What to *do*."

She smiled and looked out over the valley. "Well, what do you want? You want to force him to accept your apology? Think like you think? Be what you want him to be? Because those things are impossible."

Ah, I began to see what she was getting at.

I sat and thought. What *did* I want? I remembered how much fun I'd always had around him, even in Abundance Creek when I'd only just met him. I thought of his smile and his laugh and his eyes.

"It's weird," I mused aloud. "Even when I'm mad at him, I'm not, like, so mad I never want to see him again. I just want us to figure things out and move on. He makes me happy. Even when he's not around. I like it."

"Do you love him?"

The question should've surprised me. For months, my only

thoughts on love had revolved around Dirk and why he *didn't* love me anymore. Even though he'd recently tried to convince me that he did, I didn't believe him. And though I knew I'd loved him once, I was beginning to realize that I no longer did. But what about Matt?

"I'm afraid to. What if he doesn't love me? What if my heart gets broken again? What if I do something to screw it up? What if I *already did*?" Panic took my breath away.

"Now you know how Matt feels."

I frowned and glanced quickly at Patty. "What do you mean?"

"He's probably never told you anything about his family."

I shook my head.

"No, he wouldn't." Patty sighed. "Because he's afraid of the stories." She shook her head and smiled, then looked at me and asked, "Does he hiccup around you?"

I giggled. "Does he *hiccup*? No, why?"

"When you two are flirting or kissing, he doesn't hiccup or cough or anything?" Patty chuckled when I shook my head in confusion. "Then Matt's afraid he'll become impotent."

"What?" My shriek echoed across the valley.

Patty laughed at my expression. "I know, it sounds ridiculous. It *is* ridiculous, of course, but the Engel's have a legend to explain generations of broken families. They say if an Engel man hiccups around a girl, he probably won't have the nerve to marry her, but if he does, there's only a small chance it will last."

I stared at Patty like she was crazy. "Who lies awake at night coming up with these things?"

Patty smiled and kept going. "If he doesn't hiccup or cough around her, and he marries the girl, they'll be happy for a couple years, probably have a child or two, but then he'll become impotent. That will, of course, be so humiliating that he'll leave her."

"You're making this up," I said, laughing. "You're just trying to make me laugh so I'll feel better."

"I wish. Remember I told you Matt's mother and I were friends? She couldn't decide if she liked Ted or Will best. Both boys pursued her, but Ted couldn't stop hiccupping when they were alone together. He was afraid of the legend, told me later he loved her too much to risk ruining her life, that his entire family history proved the legend was real."

I wondered if Matt really believed any of this. Broken homes can cause more broken homes. Hiccups can't.

"Will asked her to marry him and, since Ted never asked, she married Will. Within two years, Matt was born and Will was gone. He wrote her a letter telling her about the legend. Said that's why it wasn't his fault."

"I take it Uncle Ted's been a bachelor all his life?" I asked skeptically.

Patty nodded. "But I know he desperately wanted to marry Matt's mother after Will left her."

I frowned, trying to figure out how modern men could believe such nonsense. "But it's not real," I said. "It's a self-fulfilling prophecy, not a real curse or something."

"I know." Patty shrugged.

"And Matt knows about this? And believes it?" I couldn't wrap my head around that idea.

"He knows about it," Patty said. "I don't know what he believes. He doesn't talk about his family or their history."

I was quiet for a moment, trying to digest this bizarre twist. "Well...he doesn't hiccup, but...when we're kissing it doesn't feel like impotence will be a problem for him."

Patty covered her mouth with her hand and tried to hide her laughter. I giggled. "Problem is," she said, "that's part of the legend. Stud becomes gelding."

I laughed, then sobered. It was funny, but not if Matt believed it. "So, maybe he likes me and is afraid of what might happen?" I had a thought. "And maybe that's why he was so mad at me when I said I wasn't going to sleep with him," I said quietly.

I sat on the rock, staring out over the valley, weighing it all in my mind. Poor Matt. What a horrible story to hear, and maybe fear or believe, growing up. But how did understanding him help our present crisis?

"I'm still not sure what to do, Patty. Matt seems too smart to be superstitious. But I rather doubt he'd take it well if I started discussing his family secrets."

"I don't know what to tell you, sweetie. We all have baggage. The key is to find someone who will let you carry some of theirs, and who you'll let carry some of yours. Then, together, you choose to leave some of it behind. Don't walk away from a good relationship just because it's difficult."

"You aren't suggesting I forgive Dirk and let him win me back, are you? He was giving me a speech about forgiveness earlier." I didn't know what I was going to do if Patty agreed with *that* statement.

"Marriage is a promise to not give up until you die. Dating carries no such promises. If you still love Dirk and trust him and believe the two of you can put his infidelities behind you — *permanently* — that's one thing. But you don't owe him anything, not even a second chance. Do you understand the difference?"

I nodded. I felt like the weight of the world — the *guilt* of the world — had lifted from my shoulders. I felt *free*. "I feel so much better," I told her. "I still don't know what to do, but I'm not ready to give up on Matt yet."

"Good." Patty laughed with me. "I don't know what you should do either. But you'll figure it out."

More than ever, I wanted to work things out with Matt. I couldn't wait to get home and call him.

CHAPTER 27

*W*hy in the world would I call him?

I stared up at the ceiling, thinking. After coming home from my morning hike with Patty, I took a long shower. I always think of great ideas in the shower. But I couldn't figure out what to say to Matt when I called. I needed to come up with a reason. Something that wouldn't sound stupid. I lay on my bed, staring into space, trying out different possibilities.

"Hi Matt, good to see you last night." Yeah, right.

"Hey, listen, I've thought of a name for your puppy, if you haven't thought of one already." Yes? And the name is? That's what I thought.

"What do you think of the color red, Matt? It reminds me of intense suffering, which is what I've been going through since the last time we talked."

That one might actually work, whispered a Voice.

I rolled over and pounded my pillow. I pretend-cried as I lay there. You know what I mean. You've done it. That sound when you're imitating a child crying: Hh-hhuuuuhhh-hhuuuuhhh.

My stomach growled.

The fact that it sounded like it was replying to the crying made me laugh. I smothered my laughter in my pillow. There was nothing funny about this. Unless you counted Matt's family's legend. And I hardly think the way to iron things out is to tell him how ridiculous it is.

I was tired. I was hungry. And I couldn't think of one good reason to call Matt.

But I *had* to.

I miss him, sighed Little Miss Lovesick.

"Me, too," I sighed aloud.

You really should keep some snacks by the bed, piped up another Voice.

Not unless you want to buy some larger clothes, said another.

Maybe I could explain about the emotional baggage. Somehow let him know that I'm not pressuring him for anything, just want to share the load. Of course, I'd have to make sure not to let on how much I know. Patty mentioned I might want to keep our conversation a secret for the next couple *years*. That whole privacy thing he has going.

I'll tell him I'm sorry he's angry. That was certainly the truth. Hey, maybe we should get something to eat. He seems to be in a good mood when he's eating.

I opened my eyes and rolled onto my back. My stomach growled again. Speaking of food. I rolled out of bed (the place where I do my best thinking, regardless of the fact that I'd been up for hours, hiking and all) and padded into the kitchen.

I made a piece of peanut butter and jam toast and drank a lemonade (out of OJ). I stood at the counter staring out the window, trying to come up with the right words.

"Don't hang up. It's me. I'm sorry about last night."

Nah, there's nothing to be sorry about. You didn't know he was there. You didn't do anything wrong.

Don't be a rug, remember? said Sergeant Pride.

I finished my toast and tarried over the juice. Chicken. That's me. Hmm, maybe I should say that.

"Matt, I'm just a big chicken. I'm afraid to say what I really think or what I really feel because people just don't. No one does."

I finished my juice and picked up the phone. True or not, it wouldn't work. Let's go back to option one.

The phone began to ring and I began to shake. This was a very bad idea.

"Hello?"

Hang up! screamed a Voice.

I took a deep breath. "Don't hang up. I want to apologize."

Silence.

"Matt, I'm not sure that we started out on the right foot. First, the vacation flirting when I didn't think I'd see you again. Then the weirdness when we saw each other at GT's. And now the problems we've created with our emotional baggage."

Once I heard myself say it out loud, it sounded exactly right. And undeniably stupid.

"If I could make everything perfect, if I could start over with you as a happy, healthy woman with no issues and no past, I would. I'd make us people who could tell the truth all the time, the right way, without misunderstandings."

I paused. I sounded like I had my heart on my sleeve. And like I watched soap operas all day.

I sighed. "But I can't make things perfect." I half-laughed. "I can't even make things just okay. But I can apologize for my part in making you angry. I'm sorry."

I waited. I could barely breathe.

"I don't know what you want me to say."

Typical guy answer.

"Say whatever you want, so long as it's the truth. I think we're good enough friends that we can handle it."

There was another silence, then — "I don't want to do this anymore."

My mind raced. Do what? Talk on the phone? Be honest? See each other?

"Uh, what exactly are you referring to?"

"This. The dating game. I told you at the beginning that I don't play games."

Uh, okay. Confused. What games? He's the one acting like an idiot now.

"Sorry, you lost me."

"The whole set up — you getting another guy to drool over you when I'm sitting right there." He sounded frustrated now, and more angry by the second. "Girls who try to make guys jealous to try to cure some kind of imagined commitment phobia. Everything is calculated to find the moment to move in for the kill. I've dated girls like that before and I'm not doing it anymore."

Now I was the one who was mad! But I was determined to be the calm, rational one here.

"First of all, I don't know what you think you saw, but there wasn't anyone drooling over me. Trent's a co-worker, for Pete's sake! Second—"

"I saw him. The guy has the hots for you."

"*Second* of all, I'm not trying to cure you of anything, least of all your self-described commitment phobia. Though if—"

"I don't have commitment phobia!"

"—I had to give my opinion, I'd say you're right on target."

"I'm not afraid of commitment. I'm afraid of psycho women who—"

"Are you calling me a psycho?"

"—will do anything to get a man to marry them!"

"Who's trying to get married? *You* won't even admit that we're dating! According to you, we're just eating together a lot."

"You want honesty? Fine, here's honesty! I'm not the

marrying type, okay? So you can go spread your net somewhere else. I'm not interested!"

"Well, you sure fooled me. For someone who's not interested, you've been seeing an awful lot of me!"

"Like you've ever said no when I called!"

"I didn't say no because I *liked* you. Past tense!"

"No problem! I won't be calling again. Don't worry, though. Your back-up groom looks like he's willing and ready."

"You are well and truly warped! Talk about psychos!"

Dial tone.

I can't believe that psycho hung up on me!

I can't believe that incredible hunk was psycho, exclaimed Lovesick. *What a disappointment.*

I hung up the phone and leaned against the kitchen counter, shaking. This was unbelievable. Simply unbelievable.

Good riddance, said Sergeant Pride.

That boy needs a reality check, said another Voice. *And an attitude adjustment.*

And a good smack upside the head, said Another.

I started to take a step to toss my juice bottle in the trash. Unsteady, I leaned against the counter. I couldn't stop shaking. I was so angry. And hurt.

And mystified as to how I could be so good at choosing the wrong men. I mean, the *really* wrong men.

I tossed the bottle away and moved to my junk drawer. I pulled out a black magic marker and walked to my briefcase on the kitchen counter.

I pulled out The Plan and twisted the cap off the marker. Reading through number six, I bit the inside of my lip and told myself not to cry. Then I obliterated Matt and any plans I thought I had with him.

CHAPTER 28

J stood at the kitchen table staring down at the paper with the huge black gash through it. I refused to cry. I'd cried enough over love in the last six months. No more tears. Just call me Johnson & Johnson.

I walked over to the refrigerator and looked inside. Nothing interesting. I opened the freezer. Frozen dinners. Frozen chicken. I moved the Bag o'Breasts to see if any ice cream was hiding in the back.

Nada. Then I remembered I'd finished the Godiva a few days ago while doing some paperwork.

I closed the freezer door and leaned my forehead against it. The cool surface felt good against my face. Some ice cream would make me feel even better. I grabbed my car keys and purse and left.

At the store, I got a cart and went up and down the aisles. So long as I was here, I might as well make it a regular shopping trip. Then I wouldn't have to come back.

I bought some Sun Chips, regular and cheddar. A few pounds of strawberries and apples. Then I noticed the caramel and chocolate dipping sauces, so I bought one of each.

I noticed a package of bear claws near the bakery and decided to pick that up for tomorrow. My mom always used to buy doughnuts on Sundays. Granted, this package would feed a family of four, but hey, it was all they had.

I went down the cookie aisle to get some Keebler Grasshoppers, and saw some kind of cinnamon shortbread cookie. I picked up one of each. A voice in my head suggested I keep in mind what a bad idea it is to shop while you're hungry.

Or depressed, whispered another Voice.

I pretended not to hear either of them.

When I got to the ice cream aisle, I looked first for the chocolate raspberry truffle. Yes! I bought two. (They don't always have it.) Then I noticed Ben & Jerry's was on sale and Godiva wasn't. Decisions, decisions.

Since they don't always have my flavor, I didn't put the Godiva back. But to not buy when something is on sale is a waste of money. I grabbed Peanut Butter Cup and New York Super Fudge Chunk.

Knowing I probably wouldn't feel like leaving my apartment today, I picked up a frozen pizza (the really good kind) and some mozzarella sticks. Then a package of frozen breaded mushrooms, in case I felt like that instead.

By the time I got to the checkout, I was glad I'd gotten a cart. You know how it is. You come in for one thing...

You're going to make yourself sick.

I shushed the voice.

You're just eating to keep from crying.

I shut that one up, too. If I was trying not to cry, I would've bought some wine. That's my *modis operandi*. But I didn't. So there.

I tried not to think as I drove home and unloaded my groceries.

There's nothing wrong with what I bought, I told myself.

The four ice creams are small. It's not like I was going to sit in front of the TV with a five-gallon container and a spoon.

When I was done putting things away, I found the book I was reading and curled up on the couch. I looked at the clock and began to read.

Exactly ten minutes (and four sneak peeks at the VCR clock) later, I got up and nonchalantly pulled the Peanut Butter Cup ice cream out of the freezer.

See, I waited. I didn't run to the store, then come home and dive right in. And it's not my favorite, so that means I'm not drowning my sorrows. I'm just eating ice cream like everyone does on a summer Saturday.

In fact, I'm actually saving money by buying at the store instead of going out.

See?

I curled back up on the couch with my book, my ice cream and a teaspoon. (Not a tablespoon.) My goal was to simply relax for the weekend. That's been my goal for days. It's not because of Matt.

Mid-afternoon, I took a break from my book to eat some yogurt. Very healthy. No worries about men or anything else that would make me run to high-calorie foods. I'm perfectly fine.

I finished the book about the time it was getting too dark to read without a light. The serial arsonist died in his own fire. Justice was served.

I lay on the couch breathing in the twilight. I don't know why, but this is one of my favorite times of the day. Maybe the half-light makes things look softer than they really are. I closed my eyes and snuggled deeper into the cushions. The ticking of the wall clock behind me began to sound intrusively loud. I didn't realize how many cars drove down my street until I lay there and listened to them all passing by.

How many were driven by a single someone, on their way to

an empty home? Was Matt home? Was he alone? Was Dirk alone? Trent?

When most single girls I knew had trouble finding even one intelligent, nice, single man to go out with, here I was juggling three. How ridiculous. Unreal. And it didn't even matter because I didn't want the ones who might want me, and the ones I might want, *didn't* want me.

You meant to say "one," said a Voice, *the "one" you might want.*

I sighed heavily. This was just sick and wrong.

On a whim, I pinched myself. Nothing. I pinched myself harder. Okay, ow, that hurt. Still nothing. I should never have read those time travel romances. They put wishes in your head that you can never have.

The fact is, I don't want a line of men outside my door. I'd never apply to be the next Bachelorette and choose a sexy hunk to marry while the world watched. I just want one man to love me forever. And I want to find one man I could love forever. Just so we're clear here, I want him to be the *same man*. And then I want us to live in a real house that we could make into a home.

I sighed again. God, what am I doing wrong? Which one of them am I supposed to be pursuing? Am I supposed to be pursuing *any* of them? Is there one soul mate for everyone? Or is that something we made up down here?

I thought about it for a moment. Actually, there is no mention of that in the Bible. I know the whole "man and woman become one" part, and the threatening "let no one tear asunder what God has joined together" part. But I've never read, "Sydney Riley, I created Mr. X for you to marry on September 17 of your 32nd year." That's not in there. Not in the parts I've read, anyway.

Big sigh. Well, it should be. God, if you know everything, why can't you let me in on some of it? I crossed my arms and prepared to pout.

That's so mature, said a Voice.

Better than crying.

Maybe tomorrow Pastor Mark will say something helpful. He'll be standing up front, about to begin the sermon. Then he'll suddenly frown, look for me in the crowd, and say, "Sydney Riley, are you here this morning? God just told me who you're going to marry. Come on down! You're the next contestant on 'God is Right!'"

I half snorted a tiny little laugh.

Or maybe after church, when we're all standing around talking, he'll come up to me and whisper in my ear. Maybe slide me a note. "Sydney, this is a message from God. He said to tell you, 'Door Number 3.' Does that mean anything to you?"

I'll light up with happiness and give him a hug and go find — well, whoever is Mr. Door Number 3.

I suppose those silly thoughts before I fell asleep were the reason I dreamed weird dreams. The one I remember the clearest is the one where I'm walking down the aisle at a beautiful garden wedding, flowers and guests everywhere, wearing a fantastic wedding gown. At the end of the aisle are Dirk, Matt, and Trent. All three of them!

Dirk was holding a sign with the words, "Will you forgive me?" written on it in big, black letters.

Matt had a sign that said, "Am I *The One?*"

Trent's sign read, "Do you like me? Check Yes or No." It actually had little check boxes, too.

I know, you'd think I was drinking before I went to bed. Aside from being embarrassed, there was one other thought that hounded me for the rest of the day Sunday.

Where could I buy that gorgeous wedding dress?

You probably guessed this already, but I don't want to keep you hanging. Pastor Mark did *not* give me a message from God Sunday. Not even a hint.

There was one moment that made me squirm and run home as fast as I could. David, my friend who I sat next to when we all went to have pizza two Sundays ago, came up to me and asked if I had lunch plans. I'm sure it was harmless, but that stupid dream was way too fresh in my mind. I made some excuse and left. Fast.

After moping around my apartment all day Sunday, I got ready for work Monday morning determined to have a good day, a good week.

A good life? Well, now that's pushing the limits of my Pollyanna attitude. After all, today was Monday and I had to spend most of the day with GT, starting at his office. Which is where Matt would likely be today.

No matter. I don't care. I dressed for success, but not to impress. Matt has more issues than I'm interested in dealing with. (We won't be discussing my issues today.)

I pulled on a pair of khaki Capri pants (the closest you can get to shorts and still be professional) and a white button-down cotton shirt with the sleeves rolled up. I looped a blue scarf under the collar and stepped into a comfortable pair of sandals.

One last look in the mirror — perfect. It was a "let's get down to business" outfit that also said, "I love summer."

Just my style.

I look stupid.

Shut up!

This insecurity thing is driving me crazy! Why isn't there a pill or something for it?

I hurried to the car and turned up the radio. Loud, so I couldn't hear myself think. Driving to GT's house soothed my nerves. About half the drive is along the bay on Peninsula Drive. The water calms me. I can never decide if I want my house to be on the water or in the woods. They both nurture that peaceful vibe in me.

When I get any *house, I'll feel a lot more peaceful.*

And a husband, reminded Little Miss Lovesick. *That will definitely make me feel more peaceful.*

I snorted. I was seriously beginning to have doubts about that.

GT's driveway was coming up on the right. For one awful glorious moment, I considered just driving past it. Like in the movies. Just drive past it and keep on driving.

Sighing, I flipped on my turn signal and pulled in.

I'll tell you one thing, whatever it takes, I will *not* look around for Matt. In fact, my plan is to not look anyone in the eye. Just get to GT's office and get to work.

The back door into the kitchen was open as usual, so I walked in and made a beeline for the office. Matt stood in his usual place at the butcher block, surrounded by paper.

I hurried around the other side of the counter and glanced at my watch as if I didn't see him. I saw him look up out of the corner of my eye, but I pretended I didn't.

Making it into the hallway that led to GT's office, I breathed a quiet sigh of relief. That was easier than I had hoped.

Just ignore the overwhelming feeling of guilt, said a Voice.

Yeah, like I have anything to feel guilty about!

How about amazingly bad manners, said a Voice that sounded too much like Mom.

I knocked on GT's office door. It was half-open and I could see he was on the phone. Poking my head in a bit, I saw him motion me in.

As I sat down, GT handed me a piece of paper. "Requirements for Yolanda's Cottage" was the title.

As I read through it, I got a little rush of energy — relief combined with excitement over my work again. *This* was doable.

GT finished his phone call and hung up. Turning to me, he said, "Better?"

I flashed him my Sydney-can-do-this grin. *Now* I had my confidence back.

"Perfect." All I had to do was search the MLS database and we'd have some real possibilities to look at.

"Fantastic. Set up your laptop in the kitchen or the living room and let me know when you have something for me to look at. Matt can show you where the Internet hookups are in each room."

Work here? In the kitchen? Ha! But GT had already turned back to his work and picked up the phone.

Of course I could work here. Sure. No problem. I'm a professional. I don't bring my personal problems to work. I picked up my bag, smiled at GT, and left the office. But I was working in the *living room*, not the kitchen. I'm sure Matt had no reason to go anywhere near the living room.

I found a comfy spot on the couch with the coffee table in front of me to lay out my paperwork and my portable printer. I just needed an outlet to plug in the printer. I looked behind the couch and found an outlet, but it was full.

A Frederic Remington sculpture caught my eye on an end table. I love Remington. Then I saw a cord coming out of the base. Where there was a cord, there was probably an electrical outlet. But why would a sculpture need electricity? I tentatively picked it up. The cowboy came off the horse and I heard a buzzing. I put the cowboy closer to my ear. Dial tone. I took a closer look. Apparently, you talked into his boots, his hat by your ear.

So that's what you buy for someone who has everything, said a Voice.

Yuck, said another. *Ruined a perfectly good piece of art.*

I followed the cord back behind another piece of furniture to the wall. The top of the outlet was empty. Yay. I pulled the printer cord over and tried to plug it in. Almost, just a little more give. I gave a little tug and heard a sliding sound. I looked up in time to see my laptop slide toward the floor. I dove for it and just caught it. I also caught my shins on the corner of the coffee table.

"Ah, sshhh-shooty!"

I shoved the computer back onto the coffee table, one hand grasping my left knee. But the printer cord caught around the laptop again, tightening so that I almost tripped. Frustrated, I yanked the cord out of the back of the printer and tossed the laptop safely onto the couch. I was bent over, rear end toward the kitchen, rubbing my smarting knees when I heard—

"What in the world are you doing?"

Spinning around, still holding one knee, I locked eyeballs with Matt.

I felt a growl in the back of my throat.

"Working," I said as I turned my back to him again. I heard him grunt and move, so I ignored him and went back to righting my toppled papers. I was seriously grumpy now. *This* is why I work in my office, or at home. I don't go to Internet cafes. I don't try to plug in at Starbucks. I know what works. And what doesn't.

I reached for the end of the printer cord lying nearby just as it skittered away.

"Hey!" Startled, I twisted around to find Matt wrapping the cord in a loop around his elbow. "What are you doing? I'm trying to get some work done here."

"So was I, until all the racket."

I sighed (huffed, really) and glared at him.

"Give me my cord, please." I thrust out my right hand to grab the cord, but he pulled away.

"That," he said pointing, "is where the phone is plugged in. Over there—"

"I wasn't trying to connect to the phone line."

"Over there," he said again (with a tad bit of emphasis this time), "is the Internet connection."

I snorted. "As if GT doesn't have wireless. If you'd just go away, I could get—"

"The wireless installation is part of the renovations," he interrupted. "You'll have to connect the old-fashioned way today."

Matt marched over to another wall next to the wet bar and pulled a blue Ethernet cable from behind a chair. He bent over and plugged my printer cord in the wall. Then he dropped the ends of both cables on the floor near the couch and marched past me back toward the kitchen.

"As if you know anything about how to make a connection," I muttered.

The fact that the cables would reach with room to spare wasn't half as encouraging as the thought that I might now be rid of Matt for the day. My blood pressure seemed to spike when he was around, even if we weren't getting along. I picked up the Ethernet cable and muttered dramatically, "And *stay* out."

Apparently not as quietly as I meant to.

"Excuse me?"

From the heat on my neck, I was pretty sure Matt was staring holes into my back. In the hopes that ignoring him would make him go away, I continued to plug in my equipment and turn it all on.

"Do you have a problem?"

Not turning to him, I said, "Yeah, a few."

Hey, good one, said a Voice.

"Well, one of them is rudeness."

Still keeping my eyes on my computer screen as I opened my web browser, I said, "Takes one to know one."

"*Excuse me?*" He sounded downright angry now, and that surprisingly raised my spirits.

I waved him away. "Yes, you're excused. Go!"

The silence was threatening, like the air right before a storm. Electrifying. Thrilling.

"I came in here to help you, not—"

"You did not!" My eyes shot to his. "You came in here to find out what I was doing! You don't—"

"—to be treated like some kind of—"

"—have to pretend you're some kind of—"

"*Enough!*"

Startled, Matt and I shut up and turned toward the hallway in horror. Well, I turned in horror. I'd just realized that I had been shouting like a third grader. In my client's home. Near his office. Where he was *working*.

"What in the world are you two screaming about?" GT roared. "Is this how you conduct business? Because I don't!"

I thought I was going to die. This was beyond embarrassing. Beyond humiliating.

God, please, if you're merciful, take me now!

GT looked like he was going to pop a blood vessel. Matt was staring at his boots, hands on his hips. I was afraid my mouth was hanging open. Then I realized my hands were covering it.

"Out! Both of you. Now! I've got a business to run — and not a babysitting business. Out!"

GT turned his glare straight to me. "We're done! You understand?"

Then he turned and stalked back into his office, slamming his door.

Oh, no...have I just been *fired*?

CHAPTER 29

I drove back to my office vacillating between feelings of dread and relief. The thing is, as much as GT drives me crazy, 1) I was excited to have found a method of working with him that seemed to work, and 2) I was beyond embarrassed to be fired in such a manner.

What was I going to tell Perry?

Just tell him that you can't help GT anymore. He'll probably be glad and not ask any questions.

And if he does?

Okay, tell him the truth. You'll be disqualified for Employee of the Month for the rest of your life. But hey, who needs their name on a plaque anyway?

I groaned and closed my eyes.

Eyes on the road! Eyes on the road, please!

Crap, what was I going to do?

The silence in my head was not a good indicator that fresh, innovative ideas were forthcoming. Until this thought popped into my head.

Don't tell him anything.

Huh, don't tell him anything. That has promise. That has a

sparkly glow around it. Yeah, I think I'm feeling better already. Don't tell him the client fired me. Don't tell him there was a big scene. If he asks about GT at all, I'll just look all professionally disappointed and tell him I just don't think I can help GT.

Better if you don't open your mouth at all, said a Voice. *Don't tell* him *anything.*

I ran some other errands between leaving GT's and getting to the office so I wouldn't appear early. On a whim, I stopped by Grand Traverse Pie Company on West Front Street and ordered a chocolate croissant and cranberry juice. When was the last time I sat down to eat breakfast on a weekday?

As I ate, I tried not to think. At least not about this morning. I really can't believe I was fired. I've never been fired before. But maybe it was for the best because…I couldn't think of a reason yet.

I ordered another chocolate croissant, deliberately *not* thinking about what my stress-eating was doing to my figure. What was I thinking fighting with Matt like that? Come to think of it, what was *he* thinking?

For a split second I remembered something my mother told me in the fifth grade. "Boys pick on you because they like you."

Ha! That is *so* not true. I can't even begin to explain how untrue that is. If that were true, it would mean Matt liked me, and he'd made it very clear he was totally over me.

I wolfed down the rest of my croissant and licked my fingers. Embarrassed, I looked up to see if anyone was paying attention. I was *so* upset, but with so many different emotions I didn't know *how* I felt. Humiliated topped the list. Ashamed was a close second. And guilty because…because…

Because it was exciting, said a Voice. *Exciting to engage in a passionate exchange with him, even if it was a fight.*

I needed therapy.

I finally got to the office just before eleven. There were a few people working at their desks, but it looked like the office was the usual Monday-Empty. That's one thing about people who have no time clock to punch. They work around their body clock instead, which often means a few people are in very early, a few work very late, and a lot come and go during the day.

Personally, I had really gotten to like it. I felt a bit like an entrepreneur. Every dollar I made was only because I really worked for it. No worky, no money. And since I was making a lot of money this year, I was feeling pretty pleased with myself. Until today, that is...

I waved at Carmen, who was on the phone, as I walked in and nonchalantly strolled to my desk. From the corners of my eyes, I couldn't see that anyone was paying particular attention to me. Whew. I set up my computer and got to work. GT wasn't my only client. There was always plenty of work to do. Yeah.

Around noon, Carmen stopped by my desk. "No flowers this morning. Think he finally got the message?"

I blinked, trying to register what she'd said. She smiled at my blank look and turned to walk to the kitchen. "I will miss the irises, though."

I looked toward her desk at the front of the office. No new flowers. Huh.

"It's about time," I whispered as I went back to work.

Maybe this really will be a good day, said the Pollyanna voice.

An hour later, a courier service dropped off an envelope for me. Inside was a typewritten note on expensive, personalized stationary.

"Dear Sydney, I received your message last week about the flowers and candy. I thought about it and realized you were right — they are a waste of money. So I've donated fifty dollars ($50) in your name to Habitat for Humanity. I know that's your favorite charity. You'll receive an acknowledgement from them by mail. I hope you have a wonderful day. Love, Dirk."

"For crying out loud," I whispered.

What in the world was I supposed to do about *that*?

Ignore him, said a Voice.

He's just trying to get you back, said Another.

You can't *tell him to not give to charity.*

Take his money, and ignore him.

For whatever reason, I decided the last voice sounded the most reasonable. Habitat was going to be pretty happy that Dirk was trying to make up to me if this continued. I stuffed the envelope in my briefcase and went back to work.

It was really hard to concentrate, though. I made it to almost four o'clock before I saw Perry come in. He went straight to his office without walking through the cubicle area, without even looking, in fact. I hurried to pack up my things and turn off my computer.

Chicken! said a Voice.

I just cannot deal with this right now. I need time to figure out what I should say. Then I can put a professional spin on it without resorting to lying. I hate lying.

Bawk-bawk-bawk. Chicken clucking echoed in my head.

Yeah, whatever. I'm outta here.

I couldn't believe my luck, but I managed to get out the door and into my car without anyone stopping or even noticing me. My nerves on heightened alert, I drove fast all the way home. As if Perry were actually going to follow me and specifically ask me about GT.

I was standing in front of the open refrigerator door two hours later trying to decide what to attempt to cook for dinner when someone knocked on the door. I rolled my eyes and sighed. I couldn't think of a single person I wanted to see.

I closed the fridge. Ed McMahon would be nice, coming to tell me I won thousands of dollars, but I don't think he even does that anymore. Arnold Schwarzenegger could rescue me: "Come with me if you want to live." Complete with accent. Wait, was he still governor of California?

I looked through the peephole and gasped. I tore open the

door and shrieked, "Emily!" For a moment, I forgot all about the fact that she was mad at me, too. All I was thinking was "friendly face."

Emily laughed and we tried to hug each other. Her hands were full of bags, though, making it a bit awkward.

"I come bearing the white bag of surrender," she said, holding up the bags.

"Chinese food?"

"Only the best for my best friend!"

"Come on in!" I said, imitating the announcer from *The Price Is Right*.

We cleared off the coffee table in the living room (when Em is over, we never seem to eat in the kitchen) and laid out the feast. Then we sat on the floor to eat...and to talk.

"So," I said.

"So," she said, looking at her plate. Then she looked up. Her eyes were shining and she was smiling like she'd won the Lotto.

"What?" I asked, a little alarmed, but crazy curious as well.

"When I said I was surrendering, I meant it in a couple ways. First, I'm really sorry I haven't been around much lately. You're right, I was sort of keeping a secret. But here I am to tell you what it is."

She grinned like the Cheshire Cat. Her fork swirled patterns in sweet 'n' sour sauce all over her plate.

"What?" I was so not interested in food anymore.

"I'm in love!" she shrieked. She fell back against the couch cushions and went all sappy. "He's so *wonderful*. And *hand*some. And *funny*. And *wonderful*."

"You said that one already. So tell me the truth. Do you really like him?" I teased.

Emily sighed dramatically. "I'm done, Syd. I'm done playing. I'm done having fun. I'm done looking. This is it."

Emily had *never* said anything like that before. Never. I was shocked into silence. But I looked into her eyes and I knew it really was over for her.

"Oh my gosh, Em. You're not kidding. You're really in love."

She sat up and smiled. I smiled back at her. Then she grinned and I grinned and she shrieked and I shrieked. Then we were hugging each other really tight and she was crying and that made me cry. And then she put her elbow in the sweet and sour sauce and we were laughing again.

"Wow. I can't believe it. So does he know? Is he aware that his life as he knows it is over?"

Em blushed. And I knew. "Nooo. You're not talking about getting married!"

"He hasn't actually asked me yet."

"But…?"

"Yeah, I think we're going to get married. And soon. We can't stay away from each other."

"How in the world did *this* happen? And when? It's Geoffrey, right? I thought you just met! Tell me everything!" Because Emily is my dearest friend, there was no way I could not be happy for her. Supremely happy. No matter if my love life sucked or not. So we hunkered down with our food and went all girly and giggly.

As it turns out, Geoffrey (yup, the one I met) is the reason Emily went AWOL on me. Ever since the 4th of July beach party, they've been going fishing together and going for walks in the woods by Lake Dubonnet and all this other romantic stuff. At least it sounded romantic to me.

And Emily certainly sounded like *she* thought it was romantic. Which is all that counts, I suppose. She couldn't stop talking about him and how in love they were. I sighed in my head.

Sorry, getting a bit droopy in the enthusiasm department. I'm really glad for Em. I am. I didn't think she'd settle down for a long time. But it sure looked like she was ready. And that's great. Really. It's just that...

"I'm really sorry, Sydney," she said seriously, "that I stopped calling you so much. It's just that..." She paused and looked worried.

Great. It was going to be about me. I tried to smile. "Go on."

"Well," she pushed some rice around on her plate while she talked. "It's just that you have been so unhappy, and I was sooo happy, and I didn't want to make you feel bad, but I...I didn't want your unhappiness to bring me down either." She looked up with a pained, guilty expression. "Please forgive me, okay?"

What could I say? If I were in her shoes, I'd probably have felt the same way, done the same thing, tried to protect my newfound happiness any way I could. "Of course." I leaned over to hug her and she hugged me back hard.

"So, is it okay, I mean, do you mind...would you like to hear everything?" Her voice ended high and giggly.

"Everything!" I said. "Don't leave out a single detail." She was my best friend, darn it. And I was going to be there for her during this monumental time in her life.

We had a wonderful evening together. We ate way too much Chinese food and talked and laughed for hours. When she left, I cleaned up a bit and went to bed.

And cried myself to sleep.

CHAPTER 30

J tossed and turned all night and woke up at 4:19 a.m. with a pounding headache. I got up and took some aspirin, then went back to bed. By seven, I was feeling a little better, so I got up and got ready for work.

I should've stayed in bed.

When I walked into the office, Carmen motioned me over.

"Perry needs to see you, but you better get some coffee first. I got the impression it's not good."

I couldn't remember her ever looking so pensive. That did *not* give me comfort. GT must've called Perry. I wondered what he said that got Perry so upset. Oh, I was not looking forward to this.

I dropped off my things at my desk. In a desperate act to put off the inevitable, I plugged in my laptop and turned it on and unloaded my briefcase. Then I went to the kitchen for coffee.

I stood at the counter for a minute. This was crazy. Yes, it's my fault, but honestly, Perry knows GT has been extremely difficult to work with.

Which has nothing to do with you yelling at Matt, reminded a Voice.

Oh, boy, how was I going to talk myself out of whatever trouble I was in? No, you know what? I'm just going to face it. I'll get it over with and the rest of the day is bound to be better by comparison.

I straightened my shoulders in typical hero-going-to-the-gallows fashion and walked straight to Perry's office. I knocked and went in.

"Morning. I heard you wanted to see me?"

Perry looked up. You'd never know that here sat a man who smiled almost constantly. My stomach twisted.

"Close the door and sit down. Please."

I complied. At least he said "please." That's something.

"I got a call this morning from an attorney for Jim and Lisa Carlton. You sold them a house at 219 S. Chestnut Street on January 19th this year. They said you told them they could put in a pool, but now they're finding they can't get a permit for one."

"I wouldn't tell someone they could have a pool when they can't. I don't think I'd even know if they could or not." I frowned.

"That's why it's called negligence."

"No, I know. I mean, I don't give that kind of advice. I offer lots of suggestions, but I always tell people they have to talk to the city about licenses and permits. That's standard."

"Well, that's not what they're saying. According to the attorney, they passed up a home that had a pool because they liked this one better and you told them they could put a pool in later."

"So what does all this mean?" Good thing I had a ceramic mug, not a paper cup. I had a death grip on it.

"I called my attorney and he's looking into it. He doesn't think they'll win, but going to court will still cost us a lot of money, win or lose." Perry looked at me hard.

Don't cry, don't cry, don't cry.

"Isn't there anything else we can do?"

"It's possible we can settle out of court. That means the sleazeballs get paid just for raising a stink." The name-calling was an indication that he was mad at them, not just me. It made me feel a tiny bit better.

"I'm sorry, Perry. I don't know what to say."

"There's nothing to say until we hear back from the attorney. I'll let you know what I find out."

I took that as my exit and left.

Holy crap, I was being sued. *Sued.* I'd never been sued before. I'd never sued anyone else either. *And I hadn't even done anything wrong.* I was sure of it.

I got to my desk somehow. My legs did their thing without me having to think about it. Then I just sat there, staring. I was numb. Then it hit me.

Perry doesn't know GT fired me.

I slumped over and hit my head on the desk. I wished there was someplace to hide. I took a couple of deep breaths and tried to compose myself. I wiped away the wet streaks on my cheeks and went back to work.

Don't think. Don't think about any of it.

Okay, I need to accomplish something today. I need to get something done. If it kills me, I'm going to find someone a house.

I went through the new listings looking for something that might appeal to any of my clients. My eyes caught a Mediterranean-style three-bedroom four blocks from the bay. It might be perfect for that hard-to-please older couple I was working with. Now that would be a good day: find the perfect house for difficult people.

I looked up their number and gave them a ring.

"Hi, Mr. Robertson. This is Sydney Riley from By the Bay Properties. How are you today?"

"Oh, hello, Sydney."

Something's not right, said a Voice.

"I'm calling to let you know there's a new listing for a home that might be perfect for you. It's on Wilson Road and has a view of the bay. Would you like to take a drive over there today?"

"Actually, we've already seen the house. My wife and I were driving by when the other realtor was putting the sign up. But thanks for calling."

Trying to get rid of me. Definitely not a good sign.

"What do you think? Do you have some questions I can answer? Would you like to make an offer on it?"

"The other realtor answered all of our questions, so I think we're all set. But thanks for your help."

My stomach was working itself into a knot. I'd been working with this couple for a month or more.

"Not what you were looking for, huh?"

"Well, no, it's fine. It's just right, in fact. But we already did the paperwork. So..."

I looked at the listing on my computer. Terry Adams. "Did Mr. Adams tell you that you don't need a realtor?"

"Uh, no. We asked him if he could help us since we were there, and he said he could. In fact, we're not going to have to pay the full commission since he's doing the paperwork for both sides." There was a pause. "It's business, not personal."

I took a deep calming breath. It didn't make me calmer, though. "Mr. Robertson, I can understand your desire to save money when making such a large purchase. But it's not just business; it's about business ethics, too. Did Mr. Adams mention that taking another realtor's clients is an ethical violation?"

"Listen, we're all set here. Thanks for your help. Goodbye."

And then the evil sound of the dial tone.

Once again, I found myself sitting speechless at my

computer. I looked at the time in the corner of my monitor. Wow, and it wasn't even eleven yet. What a day. What a freaking brilliant day.

Picking up the phone, I dialed the number on my screen. I was so mad I wasn't even thinking. Which is probably why I sounded so mean.

"Hi, is this Terry Adams?"

"Yes, it is, how can I help you?" He sounded nice, but I'm sure it was his cover for being an unethical creep.

"This is Sydney Riley at By the Bay Properties. I'm the realtor for the Robertson's." I didn't say anymore.

Pause. Then, "Oh."

"Are you familiar with ethics, Mr. Adams? The unwritten code that realtors respect each other's clients and don't *poach* them?"

"Sydney, I'm sorry. I did ask them if they had a realtor. They said they used to have one, but not anymore. I suspected they weren't being completely honest, but when I pushed, they said no."

"So you wrote up a contract and offered them a discount commission so you can sweep in and do both sides."

"I asked, they said no. I asked again because I'm an ethical guy, and they said no, they'd like me to draw up the papers. What did you want me to do? Call around town?" Now he was beginning to sound mad. And perhaps...understandably.

I knew there was a reason I never liked that couple. I was still furious and had no one to lash out at. And no ice cream, either.

"Sorry. I appreciate you trying." I tried to force myself to calm down. "Good luck with them." And good riddance.

"Sorry about that. These things happen to all of us. I had a turn at being on the other side last year."

I sighed and said goodbye. These things happen. Yeah, and they seem to happen to some of us more than others.

I don't know how I got through the rest of the day. I was in such a state from the last twenty-four hours that I was afraid to do any important work. What if I wrote up some paperwork wrong? What if I forgot something? What if I put taboo information in the MLS database by mistake? A few months ago, Trent got fined because he put something in the wrong section. It's crazy.

And I'm being sued for saying the wrong thing. That is, for someone *saying* I said the wrong thing.

Maybe I should move back home with my parents. Curl up under the covers and stay there. No dating. No working. No problems.

No way. My parents believe in tough love. I'm pretty sure they wouldn't let me back in just because I wanted to hide from the world. Sucks.

By the time four o'clock rolled around, I'd finished with email, filing, and other non-essential work. I decided to do a little web surfing and take off. Maybe even leave my computer here. Not take work home.

I looked at the clock what I thought was a few minutes later. It was 5:35! How does that happen? Every time I start wandering around the Internet, hours go by. Maybe there's some kind of hypnosis thing going on. You start reading something, and hit a link, then another link, and soon — they've got you! Of course, who and for what reason, I have no idea. I know, I'm mental.

I shut down my computer and picked up my briefcase. It really was much lighter without the laptop in it. I stood up. Leave it or take it? Leave it or take it? I stood next to my desk for a few seconds (probably looking like an idiot), then dropped my briefcase on my chair and began unplugging the stupid computer.

Better to have it and not need it than need it and not have it.

Yeah, and when I'm ninety and walk stooped over to the right from carrying this thing around all the time...

An old woman may be the first to be preserved and used as a demonstration to school children and business people, a local taxidermist stated. The idea was raised when an undertaker was unable to fit the woman's body into a casket because she spent her life carrying a heavy briefcase on one shoulder. Her neck and back grew into a permanent forty-degree angle.

I finally got it all together (physically only, of course) and got out the door. As I pulled my keys out, I looked up to find Dirk lounging against my vehicle.

I don't know if you can understand this, but I had taken so many hits that I didn't have anything left when I saw Dirk. I mean, I wasn't mad, I wasn't irritated. I was just, you know, there. My day couldn't get any worse.

I was being sued, after all.

"Hey gorgeous," he said. Then, "You look like you've been hit by a Mack truck. Bad day?"

"You could say that. What's up?" A serious departure, I know, from "What in the heck are you doing here?"

He looked away and then back at me. "I was thinking, maybe you'd like to get some dinner."

Was that hesitation I heard? Worse, was I actually considering it?

Hot food, prepared by and cleaned up by someone who is not you, said a Voice.

"We could drive our own vehicles. I'll treat, of course." He waited. "You look like you could use a hot meal."

I took a deep breath. "Where were you thinking?"

"On a Tuesday night, the Aerie at the Grand Traverse Resort should be quiet. Get a window seat, view of the bay."

I fiddled with my keys. I couldn't think anymore today.

"It's five minutes away. It'll be nice to unwind."

All the right words. "Just for a little while."

He smiled and touched my shoulder. "I'll meet you in the lobby."

I unlocked my door, wondering just what I had gotten myself into.

CHAPTER 31

*H*e didn't say, "I'll meet you at the top of the Empire State Building at sunset, Valentine's Day," but I should have known going to dinner with Dirk would have equally tragic consequences.

The evening started out as a refreshing escape from an otherwise horrible day. We were among the first patrons for dinner, so the service was excellent and the view — breathtaking.

Dirk was charming, attentive, sweet, and funny. The Dirk I remembered from the good days. Thankfully I was too worn out to compare and contrast with the bad days. That kind of study simply wasn't on my agenda tonight. I just wanted to be treated kindly. Kid gloves.

And I got the royal treatment. We ordered prime rib (which *always* tastes like heaven here) and seafood appetizers. Normally I'm not much of a squash eater, but what came with the meal was to die for. I made Dirk laugh when I pointed at the sunset and exclaimed that it was the same color. By the time we finished eating, I was relaxing and finally in a fairly good mood.

That must've been Dirk's cue.

"You know, Sydney," he said, playing with his wine glass, "things have gotten really messed up between us and I wanted you to know that I take full responsibility."

I didn't know what to say, so I looked out at the bay and didn't say anything. Somehow life's problems looked a little hazy around the edges when seen from sixteen stories.

"I love you, and you love me. We belong together." He paused.

I didn't give him any sign I'd heard him.

"I want to work this out, fix the problems, and move on."

I wanted to move on, too.

"What doesn't kill you makes you stronger," he said with a bit of a hopeful tone.

Or it just makes you want to lie down and die.

"Say something. Please."

I finally looked at him. "Do you know what the fifth stage of grief is?" He didn't answer. "Acceptance." I looked at him, trying to figure out who we were, why we were here.

The waiter quietly took our plates. Dirk looked up and smiled at him. Apparently, that's the cue that you're allowed to interrupt the conversation.

"Would you like to have some dessert tonight? We have a dark chocolate mousse torte with swirls of fudge and raspberry sauce as well as our usual dessert menu."

Dirk raised his eyebrows in my direction and smirked. He'd never seen me pass up a chocolate dessert.

"Yes?" he said.

"Yes," I said with a small smile.

"Two of the chocolate tortes, please. And I'll have a—"

"Dirk!"

He laughed. "You aren't ordering two?" He turned back to the waiter. "That's it."

"We have to at least try them before ordering seconds," I said, grateful to him for lightening the mood.

"Oh, yes, right, how silly of me."

We laughed. This really was rather nice. I wondered if we *could* start over. He must've seen a more serious look on my face because he picked up the conversation where he left off.

"I don't think anyone is given enough warning about how hard life will be. How easy it is to make a mistake that will change everything."

He folded his linen napkin, arranged his wine and water glasses, brushed some crumbs toward the edge of the tablecloth. "We could start slow, like this. Not even call it dating, if you want. We could have dinner, see a movie."

Ah, another with the "we're not really dating" line.

Leave it alone, said a Voice. *He's trying to be nice.*

Yes, he is. Sorry.

"Can I think about it?"

I'm pretty sure "relief" would characterize his expression. Though he was good about covering it with a drink. I think he was afraid to frighten me off.

"Sure. Take your time."

Yeah, he sounded relieved. It kind of made me want to say, "Yes, I could try again" right then. The lack of pressure sometimes is exactly what you need to move forward. Isn't that weird?

Thankfully, the waiter arrived with our desserts before an uncomfortable silence could ensue. The first bite was heavenly. I think it eased us out of the serious conversation and back to more neutral topics. About halfway through, I excused myself for the ladies' room.

I know it's silly, and maybe old-fashioned, and maybe just a show and not sincere, but Dirk stood when I stood. I really kinda liked it.

In the bathroom, I looked in the mirror when I washed my hands. How do you feel, girl in the mirror? Are you doing the right thing? I smiled a little and looked away. Maybe mistakes can be forgiven, even if they're the "I don't love you anymore; I love her" type of mistake.

I smiled in anticipation as I walked back to the table. I guess it worked out that Matt and I never really got a relationship started. Maybe my ability to forgive Dirk and move on was a sign that we could build a long-term love.

Of course, you wouldn't even be here, said a Voice, *if Matt were still talking to you.*

As I walked toward our table, I saw a woman talking to Dirk. He laughed at something she said and she leaned closer. She was tall and willowy (seriously, I'm not making that up) with long, dark, satin hair. Absolutely stunning.

As I got closer, I saw her pass a business card to Dirk. He glanced at it and put her card in his pocket. She looked up and caught my eye. She said something to Dirk, who looked up at me with a brightly innocent expression. Then the woman walked carelessly away.

I know. It sounds like something out of movie. (My whole life is a series of the worst movie scenes ever.) When I got to the table, Dirk was looking decidedly uncomfortable. And red in the face. I just looked at him, not believing and completely believing what I thought I saw.

"I don't know her." He stumbled over the words.

I raised my eyebrows.

"She just came over and started talking to me. I swear. I've never seen her before in my life."

"She gave you her card. With her phone number on it."

"I wasn't going to be rude. I'll toss it when I get home. Don't make this into something else, Sydney. I'm not leaving you for another woman again."

I stood there with my hand on the back of my chair, tapping my foot, trying to think. I picked up my purse.

"You're right. You're not."

"Syd, don't go." He never called me Syd. "Sit down and finish your dessert."

"I can't spend my life wondering if it's okay to go to the bathroom." I sighed. "Goodbye, Dirk."

And just that quietly, I walked away. No scene. No turmoil. They say you can see your life flash before your eyes when you're dying. I think I saw a flash, but it must have been my spirit dying because I managed to drive myself home just fine.

I TOSSED AND TURNED ALL NIGHT. AGAIN. I DREAMED I WAS A prisoner in a desert camp. I escaped from my cell, but as I was getting away, they saw me and started chasing me. They never caught me, but I never got away either. Just one long chase. I hate those dreams. They're really nightmares except they don't have anything particularly scary in them. They just fill you with a sense of dread.

I woke up about four to go to the bathroom. I felt horrible. I fell back into bed and went right back to sleep. Right back to the horrible dreams.

I woke up again around 7:30 and groaned when I looked at the clock. I really didn't feel good.

At 10:17, I rubbed my eyes open and tried to figure out why it looked so dark in my room. The clock must be wrong. I went to the bathroom, then peeked through the curtains when I went back to bed. Looked like it was going to storm. Pretty dark out.

Like how I feel, said a Voice.

I lay under the covers, curled around a pillow trying to figure out if I was getting up. I didn't feel good. In fact, I felt downright rotten. Must've been something I ate.

You're not sick, said a Voice.

I really don't feel good. My stomach hurts.

Your stomach doesn't hurt; your heart hurts, said the Voice.

My head hurts, too.

You're not sick. You're sad. You're heartsick.

I'm sick. I'm going to call in sick to work. I'll lay in bed the rest of the day, eat chicken soup, and then I'll feel better.

Chicken soup won't make you feel better, said the Voice. *It didn't make you feel better last time.*

I reached for the phone on the nightstand and dialed the office. Carmen picked up on the second ring.

"Hey Carmen, it's Sydney. I'm not coming in today. I'm really sick."

You're lying, said the Voice.

I'm not lying. I feel awful.

"Oh, hon, you sound awful."

See? Told you.

"Can you let Perry know? And take my calls?"

"No problem. Do you want to forward your cell here for the day?"

"Mm, that sounds good. When I can get out to wherever I left it, I will. If you think about, will you email me at the end of the day and remind me to un-forward it?"

"No problem. You just get some sleep and take care of yourself."

I hung up and went back to sleep. Thankfully, the awful dreaming was over. I just closed my eyes and it was like turning out the lights.

It was afternoon when I finally really woke up. My growling stomach was the villain. I thought I was going to die I was so hungry.

Told you you weren't really sick, said the Voice.

I splashed cold water on my face. My eyes were all gritty and hurt as if I had fallen asleep crying. But I hadn't.

You probably cried in your sleep.

I was too tired and too *sick* to have a conversation with

myself. Today, my plan was to ignore everyone and everything and feel better.

In the kitchen, I found my cell phone and remembered to forward my calls to the office. The little envelope was flashing showing I had new voice mails, but I decided to check them after I ate.

I found a can of chicken and rice soup and added more rice to it. When it was hot, I took a small bowl of it into the living room and sat down on the couch in front of the TV. I flipped through channels aimlessly. I love not having to share the remote.

Pillow Talk was on, so I dropped the remote and ate my soup. When that movie ended, *Bringing Up Baby* came on. By then, I was curled up on the couch with my pillow and my softest blanket. I fell asleep in the middle of *Baby*. The reason I know this is that I woke up with a jolt when thunder crashed over my head.

Oh, I hope it rains. Soon. The rest of the night. I always sleep so soundly when it's raining. I couldn't tell what movie was playing, so I flipped the channels and came upon *How To Lose a Guy in 10 Days*. I love that movie. I own it, but I'll watch it if it's on, even if there are commercials.

At the next commercial break, I went in the kitchen and opened the freezer. Ooo, breaded mushrooms. I'd forgotten about those. I turned on the oven and dumped the whole boxful on a pan. (It's not like it was that big a box.) I stuck the tray in without waiting for the oven to warm up and opened the fridge. After staring at everything, I pulled out a stick of string cheese and a strawberry-kiwi Snapple.

I returned to the couch and watched the movie. When the mushrooms were done, I dove in. I've had better in restaurants, but these were good. I got so caught up in the movie, I'd eaten the entire pan of breaded mushrooms before I realized it. I cried when Andie got all mushy about how Ben's family dotes on her.

I cried again when those nasty girls (who remind me of the Siamese cats in *Lady and the Tramp*) trick the guys into telling Andie about the bet.

I hate it when people try to break other people up. Do they do it on purpose? Are they just not thinking about the consequences? Are they really malicious or just plain old-fashioned selfish?

I wondered what happened to the girl Dirk left me for earlier this year. Wow, was it only this year? I wondered if he left her for someone else, or if she left him. I wondered if he called the woman from last night.

And who takes someone's phone number when they're out with someone else just to be polite? Does that sound like a line of crap or what?

I really wasn't feeling well, so I curled up in a little ball and channel-surfed some more. I finally flipped off the TV in frustration. (As in turned it off, not gave it the finger. Though for sixty bucks a month and there's not even something on I want to watch, I should've given it the finger.)

I sighed and pulled myself up and over to the bookcase. At the bottom, near the back, were some of my favorite romance novels. Just a few that I enjoy so much I can't help but read them again and again. I picked up *The Gift* and *A Knight in Shining Armor* and brought them back to the couch, turning on the light on the way.

Which one to read? Fall in love with a pirate who turns out to be your husband? Or fall in love with a knight from four hundred years ago after you've been dumped by the guy you thought was going to propose? The choice seemed obvious. I wanted to read again how you can find true love even after someone who *says* they love you throws you out like yesterday's newspaper. (Okay, I recycle, but you get my drift.)

I read for a while, then decided to see if anything new was in the fridge. The pizza in the freezer looked so delicious, but the whole process of having to take it out of the box, put extra cheese on it, heat it up — too much work. So I took a wiser course of action. I ordered a delivery pizza. Deep-dish crust, Hawaiian toppings, extra cheese. Yeah, baby.

When it came, I opened the box and breathed in the magnificent scent of hot cheese. Mmm, now this is happiness.

I ate two slices while I continued to read. An hour later, I reached for a third. Oh man, it was delicious at room temperature, too. Then I had another piece. Good stuff. I wouldn't say my stomach hurt, exactly, but I probably should've quit sooner. In any case, I felt better. And the girl was getting her guy in the book. That's what counted.

As I read, I tried not to wonder if *this* girl would get *any* guy *ever*.

The thought kept hounding me, so I got up and plucked a pint of Godiva ice cream from the freezer. The more I wondered if I'd ever be happy, the more sick I felt, so the more ice cream I ate. Not helping.

I got up and found the Grasshopper cookies. They'd be great with the chocolate ice cream. "Lady Godiva," I said, "meet the Keebler Elves." Then I put a whole cookie in my mouth, followed by a spoonful of ice cream, and chewed it all up together. Ahh, *now* I felt better.

I ate almost all of the ice cream and a third of the cookies, crying as the heroine loses her man. I put the ice cream back but left the cookies on the couch beside me — just in case.

I got to the part where the girl finds her guy again (albeit, four hundred years earlier). I felt awful. I was *never* going to be happy. I *knew* it. Even though I was reading a funny part, I cried anyway.

CHAPTER 32

I stood on the walkway of the castle wall in a flowing white gown. A strong breeze blew my hair around, but the flowers never came undone. Next to me stood an entirely *too* handsome man in a Scottish kilt. Wow. I've got to be the envy of every girl in three counties.

A vicar stood before us with a Bible in his hands. "We are gathered here—" But the scenery changed and suddenly I was in a little country church. The man next to me wore khaki's and a white shirt, not at all dressed up. I looked down to see the beautiful wedding gown I'd had on in that other dream.

"Do you take this woman—"

The man next to me smirked. I couldn't marry him! I tried to get away, but a crowd pressed in from behind. No matter which way I turned, there was no escape. I tried to put my hands over my ears, but they were full of flowers.

"I definitely don't. No way," he said. "Not in a million years."

There was a break in the crowd. I ran and ran and found myself in the woods. I'd be safe there. Then another man was next to me, holding me and comforting me. He started kissing me. His tongue was in my mouth and I couldn't breathe.

He pulled back for a second and I saw he had fangs like a vampire. He was going to suck the life out of me! I twisted and turned, trying to get away. He kissed me again and my stomach rolled. I was going to throw up on him.

I woke up suddenly, sweating and nauseous. It took me only a few seconds to realize that I was going to be sick. And not in a dream. If I didn't move soon—

I stumbled from my bed, dizzy and disoriented.

Oh, this is bad. Very bad. I made it to the toilet just in time.

I want my mom.

I leaned my head against the bathroom wall and moaned. My whole body hurt.

When I felt a tiny bit better, I started to get up and go back to bed. Barely into a standing position, I paused, leaning heavily against the sink. Oh, not good. My knees buckled and I leaned over the toilet again, retching.

The only positive thought that crossed my mind was, I am so glad I cleaned the bathroom recently. Of course, that thought was quickly followed by, now I'm going to have to clean it again.

I fell half asleep against the wall. Next thing I knew, Dirk was in the bathroom. When I started to ask him how he got in, he smiled. He had fangs. I woke up and dry-heaved into the toilet. I began to cry.

God, please help me. Please, please, please.

My stomach muscles hurt and my throat ached.

Please, please, please, God.

As I fought to keep from retching again, I thought how different life might be if I were married. I wouldn't be alone in the bathroom trying to keep my hair out of last night's supper. I wouldn't be sitting on the bathroom floor wishing I could reach the sink and a drink.

I wouldn't be alone.

I fell half asleep again. When I woke up, I tried to move a little, checking out how that felt. I looked toward the sink, so thirsty. "So close and yet so far" — the lyrics to that song danced through my brain. The last time I stood up, I threw up. I wasn't willing to try that again. If only someone were here.

This is how old people die, said a Voice. *They fall in the bathroom away from the phone, too far from the front door to yell even if someone came.*

A 28-year-old Traverse City woman was found dead in her bathroom today. Her apartment manager came in to have the place cleaned after the woman's lease expired. Apparently she'd died by the toilet months before.

Note to self: don't ever prepay the lease.

I wrinkled my nose. What a disgusting way to go. I've *got* to get up.

I made it to my knees, leaning against the bathtub. Shaking, but staying upright. Whatever may or may not be left in my stomach was staying down. Progress.

On my knees, I crawled toward the sink, still using the tub for support.

The tub! More water and closer.

Eagerly, I moved to the faucet end of the bathtub. I turned on the cold water and put one hand under the spout. I cupped the water to my mouth, drank, spit, drank again.

Oh thank you, God! Thank you, thank you, thank you!

I rinsed out my mouth, drank a little, and rinsed my hot face.

Sighing gratefully, I turned off the water. Slowly, I got to my feet and reached for a towel. Don't throw up. Don't throw up.

Waiting. Nausea, but nothing else. I dried my face, rested a moment, then made my way slowly back to bed.

I can handle an obituary about dying in my sleep, but not about puking up my guts in the bathroom.

Investigators believe Ms. Riley's final act was to wipe down the toilet after a night of vomiting. She apparently passed out and hit her head on the bathtub, never regaining consciousness.

God, if my last accomplishment on earth is to clean the

bathroom, help me to rethink my priorities and go to the beach instead.

I slept again, really slept this time, and didn't wake up until after ten.

Stomach muscles aching. Throat stinging. In serious need of mouthwash. I groaned into my pillow. What a way to start a day. At least yesterday I just felt yucky. Today, I felt like I'd been run over by a Mack truck. (Who was ever run over by a Mack truck, and when? Why do we always say that? And wouldn't you look and feel worse than even the sickest person if you got hit by a semi?)

I groped around on my bedside table for my phone. I explained to Carmen about my rendezvous with Ralph all night. (I once heard a sailor say that's what they called it — ralphing.) She clucked over me and promised to have someone answer my calls for a day or two. I hung up and wished again for water. I was going to have to find a way to get to the nearest source before my throat caught fire and set off the smoke alarm.

I could imagine the added interest if my death announcement included scientific investigation into spontaneous combustion. Well, at least I would have contributed something to the world by my death, if not by my life.

That's a pretty lousy way to look at yourself, said a Voice.

Well, I feel pretty lousy right now.

Because you ate an enormous and disgusting combination of food yesterday.

No, because I have the flu. Obviously.

You don't have the flu, insisted the Voice. *You've been here before. This is stress-induced. You've got to snap out—*

I turned on the radio part of my alarm clock.

I have the flu.

I carefully, slowly made my way to the kitchen and filled my biggest glass with water. Sliding back under the covers, I wished Matt were here. The old Matt. The one who liked to be with me.

My eyes closed. I pictured us in his house with his puppy. I'd plant rose bushes and lilac bushes and he'd come home to a sweet-smelling, beautiful house. And a sweet, beautiful wife who loved him. That's what he'd think anyway, that I was sweet and beautiful.

He'd kiss me and tell me how lucky he was. We'd argue about who was luckiest. Then he'd take me to the bedroom to "make up." It would be like the night I was over there before, only we wouldn't have to stop. If Matt thought that was only first base, in the dream life I'd get to find out what he meant by a home run.

I sighed. It wouldn't happen. Not with Matt anyway. It was over. All we do now is yell at each other or ignore each other. I'd end up single, or with someone like Trent who was nice and sweet and that's about it. Knowing my luck, I'd die of old age in my nineties. Alone. No chance I'd actually die of food poisoning this week.

My luck just isn't that good.

"Hi, this is Sydney — not Australia! Leave a message and I'll call you back as soon as I can."

Beep.

"Sydney, Perry. I hear you've got something. Well, don't bring it back here. Get better and we'll see you later. I'll have Trent handle your workload for now. Bye."

"Hi, this is Sydney — not Australia! Leave a message and I'll call you back as soon as I can."

Beep.

"Hey, baby, this is Mom. I hope you're feeling a little better. I called your cell phone and the receptionist said you were home sick. Call me when you're up. Love you."

Beep.

"Syd, Trent here. Call me when you can. Do you have the paperwork for the Olsen's or is it here at the office? Hope you feel better. Later."

Beep.

"Hey, sister-friend. I guess you must actually be sick. I thought maybe you were playing hooky. (laughs) I called your cell yesterday and today, but Carmen answered both times. I hope you're okay. Call me. I'll bring you some soup or something. Geoffrey says hi. (sighs) You're just gonna love him. Maybe we can have dinner or lunch or something this weekend. Hurry and feel better. Call me so I know you're okay. Bye."

I lay in bed, trying to sleep, waking up every time the phone rang. Since my cell phone was forwarded to the office, everyone was calling me at home. Screening calls via the answering machine is wonderful, but only when you're not trying to sleep.

I listened to everyone leave messages, completely uninterested in picking up the phone. The sound of my voice was making me sicker. Maybe I should change the message. *Hi, this is Sydney. Don't leave a message if it's not important.*

Little grumpy, are we? asked a Voice.

Maybe I should record, *You know what to do.* Short and to the point.

Definitely grumpy, the Voice said.

Maybe I should just turn it off and unplug the phone. Of course, Mom would eventually send over the police. This was one of the few moments I wish I had voice mail instead of an answering machine.

I fell asleep again, escaping into the darkness. I woke up when someone called my name.

"Sydney? Hey, sweetie, where are you?" Emily.

I moved a pillow off my head and blinked toward my

bedroom door. A moment later, Em was sitting on the side of my bed.

"Oh, you look awful, honey. What's wrong?"

I started to tell her I was sick, probably food poisoning, but no words came out. I just started bawling. I cried and cried until I was exhausted. I curled up into a tighter ball. My whole body hurt.

Emily held my hand while I cried. When I finally stopped, she said, "Tell me what's wrong, so I can help, okay?"

I shook my head and buried in my face in the pillow. "You can't help. I'm messed up."

"Well, you could use a shower, but I don't think you're that messed up." She tried to tease me into a better mood. Not working.

"I *am*. No one wants to love me. *I* don't even love me. I want someone who doesn't want me. The one who'd be perfect for me doesn't have sparks. Dirk saw another girl when he took me to dinner. I'm getting sued. And I threw up all night!" I rubbed more tears away from my sore eyes.

"Wait, you lost me. You're getting sued? By who? And how many guys are you seeing, anyway?" Emily got up and brought me some Kleenex.

"I told you I was messed up!" I blew my nose. The only part of my body that didn't hurt right now.

"Well, I always feel better after a hot shower. So how about I go run the water for you, then when you come out, we'll have soup from the Grand Traverse Pie Company, and we'll sort it all out, huh?"

I looked up at her being all nice to me when I didn't deserve it. "I love their soup," I said in a small voice.

She smiled. "I know you do. That's why I took off work early and brought you some."

"I don't deserve you." I started to cry again.

"Hey, stop that," Emily said, handing me more Kleenex.

"I *don't*. I've been so mad at you and you're being so nice to me."

"That's what best friends are for, remember? Now get up. I'll go start the shower for you."

It should've come as no surprise to me that Emily was absolutely correct. The shower made me feel *much* better. Between clean clothes, clean hair and some *amazing* broccoli and cheese soup, I knew I was once again in the land of the living.

"Feel like talking now?" Em asked as she took the bowls to the kitchen. She brought back two tall glasses of water. "Drink this. You're probably dehydrated."

"I had a plan, you know. The Slocum's had a plan and they got everything they wanted. So I decided to do the same. But it didn't work. I couldn't even fix myself, let alone other people." This was so depressing. Still, it felt less horrible when Emily was here. At least I wasn't alone.

We curled up on opposite ends of the couch, facing each other, like we'd done for every other heart-to-heart. Only no chocolate or ice cream or anything. Em was afraid I might throw up again.

"Why not? What didn't work?"

I got up and pulled The Plan out of my briefcase. I handed it to her and sat down again, hugging a pillow to my chest. She read it without saying anything.

"What's wrong with me? Why can't I be happy? That's all I want. But it seems like all I do is work to make other people happy, then they leave. I find people the perfect house, and they buy it and leave. I can't find people the perfect house, and they leave me for another agent. I give Dirk love, support, loyalty, everything. He gives me nothing. Well, a couple good years of keeping my hopes up, then Heartbreak."

"That's not 'nothing,'" said Em.

"It sure as heck isn't."

She chuckled. "I'm sorry. I'm not laughing at you."

I sighed. "I don't know what to do. Why didn't my plan work?"

Emily watched me silently. I knew she was waiting for me to tell her it was okay to speak her mind. That's one of the things I love about her, she never forces her opinions on people. Which is why I value her opinion.

"Tell me," I said. I swore to myself I'd do whatever she said if it even *sort of* sounded like it might work.

"People are happy or unhappy because they choose to be," she said gently.

"I didn't *choose* to be unhappy. I was unhappy because Dirk led me to believe we'd get married and—"

"Dirk made choices and you made choices. You chose to not get over the hurt."

"Okay, but Matt made like he liked me, then was all cool, then made like he liked me again, then completely blew me off! I didn't make any of that happen."

"Have you ever thought that Matt might have more on his mind than Sydney Riley's happiness?"

Ouch. I played with the edge of the pillow, remembering my conversation with Patty. "Patty told me some things about his parents. I think he's afraid he might turn out like his father." I looked up at Em. "He left when Matt was little and never came back."

Em made a sympathetic face. She rearranged herself on the cushions.

"Remember what you told me on the ride home from the fishing trip? You said you were sitting on the porch and realized you had *decided* to find some peace up there in the woods. And you *did*. But I think it's a daily choice, regardless of what's going on around you. Whether you're on vacation or home dealing with your problems. That's goes for you and Matt both. He'll have to choose to be a better man than his dad — or not."

We sat quietly, thinking. I drank some more water. "Do you think I'm like Ashley Judd's character in *Someone Like You*? You know, blaming everyone else and not realizing she caused a lot of her own problems?"

Em smiled. "You really do watch too many movies. No, I don't think you're that messed up. After all, you've never unveiled your fake identity on national television, right?"

I smiled and shook my head.

"But she got things figured out in the end, and so will you."

"She got Hugh Jackman in the end. Maybe Matt could be Hugh Jackman."

Emily laughed. "But will you find that he's a romantic-at-heart TV producer, or a cigar-smoking mutant with claws?"

I finally laughed. Oh, that felt good. "I think I'd take Matt either way." I sighed. I didn't feel that good anymore. Because I wasn't ever going to get Matt. I told Emily so.

"Do you love him?" she asked quietly.

I shrugged. "Don't want to think about it." I traced the pattern in the couch cushion. "When we came back from the fishing trip, I made a list of qualities I'd like to find in a man." I didn't look at Em. "Based on him."

She looked thoughtful. "If you ask me, part of the reason your plan didn't work is because you did it all by yourself. I think these things require group effort. That's probably why it worked for the Slocum's — they did it together." She looked at The Plan, then put it on the coffee table. "So you and Matt had a fight, right?"

I grunted. "You could say that."

"Do you think you could get him to talk to you again? Have lunch?"

"Not in a million years."

"Perfect!"

I looked up. "How is that perfect?"

"'Cause you've got nothing to lose!"

CHAPTER 33

Since I had already completed (or messed up) most of the items on The Plan, Em and I only worked on two areas for The New Plan — GT and Matt. She didn't really have any thoughts for helping me with GT, but when I told her my idea, she thought it was wonderful and wrote it down.

Then we worked out a plan to win Matt back — if it were possible. It was daring, with a huge chance I'd be humiliated again. But Em was right. I'd never run into him in all the time I'd lived here until we both ended up working for GT at the same time. If he chose to blow me off, there was a really good chance I'd never see him again. That was the only thing giving me courage.

Perry called Friday morning and told me not to come into the office until Monday. Didn't want anyone else to get sick. I didn't try to explain, but thanked him for his kindness. I sat at the kitchen table and did an Internet search on the house GT liked so much. An hour or two and a couple of phone calls later, I leaned back in my chair and took a deep breath. I'd never done anything like this before.

I picked up my phone and dialed.

"Hello?"

"Hi, is this Mrs. Andrews?"

"Speaking."

"Hi, my name is Sydney Riley. I'm a realtor with By the Bay Properties. I have kind of a strange question for you."

By Friday night, I was feeling much better and agreed to go out with Em and Geoff. Sorry, *Geoffrey*. He treated us to a little Italian place that was crazy busy. When the maître d' greeted him by name, I realized he wasn't kidding when he said he came here all the time.

I looked for all the things Emily had gushed about in her man, and — I can't lie — I looked for hidden faults as well. I kept reminding myself, *I choose to be happy for Emily, I choose not to be jealous.* Surprisingly, the fake-it-until-you-make-it advice of my old teacher was still working. I had a great evening. By the end of the night, I had no doubt that the two lovebirds were equally smitten.

They're so *cute*, sighed Little Miss Lovesick.

It was true. They were.

Saturday, I decided to try and catch up a bit at the office, just for an hour or two. I threw on shorts and a polo shirt thinking I might wander around downtown to catch some sun and a bit of exercise. Which I desperately needed after my binge eating lately. Some of my shorts were too tight for comfort. I planned to work on healthier habits all around.

As I was leaving, a young couple walked in. "Can I help you?"

"Hi, we were just walking by," said the guy.

"We were wondering how to find out, you know, what you need to have, or do, or whatever, to buy a house," the girl said.

"Yeah." He put his arm around her and they grinned at each other. "How does this work?"

I tried to tame my smile so it wouldn't look like I was laughing at them. If they were old enough to drink, I'd be surprised. They looked so darned *earnest*.

"Come on back and we'll see what we can do." I turned to lead them back to my desk.

"Oh, but weren't you leaving? We don't want to interrupt. We can come back." The girl hung back.

"Yeah, we probably can't get anything now anyway."

I smiled and urged them to follow me to my desk. "Let's at least talk about where you're at and what your plans are. You might be surprised at how qualified you already are. If not, I can help you create a plan for getting a house later."

They smiled at each other again and shared a quick, excited kiss.

I choose to be happy. I choose not to envy them.

The voices in my head finally had something *helpful* to say.

Marty and Scout McAlester (she's Marty and he's Scout — don't ask; I don't know) had fairly good jobs for their age. Scout was assistant manager at a restaurant (amazingly, he *was* twenty-one) and Marty worked as a receptionist at a dentist's office. She was going to school at NMC at night to become a dental assistant. Their plan was for Scout to get his food service degree when Marty finished.

Though they couldn't afford to buy a house now, they seemed eager to take any advice I was willing to give. By the time we finished, they had a plan for building credit and getting a savings account started just for the house.

"Thank you so much," Scout said, pumping my hand with exuberance.

"This is great," said Marty, looking at the notes they'd taken. "We'll call you as soon as we can. Thanks so much for helping us today. This is so cool!"

They rushed out, eager and excited. I sat at my desk watching them. I could just see the glass front door if I leaned far enough to the left. They paused as they exited to give each other a hearty kiss. I chuckled. Then I took a deep breath.

That was great. Honestly. I closed my eyes and smiled, picturing them sitting here discussing whether they could open a savings account today, or if they'd have to wait until Monday.

This is happiness, said a Voice.

I opened my eyes and blinked. Well, yeah, I guess this *is* happiness. I smiled again. I loved helping people like this. I'd gotten tangled up inside focusing on my own wants and needs. But now I remembered again that I enjoyed helping other people find happiness, too.

I felt a little pang that it had taken so long for me to see how far off course I'd gotten. Thinking about the number of houses I'd sold since I moved to Traverse City, I had to admit — I was pretty good at this. How many people get to enjoy their work and be good at it, too?

The rest of the weekend was relatively uneventful. I saw David in church sitting next to a very cute blond. I caught his eye from across the room later and raised my eyebrows at him. He grinned and turned away. I couldn't tell for sure because of the distance, but I think he even blushed.

Later, soaking up some sun while I pretended to read, my cell phone rang. The call I was waiting for. I made some notes, thanked them and hung up. Then I smiled for about five minutes straight.

Monday morning, I woke up nervous. I'd slept fitfully. Tired, but awake long before the alarm went off. I wasn't sure what to expect today. Should I go to GT's house and try to apologize, try to get him back as a client? Should I go into the office and pretend nothing happened, pretend that we parted amicably? But then what about The New Plan Em and I had crafted?

As I waited for my toast to pop up, my cell phone rang. (I

have to admit, those few days of not hearing it ring, not having another appendage — a bit of heaven.)

"This is Sydney."

"Sydney!" GT's voice boomed in my ear. "I hope you're feeling better. Are you on your way here yet?"

"Oh." I paused, trying to think through what was happening. Wasn't I fired? Maybe not.

I looked at my watch. 9:15. Technically I should already be there. "I'm sorry, GT. To tell you the truth, I thought you fired me. Did I get that wrong?"

"No, no, that was a misunderstanding. I got it out of Matt what's going on between you two. I told him he's ten times the fool to let you go. But I'll take care of that later. How soon can you be here?"

It made me nervous that GT the matchmaker had spoken to Matt. About us, I mean. And *what* was he going to take care of later? "Uh, I can be there in half an hour. Will that work?"

"I'll see you then." GT hung up before I could ask any more questions. My mind was overwhelmed with a swirl of thoughts and emotions. Did he mean that he fired me but he realized he shouldn't have? Or did he mean I misunderstood about being fired? And what exactly did he say to Matt?

I buttered my toast, grabbed a napkin, keys, and briefcase, and headed out the door. If all went well, I'd make GT a happy client today.

When I got there, I walked through the empty kitchen and back to the office. GT was on the phone. He mouthed, "I'll meet you in the kitchen in a few minutes," so I backed out of the office and wandered toward the kitchen.

I say wandered, but what I did was walk as slowly as humanly possible. In my mind, the kitchen was Matt's territory. I probably needed to apologize to him, but I wasn't sure how. (*That's* become a mantra in my life recently.) What should I say?

I was staring at a picture in the hallway, thinking, when the subject of my ruminations barreled into me. My left shoulder smashed into the wall. Matt reached out and caught me as I started to tumble backwards.

"Umf! Excuse me! Are you okay?" His face was at least six inches away, but I could smell his shampoo or aftershave or something. The scent — *not* his proximity — made my heart race. Oh, who was I kidding? Of *course* it was his proximity!

His hands still grasped my shoulders, warming my cool skin under my cotton shirt. My breathing felt shallow, too light for someone who needed to keep her wits.

I moved my left shoulder, which stung a little. Reaching up to rub it, my hand touched his. Nine-volt batteries again.

"Sorry, I didn't see you. You all right?" Matt didn't move away. His voice sounded funny, and he rubbed my shoulder some more. I had the strangest sense of déjà vu from when we met in Abundance Creek. Then, I didn't want to meet a man. Now, it was looking like the man wasn't so happy to be meeting me. Matt moved back a step and dropped his hands.

Stop it, I told my pounding heart. Like that would work.

"Hi," I said. D'oh! I sounded all girly-girl. And I didn't even answer his question. What a doofus. "I'm fine."

Yeah, you sound fine, said a Voice. *He's going to know.*

Know what? I couldn't think when he was staring at me.

That you're completely freaking in love with him!

Oh. Right.

It occurred to me that we were standing there staring at each other while I was having an internal dialogue. Or would it be a monologue since the Voices are all me?

"Hey, uh—" I stopped. I wanted to apologize, but I didn't know how. Or when. Or if. No, that's not true; there is no if. I really did need to apologize.

"I, um, really want to, uh, apologize." I stumbled all over my words, my eyes falling to his shirt buttons. The guilt lay too heavy to keep my eyes up. I heard him clear his throat. I can't do this! What should I say?!

"I've, uh, been—" I cleared my throat. I've been messed up in the head, I wanted to shout. I've handled everything badly, and I want to start over.

I took a deep breath. I looked into his eyes, beautiful blue, intense, lovely. Oh, I want to tell him everything. Right now.

No! said a Voice. *Stick to The New Plan!*

I took another calming breath, eyes on his shirt again. "I'm sorry that I've acted so badly around you. I hope you'll forgive and forget."

I chanced a look up and internally breathed a sigh of relief. No anger, no condemnation, perhaps even a touch of compassion — or something like it.

I thought maybe Matt was thinking about saying something, but before he did, GT came around the corner. He stopped and grinned when he saw us.

Oh my gosh, I'm going to die.

No cute little obituaries popped into my head this time. All I wanted was to get out. I'd made peace with Matt as best I could. Now it was time to get back to work.

I put on my professional face and turned to GT. "I may have some good news for you, GT. Would you like to talk in your office?"

"I'll be there in a minute, darlin'." GT stood with his arms folded across his chest, grinning like he expected a show. I was *not* going to give him one. Not again.

I briefly met Matt's eyes, smiled a bit, and hightailed it back down the hall. I heard an "Ow!" behind me and a lot of whispering.

Oh, geez, this is beyond embarrassing!

I sat down in GT's office and put one hand over my eyes. What am I doing? That was so stupid. I should've emailed him or — or left him a voice mail or something. Please, please, please, don't let GT mention it!

GT entered and sat down behind his desk. "So, what's the good news?"

Back to business. Business, I can handle. In fact, this particular piece of business made me fairly excited. I leaned forward.

"Well, you know that house we drove past a few weeks ago over on Sunset?"

"The one I said I liked? With the big yard?"

"Yes, that one." I chuckled. "I don't know if you realize how many times you've brought it up. You want a yard like that one, shade trees like that one—"

"Is it for sale?" GT leaned forward excitedly.

I smiled. "Yes and no. To make a long story short, I took a chance and called the owners, asked if there was anything that would entice them to move."

"And?"

"If the price is right and you're willing to wait for them to find what they're looking for, they're willing to talk. To you. They weren't planning on putting it on the market for another year or so."

GT thumped his hand on the desk so hard Matt probably heard it in the kitchen. "Well, let's go get it!"

I laughed. I *really* love my job!

CHAPTER 34

"*I* think he thinks I'm getting senile, but I found out for you," said Patty a few days later.

I'd been waiting breathlessly for her call. (Literally having a hard time breathing!) It was the key to the final phase of The New Plan. Emily was right. Things were working much better now that I had friends helping.

"He can't go out this weekend because they're working overtime. Next weekend is Labor Day, so the whole crew has the weekend off. He's planning on taking the boat out on Saturday."

"Any idea when?" I made notes on a pad from my briefcase.

"I asked him if he wouldn't mind taking Bob and me out," said Patty, "but that we wouldn't know for sure until that morning if we could go. He figured he'd probably leave about seven and get back around one or two. The boat doesn't have a cover, so it gets hot out on the water in the middle of the day."

I blew a breath through pursed lips. "Wow. Thanks, Patty. I owe you!"

"If this works, the only thing you owe me is bringing him over here for dinner."

I laughed. "Deal!"

"Now, are you sure you know where you're going?" she asked. She'd already explained it to me twice, but she said the marina where Matt kept his boat was a frustrating maze of docks.

"I'll go down tomorrow when Matt's working and make sure I can find it." I underlined the directions on the pad. Then I put a star next to them. Then I wrote "Matt" next to the star. I curbed the urge to doodle any more. If this didn't work, my heart...well, I couldn't think about that right now.

"All right," Patty said. "Don't forget to call me and tell me how it all works out. And you come over for dinner one night with or without that scallywag, understand?"

I really, honestly, truly love Patty. What a great friend! "I will," I promised.

I hung up and stared at my notes. My stomach lurched. I hugged my knees up against my chest. Did I have the courage to do this?

I dialed Emily. "Hey, you have a minute?"

"Did you find out?" She sounded breathless, too.

"Just now."

"Where are you?"

"At the kitchen table, feeling like I'm going to vomit."

Em laughed. I grinned.

"In some sick way, that's probably a good sign. Okay, here's the deal. Geoffrey and I are going to keep you busy as much as we can until it goes down. By the way, when will that be?"

"Not until Saturday of Labor Day weekend." I underlined the date on my pad. Over and over again. Oh, getting nauseous, need to stop.

"Okay, that's only about ten days. No problem. Anyway, come over to my place tonight about six. We'll have dinner and watch a movie. Brace yourself, though. No chick flicks."

"Aww, you're kidding. Well, I don't think I can make it then."

Em giggled and lowered her voice. "The good news is he loves sci-fi as much as me!"

I laughed. "If you make me watch *Alien 3* tonight, I won't come to the wedding."

"Sydney!" she said in a loud stage whisper.

"What? He can't hear me. Wedding, wedding, wedding!" I all but shouted. It echoed in my kitchen.

She giggled. "Six tonight at my place. Bye!"

"Bye." I laughed and hung up. Now that I was getting used to Emily-in-Love, I was getting a big kick out of it. She was just as fun, but easier to tease.

SATURDAY OF LABOR DAY WEEKEND. THAT'S TODAY.

I rolled over in my bed and put a pillow over my head. I didn't have the courage. I couldn't do it. Even if I could make myself get there, I'd throw up on his shoes — or worse!

What if he says yes?

What if he says no?

What if he says yes, insisted Little Miss Lovesick. *I won't know what to do.*

Now *that* would be a shocker.

I pulled the pillow away and stared at the ceiling. Every time I got cold feet in the last ten days, Emily would remind me that if I want the best in life, I have to take risks. Did I think Matt was the best I could do in the "happily ever after" department? Then I had to try.

"He's better than the best," I whispered to myself.

I made a scared whining noise in the back of my throat and got up to take a shower. It's a good thing Emily knows me so well. She insisted that I go to breakfast with her and Geoffrey. They'd entertain me (i.e., babysit me, i.e., make sure I don't run away) until eleven or so. Then they'd take me down to the marina and wait for my call.

Geoffrey loaned me a folding fishing pole that I could stuff in my backpack. Em made sure I had plenty of water and sunscreen. I tossed in a book to keep my mind occupied during the potentially long wait.

They dropped me off around noon and waited to make sure Matt hadn't returned earlier. I called and told them to go, the boat wasn't in the slip. Then I got set up and tried to relax.

"You can't fish in the marina." A big burly man paused behind me.

"Yes, I know. I'm waiting for someone."

He grunted and moved on.

I couldn't concentrate on my book. I was afraid I'd get too involved and suddenly he'd be standing there and I'd mess it all up. After an hour and a half of increasing misery, I thought I saw Matt's boat motoring through the entrance to the marina. I stuffed the book and the water bottle into my backpack. I stood up and nearly tripped over my phone. I'd forgotten I had it in my lap thinking I'd call Emily for an extra dose of courage. Too late for that.

I shoved the phone in the backpack and pulled out a yellow plastic fish. It looked a little like Flounder in *The Little Mermaid*, but not as cute. I made sure the Zip-lock bag was wedged tightly into its mouth, then I inserted the hook in the little hole I'd made.

I carefully lowered the fish into the water. I'd put rocks inside it so it wouldn't float. I watched it disappear under the water and my stomach filled with butterflies. So far, so good. I let out the line just enough so Matt wouldn't be able to see the fish. By the time I finished, I could see him heading my way. He definitely hadn't seen me yet.

You could still run!

For a split second, I considered it. On the one hand, Emily

and Geoffrey were waiting to rescue me. On the other hand, I
was afraid they'd just deliver me back to the gallows again. No, I
was going to follow through with this. And then I would *choose*
to accept whatever happened.

Matt looked over and saw me. I felt like a deer caught in the
headlights. Danger straight ahead! Can't move a muscle! I
couldn't see his expression well enough to know how to act.
Should I smile and wave? Get ready to talk fast and try to
convince him? I realized I was chewing on my lower lip when I
bit it too hard.

The boat glided into the slip. Matt stood less than ten feet
from me.

Absolutely *positive* I was going to hurl.

"Hey," he said. He smiled a little and looked at my fishing
pole. "Thought you didn't like to fish."

Perfect! He'd made an opening. Now I was supposed to say
— Dang it! I couldn't remember! *Crap!*

"Depends on what I'm fishing for." Something like that.
What was the rest of it? "Some things are worth the trouble."
Geez, I hoped he felt *I* was worth the trouble.

"You know you can't fish in the marina, right?" He threw a
rope around a pylon and tied up the end of his boat.

"I'm fishing for something very special, though."

He grinned. "Oh, really?" He tied the front of the boat to a
pylon attached to the dock.

I finally really noticed him when I wasn't trapped in his gaze.
Wow. Swim trunks. I mean, duh, of course he was wearing
swim trunks. He was out on the water. But that's *all* he was
wearing. I'd never seen so much of him before. His dark hair
was wet and slicked back. His entire body was a glowing island
brown.

That should be a new Crayola color. I'd *definitely* start
coloring again.

When he turned toward me, I noticed his chest was — well,

wow. His muscles stood out everywhere. And he had just the right amount of dark hair on his chest and stomach. Oh, how my palms itched...

He chuckled. "You okay?"

He saw me staring. My eyes jerked back to his again. "Of course, yeah, fine." I was babbling. Remember the script! What was I saying? Oh yeah. "Maybe you could help me out."

His friendly attitude fueled my hopes that this could work. I gave him a cheeky grin. "Do you have a fishing net?"

Matt finished tying up the boat and stood looking down at me, hands on his hips. "I might," he said, returning my grin.

He picked up his net and I pretended to reel in my catch. "Oh, look! I caught something." I made a funny face of pretend shock. It had the desired effect — Matt laughed.

"That's some, uh, fish," he said. "Gee, let me help." He scooped the plastic fish out of the air.

"You know how I am about fish," I said, wrinkling my nose. "Could you take it off the hook for me?"

Matt raised an eyebrow and did as I asked. I was trying not to laugh and trying not to faint at the same time. I was supposed to tell him to open the fish's mouth now, but I was too nervous. I just stood there, grasping the fishing pole in a white knuckle grip, trying to get the words to come out of my mouth.

"Oh, look," Matt said, playing along, "there's something in the fish's mouth. I wonder if I should take it out?"

"Oh, interesting." I heard my voice sound higher than usual. I think because my throat was closing up. What should I do? I didn't know if I could watch him read my note. Maybe I should tell him to read it later and call me.

Actually, that sounded like a brilliant idea. No pressure on Matt. Why didn't I think of this earlier? He doesn't like pressure and the point was to show him I don't want to pressure him. I just want to let him know that I'd like to stick around, see if things could—

He's reading the note! yelled a Voice.

Stop him! yelled Sergeant Pride.

Insert disaster story here.

I leaped toward the deck of his boat. "No, wait, I—"

The heel of my sandal caught in a crack in the dock. By the time my shoe came loose, I'd *completely* lost my balance. My last thought before I hit the water was, whatever you do, *don't lose Geoffrey's fishing pole.*

I held my breath right before I hit the surface. Disgusting dirty water closed over me. I tasted gasoline and dirt and dead fish. Fought my way to the surface. Need clean air. Gasping and sputtering and coughing, eyes burning. The fishing pole! Ah, still in my hand. Good job.

I fought to stay above the water and heard another splash. The gasoline-tainted marina water stung my eyes and I couldn't open them. I started trying to swim with the fishing pole still in my hand.

"Sydney!" Matt yelled from behind me.

I turned in the water but before I could swim toward his voice, I felt his arms around me. Safety. I felt myself relax.

"I got ya." Laughter bubbled behind the words. "What a land lubber." Matt swam a couple of yards to his boat, pulling me along with him. Despite the disgusting water and embarrassing display of gracelessness, it felt great to have his arms around me again.

I knuckled my eyes until I could see out of one. "Am not!" Then I realized how ridiculous it was to argue that point. I giggled. "Maybe."

Matt grabbed the ladder at the back of his boat and pulled me over so I could climb up. He took the fishing rod from my hand and carefully tossed it onto the seat. Safely up in the boat, he pulled me into a rough hug. "Are you okay?" He laughed. "You are such a klutz!"

"Only around you!" I sputtered, embarrassed.

Who cares? exclaimed Lovesick. *You're in his arms again!*

She was right. I smiled. With one eye open. The other one still refused to return to duty.

Matt smiled back. A big dimple-causing, heart-stopping smile. My favorite smile in the whole world.

Without thinking, I wrapped my arms around his neck and kissed him with all of my heart. Matt pulled me closer, kissing me back with gusto. Joy must be like helium, because I couldn't feel the deck under my feet.

When we came up for air, we laughed and grimaced and wiped our mouths. "You taste like gasoline," I told him.

"You smell like dead fish," he said with a grin. "But I don't mind," he added.

"Sorry about that." The reason why I fell into the marina resurfaced. "I just wanted to tell you to read the note later and then call me."

Matt's smiled faded a little. "Too late." He pulled me close again and rested his cheek on my hair. "I didn't see you fall because I was busy reading the nicest letter anyone's ever written me."

I held my breath. Really? Oh, please, please, please!

"And?" I prompted when he didn't say anything more.

He chuckled and pulled back to meet my hopeful gaze. He wiped water from my face with one hand. He kissed my forehead, then gazed down at me. The softest, sweetest gaze ever. His lips came down on mine. The softest, sweetest kiss ever. Even if it did taste a little like gasoline.

I felt life flowing back into my veins. My heart began to beat again. I felt like the sun was shining on me from the inside out.

"I love you." I hadn't meant to say it out loud. The poetry of the moment got to me. The New Plan was to give Matt time to see if...well, if loving me was a possibility. I opened my eyes to gauge the damage.

"I'm sorry that I've been — It's just GT and Patty kept

pushing me and—" Matt sighed against my hair. "Anyway, I give up. I don't want you to walk away."

I sucked in my breath and felt my face turn into one big happy grin. I must've looked like one of those big yellow smiley faces. Celebratory fireworks exploded in my eyes, in my chest—

"But I have some conditions."

Everything stopped. Conditions? He looked kind of serious.

"First." He pushed me away enough to look down at my feet. I realized part of the reason my world was tilted was that I had only one sandal. "I'm buying you new shoes. And I reserve the right to tell you when to wear them."

The Ferris wheels and firecrackers and cotton candy started spinning again. I felt my face heat up as I smiled at his shoulder. "I think I can buy my own—"

"These points are non-negotiable." Matt lifted my chin up and winked at me.

I rolled my eyes. "Fine." I tried not to laugh.

"Second—"

"There's more?" I pretended to be annoyed. "For heaven's sake, Matt—"

"*Second*, I'm not giving up my home. If we decide to-to go all the way," his voice broke and he cleared his throat.

Oh my gosh, he loves me! Little Miss Lovesick whispered.

"It's a good house. It's solid, doesn't need any repairs. And I think maybe you like it, so...if you really need something changed, I'll do that, but I really think..."

I put him out of his misery. "I love your home, Matt." I saw the relief in his eyes.

"Third." He broke eye contact.

My stomach tightened with nerves. Even more serious than keeping the house. I hoped it was something I was willing to agree to.

"If we were to...If I ever get married, it's going to be permanent. End of story. So whatever woman..." He cleared his throat again. "If you wanted to...be with me, it'd have to be forever. No cop-outs or lame excuses or even good excuses. We work through things, whatever it takes."

He paused, but he still didn't look me in the eye. If he had, he would've realized there was nothing to worry about in this department. But he didn't, so he finished his demand. "I know not everyone feels that way nowadays, so take time to think about it before we get to that point."

"Fourth—"

"Matt—" I moved one hand from behind his neck and ran it over his cheek. I tried to get him to look at me again.

"Just let me finish." He met my gaze. His eyes had a mischievous gleam. "Fourth, you're going to have to spend a lot more time with Rover."

I burst out laughing.

"She needs a woman's touch. You wouldn't believe what a tomboy she's become. She—"

I pulled his head back down and kissed him hard. Aside from the fact that I'd really like for us both to take showers and try this again, I didn't think life could get any better. From the way he got into that next kiss, I think Matt just might've felt the same way.

"I can't live without you any longer," he whispered, his mouth near my ear.

My heart blasted out of my chest like a rocket headed straight for the moon! Thank you, God! Thank you, thank you, thank you! I squeezed Matt tight.

"I guess we should go clean up — and get you on dry land." Matt shook his head. "I don't know what I'm going to do with my boat. Maybe I'll buy you some of those inflatable arm bands for kids."

"Yeah, I don't care right now. Kiss me again, please." I stood on tiptoe. My single-sandal state left me off balance and I compensated, causing the boat to rock a little.

"See what I mean? Am I going to spend the rest of my life—"

"I want to *start* the rest of my life *now*."

"—rescuing you from various bodies of water?"

"Then kiss me and I'll stop jumping around!"

"What have I gotten myself into, huh?"

I sighed very loudly and pulled his head down. How was I going to make him fall in love with me if I couldn't kiss him?

Little Miss Lovesick giggled and sighed. *Looks like I caught what I was fishing for.*

A PEEK AT CHERRY ON TOP

A TRAVERSE CITY IN LOVE CHICK LIT SHORT STORY

This free short story is available exclusively for my fans and followers
at
https://kittybucholtz.com/freebook

I really couldn't be happier.

My job is fun and pays well — check. My parents and sister and I get along just fine — check. I have plenty of friends — check. I even own my own home, a condo on the water in

Traverse City, Michigan, one of the prettiest towns in the Midwest — check.

Work, family, friends, home — there's nothing left. Zero complaints.

Which means this feeling of restlessness that's been nibbling at me lately is probably just in my head. Maybe I'm just antsy to start my MBA in the fall.

A vacation would probably cure me.

Lucky for me, I just happen to have one planned for next week.

Well…working vacation.

Two words that should never be paired. Like fat-free ice cream. Affordable healthcare. Honest lawyer.

And yet, here I stood in the conference room at work, smile in place, agreeing to test out some food over my time off and create a few social media posts to feel out what consumers already think of this brand. Most of the items need to be combined with other foods to actually eat them. I don't enjoy cooking, but it's a necessary evil for survival unless you eat out a lot. All my extra money is being socked away, so cooking is both more necessary than ever and therefore more evil.

Except for this next week on vacation. I'd planned a vacation from cooking, and that would start tonight as Traverse City's National Cherry Festival begins.

Nonetheless, I would be required to think about our new client's food, take pictures of the food, tweet about the food, think about how I would make other people want to go buy the food. Again, not what I planned on doing this next week.

Vacation, people. It literally means *not* working.

I took a breath, adjusted my glasses, and refocused on how I love my job and don't have anything to complain about.

My boss, Chris, smiled at everyone gathered around the conference table. "Yacko's generously provided samples for every employee. Two kinds of taco sauce, three salad dressings, a marinade, spaghetti sauce, and salsa. Everybody take some."

My co-worker and friend, Ted, who had the unfortunate last name of Dundee, immediately reached for the salsa and the marinade.

"Isn't Yakko the name of one of the *Animaniacs*?" I asked as I took one of each kind of taco sauce and a bottle of raspberry vinaigrette. At least with these, I could put them on food I could purchase. No cooking required.

"No, Zoe, that's Wakko," Ted replied, reading the ingredients label on the marinade. He's really into outdoor grilling. No doubt the marinade would be opened tonight. I almost wished I didn't have plans. Ted's magic with grilled meat could make a vegan's mouth water.

"You're both right," Chris chimed in. "It's Yakko, Wakko, and Dot. But this Yacko is spelled differently."

I shook my head as I stared at my boss. He was old enough to be my father, but he never acted like an older man, not like my own father anyway. He knew more TV and movie trivia than anyone I'd ever met. And not just boring stuff like a movie's budget or its opening weekend gross. He knew stuff like how Tom Cruise was the original choice for *Iron Man*, and how *Friends* was originally called *Insomnia Cafe*. Definitely mistakes corrected, in my opinion. "Is there anything you don't know, Chris?" I asked with a chuckle.

He grinned. "Hey, media is my business. I gotta keep up with things, right?"

"So long as no one thinks of yakking." Cary, an intern from Northwestern Michigan College, looked around the room. He always tried to be part of the conversation, which was good, but he didn't always pick the right entrance. "You know, vomiting. Yakking it up."

Ted raised his eyebrows at the guy. "Yakking it up is talking. Do you use 'yak' for 'vomit' now?" Ted leaned closer to the new guy and whispered loudly, "Either way, you don't talk about vomiting when you're in a meeting about a client's food."

Cary nodded and picked up two jars. His face burst into color. I patted his shoulder, hoping it would make him feel better.

"I read somewhere that someone makes tacos out of yak meat," Melody mused from the back of the room. "You know, the big animal that looks like a wildebeest."

"You mean a water buffalo?" someone asked.

"No, the other name for wildebeest is gnu," Ted said. "A water buffalo is something else." I raised my eyebrows at him. "YouTube." He grinned.

"Right, right," Melody nodded. "I get those confused." She rolled her eyes at me. I scrunched up my face at her, wordlessly saying, *where do these guys get this stuff?* She laughed.

We have the oddest conversations at work. They tend to zig-zag all over the place, but they're always interesting and usually fun. And we tended to learn a lot from each other. Perhaps not much of importance — like the names of cartoon characters — but you never know when a piece of "unimportant" information will be useful when you're putting an ad or a tweet together. Thanks to Ted and YouTube, I now know that a wildebeest and a gnu are the same thing. Might have to use that somewhere.

Though…probably not.

"All right, folks, I know some of you are headed out of town to avoid Cherry Festival," Chris gestured to Melody, "and some of you can't wait for it to start." He looked at me and rolled his eyes, laughing.

I grinned and shrugged unapologetically. My plan was to see every parade, eat every cherry-covered and cherry-infused food, ride the ferris wheel at the carnival, and listen to as many of the bands at the Open Space as I could this week.

"So if you'll please take a short lunch and focus on finishing the work that needs to be done before Monday, you can start heading out at two."

"Yes!" I did a little arm pump.

Okay, *that* kind of working vacation I loved. The kind where you're getting paid to be at the office working, but you're really on vacation.

Chris chuckled as Ted gave a whoop and bounded off to his desk. The rest of us quickly followed, calling our thanks as we went.

By five minutes to two, most everyone had their desks cleared, computers turned off, and purse and bag in hand. Chris waved us out with a cheerful laugh at 1:59.

Vacation had begun.

The July day dawned with the perfect mix of blue sky, sunshine, and a light breeze, so I'd happily ridden my bike to work. And since Cherry Festival traffic always clogs the streets by Friday afternoon before the official Saturday start, I was even happier to bike home, avoiding the tangle of cars choking every major road in town. Plus, Traverse City is arguably the most beautiful place in the world, particularly on a summer's day. Riding my bike anywhere is a pleasure.

From work, I turned down the fairly safe and bicycle friendly Washington Street, one of the loveliest streets in town due to all the Queen Anne Victorian-style homes. That kind of house reminds me of fairy tales and all the kinds of magic life could hold, so I like to use that section of Washington any chance I get.

Crossing over Railroad Avenue, I headed south on the bicycle path that ran parallel. The smell of pizza hung in the air as I passed near the converted train depot — The Filling Station Microbrewery was my kitchen away from home. Though, seriously, after this week I'd have to focus on eating at home to save money for my fall colors trip with Dean and the crew in a few months.

I passed the library at the north end of Boardman Lake (where I like to believe I can smell old books in the air), and pedaled down Woodmere, cut over to the Boardman Lake Trail, and coasted along the lake to the condo complex I call home.

I still almost can't believe I own my own condo. My parents were great at teaching me about money. Mostly they said, because their parents hadn't so my parents made a lot of mistakes in the first few decades of their lives. I learned to save early and I was already reaping the benefits.

I locked up my bike outside and hurried to change clothes and pick up my pre-packed messenger bag. It held a sun hat, sunscreen, a beach towel, a windbreaker for later in the evening, an insulated water bottle, and some protein bars. The last were more out of habit than anything else.

I hate being hungry because — I'll be the first to admit it — I get hangry. It's one of the things I hate about myself. Being a friendly, even-tempered girl-next-door — that's who I am. When I get grumpy and snarky, I tend to joke around in a way that sounds mean instead of funny. *Not* who I am. Dean says I'm not that bad, but he's the one who suggested I put a protein bar in my purse so I'm pretty sure he's being nice and downplaying my contentiousness. Always having a snack at hand, preferably something not entirely sugar-based, keeps the monster at bay.

All the way home I'd been saying "taco sauce, taco sauce" to myself so I'd remember. I dropped the two bottles into a corner of the bag so I could try them tonight at the taco truck, send out a tweet or two, and get a bit of goodwill started with our new client.

"I love my job," I reminded myself out loud. Despite the fact that I was officially on vacation.

Double-checking my hair, the weather on my phone, and

making sure all the lights were off, I locked the door and hurried over to Dean's condo in the next building.

Dean and I have been friends for years. We'd both gone to Northwestern Michigan College, the local community college, where we'd been able to get bachelor degrees by attending classes from other universities through their University Center. We met while taking a pottery class for an elective credit, and discovered we thought a lot of the same things were funny, weird, or stupid. Our friendship solidified, though, when we realized we both wanted to do good in the world through our work, not just pocket a paycheck every Friday. (I'm sure social media could become a positive force for global social change, and Dean believes micro-businesses can change the world one poverty-locked family at a time.)

Most of our friends think it's strange that we never tried dating each other since we have so much in common. But we agree on that, too — it would be too weird. We aren't attracted to each other that way. We like brainstorming entrepreneurial ideas and thinking about philosophical questions, but he just isn't my type. And I'm sure he feels the same about me.

Nonetheless, he's probably more my best friend now than Shelby, whom I've known and loved since kindergarten. She fell in love in high school, got married after graduation, had kids, and is living a completely different life in Cadillac, where we grew up. I have no concept of the merits of breastfeeding versus formula, and she doesn't care about how new developments in neuroscience could affect social media. So we text each other once in a while, and sometimes I visit when I'm home. I miss what we used to have and don't see how we'll ever get it back. Mom says this is just how life happens, it's a bummer, but what can you do.

Back to Dean. I knocked on his door, barely waiting for his "Come in" before I entered. I threw back my head and opened my arms wide. "Hap-py va-ca-tion!" I let each syllable lengthen as if I were announcing a guest on Jimmy Fallon's *The Tonight Show*. Dean whooped from the kitchen.

Following the sound, I hurried in and we high-fived. Dean is only a few inches taller than me, which is great for high-fives and hugs — I don't have to stretch up on my toes like when I hug my dad — and his brilliant red hair is outshined only by his sunny smile. He zipped his Outlander backpack closed and shoved his water bottle into the side pocket. "Ready for Friday night fun?" His smile beamed out and warmed the whole room.

"It's only 2:30, but — yes!" I hopped a little on my toes. "I totally can't wait to hear Karma Karma live. I *love* their music."

Dean chuckled as he pushed me out the door and locked up. "You don't say. Oh, wait, you *do* say. Daily. For weeks."

I laughed as I unlocked my bike and tossed my bag in the basket. "Lead or follow?"

"Go ahead. You always complain I ride too fast."

"It's like you're trying to do the bicycle version of *The Fast and the Furious*," I said, heading out.

"Not this week," he called from behind me as we turned onto the bike path. "Nobody's going anywhere fast for awhile."

Like me, Dean loves Cherry Festival and doesn't mind the crowds. He works full-time from home, and I work from home two or three days a week, so we both enjoy getting out and seeing people in real life. I wouldn't say either of us are foodies, exactly, but we both love food and that's one thing the festival has in spades.

My favorite is probably the cherry bratwurst with cherry chutney sauce. Holy cow, I could eat those forever. Every single restaurant and store in town has cherry products. A friend of mine worked at the Holiday Inn for a few years, and he assured me there is nothing to eat that doesn't have cherries mixed in or on top this week. Maybe the scrambled eggs. But I wouldn't put it past someone to find a way to add cherries to the omelettes.

Today we would start at the food trucks, meeting some

other friends for a late lunch. Then we'd wander downtown, through the carnival area, take the Grandview Parkway tunnel to the beach, and then wander through everything set up in the Open Space. I already had a list of things on my phone that I wanted to see, do, or eat this week, but not everyone likes to be so organized. I think most of our crowd just wants to take it as it comes, but that's a good way to miss something amazing just because you didn't take the time to read the Events calendar.

Come to think of it, my friend Sydney was probably the only other person I knew who had also made a list. She and I wouldn't be missing anything, that's for sure.

It took awhile for Dean and I to find a place to lock up our bikes anywhere near The Little Fleet food truck area — there were bikes everywhere! Then he stood on the split-rail fence searching the crowd.

"There they are." He pointed up Wellington Street. He whistled hard, and I put my hands over my ears. "Matt! Sydney!" He waved his arms.

Eventually, I saw a group of our friends appear in the crowd. I rushed over to hug everyone.

"Anyone know what they want to eat?" asked Dean, ever the organizer.

"Tacos!"

"Tacos, definitely."

"I'll eat anything," Matt added with a shrug.

"I've got to try some new taco sauce for work so I brought it with me." I pulled one of the bottles out of my bag.

Dean took it and read the label. "Well, I love Garcia's Tacos, and I'm not spoiling them with store-bought sauce."

"It's taco sauce, Dean, not béarnaise sauce." I laughed as we went to stand in a very long line. I'd never eaten at Garcia's Tacos, but I loved tacos and burritos in general and I was hungry. They'd be fine.

Dean tutted. "You haven't had *these* tacos, have you? You're in for a treat."

As we waited, we caught each other up on our lives. Jeff was totally psyched to have rocked an interview for a promotion at work. Matt told the story of Sydney's parents' visit and how her dad tried to intimidate him while they grilled steaks in Matt's backyard.

"I wouldn't say 'intimidate' exactly," Sydney interrupted.

"You weren't there."

"I was in the kitchen with Mom with the door open," she argued with a laugh.

"No, really, he threatened me, honey," Matt insisted.

"Really?" Sydney's face softened from laughter to the face of a little girl who wanted Daddy's love. She'd told me she didn't think her parents believed in her or trusted her to make good decisions with her life, a sore point that kept her from visiting much.

"Aw, Syd," I said, putting my arm around her shoulder, "that's so sweet. Daddy's protecting his little girl."

She hugged me back, then moved into Matt's arms. I could almost see her heart on her sleeve. Maybe this would help ease the tension between her and her dad.

"And you, Zoe? Anything new besides what we see you tweeting or posting on Insta?" Joanna asked.

"Nope, I'm boring," I said. "I'm the no-news girl today."

"It's true, she's boring," Dean added. "No parties at her place, wild or otherwise. No midnight guests. No unmarked packages delivered."

Jeff raised his eyebrows at Dean. "Nothing creepy about how you would know all that. Not creepy at all. Stalker."

We kept teasing each other, joking around, talking about nothing in particular, until we were near the front of the line. By now, I was genuinely hungry and not just eating because it's what you do at festivals. We could read the menu from here.

Traditional soft tacos. Trio of hard tacos. Fish tacos. Vegetarian tacos. Optional cherry salsa on any of them.

Hmm. Well, you get two soft tacos or three hard shell, and I wanted to be hungry later for Moomer's. I swoon over their Cherries Moobilee , cherry ice cream with bits of cherries and chunks of fudge. To die for.

Eyes still on the menu, I started to say, "Two traditional soft tacos, please." But when I made eye contact with the man behind the counter, I don't know, maybe I was still thinking about the ice cream because I felt a swoon coming on.

Rich brown eyes ringed by thick black lashes captured me in some kind of magic taco spell. A smile that made the gorgeous sunny day gloomy in comparison. A growing dimple in one tanned cheek as his lips moved over straight white teeth. If his eyes cast a spell on me, his smile made me hope I'd never be set free. The earth seemed to move.

I stumbled and someone caught me. Dean poked me in the shoulder, poked again, and snapped his fingers. "Earth to Zoe. He's waiting for your order."

I blinked and sucked in some oxygen. The piano music and birdsong running through my head abruptly halted. I still hadn't lost eye contact with Mr. Gorgeous. "Um...I...hi." I pushed my glasses up my nose.

He grinned. "Hi."

I grinned back.

Dean leaned his arm on my shoulder. "There's a long line of people waiting. Hungry people like me. Soft or hard," he pressed when I still didn't order.

My eyes traveled down. Soft lips. Hard shoulders. Strong hands. I couldn't see much more but he looked like his body was more hard than soft.

"Let's start with the easy question," he said, and his voice reminded me of music with a bass beat. "With or without cherries?"

Wow, what was wrong with me? I hadn't felt this way since the seventh grade when Troy Brown came back from summer vacation all lean and muscular, baby fat long gone.

Dean leaned close and whispered in my ear. "Are you going through baby names or honeymoon destinations?"

It was enough to knock me out of the alternate universe I'd gotten stuck in. I slapped Dean's stomach with the back of my hand and ordered.

"T-two traditional"—I cleared my throat, the heat of the day obviously drying out my mouth—"soft tacos. Please." I remembered my manners at the end.

But I also heard the extra throaty sound in my voice. I felt heat rising in my cheeks.

Mr. Gorgeous winked at me. "Good choice." He ran my order and I fumbled to tap my card against the payment device. When he turned away to get my food, I heard laughing around me.

I swiveled to see all my friends in various stages of mirth. My cheeks burned worse than summer's first sunburn.

"Here you go, Zoe."

I turned back to find the man of my dreams reaching out to me. Well, handing me a plate. I tried to avert my eyes when I took it, but at the last moment I caved.

Our eyes met.

Our fingers touched.

Sparks flew.

At least on my end.

More than anything I wished we were in a situation where I could have a longer conversation with him, see if this connection was something more than a random burst of energy in a universe full of electrical charges. More than dopamine and serotonin and…

I got lost in that alternate universe again and lost track of all the geeky things I know and love about neuroscience. All the research that explains attraction as chemicals and electrical impulses drained out of my head. The only thing left was the one thing I feared...and longed for.

That rosy colored tunnel vision that included only this man with the beautiful smile. Nothing else.

"Thanks," I said, barely above a whisper. I cleared my throat again. I needed some water.

"Enjoy." He was still looking at me when I turned away.

I smiled. I couldn't help it.

I moved toward a nearby picnic table to wait for my friends. A peek over my shoulder showed Mr. Gorgeous taking Dean's order — then he glanced toward me again. I grinned and turned away, trying to hide...whatever it was.

It's just the dopamine rush, I told myself, still grinning.

Wow. What a way to start the weekend.

Right before I took a bite of my taco, the enticing scent of cooked meat and vegetables swirling around me, I remembered my work. I set my plate on a corner of the full picnic table, smiling my thanks at the mom sitting with her kids who moved to make room, and pulled the two bottles of taco sauce from my bag. I poured some on the tacos, one sauce flavor on each, trying to focus so I could remember which was which when I tasted them.

I bit into one taco and chewed. Not bad. For store bought food. The taco sauce didn't taste much different to me than any other I'd eaten. I set it down and took a bite of the other one. Smokier taste. It overtook the other flavors of the taco and kind of made it all about the sauce. Bummer. Not really how I enjoyed eating tacos.

I finished that one so I could get it over with and enjoy the first taco with the better sauce. Meanwhile, my friends joined me one by one and ribbed me some more about my embarrassing slip-up.

"Slip-up?" Dean all but cackled when I tried to shrug off that immediate and intense attraction I'd felt with such a casual phrase. "More like some kind of power surge went through your brain and shorted everything out."

"I was just excited to be out in the crush of Cherry Festival crowds," I explained, acknowledging only to myself the full-on lying. "I couldn't hear him very well, and he couldn't hear me. There's gotta be three hundred people just in the food truck area."

I widened my eyes and nodded around me as if that would convince everyone.

"He heard me," Matt said before he shoved the rest of his taco into his mouth.

I rolled my eyes. "That's because you have a deep voice. The sound travels better."

"He heard me," said Sydney and Joanna in unison.

I gave them a you're-supposed-to-be-on-my-side look. Joanna just laughed.

"He's very cute," Sydney added. "You should get his number."

"Hey!" Matt protested. "I'm right here."

Sydney kissed his cheek. "You're the handsomest man I've ever loved."

Matt pretended to be only somewhat mollified. "I was looking for 'the handsomest man you've ever met' but I'll go with 'loved.'"

Joanna looked back at the taco truck. "You have to admit, Latino men do tend to be good-looking." She turned back to me and Sydney. "But Scottish men have the best accent."

"Oh, yeah." We nodded emphatically.

Dean rolled his eyes and popped the last bite of his hard taco into his mouth. When he was half-done chewing, he said, "This conversation has really gotten away from us. Where are we going next?"

"Hold on, I gotta tweet!" I wiped my hands on a napkin and tried to be quick. I composed as I typed, trying to make sure it sounded upbeat without moving into the territory of lying. I didn't love the sauce, but I had to make our new client feel some love. I finished typing, tagged Yacko's and Garcia's Tacos, and added #whatsfordinner #tacosfordinner #cherryfestival to the end. Instagram, Twitter, done!

We separated our trash into the recycling containers, took a quick group photo, and headed to the riverwalk and downtown. A great start to my favorite week of the year.

I told myself not to look back, but I turned slightly, pretending to adjust my bag. I raised my eyes toward the taco truck while moving the strap around on my shoulder. I let myself smile just a bit. He really was a little bit swoonworthy.

Then he glanced up and looked right at me. Had he been watching me? He smiled and waved.

I heard a voice in my head telling me to just keep walking. But I smiled wider and waved back at him.

A great start to the week, indeed.

Finish reading this free short story, available exclusively for my fans and followers, by going here:
https://kittybucholtz.com/freebook

ALSO BY KITTY BUCHOLTZ

CONSIDER BUYING BOOKS DIRECT FROM KITTY! GO TO KITTYBUCHOLTZ.COM/BOOKS

Traverse City in Love

Cherry on Top (free short story)

Little Miss Lovesick

Death and Tacos (coming soon!)

The Strays of Loon Lake

Welcome to Loon Lake

Love at the Fluff and Fold

Adventures of Lewis and Clarke

Superhero in Disguise

A Very Merry Superhero Wedding

Unexpected Superhero

My Bullheaded Superhero Valentine

Also…

Adventures of Lewis and Clarke: The Beginning (the first three books)

A NOTE FROM KITTY

I hope you enjoyed reading *Little Miss Lovesick* as much as I enjoyed writing it! There's something about laughter and romantic gestures that keep my romantic heart pounding. Just ask my husband!

If you enjoyed this book, check out my Adventures of Lewis and Clarke superhero urban fantasy series. The short story prequel, *Superhero in Disguise*, is the story of how Tori and Joe met on Halloween. *A Very Merry Superhero Wedding* is about their Christmas Eve wedding during a Christmastime crime spree. And *Unexpected Superhero* tells the story of what happens when Tori finds out why she's different. (You can read all three stories in the omnibus, *Adventures of Lewis and Clarke: The Beginning*.) Then their best friends, Bull and Hayley, finally go out on a real date in *My Bullheaded Superhero Valentine*.

My books are available as ebooks and in print at most online retailers. *Unexpected Superhero* and *Little Miss Lovesick* are also available as audiobooks. All the ebooks, print books, and audiobooks will be added to my own web store over the course of 2024. Purchases there support me and my work in a significantly greater way so I'd love it if you'd like to buy from me directly (kittybucholtz.com/books)!

You can also join my free or paid membership community over on Patreon (links at the end of About the Author). Read chapters early before the books even come out, discuss the stories with other readers, see fun art about the settings of the books, and more!

Would you like to read *Cherry on Top* for free? It's set in the same town as *Little Miss Lovesick* during the famous National Cherry Festival. It's my gift to you when you join my reader newsletter at kittybucholtz.com/freebook. Enjoy!

And if you really want to make my day, I'd love for you to post your thoughts about any of my books in a review. Thanks so much!

Just so you know, I rebranded all my books in 2024 to be "sweet" — so no swear words or overt sex scenes. I hope you enjoy the change.

Thanks for spending part of your day with me. I hope you have a great tomorrow!

Happy Reading!

ABOUT THE AUTHOR

Kitty Bucholtz writes sweet romantic comedy and superhero urban fantasy, often with an inspirational element woven in. Her stories feature women whose sense of humor and nervous gutsiness get them into and out of all kinds of trouble. She grew up forty miles east of Traverse City, Michigan, the setting of this book. She went to college there, met and married the love of her life, and waved goodbye to everything she knew when she and her husband, John, struck out for parts unknown.

Their romantic adventures have included a scolding at Parliament House in Belfast for canoodling, three trips Down Under where her handsome hubby made animated movie animals look real, and a delicious taste of European life living in Sweden. After earning her M.A. in Creative Writing in Sydney, she formed Daydreamer Entertainment and began self-publishing. Founder of Write Now! Workshop and Write Now! Workshop Podcast, she loves to teach and coach writers.

Only God knows where they'll wind up next – but they're pretty sure it will be another cool chapter in their adventure!

If you enjoyed this or any of Kitty's books, please leave a review—they are a tremendous help to both writers and readers!

Connect with Kitty today!
kittybucholtz.com
kitty@kittybucholtz.com

Get your copy of the free short story *Cherry on Top* at kittybucholtz.com/freebook today!

patreon.com/kittybucholtz

tiktok.com/@kitty_bucholtz

facebook.com/kittybucholtzauthor

bookbub.com/profile/kitty-bucholtz

amazon.com/author/kittybucholtz

x.com/KittyBucholtz

instagram.com/kittybucholtz

goodreads.com/kittybucholtz

youtube.com/kittybucholtz

www.ingramcontent.com/pod-product-compliance
Lightning Source LLC
Chambersburg PA
CBHW051335250626
47155CB00007B/2610